Bough Cutter won first place in the *Great Lakes Best Regional Fiction* category of the 2022 Independent Publisher Book Awards.

BOUGH CUTTER

A NORTHERN LAKES MYSTERY

Award-winning Series
NORTHERN LAKES MYSTERIES

FIGURE EIGHT
SPIDER LAKE
BOUGH CUTTER
MUSKY RUN

Visit www.feetwetwriting.com to sign-up for
email updates and read more from Jeff Nania.

f @jeffnaniaauthor   @jeffnania

JEFF NANIA

BOUGH CUTTER

A NORTHERN LAKES MYSTERY

Feet Wet
Writing

Feet Wet Writing
Portage, Wisconsin 53901
www.feetwetwriting.com

Book Design: Fine Print Design
Cover Design: Chris Nania

Fourth Printing
May 2023
Printed in the United States of America

For more information or to contact the author visit www.feetwetwriting.com.

Library of Congress Control Number: 2023936840

ISBN: 978-1-960681-04-1 (Paperback)
ISBN: 978-1-7363373-4-9 (Hardcover)
ISBN: 978-1-7363373-6-3 (Ebook)
ISBN: 978-1-960681-05-8 (Audio)

For Camille Inez Chalifoux—
I can't wait to teach you
how to catch bluegills off the dock.

ACKNOWLEDGEMENTS

It would be impossible to thank all the people who have been a part of the success of my first two books, but I want to tell you from the bottom of my heart you are as much a part of the Northern Lakes Mystery series as I am. 2020 has been a challenging year, and I hope my stories have allowed you to escape for even a little while. Our books are for sale at many places, and we are glad that you buy them wherever you buy them. However, during the last year many of our treasured community bookstores have really faced some challenges. As these stores reopen, if you get the chance, stop by, see what they have to offer, and maybe even pick up a Northern Lakes Mystery or two.

During the writing of *Bough Cutter*, I imposed upon many of my friends and family who helped make certain that technical details of the story were correct: Sheriff's Captain Ret. Tanya Molony, Sheriff's Lieutenant Ret. JJ Molony, Sheriff's EOD Deputy Ret. Jeff Wolf, FBI Special Agent Ret. Kent Miller, Dr. Michael Chalifoux, and EMT Amanda Halatek. A special thanks to Niizhoodewii Denomie for her expertise in Ojibwe language and culture. Thanks to the Huffaker Five and Marilyn Davis for making sure the story was worth telling and to Karin O'Malley, Karen Ferrell, Terry Rydberg, and Shannon Booth for making sure that the final draft was really the final draft. Any errors are my fault, not theirs. Finally, thanks to Kristin Mitchell at Little Creek Press for first giving me the chance to turn my words into a book to put into the hands of readers.

My entire family and the traditions we share are very much part of this story. I especially want to thank my family members, my wife Victoria (the brains behind this outfit), my son Chris who designed another incredible cover, and Rebecca, Jim, Jay John, and all the extended Nania family for their unwavering support.

Thanks again to Tommye Heinemann for keeping the tradition of Spider Lake alive.

CHAPTER 1

Nearly every chair was full in the Musky Falls High School cafeteria. Merry chatter filled the room as friends, neighbors, and family members reacquainted after a busy summer season, waiting for the program to begin.

The crowd quieted as a smiling woman walked up to the podium with a purposeful stride. Her blonde hair was in a ponytail, and she was wearing a bright green tie-dyed sweatshirt emblazoned with *Northern Lakes Academy*. She faced the room and introduced herself and her students.

"Welcome. My name is Julie Carlson. I am the teacher at Northern Lakes Academy, and these," she said with a sweeping gesture to the chairs behind her, "are my students."

"Tonight, they will present the research project they began last spring and will continue through the rest of this year. Each individual or small group designed and researched an aspect of the larger project based on firsthand, real-world circumstances. The individual and collective outcomes of the students' research and investigation must lead to a potential solution they can implement by working with community partners. So, without further ado, let me turn the program over to the students."

Julie Carlson didn't mention that besides being the lead and only teacher at Northern Lakes, she was also the love of my life.

She smiled and stepped down and took a seat with the audience. A girl about fourteen years old took Julie's place at the podium. She wore a sweatshirt two sizes too big and had purple hair on one side of her head and blonde on the other.

"Welcome to the Northern Lakes presentation night. My name is Amber Lockridge. I am an eighth-grade student at the school, and this is my second year. Our school researches a local topic of interest three times a year. It can be any topic as long as it fits the guidelines we developed with Ms. Carlson.

"Tonight, we are here to tell you what we have learned about the Wisconsin State fish, *Esox masquinongy*, better known as the muskellunge or musky. The muskellunge has become a source of significant revenue for the local economy. Recreational fishing brings in about 1.4 billion dollars in revenue annually to our state, and it is estimated that musky anglers generated 425 million dollars of that revenue. Just as importantly, muskies have played an important role in our history. My classmate Jacob will tell you about the history of the musky."

A boy about the same age as Amber took the podium. He was doing battle with his straight black hair to keep it out of his eyes.

"My name is Jacob Fastfish or Gizhii-giigoonh. Long before the musky was the state fish of Wisconsin, actually long before Wisconsin was Wisconsin, and even before Wisconsin was known as Meskonsing, the Ojibwa called the musky the maashkinoozhe, meaning 'ugly pike.' Stories of the great fish, its tenacity and ferocious attitude, have accounted for countless legends and fish tales across the north country. According to written history, the world's record musky was caught in Sawyer County, Wisconsin, in 1949 by a guy named Cal Johnson. The fish was sixty and one-eighth inches long, weighed over sixty-seven pounds, and was probably over twenty years old. It was caught on Lac Courte Oreilles, also known as Ottawa Lake by the Anishinaabe. It's a five-thousand-acre body of water in northern Wisconsin and a perfect place for muskies. Now my classmate Lynsey will tell you more about muskies."

"Hi, my name is Lynsey Jones," she started right off. "There are currently seven hundred seventy-five lakes, rivers, and streams in our state that have musky populations. It is thought that one acre of surface water will support one mature musky. Although depending on available food, they will range much further. They prefer a rocky bottom near heavy weeds to ambush prey. A musky will lay between twenty thousand and a quarter of a million eggs each year, depending on the health and size of the individual fish. When the eggs hatch, the fry are readily eaten by northern pike, large and smallmouth bass, perch, and sunfish. If a musky survives the first year, a hatchling will grow to eleven inches. The bigger they get, the fewer predators they have, and they can reach forty inches long by the age of nine. Now my classmate Danny will tell you about musky fishing."

"My name is Danny LeTroy. My dad is a musky fishing guide, and so is my grandpa. We take people out musky fishing all the time, but there is no guarantee the people we are guiding will catch a fish. Sometimes we don't even see one. Muskies are the trickiest fish around, and even if you hook one, you are in for a fight. They will jump straight out of the water and try to shake the lure. Another trick they use is instead of pulling the line away from you, they will run at the boat and make the line go slack so you have to reel super fast to tighten up the line. They will dive under the boat and tangle the line in the prop and break it off. There is one trick you can use that will help you catch a musky. When people are casting lures for fish, they throw it out, reel it back in, and throw it out again. Every once in a while, they will see a musky follow their lure or swipe at it right next to the boat. Most of the time, they don't strike. My dad and grandpa will then have their customers finish the cast, and when the lure is right next to the boat, they swirl it around in a figure-eight pattern. It gives you one more chance to get a fish. If a musky is following your bait, the figure eight will sometimes get them to strike. Once they hit, jerk the rod hard to set the hook and hold on, 'cause it's going to get pretty exciting. My grandpa says catching a musky always depends on a combination of skill and luck. The bigger the fish is, the more luck you'll need."

A figure eight. One more chance. This path that loops around and leads back into itself seems to be the one I follow. But even when I seem to be on a predictable path, events turn life upside down unpredictably.

An old friend of mine, Manny Pinski, was the rabbi at a Jewish temple located in my old police beat. He had gotten word that I had some troubles and suggested we get together and talk.

We met at a run-down park on the south side of the city. Broken bottles, used syringes, and trash littered the ground. Sitting on a bench together, I told Manny how I felt like my life was spiraling out of control. Plans for the future, or the next day for that matter, seemed to be thrown to the wind. He listened patiently and nodded.

He addressed the situation in his clever way of combining a story into a lesson.

"John Cabrelli, your trials and tribulations have given me inspiration for my next derasha. When my people next come together, I will tell them to go out and buy a notebook, spiral-bound, with one hundred pages—no, no, three hundred pages. Then I want them to get a pencil, a number two Ticonderoga—no, wait two pencils in case the lead breaks in one—and sit down and write the story of their life from this day forward. Every detail they can think of. You know why I want them to do this, John?"

"No, Manny, I don't."

"I want them to do this because God needs a good laugh, John."

Life had indeed become a series of unpredictable twists and turns—figure eights aplenty. I now found myself in a role that I had filled before, but not at my current location and place in life.

———

Danny stepped down, and other students took their turn at the microphone. With their journals in hand, each student read a story recounted to them by a local person and their most exciting encounter with a musky. Some stories were hilarious and got the crowd laughing. I especially enjoyed the story of a young boy who was fishing panfish with his dad off a boat dock on Spider Lake. He was reeling in a bluegill with his brand-new kid's fishing pole when a musky came up from the bottom of the lake and grabbed the bluegill. The boy held his rod tight and tried to reel it in, but the musky turned and ran, breaking the line.

The final two speakers were a boy and girl, working as a team to explain the next step.

The boy started, "Northern Lakes Academy has joined in a partnership with the Department of Natural Resources in a project that will provide critical information regarding the future of muskies. We will work together with them at the George Meyer Fish Hatchery to insert passive integrated transponders, known as PITs, in fingerling muskies. The PITs are tiny and have no negative impact on the fish. There is no battery, so the PIT will hopefully work for the life of the fish. The muskies with PITs will be released into a monitored lake. A musky captured in the process will be scanned for the presence of a PIT, using something that looks like a supermarket scanner. If the fish has a PIT, the number will be recorded, and the fish will be measured and weighed then released.

The girl stepped up. "Anyone who wishes to can join our

partnership and adopt a fish. If your fish is recaptured, you will be notified along with your student partner. Our goal is to raise one thousand dollars through the adoption of one hundred fish. We have already made pretty good progress toward that. This year we ordered extra Northern Lakes t-shirts and sweatshirts and sold them. We have raised two hundred fifty dollars. In addition, a local citizen who wishes to remain anonymous donated one hundred fifty dollars. So we are only six hundred dollars from our goal."

The crowd gave a round of applause at the early success, and the kids were beaming. I couldn't help but smile at Julie. I had spent one hundred fifty dollars on worse things.

The boy finished. "As you walk around the room to look at each person's project, you will come to Lars Timson, DNR Fisheries biologist, at the front table who has handouts and can explain the project and history of the program. There will also be a bright orange can on his table with a slot in the top for donations."

Julie walked up front. "Thank you all so much for coming out tonight. Please stay around and have some refreshments while you look at the individual projects."

After the applause subsided, Julie stepped down and waved me over. Standing next to her was a man with a walrus mustache.

"Sheriff John Cabrelli, let me introduce you to Lars Timson. Lars is taking the official lead on this project," Julie started. "He has a question to ask you."

"I am pleased to meet you, Sheriff Cabrelli."

"And I you, Lars. Just John is fine, by the way. What can I help you with?"

"We would like to do a special project with the school. If possible, working with the kids, we would like to release these fish in the bay that feeds into Spider Creek. The release area would be right in front of your cabin. The sampling point we have used in the past is west of your property, but if you would allow it, we would like to move that point to the mouth of Spider Creek and set everything up on your property for the day. It would give us lots of space for our folks and the students. No permanent structures or anything. We would set up on the spot a couple of days a year. That's the long and short of it. If you want to think it over, take your time. I better get back to my table. Just let me know."

I moved from the city to the wilds of northern Wisconsin to a cabin I inherited from my uncle Nick and aunt Rose. The property was located on a pristine lake, and as a young boy, I remember standing on the dock looking out across the broad expanse of water. The distance to the opposite shore seemed like miles. When we swam, Uncle Nick had told me that someday when I was older, he and I would swim back and forth across the lake. I couldn't imagine how I could do it. Now during warm weather, I swam across and back almost every day.

"I already know the answer, Lars. Use the property whenever you want, so the answer is yes," I replied.

"Thanks, Sheriff, or I mean John. Thanks a bunch."

Several people were waiting at his table, so he hurried off to talk with them.

"That was very nice of you, John. Lars has sure been a help with this project," Julie said.

"Anything to help with the kids is good with me. You know you could have said yes yourself. I mean, we do live together, and the spot he wants to use is out in front of our cabin," I teased.

"I don't want to overstep my bounds, Sheriff, and while I would like very much to sit here and visit with you, I have to get back to business with the kids." Julie turned on her heel and was gone.

As the recently appointed sheriff of Namekagon County, attending events like this was part of the job description. Some others in positions like mine dreaded them. I, on the other hand, enjoyed them thoroughly. Len Bork, the Musky Falls Police Department chief and his wife, Martha, sat next to me during the presentation. I noted that when Martha came in, she had a plate stacked high with her delicious sugar cookies. I needed to find out where she put them before they were all gone.

For a minute, I looked around to appreciate the trappings of the new life I had made. The people circulating around the cafeteria were members of the community to which I now belonged. I had met many of them. They were good folks. Solid.

How I ended up here was a long story, and the young girl who played a central role in that story will never leave me. Leaving my life in law enforcement behind, I had hoped that maybe this place that had meant so much to me growing up would help me find peace. It didn't turn out to be so peaceful after all, but I had survived.

Jim Rawsom, the real sheriff of Namekagon County, survived too but had been severely wounded and faced a long recovery. The county board asked the governor to appoint an interim sheriff until Rawsom recovered or couldn't return. Without my knowledge, Chief Bork, my old partner Lieutenant JJ Malone, and the sheriff himself recommended me for the job. I hadn't intended to go back into law enforcement, but I found it appealing when I was offered the appointment. If I accepted the position, I would finish out the remaining three years of the term or until Jim was cleared to return to active duty.

Jim was a hometown boy who had risen through the ranks. He ran in the election for the position and was elected by a landslide. He had proven himself to be worthy of the trust people had put in him. So, before I accepted the job, we called all the troops together for a meeting at the sheriff's office. Almost all the deputies in the room had been with me when we executed a warrant to take down a violent killer at the Stone estate where the sheriff had been wounded.

I hoped they would give me a fair chance to earn or lose their respect and loyalty.

Jim Rawsom, using his cane for support, started off. "John Cabrelli has been offered the job as interim sheriff. He has not accepted nor declined the appointment. He would not decide until he talked to you people. So hear him out. John, you have got the floor."

I stood in front of the group, but before I could speak, a young deputy who had been wounded during the execution of the warrant raised his hand.

"Mr. Cabrelli, I would like to speak on behalf of all of us here if that's okay," Deputy Holmes requested.

"Is that okay with you folks?" I asked the group. All nodded in agreement. "Go ahead, Deputy," I responded.

"Mr. Cabrelli, you have proven yourself to us. You could have easily said that all these things we were facing were no longer any of your business and turned your back. After what you've been through, no one would have blamed you. But you didn't. You stepped up and put it all on the line, just like we did. We are all ready to stand behind you. We would be honored to serve under your leadership."

With Julie beside me and surrounded by friends, I was sworn in on the courthouse steps a few days later.

Like my predecessor, I was a patrol sheriff and worked side by side with my deputies on the day, evening, and night shifts to learn the county and meet the citizens. In my old department, I had seen many people rise in the ranks, where they found themselves in an office and distanced from the troops in the field. I had no intention of allowing that to happen. ✦

CHAPTER 2

Namekagon County was thirteen hundred and fifty square miles of mostly forests, lakes, rivers, and streams—a stunning landscape with a population of sixteen thousand citizens. Musky Falls was the largest city and the county seat.

Between Memorial Day and Labor Day, thousands of tourists came to Namekagon County to enjoy the lakes and rivers and hiking and biking trails. This time of year, however, had more of a local flavor. That didn't mean there were no tourists; the contrary was true. The north country was truly a spectacular sight in fall. Plenty of people came to bask in the autumn colors of smoky gold tamaracks, sugar maples, and poplar leaves quaking in the breeze. Hiking boots, checkerboard flannels, and sweaters replaced shorts, t-shirts, and sandals. The hustle and bustle of summer was replaced by a slower, seemingly more observant pace. Days grew shorter, and an early fall snow could come at any time.

Fall triggered the hunter-gatherer spirit of most everyone in the north country. It was time to make sure there was enough wood on the woodpile to get you through to spring. Canning jars of blueberries and other wild fruit were counted. Everyone prepared their hunting gear. While camouflage was worn year-round here, this time of year, it was more abundant. Hunters were responsible citizens, but come fall, an inordinate number of sick days were used, and the pews on Sundays had a little extra room. School absenteeism was more commonplace.

Anglers anxiously took advantage of the mild fall weather and plied the waters of northern lakes for fall-fattened muskies and walleyes. Hunting seasons for ruffed grouse, bear, deer, and waterfowl had opened or soon would. Most conversations at the Moose Café and Crossroads Coffee centered on the upcoming or ongoing hunting seasons.

There was an entire group of citizens who became more visible in the fall. It seemed that everyone in Namekagon County owned a dog or two, and I wouldn't be surprised if the canine citizens outnumbered the human ones. Hound dogs stuck their heads out of the openings in dog boxes in the back of pickup trucks. They were anxious and ready to travel the backcountry with their handler, sorting out thousands of scents, looking for the one they lived for—the smell of a bear—announcing success with hound dog howls.

The northern lakes and rivers were also a destination for waterfowl hunters. Wild rice flowages, big water, and shallow wetlands host thousands of ducks and geese during the fall migration. Water dogs, mostly Labs and Chesapeakes, were the choice of waterfowlers. These dogs were unfazed by the cold water, and they lived to retrieve ducks and geese knocked down by their hunter.

Bird dogs rode in backseats or portable kennels. Pointers and close working flushers were ready to go in search of ruffed grouse and woodcock. Bird populations were high. Some said the best in over a decade. With thousands of acres of land open to the public, even the most determined hunter could not hunt it all in a lifetime.

Hunting with dogs in the north country, as of late, faced some unusual challenges, and the situation had become more difficult and dangerous. Some of the best hunting was in the backcountry, the home territory of gray wolves, the largest wild canine on earth. These packs roamed freely across the landscape, covering large territories. Until recently, they were protected by the federal Endangered Species Act, and the number of gray wolves had grown significantly. As a result, there had been an increase in the number of wolf attacks on domestic animals. Bird dogs and bear hounds cover lots of ground, sometimes running head-on into a wolf pack. These encounters rarely end well for the dogs.

Wolves also were suspects in the decline of the deer herd. Hunters harvested fewer deer, and in some areas available doe tags had been reduced to bolster the number of breeding females. Hunters were encouraged to take mostly bucks.

For the past several years, it has been against federal law to kill a wolf unless, as locals put it, "your leg is in its mouth." Whether they liked wolves or not, most people were law-abiding and adopted a live-and-let-live attitude. After all, wolves, known as ma'iinganag to the Ojibwe, had roamed this land for over ten thousand years. However, some folks had taken wolf management into their own hands and subscribed to the concept of the three S's: shoot, shovel, and shut up. Even though wolves are a formidable animal, there had yet to be a case of a healthy wolf attacking a human in Wisconsin. But there have been some pretty close calls.

Namekagon County sheriff's deputies worked closely with local conservation wardens. There were only two wardens to cover the entire county, and by statute, the deputies were allowed to enforce game laws. Some of my staff even carried deputy warden credentials working part-time for the DNR when they were off duty. With backup sometimes miles away, patrolling so much country required all law enforcement officers to work together. A sheriff's deputy on a call might be backed up by a Musky Falls city officer, a Wisconsin State Trooper, or a conservation warden and vice versa.

It was the beginning of October, about one in the afternoon of a very quiet day, when I got a call from dispatch to switch down to our secure radio channel.

My call number came first, "301," said the dispatcher.

"301, go ahead," I replied.

"Sheriff, meet Conservation Warden Asmundsen and a grouse hunter in the parking lot at the Birchbark Bar. The grouse hunter and his hunting partner were hunting off Ghost Lake Road and came on an SUV that contains a body. One hunter stayed with the vehicle, and the other went over to the bar to call it in. They will be standing by in the parking lot."

"Have they determined that the individual in question is deceased?" I asked.

"One of the hunters opened the driver's door of the SUV. The one who called it in is a retired dentist from Eau Claire, so he has had a fair amount of medical training, but he didn't need it. He said the body was very decomposed and had a solid population of maggots cleaning things up."

"Okay. Notify the ME's office and put them on standby."

"Ten-four, Sheriff. What is your ETA to the Birchbark?"

"About twenty minutes if I fly. I am en route."

"Ten-four," dispatch replied.

My Chevy Tahoe squad car was a police interceptor. It was equipped to be operated on the backroads. Four-wheel drive, all-weather tires, a steel welded crash bar, and a twelve-thousand-pound winch were standard equipment. Northern Wisconsin was known for its weather extremes, fifty below zero and eight feet of snow. The Tahoe was just the vehicle for that. It had plenty of horsepower but lacked the sports car handling I had come to know from driving a Crown Vic.

I hit my flashing lights and took off toward the Birchbark. There wasn't much traffic, and I cruised at eighty.

As I pulled into the parking lot, I saw the conservation warden leaning on his pickup truck talking to a guy wearing a bird hunting vest. Hunters covered a lot of country and some pretty remote areas. It was inevitable that they would come upon something that required the attention of law enforcement.

I stopped my squad next to them and got out.

"Hey guys," I said.

"Hello, Sheriff," they responded in unison.

The warden was a veteran, closing in on his third decade in law enforcement. He was tough as boot leather and had no tolerance for people who violated our natural resource laws. My predecessor had provided background on the people I would be working with and had spoken highly of Warden Clark Asmundsen. Asmundsen was very adept at tracking and had run a fair number of miscreants to ground over the years. In one now legendary case, he had followed a wanted felon into the national forest. The person he was pursuing was a suspect in a homicide in the southern part of the state. A trooper had stopped a vehicle for having only one headlight. When he went back to his car to run a check on the guy, the suspect bailed out and took off into the woods. The trooper called in the foot pursuit, and Asmundsen, who was nearby, showed up a few minutes later.

There was over a foot of snow on the ground, and he strapped on his snowshoes. The trooper stayed with the suspect's car, and Asmundsen took off at a dead run, snowshoes and all. Following the bad guy's tracks in the deep snow was easy. The warden kept the pressure on, and he could see that the felon's strides were getting shorter and shorter, clearly a sign that he was running out of steam. The warden caught a glimpse of his quarry on two occasions and, knowing he would soon overtake him, pushed even harder. Asmundsen came to a small clearing, and there slumped on the ground was the suspect, breathing hard and exhausted, with no energy left to resist. The warden cuffed him without a problem. He radioed ahead to have a squad car meet him at a forest crossroad he was near. Then he hoisted the bad guy up and dragged him another mile through the woods to the waiting officers. The story goes that the officers who took the suspect offered Asmundsen a ride back to his truck, but he declined and headed back into the woods, claiming it was a good night for a hike.

"Go ahead and tell the sheriff here your story," the warden instructed the hunter.

"We were bird hunting on a two-track that runs off of Ghost Lake Road. We've been hunting this same covert for years. I can't recall ever running into any other hunters. Anyway, the birds weren't cooperating, so we pushed on, looking for a stand of young poplar trees we knew about. We came over a rise in the trail, and Odie, my English setter, and my partner's Llewellin setter, locked up on point. Two birds flushed. My partner got one, and I missed the other. The bird I missed didn't fly far, and after the dogs retrieved his bird, we headed over to where we had seen the grouse land. That's when we saw the truck. It was on the dead end of the two-track. A newer, fancy SUV, but it was pretty much covered with leaves and dust. There was also a sizable tree branch laying across the hood. The windows were tinted, but I could see someone was inside. I probably shouldn't have, but I opened the driver's side door to see if the guy needed help. When I did, a cloud of flies flew out of the truck, and others started buzzing around the body. The smell was overpowering. It was clear he was beyond any help I might offer. I could see maggots and the body was in an advanced state of decomposition. If I had to guess, I would say it had been there at least a month. It's not a very educated opinion on my part, but taking into account the warm months of late summer and early fall, it seemed consistent with what you might expect," the retired dentist relayed.

"If you guys don't mind, I would like it if you could take me to the scene."

"Sure thing, Sheriff," the warden replied. "One thing though, I think there is another way into the area they are talking about that will be easier to get through. There is a long-abandoned guest lodge just a mile from here. I think the old driveway works its way back in the woods and hooks up to the trail he's talking about."

"Works for me," I replied.

The old driveway took us right to the road where the SUV was parked. The hunter's partner and the dogs greeted us. I approached the vehicle and called the plate number into dispatch. I opened the driver's door and found the victim much as the dentist had described. Then I started photographing the entire area, including the vehicle, from every angle. It is surprising how many things are revealed by clear photographs that you may not have noticed even though you were at the scene.

The vehicle plate came back on a three-year-old Cadillac Escalade registered to a Devin Martin from Milwaukee. The dispatcher immediately ran a criminal history on the name Devin Martin. Several individuals shared the name, but one in particular from Milwaukee had a lengthy criminal record.

The warden recorded contact information for the two hunters while I began examining the scene in close detail. I could not make out the victim's features. From what I could tell, it appeared to be a Caucasian male, thin build, with black hair. The insect world had all come to the buffet and had things covered. I knew the condition of the flesh would help the medical examiner determine how long the body had been there. I began photographing the corpse and immediately could make out the butt of a handgun down off the edge of the center console. Then I noticed a long stem of some sort of grass or woodland plant. The stem was inside the vehicle, pinched in place by the passenger door. I walked back around the vehicle and looked closely at the door. It was not completely closed. The door was about a quarter of an inch from completely latching. I photographed the door in its position and the weed as best I could.

I walked back to the hunters and asked if they would mind going to the sheriff's office to give a statement. Both readily agreed. I thanked both men for their cooperation and gave each a business card.

"If either of you remembers or thinks of anything else, don't hesitate to call me, no matter how insignificant you think it might be. Before you go, I have a couple of questions for you. Did either of you open the front passenger side door?" I asked.

Both reiterated that they had only opened the driver's door, which was the only physical contact they had with the vehicle.

"Did you notice a pistol laying near the console?"

Both again said they hadn't really looked around once they noted the condition of the body. I figured they were being straight with me. Perpetrators or co-conspirators in a crime rarely reported the victim and cooperated fully with law enforcement. The exception would be some sociopaths who had made cooperating with police all part of their sick game. I could be wrong, but these guys did not appear to be murderous criminals plying their trade in the Northwoods. The hunters headed to the sheriff's office.

The scene always told a story. Here was a late model, top-of-the-line Cadillac SUV, dressed out with huge chrome rims and thin profile tires. Where leaves and dirt hadn't covered the truck, the finish appeared to have been buffed to a high gloss shine. This was not the typical truck that someone would choose for cruising the backwoods. There was a gun in close proximity to the dead man's right hand. Most people are right-handed. Maybe this guy had powered his fancy SUV out through the bush until he had come to the right place, then had ended it all. At first glance, it was looking like a strong scenario. But there was something else. Someone had opened and partially closed the passenger's front door, catching the plant. The victim may have done it himself. Got out for one last look at his fancy car before he did himself in. Or someone else may have come upon the Cadillac and opened the door. Once they saw what was inside, they decided they wanted no part of it, shut the door, and moved on. Or maybe someone who had been a participant or had critical information about what happened to the guy behind the wheel was in the car—all questions that needed answers. •

CHAPTER 3

In Wisconsin, if a law enforcement officer comes upon a death that is "unexplained, unusual, or otherwise suspicious in nature," it must be reported to the coroner or medical examiner assigned to the jurisdiction in which the death occurred. The coroner is an elected position. Anyone can run for that position as long as they are over the age of eighteen and don't have a felony conviction. They don't have to know anything about forensic investigation.

In my county, a local livestock dealer and part-time realtor held the coroner's position for over twenty-five years. His brother owned a funeral home in Musky Falls. By all reports, the coroner was competent and professional in carrying out his duties. Wisconsin law does not allow a funeral director acting as coroner to offer funeral services to the victim's family. The coroner did not offer funeral services. He did, however, occasionally provide to the bereaved the business card for his brother's funeral home, and rumor had it he was compensated for the referral on the side. This didn't appear to be an issue with the local community until a funeral home from Superior opened a branch in Musky Falls. The owner of the new state-of-the-art, full-service funeral home noticed immediately that it seemed everybody who died in Namekagon County went to the coroner's brother's facility. He grumbled to the county board, prompting two members to call for an investigation to see if their duly elected and compensated coroner was double-dipping. Another member added fuel to the fire when he shared that he was recently beaten out of first place in a bass tournament by the coroner who happened to be running around in a new decked-out fishing boat with the name of his brother's funeral home professionally lettered on both sides. He wasn't accusing the coroner of anything but, under the circumstances, felt he should bring it up.

The discussion was enough for the coroner, and consequently, he withdrew his candidacy in the next election. That seemed to satisfy most, but his withdrawal set tongues wagging. The deadline to be put on the ballot for the coroner's race was rapidly approaching, and no one was jumping up. Finally, Olaf Gjertson, the local butcher who was known to run errands around town in his blood-stained apron, walked into the county office at the last minute and said, "How do I get them papers to fill out to be the 'corner'?"

The clerk called the county board chair, and he added an agenda item to the upcoming county board meeting. They had been considering replacing the coroner's position with a medical examiner—someone highly trained in forensic procedures and who would serve at the pleasure of the county board. Although unsaid, it appeared as if Olaf's desire to run for public office was just the thing needed for a unanimous vote to replace the coroner with an ME.

The timing was perfect, and Namekagon County was lucky. A young physician and his wife had found the north country too alluring to resist. He was at the end of his contract with a giant hospital on the east coast, and his wife had recently completed graduate school and was looking for a position as a counselor working with kids. The big hospital offered him a contract with a four-year commitment. It was attractive, but not as attractive as living in the

Northwoods splendor and being able to fish muskies whenever he wanted. They packed up and moved to Musky Falls. He was offered a job in the local hospital emergency room and was working there when the notice went out for the part-time ME. The fact he was well qualified and the only applicant was not lost on the county board. They hired him before the ink was dry on his application.

I had dispatch send our new medical examiner, Dr. Mike Chali, to the scene.

Warden Asmundsen offered to stick around but added that the wardens had mobilized to work deer shiners after he received several reports of a group cruising backroads at night. When they spotted a deer standing in a meadow or crop field, they would shine a powerful spotlight in the animal's eyes, immobilizing it for a few seconds but long enough for someone else in the vehicle to stick a rifle out the window, take aim, and shoot. The perpetrators did not even attempt to retrieve the deer they shot, leaving them to rot. People here have no sense of humor when it comes to things like this, nor does the warden force. Low deer numbers made this worse. Asmundsen took off to meet up with his crew for the night maneuvers.

I stayed with the vehicle and body. It was over an hour before the ME got close enough for me to direct him in. He drove easily down the woods road in his restored 1980s vintage Toyota Land Cruiser.

Despite the routine nature of the work around the area so far— drunk drivers killed in accidents, two suicides, and tragically the death of a local teenager from a drug overdose—Dr. Chali demonstrated thoroughness. Becky, his wife, landed a position as a mental health counselor at the crisis center in Musky Falls. Part of her job was to develop a community action group for kids and adults who would meet at the community center every other week. Julie volunteered to help her, and they had become good friends. Both were concerned about the increase in the number of kids and adults struggling with drug addiction. While a familiar problem for urban dwellers, it was somewhat new to rural areas. Community concern was voiced regularly in the local paper and at county board and city council meetings. Law enforcement had become the focal point of many of their concerns, essentially falling back to the age-old position taken by those who saw their lives and community being challenged: throw the bastards in jail. The truth is, most people still expect when they call a cop, one will show up and do something.

"Hi, Mike. Thanks for coming out," I said.

He listened intently as I explained my suspicion of the circumstances.

"Sheriff, it sounds to me like you have good reason to be suspicious. Let's see what we can find."

He removed a set of white coveralls with elastic cuffs at the wrists and ankles from one of two large aluminum-clad suitcases he brought. Once he donned the coveralls, he slipped a pair of white booties on over his boots, and then put on a hairnet, a face mask, and surgical gloves. He hooked a microphone on his shirt collar and began to film and narrate the scene using a small video camera. He was meticulous in his approach, doing everything he could to protect any evidence.

He finished with his video and called me over.

"Sheriff, let me tell you what I think we are going to need to do. I am going to enter the vehicle from the back doors and begin an examination of the body. I do not want to enter the front passenger's door because of your astute observation regarding the plant. I need to get a closer look to make an initial determination if I can. The condition may make it impossible outside of the examination room, but I need to try. While I am doing this, would you please video my every move and anything else I ask you to?"

"Okay, I will," I responded.

The doctor entered the SUV. I started recording. Shortly after getting started, he spoke to me.

"Sheriff, on the passenger's side of the vehicle in approximately the middle of the floor mat, there is a brass shell casing. Near the victim's right hand is a black semiautomatic handgun laying between the seat and console. Please video these items at their respective locations. First distant, then zoom in as best you can."

"Got it, Doctor," I replied.

"The victim appears to be a white male. Estimate of age is mid to upper thirties. Sheriff, I am going to see if he has some form of identification on him. There is a chain hooked to a belt loop in his pants that goes to an area that is near his right rear pocket, probably a wallet."

Then he moved closer to the body.

"There is what appears to be an entry wound on the right side of the subject's head. It is irregular, with portions of the skull broken away; There appears to be powder tattooing in the remaining flesh around the wound. It also appears as though some flesh and tissue were carried into the area. The wound area has seen significant activity from scavengers, in particular maggots."

The ME tried to move to a spot right behind the body.

"Sheriff, there is a large duffle bag on the floor behind the driver's seat. Please video the bag. I am not going to disturb it. I will need to crawl up onto the seat to examine the rest of the subject's skull for an exit wound."

He looked over the victim's head and then began to gently move his gloved fingers around and under the hair. After a few minutes, he stated, "No exit wound is apparent at this time. Sheriff, do you want me to retrieve the victim's wallet at this time?"

"Yes, Mike."

While he was unhooking the wallet from the deceased's belt and pulling it from his pocket, I gloved up and got a large clear evidence bag. I held the bag out for the ME, and he dropped the wallet in.

He got out of the vehicle, walked some distance away, and brushed away the maggots that had crawled onto his coveralls and gloves.

I reached into the evidence bag and opened the wallet. There was a driver's license. The ME walked over to me and turned on his mic.

I gave my narrative.

"Dr. Chali, ME of Namekagon County, has retrieved a black leather wallet attached to a silver color chain from the victim. The wallet was deposited in an evidence bag. I have opened the wallet inside the bag and retrieved a Wisconsin driver's license. The name on the driver's license is Devin L. Martin, six feet tall, one hundred seventy pounds, brown eyes, black hair, 37 years old with a Milwaukee address. The name is consistent with registration of the vehicle." I removed my hands from the evidence bag and sealed it.

"So, what do you think?" I asked the ME.

"It appears as if the victim received a gunshot wound to the right temple, possibly self-inflicted. I could not find an exit wound, so the slug may still be inside. Hopefully, we can retrieve it. Then the lab folks can maybe get a match with the gun in the car. Determining how long ago he died is going to be a little more difficult to establish. Flies begin to lay their eggs just a few days after death. It takes between two and three weeks for the eggs to hatch and release maggots. Once the maggots are on the body, they move quickly and can consume sixty percent of a human body in just seven days. So, he has been here for at least several weeks. Once we get him back to the examination room, we will try to pin down a more precise date. What I see here is consistent with suicide, but I will not make that call until the full exam is complete. The subject is clearly deceased, and I will call it 4:32 p.m., October 16. John, any other information will have to come from the postmortem examination. Are you calling in a crime scene unit or handling this yourself?"

"Doc, I know this looks like a suicide, and it probably is, but I am going to call in a crime scene unit."

"Okay with me, Sheriff. I will stand by until they arrive and assist in the investigation."

I radioed dispatch. Lois, our most senior and competent communicator, responded.

"Lois, contact the crime scene unit out of Eau Claire County and see if they are available."

"I already made contact with them after you requested the ME. They are finishing a scene, and the soonest they could get going would be first thing tomorrow morning," she replied.

"How about Douglas County?" I asked.

"They are not available. They only have two techs on. Everyone else has been subpoenaed in a homicide case."

"Tell the Eau Claire crew we will stand by and await their arrival. Also, advise them that the ME's initial exam indicates death by a possible gunshot to the head. The corpse is decomposed, and we will wait to extract the body from the vehicle until they are on the scene."

"Ten-four, Sheriff. I will pass it on," Lois replied.

I said to Dr. Chali, "The Eau Claire County crime scene unit will be here first thing in the morning. You might as well head home."

"Okay, John. Give me a call as soon as you know the crime scene unit's ETA. I want to be on-site before they arrive."

He backed his old Land Cruiser down the two-track and was soon gone. I took the opportunity to run Devin L. Martin for a criminal record. He had been a busy boy. Four felony convictions, the last of which netted him three years in prison. He was released on parole after eighteen months. However, he had neglected to follow up with his P.O., and there was an active warrant for his arrest issued in August.

Whether in a big city, a small town, or the middle of a national forest, a crime scene needs to be protected against contamination. That means cordoning off the area with an officer or deputy standing guard. It is not the most popular duty for a law enforcement officer. Cops are more prone to action. Sitting around watching a car with a dead guy in it is not very exciting. But it needed to be done. In most circumstances, the protocol would be to remove the body and take it to the morgue for testing and examination. In this case, I opted not to. The body had been there a long time, and I meant no disrespect to the dead. One of the most respectful things I could do was to conduct a thorough investigation.

"301," I called on the radio.

"301, go ahead," Lois responded.

"Lois, I am going to stand by and secure the scene until midnight or so. Find someone else to relieve me from then until the crime scene team gets here. Let them know it's on overtime."

"Ten-four, Sheriff," she replied.

I got comfortable in the car and began the long wait. I tried to call Julie, but there was no cell signal.

"301," I called.

"301, go ahead," Lois responded.

"Lois, will you call Julie on her cell and let her know what is going on? Let her know I will be home late."

"Will do, Sheriff."

Law enforcement is mostly mundane. Pretty routine and often quite boring. That is, until it's not. Darkness started creeping in a little after seven. The air temperature was cool but not uncomfortable, and the big woods was peaceful. I had not heard back from Lois about someone to relieve me, but I knew she was on it and would let me know when she knew.

I had a small lunch cooler in my squad, and by about eight o'clock, I was cruising it for snacks. Julie had packed both our lunches this morning before she left for school and I went off to guard a dead body. She was no stranger to the men and women of the north country and their caloric needs and had packed me a sizable amount of food. She had lived with her cousin, Arvid "Bud" Treetall, for many years, who required large quantities of food to keep his engine running.

Julie, Bud, and I had become an unofficial family of sorts. We spent all our holidays together and had many suppers out at the cabin. I had not yet convinced Julie to take me up on my marriage proposal. She maintained that she intended to treat me like a pair of shoes. She said no one would ever buy a pair of shoes without at least trying them on. Why should considering a husband be any different? It didn't matter to me; I was happier than I had ever been in my life. She could take all the time she wanted.

True dark sets into the Northwoods at night. Moonrise and starlight would provide some illumination, but the dense forest pretty much blocked everything else out. I took an emergency blanket from the back of my squad, spread it on the ground next to a tree, and got comfortable for the long haul. Still no word from Lois.

What happened next, I am sure has been a thrilling event for humankind through the ages. It was definitely a thrilling moment for me. From what seemed only a few feet away, a sound pierced the night, crystal clear and loud enough to make the hair on the back of my neck stand up. It was the howl of a gray wolf. Another wolf on the opposite side of me responded with a howl of their own. They seemed to have me surrounded.

Even though, on some level, I knew better, I reached for my gun to protect me from the impending wolf attack I was sure would come. Wolf researchers reiterated at every chance that humans had nothing to fear from wolves. At this moment, however, that was of little consequence as I struggled to get my heart out of my throat. I sat as still as I could and was ready for the next call when it came, louder and closer—a mournful call of the north country combined with raw wildness. Although it gave me a jolt at first, I was now calm, and any vestiges of fear had ebbed. I had heard a wolf howl before, but not in such proximity. The communication between the wolves continued for a short while and stopped. I put my back against the tree and got comfortable again. Minutes later, I heard leaves crunching off to my right. Something was approaching. I snapped on my flashlight. At the edge of the clearing was a full-grown wolf facing me. His head seemed enormous. Before I could really look at him, he turned and vanished back into the night.

A voice came over my radio, and I am sure I jumped a foot.

"301."

"301, go ahead," I responded.

"Sheriff, Deputy Holmes will replace you at midnight. With a new baby on the way, he is looking for all the overtime he can get."

"Ten-four. Thanks, Lois. Oh, did you get a hold of Julie?"

"Yes, I did. She said she would put dinner in a container in the fridge. She has parent-teacher conferences starting tomorrow, so she said don't count on her to wait up."

"Thanks, Lois," I said.

"Now, if you don't mind, Sheriff, I am worn out and ready to get myself home."

"Thanks for sticking around," I said.

———

Parent-teacher conferences. I had learned that most teachers didn't care for them much. Still, Julie thought they were worthwhile, giving the parents and teachers a chance to have a productive conversation about student learning, with the end goal being to develop a plan that the parents, teachers, and the student could buy into. Almost half of her students were considered "at risk," to use the same language the school board used. Many of them faced challenges of epic proportions—poverty, broken families, drugs and alcohol. Some were not conventional learners. All were welcome at her school. It was her mission in life to help them learn how to learn. Her greatest challenge came from the fact that she had a waiting list every year. She hated the idea that any student who wanted to couldn't come to her school. To that end, she worked diligently on curing that problem by getting the okay to hire another teacher. So far, approval had not been given.

———————————

Shortly before midnight, a spotlight beam crossed the area and settled on my squad car.

Deputy Holmes exited the vehicle. "Hey, Sheriff. How you doing?"

"Good, Deputy. Good."

"What have you got here?" the deputy asked.

"Well, this is probably pretty straightforward. It looks like a suicide and probably is. But some things raise questions, so I requested a crime scene unit. They are coming in from Eau Claire County and should be here by eight o'clock in the morning. I will be back tomorrow morning by seven. If by chance they get here early, tell them not to touch anything until I get here."

"Got it, Sheriff."

"I am dog tired, and heading home to catch a couple of hours of sleep. By the way, how's your wife doing?"

"She's excited to have the baby, but we've got a long way to go. She's healthy and strong, so we'll make it through. I promised to pick up a half gallon of her favorite ice cream from the dairy on my way home."

"I am glad to hear everything is okay. I'll see you in the morning. Oh, by the way, a wolf paid me a visit a while ago. Kinda gave me a start, if you know what I mean."

"I know what you mean. You run into them when you least expect it, and it always makes me jump. They are usually gone before you even know they are there. Everybody says they won't bother people. So far, I guess that's true. Last winter, I took a call at a sheep farm north of town. Wolves had gotten in with the sheep and killed most of them. The only thing the farmer could do was shoot up in the air, and they finally ran off."

"You watch out. I'll see you in the morning." ☙

CHAPTER 4

The drive home was quiet with no radio calls, meaning Namekagon County citizens and visitors were tucked in bed.

Driving up to the cabin, I was glad to see the lights on. At night, light shining on old wood gave everything a comfortable orange-brown glow. I went inside and was more or less greeted by the love of my life. She was in the room but sound asleep in her comfortable chair with a pile of student papers on the table next to her.

I touched her arm gently, and she woke with a start.

"Oh, hi, John. I must have dozed off. What time is it?"

"A little after one, and time to hit the sack."

"That sounds like a wonderful idea. Did you eat supper?"

"No, the lunch you packed me got me through."

"I could warm something up for you."

"Thanks, honey, but to be honest, I am too tired to eat. Let's get to bed. I have to be back on the road by at least six thirty. So I need to sleep fast as it is."

We trudged upstairs and got ready for bed. She came out of the bathroom wearing what I deemed her most alluring sleepwear— green flannel pajamas patterned with bears and pine trees. I crawled into bed next to her, and she snuggled the soft material against me to ward off the cold. There could be nothing on earth better than this. Exhausted, we kissed goodnight and were fast asleep.

═══════════

Morning came too soon. Julie and I had a rule every morning: we had a cup of coffee together and discussed the day. If one of us had to leave the house at six, then we got up early and had coffee at five thirty. It was a wonderful routine for two very busy people who just needed a moment to reconnect.

"What is going on out there that kept you out so late?" she asked.

"A dead body in a car out in the woods. Looks like a suicide, but not everything is right. So, I figured I would spend my budget and call out the crime scene unit."

"Suicide is such a sad statement on life. If someone could reach out to these people at the right time, so many of them could probably be saved. The real tragedy is the pain suffered by the people left behind. I know mental illness is behind it, and I should not be critical, but I always felt it was the coward's way out. A few years ago, the father of one of my students killed himself on Christmas Day, leaving an eighth-grade girl and her mother who was struggling through recovery. They made it, but not without a lot of pain," she said.

"I don't know anything about this victim other than a possible name. We'll find out more today. Dr. Chali came out and pronounced him dead. Today we need to process the scene and see what we can find. I should be home before you are unless something else comes up," I said.

"I won't be home until late, John. The rest of my parent-teacher conferences are tonight, and I pushed my evening meetings back because I have to do a home visit. One of my students is clearly struggling with some family issues. She has been absent several days, and when she comes to school, she looks like she hasn't slept.

She is a wonderful kid and plenty smart, but her home environment has become a real limiting factor for her."

"What time do you think I might see you?" I asked.

"Not before nine, I am sure."

Just then, my portable radio squawked my number.

"301, go ahead," I replied.

"301, switch down to Tact 1."

"301, I am on the secure channel. Go ahead."

"301, the crime scene unit is running ahead of schedule and will be on the scene in about a half hour."

"Ten-four. I am on my way."

I gave Julie a quick kiss goodbye and took off down the road. There was little traffic on the highway, and I moved right along. I wanted to get to the scene first to talk with the techs before they started. Almost as an afterthought, I remembered to have dispatch page out the ME. They did, and he responded to the page telling dispatch he was en route in the transport van.

I arrived only a minute before everyone else. I asked Deputy Holmes to stick around to help out, and he agreed.

Everyone huddled together, and Dr. Chali reported on his cursory examination. On the passenger side of the vehicle, I pointed out the plant pinched in the door and explained why that made me curious.

"Someone opened this door wide enough to go over the top of this plant about eighteen inches away. Then, whoever closed the door caught the plant, and the stem ended up inside the vehicle. The door was also not completely closed. I am guessing because the stem got in the way. I don't know when this might have happened, but it is clear that someone else was here at some point and opened the door. It could have been a hiker walking by that took one look and decided it was not their business, or it could have been someone else. Other than that, you folks can have at it. We will stand by to assist," I explained.

The crime scene team began the meticulous job of surveying the area around the car. Once the area leading to the driver's door was cleared, they suited up and began the grisly task of helping the ME remove the body and attached organisms. Dr. Chali examined the right side of the head more closely this time and announced the hole in the subject's head did appear to be a bullet wound. He also confirmed that there was no apparent exit wound, so the bullet was still inside the body. The team bagged the hands of the deceased and gently loaded him into a body bag. Then the body was transferred to the ME's van and transported.

Then one of the techs called me over. He was holding the duffle bag that he had unzipped. Inside was a pile of cash and an equal pile of plastic bags containing a white crystalline substance that looked a lot like meth. One of the technicians removed a baggie from the duffle bag and tested the substance with a chemical kit. It was positive for methamphetamines. The test kit and sample were bagged for evidence.

The gun was retrieved from the front seat. It was an older model, Smith & Wesson nine millimeter semi-auto. The magazine was only partially full, with cutouts indicating it held only ten rounds even though the capacity was fifteen. There was a live round in the chamber. A nine millimeter shell casing was recovered from the floor on the passenger side of the vehicle.

A black rectangular weapon was stuffed under the back seat. It looked like an Ingram Mac-ten sub-machine gun. Closer examination showed it to be a cheaply made semi-auto copy, stamped out of sheet metal, with a long stick magazine protruding from the bottom. The magazine was partially loaded with nine millimeter rounds. The receiver was stamped "Cobray M11."

It appeared as though Martin was prepared for potential violence and had taken great precautions to make sure he was able to protect himself. Not the actions of someone who intends to commit suicide.

Then again, who knows what is going through anybody's head at a given time. Maybe he was sampling his product and got crazy. Who knows?

The crime scene crew bagged and tagged what they needed, including the plant.

"Sheriff, we are good to move the vehicle to secure storage if it's okay with you," the technician said.

"I will call a wrecker. We can store the vehicle at the department lock-up where you can finish up."

"Sounds good. We'll finish up with fibers, fluids, latents, and all the rest. Do you intend to keep the vehicle in impound for a while?" the tech asked.

"Why?" I asked.

"I was just wondering. I mean, at this point, it looks like a pretty straightforward suicide. We'll do all the collections and tests right away. If you want a full ballistic workup, that will have to go Milwaukee. We can do a cursory review, but I guess what I'm saying is there is probably no need to rush."

Crime scene teams were always under the gun. I knew that whatever they came up with here would be added to the pile of what they already had on their plate.

"Our impound is dry and secure. I don't need you to put a rush on this, but I don't want it to get buried either. Let's tag and secure the money and drugs. If the ME is able to find a slug, take it along with the gun and shell casing and go through with the ballistics. Analysis of trace, hair, fluids, fiber can wait a while."

"Works for us," the tech replied, relieved.

I radioed dispatch to send the flatbed wrecker from Bill and Jack's Garage and Guide Service to transport the vehicle. Deputy Holmes and the crime scene crew would follow it into town and lock it up.

I signed a formal evidence release for the plant and took it into my possession. I thanked everyone and headed back toward Musky

Falls. Once I had cell service, I called a friend of mine over at the university, Professor Charlie Newlin. He was a brilliant professor-type who answered the phone with a "*Quack*."

"Hey, Charlie, this is John Cabrelli," I said.

"Why hello there, Sheriff John. It is good to hear from you. Hasn't this been a wonderful fall? I think the north country in the fall is an absolutely splendid place to be. I have had my students out in the field watching migrating birds, everything from giant Canada geese to tiny neotropical migrants. It is all part of a field biology unit on seasonal adaptive behaviors of wildlife. We spend the first part of the class documenting general observations of the environment and determine how they impact residents as temperatures get colder. It can be as simple as noting a small, isolated wetland that has frozen up and then deciding what the resident species would likely be and how they would adapt. As the birds begin to move, we concentrate on them. Who is here today, and who is gone? I order phenology calendars for each student produced by the Aldo Leopold Foundation for comparative information. It is a fun way of seeing how things have changed and how things have stayed the same. I must confess, though, that I collect a great deal of information during these outings that I hope will benefit me during the waterfowl season. Noting species of birds and locations is of interest to me both as a scientist and someone who loves the taste of roasted duck or goose.

"Most recently, I have indulged my culinary bent with a recipe that is new to me. It's called Marcy's Goose stew. It is absolutely delicious. I throw in a handful of freshly picked oyster mushrooms, and it is a gourmet delight. As a matter of fact, it is what I have packed myself for lunch today. I do love the fall. I expect that we will get some real weather soon that will put a winter chill in the air. Enough of me going on. What can I do for you, John?"

"Charlie, I know your expertise is wildlife, but I need some information on a plant."

"You are in luck. My first real love has been botany. As I began my studies, I noted that habitat and wildlife were interlinked. For example, if you found a plant that a certain wildlife species liked, you could expect that to be a situation that would repeat itself. If you found a healthy patch of wild blue lupine, you might very well expect to find the endangered Karner blue butterfly in the same place. A large bed of wild rice growing in a lake would be a great place to expect to find waterfowl, and so on. I realized that if I truly wanted to understand wildlife, I needed to understand their habitat. Plants are a huge part of that. I could probably help you out with a plant question, or at least steer you in the right direction."

"Are you busy right now?" I asked.

"Nothing other than partaking of my aforementioned goose stew," he replied.

"Thanks, Charlie. I will be there in twenty minutes."

"See you then, John. By the way, I will be in the lab in Heinemann Hall. First door on the left as you are coming in."

———————————

On my way over, my cell phone rang.

"Sheriff, this is Holmes. We are at the secure storage building with Doc O'Malley. We have a problem. The garage stall is stacked high and deep with boxes. There is not enough room for us to get the vehicle in and have enough room for the evidence techs to work."

"Can you move the boxes? What's in them?" I asked.

"We would have to move them out the door. They are full of stuff from the Chamber of Commerce for Fall Fest and the Great Northern Ski Race. The storage building they were using had a leak in the roof, so they moved the stuff over here. I forgot all about it. We don't use the impound that much," Holmes replied.

"Any alternative for secure storage?" I asked.

"Not that I am aware of, Sheriff."

"Okay. Stand by. I will get back to you."

I called Jim Rawsom.

"Hey, Jim, how are you doing?"

"Well, John, things are going in the right direction, but slow. Physical therapy, as you well know, is a real job. The doctor says that we should have a better handle on things come spring, but he says my progress is better than expected. The big thing is the head wound. I continue to have vision issues and headaches. Both are better, but still there. You didn't call to listen to me whine. What can I do for you, Sheriff?"

That stopped me cold. He had never called me Sheriff before. Not at the swearing-in or since. He was the *real* sheriff; I was just filling in. We both knew that. He would heal, and I would hand over the badge. Then maybe I'd buy part interest in the Happy Hooker Bait and Tackle Shop to keep me busy. I had heard the co-owners were thinking about slowing down. I never once thought I would be the real sheriff. I still didn't.

"Jim, here is the deal. Two grouse hunters found a fancy SUV off on a fire lane. There was a dead guy in the driver's seat. The ME says it looks like a suicide, and it probably is, but I want to cover a few bases before I turn it over to next of kin or whoever. It turns out our secure storage is full of boxes being stored for the chamber while they get their roof fixed. Do you know of any alternative storage I can use?"

"Sure, call the warden. They have secure storage by the ranger station, where they store confiscated animals. The small ones go in the freezer. The big ones hang from the rafters. What makes you think this isn't a suicide?"

"I still do think that's likely, but there are some things that don't wash. First of all, this guy was doing business. A duffle bag in the back seat was stuffed with cash and meth. Second, I think there may have been someone else in the car."

"Aw shit, John, meth. We've had a real problem with dealers expanding their networks up to our Northwoods. We put a ton of pressure on them when it first started, and that seemed to work for a while, but we never got rid of them. They recruited some of our resident dirtbags and wormed their way in. It's been a real issue. About five years ago, things got worse. A local girl and some of her friends got mixed up with a guy from the cities. She was a good kid, a tough family life, but a good kid all the same. She OD'd and didn't make it. We put everything we had into making a case. All we knew was that a guy in his twenties named Jake, last name unknown, sold them drugs. He was long gone by the time we got there. We grilled those kids pretty damn hard, but I am convinced they didn't know much about him or his supplier. Just out of curiosity, you got a name on the guy you found?"

"Yeah, a tentative is Devin Martin, a white male in his thirties."

Rawsom was silent for long enough that I asked if he was still there.

"I'm here, John. I also know who Devin Martin was. We got a report from the Department of Narcotics Enforcement that he was supplying drugs to dealers in our area, mostly meth but also heroin. The report said he was usually armed. There were no wants or warrants at the time; it was just an FYI. They wanted us to watch for him. It was the middle of summer. There were so many tourists from the cities that we didn't notice him when he showed up. Then the city police department busted a couple of our local troublemakers. Both of them had meth in their possession. We ID'd Martin and stopped him every chance we got. We shook him down pretty well, but he was clean. Anyway, one day Martin disappears, and meth starts showing up on the streets. DNE came up and tried to stop things before they got started. They made a few cases, but the genie was already out of the bottle."

Out of the bottle was a gross understatement. Drugs were a poison destroying the lives of everyone they touched. The number of people dying from drug overdoses had tripled in the last ten years. It wasn't just in Namekagon County; it was all over the country. The nightly news bombarded us with national tragedies every day. I had heard many people say they could not stand to watch the news anymore. Of all the national tragedies, there was nothing worse than the cancer of drug addiction and the subsequent wasted and lost lives it represented. No one was untouched. Everyone knew someone who had perished, been arrested, or had a junkie break into their house to steal enough to sell for their next fix.

"My first order of business when I get back to the office is to call his P.O. and see what I can find out. There was a probation hold issued for him in August. Maybe that will give me a clue as to how long he has been sitting there."

"Good luck with that, John. I've gotta go. My wife is ready to drive me over to PT."

"Thanks, Jim."

"Anytime, Sheriff. Keep up the good work."

I called Warden Asmundsen and advised him of the situation. He said he would meet Holmes and the wrecker from Bill and Jack's at the storage facility. The space was empty except for a bear killed by poachers that was hanging from the ceiling.

When I arrived at the lab, Charlie was just finishing the last of his goose stew and was clearly quite happy.

"Hello, John. It is wonderful to see you."

"Same here, Charlie."

"I suppose Julie told you I am taking her students on several field days this winter. We have acquired several trail cameras. Our plan is to head out on snowshoes and place the trail cameras in areas where we see tracks. We will change out the camera cards the following week, go back to school, and project what we have captured. Each species will be assigned to the students' field teams, and they will do a research project and present it to the rest of the class. It should be a great deal of fun. Plus, I could stand to get out on snowshoes now and again."

"Charlie, I need some information on this plant. I hope you can help me."

"Certainly, John. But why, may I ask?"

"This is evidence in a criminal investigation, and we need to preserve the chain of evidence to protect the evidentiary value of the item. Everyone who examines it or touches it needs to sign off."

"My gosh, a stalk of *Solidago canadensis* is part of a criminal investigation? That has to be a first. What would you like to know?"

"Whatever you can tell me," I replied.

"It is an abundant perennial plant native to this area. Its common name is Canada goldenrod, and it is a member of the Asteraceae family. This particular specimen seems to have been harvested prior to maturity as the flowers appear to be not fully formed. Canada goldenrod grows everywhere in the lower forty-eight states, except for the southeast, I believe. I would have to check on that to be sure. It can grow in wetlands, on the fringe, or in uplands. It is everywhere around Namekagon County."

"Charlie, here is my real question. It may be impossible, but I need to ask. That plant started to grow in the spring. It grew and grew, and then the stem was pinched right there. That effectively killed the plant, right?"

"Right. It would have persisted for a while, but smashing and cutting most of the way through the stem would kill it."

"Can you tell me when the plant died?"

"Well, it died when the stem was crushed."

"No, I've got that, Charlie. Based on the plant's development, can you tell me where it was in its life cycle when it was killed? Could you give me an estimate of how that corresponds to the calendar?

Meaning, was the plant killed in June or September? Approximately when did it die?"

"Aah, I see what you are getting at. With a little work, I can come up with a reasonable estimate of when the plant was killed in the growing season. Already I can see that it had not yet completely flowered. Is this plant from the geographic area?"

"Yup, right here in Namekagon County."

"Well, let me take a look at this and put it under the magnification viewer. It is a plant species with which I am very familiar, and an interesting one at that. It has been thought to have broad-spectrum medicinal applications. It is used to treat urinary tract issues, sinus pain and congestion, and a topical wound application. I could do a little research to give you more information on the history and range of the plant if you want me to."

"That's all very interesting, and I would love to hear more about the plant sometime, but now I just want to know when this particular plant died. I would like to know as soon as you can tell me. It's important."

Students began to file into the room and take their spaces at the lab tables.

"This is my lab class," Charlie said. "If it is okay, I will engage them in the investigation of the *Solidago canadensis* sample you brought me."

"That's fine, Charlie. Just keep the circumstances to yourself."

"Will do, John. I will need to keep the plant with me, of course, for examination. Will that require we do something, or do you have to come along with me to preserve your evidence?"

"The truth is, I am not sure that the plant has much evidentiary value. I am most interested in whether it supports a theory I have regarding a case. What you determine will have an impact on how I pursue things. It will help me understand when the event occurred. Just to be on the safe side, I am going to sign the plant off to you to maintain the chain of evidence."

I signed over the paperwork and walked toward the door.

"You know, John, environmental science is a great deal like a police investigation. You gather evidence and anecdotal information. Examining the scene of the crime is like examining habitat. Once we have all the little pieces, we try to put them together. Often the most interesting things we find have nothing to do with what we are looking for. They are, however, interesting just the same. But the big difference between what we do is not lost on me. You are dealing with life and death every day. What you do changes things in real time, minutes or seconds. My research often involves life and death but in a very different setting. For example, the Kirtland's warbler was on the brink of disappearing from this earth, and all of a sudden, a new breeding population was found, and our hope is renewed. But people like me are very aware that a lot of what we do determines our world's overall health. Wildlife is often the first indicator of environmental health issues. I will be glad to help you, and I hope we can give you conclusive results. Until then, John, remember the magic words: please, thank you, *quack, quack, quack,* and *honk, honk.*" ◆

CHAPTER 5

Lois met me as I walked in the door of the office.

"Here are your messages, Sheriff. Chief Bork wants a call as soon as you get in."

I dialed his number.

"Hey, John. What do you have going out by Ghost Lake?" he asked.

I filled him in. He reiterated what Rawsom had told me about Devin Martin with a couple of pretty significant additions.

"We watched for him and made sure he knew that we knew who he was. Gotta be a little careful, you know, not to be profiling. Anyway, we got some information from Milwaukee. They told us Devin Martin was an up-and-comer in a drug gang. The story is that during his last stretch in prison, he hooked up with some new business associates, and they got together when they got out. I don't feel the world will really mourn the loss," Len said.

"Do you remember who gave you the information about him?"

"I most surely do. It was Agent Anthony Ricardo from the Department of Narcotics Enforcement. I've only met him a couple of times. He's pretty surly, but word on the street is that he is really good at what he does," Len replied.

"What is it that he does?" I asked.

"He puts drug dealers out of business, and from what I've heard, he isn't too picky on how hard he steps on their toes. I know for a fact he's still around. I'll send his contact information over to you," Len replied.

"Sounds like my kinda guy. Anything else going on, Len?"

"Nope, most locals are out hunting and trying to put in some fat fall fish. The bear hunters are out now. You'll probably get some complaints of dogs running loose. Fall is a pretty quiet time, which gives you the chance to wind down after the tourist season."

"Not much on our end either, except this suicide."

"We keep things quiet, and that's the way I like 'em," Len said. "By the way, Martha wants you and Julie to come over for dinner real soon, so give me some dates."

"Will do, Len. Talk to you soon."

I hung up the phone and was just going to contact Lois to get the number for Devin Martin's P.O. when it rang again. I answered.

"Hey, Sheriff. Doc O'Malley."

"Hey, Doc, did you get that SUV put away?"

"Well, yes, I did. I put it in the secure area over by the ranger station. It is locked up tight."

"Good. Thanks for your help."

"Sheriff, the only thing is that I noticed something about that fancy Cadillac. When I went to write down the VIN for my tow record, I was shining my flashlight on it, and if I held it just right, something looked off. I think the VIN plate has been changed. I looked for the one from the driver's door, and it was gone. I didn't look any further because I didn't want to mess up anything. But I think someone might've switched the numbers. It is hard to do so that no one notices, but there are guys who are pretty good at it. I think your fancy Cadillac might be stolen."

It wasn't the least bit far-fetched. The driver was a convicted felon in possession of firearms and drugs. Why wouldn't he drive a stolen car?

"Boy, Doc, that is a good find. I appreciate you letting me know."

"No problem, Sheriff. I gotta get back to work here. If you need me, give me a call."

I went straight to the office and sat down to make some calls regarding Devin Martin.

My first was to the probation officer who held his paper. Being a probation agent is a thankless but necessary job. The prisons were full, and we needed to keep track of the bad guys and girls as best we could.

I dialed the number for Greta Williams.

A rough, smoke-soaked voice answered, "Williams."

"Agent Williams, this is Sheriff John Cabrelli from the Namekagon County Sheriff's Office."

"Namekagon County, you mean like way up north, just about to Canada?"

"Well, up north for sure."

"What do you want, Sheriff? One of my folks pee on a tree in public?"

"Nope, not that I know of. But in the morgue, I have a guy assigned to you, Devin Martin."

"Devin Martin?"

"Yes, Devin Martin."

"Give me a minute, Sheriff."

I waited and heard her clicking away at computer keys in the background.

"Yeah, Sheriff, here he is. Devin Martin. He was added to my caseload but never showed up for his first meeting, so I violated him in August. Never laid eyes on the boy. Don't know nothing about him other than what is in the file. You sure he's dead?"

"We have got a tentative ID from the wallet and a vehicle registered to him. We are at about ninety percent."

"Who killed him?" asked the agent.

"Looks like he killed himself. We found him dead in a car with a couple of guns, some cash, and a bunch of meth."

"Well, you hit the jackpot. Sounds like good riddance to bad rubbish," she said.

"Agent Williams, could you please send me his file?"

"Be glad to, as long as when you are sure on the ID, you let me know so I can cross him off the list. Namekagon County Sheriff's Office, attention ... uh, what was your name again?"

"Sheriff John Cabrelli," I replied.

"I will send the file over to your office, attention Sheriff John Cabrelli." The phone clicked off.

My next call was to the Wisconsin State Patrol trooper supervisor for our area.

"Sergeant Kruger," he answered.

"Sergeant, this is John Cabrelli."

"Hey, Sheriff, how are you doing? Keeping all the troublemakers in Namekagon County in line?"

"As much as possible," I replied. "I need your help with something. We have a body that showed up in a possibly stolen vehicle. Doc O'Malley from Bill and Jack's Garage was recording the VIN for his tow log and believes that the number has been altered. Do you have an inspector who can help us determine if the vehicle is stolen?"

"We sure do. An inspector from Madison transferred up here last year. He really knows his stuff. Hidden VINs, altered numbers, you name it. I will send him your way if you let me know when you want to meet."

"If he's got the time, now would be good. It's kind of a priority."

"I will check with him, John, and let you know. Say, how's Jim Rawsom doing? I have been meaning to get over and see him."

"He is making progress every day," I replied.

"Well, if you talk to him, tell him hello, and let me know if I can be of any help."

"Thanks, I will."

It was just a few minutes later when I got a call back from the motor vehicle inspector. I filled him in, and he said he would catch up with the warden and get access to the impound lot. The crime scene unit would be done by noon, so it was all his after that. As soon as he could figure things out, he would let me know.

For the moment, I had things pretty well under control, and I needed a little break. I stopped to get a cup of the Northwoods dark roast, then took off down the highway back to my cabin on Spider Lake.

I pulled into the yard and felt a chill of happiness. I had come a long way in a short while. I loved this place, and I loved the woman I shared it with. It was my sanctuary, my home. The lake was my tonic. Whether sitting on the dock watching a sunset, paddling our restored cedar strip canoe, swimming in its cold waters, or fishing for muskies, the lake offered endless opportunities for recreation and renewal. As I walked to the cabin, light snowflakes slowly and lazily fell to the ground. The air was cooling off, and winter would be here soon.

I started a fire in the woodstove, sat in my uncle Nick's chair and picked up the latest copy of the *Wisconsin Outdoor News*. On the front page was a series of clear photographs from a trail camera of a cougar taking down a whitetail deer. There had been many reported sightings of cougars in the area, even back when I was a boy. These photos were taken only a few miles from my cabin. It only made sense that these large carnivores would move into the area. Millions of acres of unsettled wilderness, thousands of lakes, rivers and streams, and food provided a great habitat. Healthy wolves were not known to attack humans, but that was not the case with cougars. In other states, cougars had identified humans as slow moving, easy to catch protein sources, and people had been mauled and some killed.

I pulled off my boots and faced my feet toward the fire. I hadn't realized how tired I was. I turned my portable radio down low, loud enough that I could hear any important traffic, but not too loud.

Toward evening, my pager went off. I called in from my landline, and they patched me in to the motor vehicle inspector.

"Sheriff, you are correct. The VIN has been altered on this vehicle. I was able to locate the hidden VIN on the frame. The vehicle was stolen in Georgia about eight months ago. We are trying to track down the SUV that the phony VIN came from. I will forward you my report. Also, just for your information, it was not a real high-quality number switch. All the adhesive VINs were removed, and the one on the dash and the one in the engine compartment had the tags put over the top of the originals and were held in place by some kind of adhesive, maybe like JB Weld. For the record, I gloved up before I touched the vehicle, and I kept my examination to the minimum. I didn't want to contaminate anything."

"Thanks, Inspector. I appreciate your help."

"You're welcome, Sheriff. At your service anytime."

———

Nothing here was surprising. A drug dealer driving a stolen car isn't unusual. The cash from the duffle bag had been counted, and it amounted to eighteen thousand dollars. The twelve bags of meth weighed in at several ounces each, and a couple of dozen "eight-balls" or one-eighth-ounce bags. Eight-balls were a common street quantity. It was also an amount a producer might use to let a potential dealer test his product. It was easily thirty thousand dollars' worth of product.

I started whittling down the possibilities regarding the circumstances of the drug dealer's death. Robbery was out simply because no robber is going to leave a pile of cash and drugs. Maybe the guy tried to sample the product, which made him crazy, and he shot himself. We would continue to gather information until there was no more to gather and then decide whether our death investigation turned into a criminal case.

I added wood to the fire to ward off the fall chill and gazed out the picture window that faced Spider Lake, watching the gentle snow, a harbinger of things yet to come. It wouldn't be too long before the lake would freeze solid, and snow would come in quantity. But based on recent weather patterns, when that would occur was anyone's guess.

I didn't know when to expect Julie, but I planned to wait up for her even as tired as I was. My police radio squawked, and one of my people on patrol was dispatched to an accident with property damage only, meaning no injuries. Otherwise, things were quiet.

CHAPTER 6

A welcome sight pulled up in front of the cabin. I slipped on some boots and went out to help my sweetie carry what I knew would be a huge pile of schoolwork she was unloading from the back seat.

"Hey there. Can I carry something?"

She turned toward me with a smile and dropped a twelve-inch-high stack of student folders into my arms. "That's it for tonight, John."

Back in the house, I set them on the table next to Julie's chair, a chair that had once belonged to my aunt Rose. My uncle Nick had a chair next to hers that was now mine. They were situated so you could get the most benefit from the fire in colder months, the breeze off the lake in the summer, and the lake view out the picture window.

Julie took off her boots, hung up her coat, plopped down, and let out a sigh.

"Can I get you anything, Julie?" I asked.

"I would love a big glass of wine. It has been a long day."

I poured her a glass of her favorite, Musky Merlot from a local winery.

She had her feet on the footstool and her head resting back, looking at the ceiling.

"How did conferences go?" I asked.

"There were no real big surprises." Julie made a practice of keeping up with the kids and their families and knew what to expect.

"I feel like we are making progress. The volunteer program I put in place for the parents in our school is paying dividends. Most of the parents seem more engaged with their kids and the education process as a whole. The number of parents volunteering has increased. I think that is mostly due to peer pressure and the fact that they have found the school to be a welcoming environment. I still have some problems, though.

"Danny showed up at school for his conference with his dad, who was clearly drunk. He wasn't a problem, but I knew talking to him was a waste of time. He kept repeating over and over how he never went to school and turned out alright, but he wanted something better for Danny. They were the last conference I had at school today, so I gave them both a ride home. Danny's dad didn't care for the idea and said he was fine to drive. Then someplace in the back of his alcohol-soaked brain he remembered that my significant other was the sheriff, and he agreed to the ride.

"After I dropped them off, I drove out to Amber Lockridge's place way out on Highway B. Her mother doesn't have a driver's license right now, so we agreed to meet at the house. I pulled up in front of their house, and Amber came out in a hurry, slamming the front door behind her. She stopped me before I could get out and said she was sorry that I drove all the way out, but they needed to cancel the meeting. It seems her mom was sick.

"I asked her what was wrong with her, and Amber said she just had the flu, but that she is very contagious and didn't want me to get it. Her mom told her that she would call into school for another appointment.

"I had a feeling that something else was wrong. But Amber was adamant that she was fine, and her mother just had the flu. I asked to talk to her mom for a minute, just to make sure she was okay. Amber stood in front of the door and gave me an emphatic 'No!' Then she went inside and closed the door behind her," Julie finished and let out a long sigh.

She continued after a moment, "Amber and her mom have had a tough go of it. Her mother and father never married and lived together on and off. Her dad was bad news. I know he had a police record, I think for selling drugs. I don't know for sure. I also don't know if her mother has a drug problem, but that's the local rumor."

"Was? Where's the father now?" I asked.

"He's dead. I'm not positive, but I think he drowned. I don't even know how long ago. I do know it was before I met Amber."

"So it's just Amber and her mother living out there?"

"As far as I know," Julie answered.

"How does she get to school if her mother doesn't drive and she lives way out in the country?" I asked.

"Her grandparents, Ed and Stella Lockridge, bring her and pick her up every day. They also volunteer in the school from time to time, especially when it comes to outdoor biology lessons. They are a wealth of knowledge about the outdoors. Bud knows them pretty well. Like many people up here, they are good folks, making their living pretty much off the land. In the summer, they can and freeze everything they need then drop the rest off at the food pantry. In the fall, they shoot a couple of deer for the freezer. Pretty much takes care of what they need. They also run a trapline. Every year we have the local warden come in as part of teaching hunter safety, and the Lockridges bring in tanned furs from all sorts of animals for the kids to see. When they first started coming, the students were a little standoffish."

"Why is that?" I asked.

"Her grandpa has a long white beard and long white hair. The only color to his hair is a brown ring around his mouth from smoking. Her grandma has long gray hair down to the middle of her back that she wears in a braid as thick as your wrist. Their clothes are worn but clean, and they are good with the students. The kids have warmed up to them, and it seems like Amber is proud they come. They are skillful in outdoor ways. Every year at school, we have a lumberjack challenge. Working in teams, the kids perform a series of tasks: make a fire, cook their own lunch, build a shelter out of logs and branches. Once that's all done, we end it with three competitions: log roll, crosscut saw, and axe throwing. I asked the Lockridges this year if they would help prepare the kids for the day. It turns out that Ed used to compete in lumberjack contests. A local logger dropped off a big tree stump for the kids to use for a target in the axe throw. Ed picked up the axe, and the students gathered around him. After explaining what they had to do, he gave them a demonstration. He took the axe, raised it above his head, and let it fly. The axe hit right in the center of the bullseye we had drawn on the stump. It was buried so deep it took one of the bigger boys to pull it out."

"Sound like folks I would like to meet someday," I said.

"They don't live too far from us as the crow flies. Maybe ten miles away on Spider Creek."

"Any chance they could take over as Amber's guardians?" I asked.

"It is not something they will consider. I already broached the subject. They said that without Amber, their daughter would not survive. It's the only thing she has left. The good news is that Amber is a great student and smart as a whip. She is already taking advanced placement classes online. We have cooperative agreements with many companies and organizations that help students continue on a successful path once they leave here."

"Julie, you are truly a hero. What would these kids do without you?"

"I am no hero, John. The kids who pull themselves out of challenging circumstances are."

She settled back and took her first sip of wine. I had warmed up enough dinner for both of us when she was ready. Then the house phone rang. I was hesitant, but I picked it up.

My hello was answered with a "*Quack.*"

"Hello, Sheriff. Charlie Newlin here."

"Thanks for calling, Charlie. Do you have some news on the plant?"

"I certainly do. The plant had begun to flower when it was killed. The flowers had not yet opened, and the pollen was not yet exposed. The plant's stem was almost completely severed with a small crushed area that kept it attached to the stem remaining in the ground. So the plant would have used up the remaining nutrients in short order. The internal tissue in the stem measured—"

I interrupted him. "Charlie, hold on a minute. I am interested in all of this, but I just need to know when the plant died."

"Oh, of course, Sheriff. The plant died in the middle to late part of August. No later than the end of the month and no earlier than the second week of August. We would like to continue and try to pinpoint the date if you don't mind. The students are very engaged with this project, and I am not one to ignore the importance of enthusiasm when it comes to science."

"This is great information, Charlie. Where is the plant now?"

"It is sitting atop my antique oak bookshelf, sealed in its plastic bag. It has never left my sight, and I would be glad to testify to that in the highest court in the land," he replied.

"How long do you think you will need the plant to finish your studies?"

"I have requisitioned the vans for tomorrow. With your permission, we would like to go to the scene of the plant's demise to gather additional evidence."

"Let me think for a minute before I answer," I said and paused momentarily to consider the request. "I will check with the crime scene crew to make sure they are done with the scene. If they are, I will have them send you the coordinates and you can have at it. Keep your eyes open for anything else that might turn up. More eyes on the scene the better."

"Oh, my gosh! This plant is really part of a crime scene?"

"It is part of a death investigation, yes," I replied.

Professor Newlin confirmed my suspicion. The passenger's door had been opened and closed approximately a month before the grouse hunters came upon the vehicle. It was not a definitive piece of case closing evidence, but it was something. The question was, opened and closed by whom?

———

Julie and I ate our dinner in relative silence, both deep in our thoughts.

Then she said, "John, I am not asking you to do anything, so don't. But I am wondering if Amber's mom is involved in drugs right now."

"I am pretty sure I could find out," I replied.

"I am not comfortable snooping into my students' lives. I am their teacher, and there are limits to what I should be doing. I wouldn't do anything to compromise my relationship with any of them. Trust is a real issue, and they need to trust me."

"I agree with everything you're saying. But you are talking to an investigator, and I will always check things out. I try to do it carefully, but you never know. If you are interested, why don't you just search public court records first? It is an easy search form. Just type in the last name and first name to get started. Then whittle down the results by dates of birth that correspond to the approximate age of Amber's mom. There is no record of your search. We use CCAP all the time for quick records searches. I can pull up the website if you want."

"John, I just don't know," Julie replied with hesitation in her voice.

"How about this: I will look for you, and if there is anything important, I will let you know?"

A look of relief washed over Julie's face. "Her name is Crystal

Lockridge. I think she is in her thirties."

I turned on my Toughbook laptop and got into court records quickly. Crystal Lockridge was definitely a presence on the court records. She had two convictions for theft by fraud, one conviction for battery, another for child abuse, and three convictions for possession of a controlled substance. Notably, no charges or activity existed during the last few years.

"She's here, Julie. Do you want to know?"

"Is it bad, John?"

"Well, it's not good. Although there has been nothing for a while, and she is not on probation. I could pull the files on all the cases. It looks like most of the charges came out of my department or the city PD, so I can read them to get more details if you want."

"No, let's just let it go for now."

Julie went upstairs with her second glass of wine, a rarity, and ran a hot bath in the whirlpool tub. Then she settled in to relax.

I used the opportunity to get into my department's files and educate myself on Crystal Lockridge. I did not consider this to be betraying Julie's trust. I felt it was more due diligence on my part.

The theft by fraud charges were regarding unauthorized use of a credit card. She had stolen the card from her significant other at the time, a guy named Travis Winslow. Travis Winslow first stole the card from an elderly woman he did odd jobs for. Crystal used the card with abandon until the law caught up with her. She agreed to pay restitution and serve ten days in jail.

The conviction for battery came close on the heels of the credit card issue. The significant other she had stolen the card from confronted her at a bar. She must have had enough of him because she pounded some knots on his head with the closest available blunt object: a pool cue. He disarmed her and slapped her around. Sheriff's deputies got to the tavern on the edge of town and took them both to jail.

The charge for child abuse was something different. Crystal had a brush with an overdose. Amber was nine at the time. She could not wake her mother and did the only thing she could do, and that was call 911. EMS and a patrol deputy showed up. They hauled Crystal off to the hospital and called the Namekagon County social worker on duty for Amber. The trailer they lived in, according to the report, was "akin to a toxic waste dump." A check with the school district indicated Amber had not been to school in over a month. Amber's grandparents came when the social worker called them. She was temporarily placed with them. The investigating officer who noted everything about the living conditions asked the social worker to contact crisis intervention and get an evaluation in the works.

The next three charges read like they were from the addict's handbook. She is stopped for speeding by the state patrol. The trooper runs her name, and low and behold, her driver's license is revoked for failure to pay a previous fine. He arrests her. During the search incident to arrest, the trooper finds two meth eight-balls.

She goes to court on the traffic charges and agrees to pay a fine within sixty days. A preliminary hearing is set for the drug charges, and they let her sign a five-hundred-dollar signature bond. The problem is she is dead broke and doesn't have the money to pay the traffic fine, much less the money to make good on the bond. So, she misses the court date and doesn't pay the fines. After ninety days, they issue a warrant for her arrest, adding bail jumping to the growing list. A couple of months after the warrants are issued, she is involved in an altercation at a downtown bar. The police are called, and a Musky Falls officer recognizes her. He runs her name, and all the warrants pop up. He arrests her, and when he searches her, he finds a baggie containing methamphetamines. In addition to the previous charges, she is now also charged with possession of a controlled substance and disorderly conduct for the incident that brought them all to the bar in the first place. She begins to spiral down.

She is facing all these charges, and something interesting happens. The State Department of Narcotics Enforcement was working with my department and the Musky Falls PD on some undercover drug stuff. According to the report, Crystal, who doesn't have any visible means of support, is popped by an undercover agent. At the bust, Crystal attacks the agent and takes off running. She is tackled by backup. In the backpack, she was carrying twenty one-eighth-ounce baggies of meth packaged and ready for sale. It seems that Crystal had become a dealer. Based on the court report, it appears as if she bought her way out of a felony possession with intent to deliver with some cooperation.

Then that's it. Nothing further on the record, anyway. I had some questions, and when I went into the office in the morning, I would check out a couple of things. Just for the heck of it, I wanted to find out who Travis Winslow was.

Julie came out from her bath wrapped in a fluffy robe, rosy-cheeked, and looking relaxed.

"Did you find out anything on Crystal?"

I was caught, and the look on my face must have told her so.

"Relax. I knew the minute I asked whether you could do it, you would at the first opportunity. You are who you are, John Cabrelli."

I told Julie what I found out. A girl who lives her life looking for silver linings was encouraged that Amber's mom appeared to be clean.

"Maybe she really had the flu, and I was just too harsh."

"Maybe so," I replied.

The cabin was cool. Although the logs that made up the structure were perfectly set and the cabin was masterfully built and tight against the wind, cold air coming down from the arctic put a chill in the air. We crawled under our five-point Hudson Bay blanket and were soon asleep. ❖

CHAPTER 7

In the morning, we awoke to a light dusting of new snow that had snuck in overnight. The temperature had dropped to a frosty twenty-five degrees, according to our thermometer. I got to making a fire while Julie started whipping up some breakfast. She was making a pile of bacon, eggs, toast, and pancakes. The smell of freshly brewed local roast coffee filled the air.

"Are you expecting company?" I asked.

"Did you forget Bud is coming out this morning to help you bring in the boat dock?"

It had slipped my mind completely. "Oh yeah, right."

Bud was more like Julie's brother than her cousin. He was a mountain-size man, known far and wide for his strength and ability as a handyman. There was nothing he could not repair or build. As big as he was, Bud was a gentle soul and friend to all without a mean bone in his body.

A few minutes later, his giant four-wheel drive, crew cab, one-ton pickup pulled into the yard with his snowplow attached. He shut off the diesel and, at the top of his lungs, boomed out, "YO HO!" He was practicing for the annual YO HO contest held each year before the Nordic ski race.

I opened the door and in he came.

"Geez, you guys, the weatherman didn't say a word about snow, but we sure got some. The wind is supposed to kick up during the day. As light as that snow is, it'll really be moving around. Anyway, I figured I might as well put the plow on. I will probably need it sooner than later. Old man winter is just around the corner. Ah, what is that I smell? Pancakes?"

"Sure are, Bud."

"Rose's recipe?"

"Of course. Would you expect anything else?"

"Nope. I sure am hungry."

Julie was a cook renowned for her breakfasts and walleye dinners. Either one was so good you could hardly stand to eat it. She presented us with heaping platters of pancakes and smokehouse bacon that had come from the neighbor down the road. The syrup was made from tapping the sap from local sugar maple trees. Each spring, when the sap began to run, her students would tap into the trees. They would attach a clear hose to each tap and run it into a five-gallon bucket with a lid. Once the buckets were full, they dumped the sap into a large cooking vat elevated on some concrete blocks over a wood fire. When the vat was full, they began the process of boiling down and adding sap. It took about forty gallons of sap to make one gallon of syrup. Their goal was to produce enough syrup for each student to take a quart home. They also distributed half-pint jars wrapped with ribbons to local, mostly elderly people. The whole activity was a big hit with the kids and the community.

I would have gladly testified under oath that the maple syrup on top of those pancakes was the best I had ever tasted. After breakfast, Bud and I dutifully began to help clean up. Before we could start with dishes, Julie stopped us.

"I can take care of these dishes. You two better get going if you're going to get the dock in. Don't you also need to winterize the outboard motor?"

"Yep, we've waited long enough. We'll do the boat first," Bud said.

We walked out onto the dock. Our little fourteen-foot F-7 Alumacraft was on a boat hoist with the old fifteen horsepower flat top Evinrude mounted securely on the transom.

A little snow had covered the deck and the seats. I started brushing it off and throwing it into the lake.

"I wouldn't worry much about getting rid of that snow. A quick trip up the lake will take care of it."

Bud brought the orange six-gallon fuel can from the shop, set it on the dock, and opened the cap. He carefully measured the right amount of two-stroke fuel stabilizer and dumped it in the tank. Then he lifted the tank and shook it up, mixing the contents thoroughly. I put the fuel tank into the boat, and I hooked it up to the engine. Bud cranked the hoist down until the boat floated free.

"John, run her up to Big Spider, swing around Picnic Island, and come back. That ought to be plenty of running to get the fuel treatment where it should be. I'll get the lower unit pump and lube ready."

I sat down on the rear bench seat and got myself centered. I squeezed the in-line fuel bulb until it filled with gas. With the throttle at the start mark and the engine in neutral, I pulled out the choke. Three pulls of the rope and the old engine purred to life. I ran it with choke out and let it warm up a little. Then I pushed the choke back in, and the motor settled into a steady hum. Bud shoved me off from the dock, and I took off toward Big Spider Lake.

The snow began falling again, this time a little more in earnest. Navigating the lake during a snowstorm was a new experience for me. The snow dampened the sound, and it was almost as if I were traveling down a winter tunnel. As I approached Picnic Island, I was out in the open, and the wind increased, and visibility got a bit more challenging. I reached the end of the island and turned to the starboard to round the rocky point without hitting the submerged boulders I knew rested there.

I came around close to shore and was shocked when a large wooly beast jumped off the land and into the water, swimming directly at me. I shut down the engine to avoid a collision, and it was then I realized the situation. I had accidentally turned my boat into a flock of about three dozen goose and duck decoys. The wooly beast turned out to be a big old Chesapeake Bay retriever. I avoided hitting the dog or running over any of the decoys and apologized to the duck hunters. They smiled and waved me on, and in a minute, I was on my way back to the cabin. Bud had instructed me to run the motor full throttle part of the way back, and when I cranked it wide open, the little boat skipped right along.

The snow-dusted trees towered above me. The snow that fell on the water melted and immediately became part of the lake. I was again awed by this place where I lived. It was nature at its pinnacle—rough, wild country painted with a gentle brush. I could not have asked for anything better. This was my home and always would be.

I pulled the boat up to the dock. Bud grabbed the gunnels while I unscrewed the motor from the transom and disconnected the fuel line. The motor, although small, was heavy, and I took my time setting it down on the dock, followed by the gas tank and fuel hose. Then I jumped out.

"Okay, John, let's each grab a side of the boat and pull it up."

The boat dragged up on shore and then over to the sidewall of the workshop. Once there, we leaned it on the building, bottom out to prevent any rain or snow from accumulating in parts of the boat where it might freeze and cause damage. The boat would stay there until next spring.

Next, we had to bring in the dock and boat lift. Bud was a genius at these things. He went behind the shed and retrieved two long aluminum planks. I helped him stick the planks under the wheels mounted on the dock underwater. Our dock was pretty short, with only two twelve-foot sections. Once the planks were in place, Bud jumped in his truck and started it up. He drove it back and forth, correcting the position each time until the front of the truck was the exact distance it needed to be from the dock and as squared up as possible. Then Bud lowered the snowplow to gain access to the front-mounted truck winch. He flipped the lever on the winch to free the spool so he could easily pull out the cable. Once he got to the end of the dock, he attached the towline hook to a loop welded to the dock. He locked the winch back in gear and looked at me and smiled.

"Nick and I figured this out. Manhandling those dock sections is a real pain. He started experimenting with different ways to get this job done with as little work as possible. The first thing he came up with was using some sort of ramps. No matter what we tried, we could not get it to work. Then he found these ramps for sale at the local surplus store. The cylinder welded on the bottom lets them pivot like a teeter-totter. The dock goes so far, and when it seems like it's going to jump off and slam into the ground, the front end of the dock we been pullin' on tips down on that round piece of pipe and just settles right down. Then we just winch it in and let it set onshore. In the spring, we do the reverse using the boat to pull the dock back."

Uncle Nick was a brilliant man, an engineer and inventor by trade.

Bud started the winch, and it slowly pulled the dock section onto the shore. It climbed the incline until it got the pivot point and then dropped down on the ground after teetering for a second. The winch easily pulled it to its winter resting point.

"The next thing we've gotta do is drag this hoist up on land. It is so clumsy to handle that the only way to get it up here is by putting on waders and giving it a boost. We can get Julie to run the winch to keep it from falling back on us."

Rather than walk up to the house, Bud continued his yelling practice, "Julie!"

She came to the door, wiping her hands with a dishtowel. "Geez, Bud, quiet down. You will wake every bear in the area," she scolded.

"Oh, sorry. John and I are going to pull out the hoist, and I was wondering if you could run the winch while we lift it onto the shore. Not really pull with it, just kinda click the controller to keep the cable tight so the hoist doesn't slide back into the water."

Julie, always the willing helper, didn't bat an eye. "Let me get my coat on, and I will be right out," she said.

The hoist came up without a problem. On my brief boat ride, I noticed almost half of the lake's places still had boat docks in. Woe to the guy who didn't get his pier in before freeze up and found it frozen in the ice one morning. Come spring, it could be fine, or the ice could have twisted it like a pretzel.

We thanked Julie, and she went back into the house.

The last thing to do was drain the lower unit on the motor. Bud set the motor inside the shop on the motor stand. He put a pan directly underneath the prop and removed a round screw from the bottom of the gear case, and then he removed an almost identical screw from higher up on the gearcase. Once done, heavyweight gear lube began to drain into the pan. Bud looked at the fluid coming out and seemed satisfied.

"If that lower unit lube was kinda creamy looking, that would mean that seal is leaking and letting in water. That's bad. Yours looks real good, though. See, it's pretty clear."

This was my first time doing this, so Bud took his time explaining.

"The reason you change the fluid is to put in new stuff, but also because you have got to make sure there is no water. If you didn't drain it and water had gotten into the gear case, the first night it gets twenty below, that water freezes and cracks the lower unit. Now you're into some serious money," Bud explained.

"Here, John," Bud handed me a sixteen-ounce jug of marine lower unit gear lube with a hose attached. "That one end has a screw fitting. Screw that into the lower hole, the one the bottom plug came out of."

I screwed in the fitting, and Bud told me to begin to pump the top. Every time I pushed down and released the pump, it shot some new gear lube into the lower unit. Eventually, it started coming out the top hole in a steady stream with every pump. I replaced the filler plugs, and the motor was ready for another year. I had a lot to learn about living year-round in the north country, and I could not have a better teacher than Bud.

I put on my gear and took off for the office. When I was on the road in an area with cell service, I called Len.

"Chief Bork," he answered.

"Len, it's John. I am coming into town and wondered if we could get together for a minute."

"Sure, John. First, I have got to run some errands for Martha. They are making baby blankets for their annual knitting marathon. The yarn came into the Yarn & Book Nook the other day, and I promised to haul it all over to the community center and help set up the tables and chairs. Say, now that I think of it, why don't you meet me there?"

"On my way," I sighed. Police work in a small community involved as much volunteer work as policing. No one was the least bit shy about asking for help, and the only acceptable answer was, "I'd be glad to help."

After setting chairs and tables in a circle under the watchful eye of Martha Bork and her crew, we unloaded bales of yarn. Then we were both dismissed for the moment.

The knitting marathon attracted over fifty knitters, men and women, young and old. They started on a Friday morning and knitted for three straight days, only stopping for a bit of sleep and food. The VFW recruited volunteers and did all the cooking to keep the knitters fed. At the end of it all, the knitters turned the giant piles of yarn into colorful knitted blankets. The local fire department delivered the larger ones to local nursing homes and senior centers. The smaller ones were given out at the hospital and for families in need. It was a grand tradition that began before World War II. Several of the knitters were over ninety; one had passed the century mark.

"Let's go over to the coffee shop, John. We should be safe there. They have fresh coffee here at the community center, but I don't think we should hang around. Those old gals see two men standing around doing nothing, and it becomes their mission to replace our idleness with activity."

Len Bork was one of the best men I had ever met in every regard. He had told me once that he was a Bible reader and a Bible believer. That appeared to be so, but Len Bork had something else. Hero's blood ran through his veins. His community had faced some hard times. Len's boss, the chief of police, turned out to be corrupt and almost tore the community to pieces. After thirty years with the department, Len looked forward to spending his remaining years hunting, fishing, and traveling the country with his wife. But when his community, his home, and neighbors were in need, he was the first to step up and lead. He was appointed chief, and it looked like he had no immediate plans of moving on.

We sat down in the back of the Crossroads Coffee Shop, Len with a scone and me with coffee. I was still full from breakfast.

"What can I help you with, John?"

"You know a local guy named Travis Winslow?"

"Travis Winslow, I haven't heard that name for a while. Sure, I know him, or I guess I should say knew him. He's dead."

"How did he die?"

"He drowned," Len stated.

"Swimming or boating accident?" I asked.

"Neither. Winslow was always into something, anything to make a crooked buck. He was a druggie and a small-time dealer. Anyway, he had an under-the-table deal with a couple of local restaurants. He'd go out at night when the walleyes were spawning. Using a headlamp for light, he speared the fish and threw them in a big cooler. When he had enough, he'd sell them to the restaurants for cash. One night he was spearing up by the dam at Crooked Lake. The dam is only three or so feet high, but he must have been trying to walk across it. It looks like he slipped off the dam and hit his head on the way down. The official cause of death was drowning. That was it. A guy from the DNR was checking the dam the next day and found two big coolers full of walleyes. He got to looking around and saw Winslow on the bottom under the outflow of the dam."

"When did it happen?"

"I would have to look for sure, but I think about four years ago."

"What did he have to do with Crystal Lockridge?"

"To start with, I think he was Amber Lockridge's father. He and Crystal were an on-again, off-again couple. The only thing they had in common was attracting trouble and doing drugs. It seemed like they would start to get their act together, but it never lasted," Len answered.

"He was Amber's father?" I asked.

"I don't know for sure, but I think so. Like I said, he tried to get it together. He had several jobs, mostly unskilled labor. He didn't last too long at any of them. Winslow was a junkie, and like every other junkie, the only thing that mattered to him was getting high. Toward the end, we kind of figured that he was dealing. He didn't have a job but had money. I think he got Crystal hooked up in selling too. She got busted with a bunch of meth that everybody figured she was holding for him, but who knows."

"I know some of it. I read the case file."

"She cooperated, and since she had a daughter, they cut her a break. DNE charged Travis and, based on the information from Crystal, recovered a pile of drugs. Other than that, it never came to anything 'cause in the meantime, while Winslow was out on bail, he slipped off the dam and drowned."

"What about the Lockridge family? What is the story with them?" I asked.

"As far as I know, Ed, Stella, Crystal, and Amber are the only Lockridges left around here. I think Ed and Stella got married when they were really young. Stella was raised on the reservation. I don't know much about Ed's family. They are different, the sort of folks who live off the land as much as they can. They hunt and fish, run a trapline, sell tanned furs and sometimes hire out to fishing lodges for short stints as a guide and cook. I can tell you one thing about them for sure. They are the salt of the earth. Ed and Stella are good folks, always willing to lend a hand. Why are you interested?" said Len.

"Julie went over to Crystal Lockridge's house for a parent-teacher conference with Amber. When Julie got there, Amber wouldn't let her in, claiming that her mother had the flu. Maybe that was the case, but Julie made it sound a little more desperate than that. Amber wouldn't even let Julie talk to her mother for a minute. Based on Crystal's history, well, you know."

"It wouldn't be the first time she slipped backward. I don't know Amber. Is she a good kid?" Len inquired.

"Julie says she is as smart as can be and no behavior issues. I guess she was just concerned."

"I'll keep my ear to the ground, and if I hear something, I will let you know."

"I would appreciate that, Len."

"While we are talking, what's the update with the body that showed up out on Ghost Lake Road?" Len asked.

"So far, everything is still pointing to suicide. I don't know if I told you before, but it turns out the car was stolen out of Georgia, and the VINs were altered. The ME thought he would be done today. I am going to try to convince the crime lab to ship the whole package—guns, shell casing, and bullet—down to the lab in Milwaukee for testing. I'm guessing it won't see the top of the pile for a while. I got the file from Martin's P.O. His known next of kin included a brother and mother. His father was listed as deceased. His brother was easy to find; he is a permanent guest of the state penal system, doing life twice. The mother took some more checking, but we eventually came up with a land line and address. I sent it on to the ME for the notification."

"Keep me posted. I hate to leave you, but I have got a pile of stuff on my plate. Call me if you need me," Len said and stood up to leave.

"Thanks, Len. I will," I replied. ✦

CHAPTER 8

On my way back to the office, my phone rang. It was the call I had been waiting for.

"Dr. Chali, what have you got for me?" I asked.

"Here is the long and short of it, Sheriff. One slug to the right temple was the cause of death. It appears to be a nine millimeter, which would match up with the pistol recovered from the car. That's just a visual on my part with some measurements. The ballistics lab will have to make the final determination. The bullet looks like solid lead. It expanded significantly, and that is why it didn't exit. I'll wait until the ballistics stuff comes back, but right now, I am going with death by a self-inflicted gunshot wound. Regarding the ID of the victim, it's confirmed, through prison medical records. Also Devin Martin's DNA is on file from a prior sexual assault charge, so we are running a comparison. I'll let you know when we get those results. Incidentally, Sheriff, I took tissue samples to send into toxicology. The powder tattooing near the entrance wound was not consistent with a contact discharge. More likely, he held the gun a few inches away when he pulled the trigger. Thanks for the information on his next of kin. The Milwaukee County ME's office is attempting to make contact."

My next call was to Sandra Benson, the lab administrator at the crime lab in Eau Claire County. The receptionist put me right through to her.

"Dr. Benson," she answered.

"Dr. Benson, this is Sheriff John Cabrelli from Namekagon County."

"Sheriff Cabrelli, you are the appointee who took over for Jim Rawsom. Jim was a heck of a good man."

"He still is, Dr. Benson. We are all hoping and praying that he comes back to pin on his sheriff's star again."

"It is good to talk to you, Sheriff. I am just getting the swing of things around here myself. As you may be aware, I was recently promoted to fill the director's position here at the lab. Now, what can I help you with?"

"Your folks did the scene at a death investigation. A decomposed body was found in a vehicle out in the national forest."

"Yes, Sheriff, I am familiar with the case. Suicide, right?"

"Yes, Dr. Benson, it appears to be a suicide. But before we close the door on this case, I was wondering if you could send everything to the firearm lab, just to make sure we are covering all our bases."

"Do you have any reason to believe that it is anything but a suicide?"

"Nothing concrete, but I will feel better once the tests are run."

"We can't do the testing here. Everything firearm related goes to the Milwaukee lab. Technically, we have the equipment and ability to perform the tests, but even if we could do the testing here, we couldn't get to it for at least six months. As it is, it will probably be at least three months before you hear anything back from Milwaukee. Unless you put in a priority request, which you could do but would likely be rejected unless you have something that will tip the scales from suicide to homicide."

"Three months? You're kidding. Dr. Benson, is there any way you could help me out with this? Maybe just the bullet and case comparison—the short version."

"I am sorry, Sheriff. We are all frustrated by the process. Unfortunately, we can't help. We are too backed up. I was appointed to this position, and my first charge was to prioritize our activities, starting with the backlog of sexual assault kits that remain untested. We need to take as many predators off the street as we can."

Every cop in the state knew about the fiasco regarding processing sexual assault kits for potential evidence. At last count, over six thousand had yet to be processed. These kits contain potential evidence that will identify predators and help bring them to justice. It had all been tied up as part of politics. Now things were rolling forward. A new attorney general was pushing the issue hard with poignant comments about not putting politics ahead of victims. The very first kits tested resulted in several arrests. Arrests in sexual assault cases are a big deal, especially when something like DNA evidence comes into play. The issue is that most people who commit sexual assaults are likely repeat offenders, but that is not how it presents itself. A law enforcement officer takes a sexual assault complaint, and most cops take this stuff very seriously, and they do a thorough investigation.

Depending on the circumstances, the reported assault is then sent over to people trained in investigating sensitive crimes. Everybody is working hard to ID the perp to get him or her off the street as soon as possible. Nobody likes sexual predators. Even in prison, they occupy space somewhere below the lowest rung on the ladder. The thing is, many of these pieces of human excrement are habitual offenders. So a cop takes a report of an assault one day. He does everything he can to identify the suspect. A month goes by. A cop in another area catches another sexual assault. He does his best. Then another six weeks later, same deal. Unless there are distinct definable characteristics, these all go down as separate incidents. Suddenly, they start testing for DNA from the evidence they recovered and compare it to other samples. They start getting a bunch of matches from other sexual assaults. Pretty soon, you find out that the perpetrator in all the cases is the same person. What everyone thought was a series of separate crimes turns out to be the work of a habitual predator. Now everybody is looking hard for him.

"Yeah, I understand. If you would, transfer my stuff as soon as you can. Don't let it get away on you, okay?"

"Sheriff Cabrelli, I can assure you that we will get the firearms, casing, and bullet down to Milwaukee as soon as we get the opportunity."

"What if I take the stuff to Milwaukee? Could you make a call for me to help with that?"

"Sheriff, everyone is busy, Milwaukee included. I don't want to be insulting, but your death investigation is probably what it looks like. I know good cops want to make sure they cover all the bases. Sometimes we have to prioritize. We haven't got the time to chase after something that's not there. Sorry, Sheriff, but that's the way it is."

"I get it, Dr. Benson. Let's do this: pack up my evidence, prepare the transfer forms, and I will be down at your office first thing in the morning to pick it up."

"Sheriff, that is neither necessary nor warranted."

"Pack up my evidence, prepare the transfer forms, and I will be by in the morning. Let's say, around nine. That work for you?"

"Sheriff Cabrelli, you are trying my patience. I said I would get to your evidence when I can."

"One thing I have noted about myself: I have some recognized expertise in trying people's patience. I am trying to get better, but no real luck yet. I will see you in the morning."

I began to hang up.

"Sheriff, wait a second. We have some tools that need to be examined from a home invasion that resulted in two homicides. It is going out first thing tomorrow to Milwaukee. I will send your stuff along with it. Will that satisfy you?"

"Yes, Dr. Benson, it does. Thank you very much."

"You are welcome, Sheriff. Now, if you don't mind, I would like to get back to work," and she hung up.

I understand the pressure the lab people are under, the good work they do, and the challenges they face. Unfortunately, my world just keeps on spinning even if theirs stops.

I called Dr. Chali to advise him of the new situation with the evidence.

"Good move Sheriff, I think your suspicions have merit. I am absolutely open to looking at any new information that may impact the Martin death investigation. Oh by the way the Milwaukee ME's office has attempted personal contact with Tina Martin three times with no success. They believe she may have moved."

I thought for a minute.

"Mike I know it's not the way things are done normally, but can I try to make the contact?"

Dr. Chali thought for a second.

"I guess I don't have any problem with that, but I can't help but wonder whether or not driving to her house in Milwaukee is going to get you anywhere."

"Well we've tried personal contact, with no success. What if I call her on the phone?" I asked.

"Personal notification of a death is really an important part of our responsibilities. A phone call just doesn't cut it," he replied.

"Better a phone call than nothing. I am the lead on the case, she may have questions for me. She probably won't even answer the phone."

"Go ahead, Sheriff. Give it a try," Dr. Chali said.

I closed my office door and called the number I had. After half a dozen rings, a rough voice with slurred speech answered.

"Hello."

"Tina Martin?"

"Who wants to know?" she replied.

"My name is John Cabrelli. I am the sheriff of Namekagon County. Is this Tina Martin?"

"What do you want with me?"

"I am calling about your son, Devin. Is Devin your son?"

"What did he do now? Is he in prison again?"

"Ms. Martin, do you have a son named Devin?"

"Yeah, he's my kid. For better or worse," she replied. Then she chuckled, "No, that's what they say for marriage, isn't it? I wouldn't know; his father never bothered to marry me. So, what did he do?"

"Ms. Martin, I'm sorry I have some bad news. Devin is dead."

There was silence at the end of the line. Then I heard a mournful sob.

"My boy is dead? You sure?"

"Yes, ma'am, I am sure. The medical examiner has made a positive identification."

"Did he OD? Is that what he died from?"

"I am sorry, Ms. Martin. He died from a self-inflicted gunshot wound."

"He killed himself? Are you trying to tell me he killed himself?"

"We are waiting for some tests to come back, but they are just a formality. Everything indicates suicide."

Wracking uncontrolled sobs came from the other end of the line, the kind that come whether you want them or not.

I gave her some time. The sobbing stopped.

"Ms. Martin, the body can be released in the next couple of days. Do you have any thoughts on how you might like to handle that?"

"I don't know right now. I would like to bring him home if I could. You have any idea how much that might cost?"

"No I don't. You are going to have to contact a funeral director in Milwaukee to help you with that. They will be able to help you figure things out."

"Yeah, that would be good." Then the sobs came again, and she said she needed to go.

Devin Martin was a convicted criminal, a drug dealer, and probably guilty of any number of crimes he was never held accountable for. A hard man, no doubt. Today he wasn't any of that; today, he was his mother's little boy.

───────────

I got ready to get out on the road, but before I did, I checked in with everyone in the office and communications center. The world was quiet. The weatherman predicted intermittent light snow would stop midday, and the sun would come out. The temperature would rise to the mid-thirties.

The streets of town were not hustling and bustling, and the crowds had thinned considerably. I pulled up and parked in front of the local jewelry store. When I walked in, the person I was looking for was sitting behind the counter, peering at a ring through a single lens squinted in place.

"Well, Miss, I am sorry to tell you that this ring is worth very little," he said to a girl on the other side of the counter.

"He told me he paid over a thousand dollars for it!" exclaimed the young woman, clearly agitated.

"I don't know what he paid for it. I can only tell you what I value it at. The truth is, I don't want the ring. It's not the kind of thing my customers expect from me."

"The diamond in the center is huge. It has got to be worth something!" she pleaded.

"That's the problem. The diamond in the center is not a diamond. It looks like a diamond, but it is a fake called cubic zirconia. To me, the center stone has no value. The ring itself is sterling silver and is worth something. Silver is selling for about eighteen dollars an ounce. The ring weighs about a third of an ounce. I could give you twenty-five dollars for the ring."

"But he said he paid a thousand dollars for it," she said and then started to sob quietly. "I should have known it all along. I paid for my bus ticket to get here. He said he would pay me back, but he didn't. I am so stupid, packing up and coming up here to hook up with some guy I only met on the Internet. I am so stupid."

Ron Carver, the master goldsmith and jeweler behind the counter, had been there and done that—at least twice. He was a successful businessman and did not become that way by making foolish purchases. He was not someone that would be classified as a soft touch, except when it came to a sobbing woman.

"Miss, how much do you need for the ring?"

"I just want enough to pay for a bus ticket home."

"Will a hundred dollars do it?"

"No," she sobbed. "The ticket is one hundred forty dollars."

Ron opened his wallet and pulled out two hundred-dollar bills and gave them to her. Then he turned to look at me.

"The sheriff here will be glad to give you a ride to the bus stop. Won't you, Sheriff?"

"I would be glad to. I'll be right back, Ron."

As soon as we got in my squad, I called the dispatcher and had them record that I was making transport of a single person to the bus depot. I arrived four minutes later, and she got out. I advised dispatch that I had concluded transport.

I stopped back at the jewelry store. Ron was already back at his workbench.

"Come on back here, Johnny boy. I have got a real deal for you," he said.

"What's the deal?" I asked.

"I just took in this ring, sterling silver with a beautiful center stone. It would look perfect on that sweet little Julie Carlson's finger. Yes, it surely would. I can let you have it for a real bargain. Let's say two hundred dollars, and at that, I am not making a nickel on it. So what do you think? I can even put it in a fancy box."

"You mean the ring that you just told that poor girl was worthless? That's what you want to sell me?"

"That's the one."

"I thought you said it was worthless?"

"It's not *worthless*. It's probably worth twenty bucks or so."

"Thanks, Ron. I think I will pass."

"You can't blame a guy for trying." Then he opened a drawer under his bench and threw the ring in with at least a couple dozen others. "A lot of broken hearts come through that door. What can I do for you, Sheriff Cabrelli? I am at your service."

"Nothing, really. I thought I would stop and check in with you."

"Things are slow, but it will pick up in a few weeks when deer season gets here. Plenty of guys come in to pick something up for their wives. Mostly guilt-driven after having spent a week or so drinking and carousing in the great north. I even set up a deer hunters' special display—nice stuff but moderately priced."

One of Wisconsin's great traditions is the annual nine-day deer gun season, during which over six hundred thousand deer hunters take to the woods. Oftentimes, several generations hunt together, cook good food over an open fire, and share stories of hunts past while making memories for next year.

"I remember my first deer hunt. I was twelve years old. Uncle Nick and I had taken a hunter safety course together. He taught me how to shoot a rifle. He believed that you needed to understand every facet of shooting. I used an old 721 Remington bolt action rifle, chambered in 30–06, America's most popular caliber. In his shop, we used brass shell casings, gun powder, primers, and bullets to assemble our ammunition. Uncle Nick was convinced that our handloads were superior to anything you could buy at a sporting goods store. We practiced at the range and made sure the rifle was sighted in perfectly. Based on our loads, if we sighted in two inches high at one hundred yards, that would work well for where we would hunt. Opening morning, we woke well before the sun, and Aunt Rose cooked us a huge breakfast. She packed food and thermoses filled with hot chocolate and coffee in our day pack. We trekked across the ice on Spider Lake to the opposite shore and climbed to a ridgetop. Once on the top, we could see the lake below us from both sides. If a deer came out, and it was in range, I could shoot it, but not unless I wanted to. That year the only deer we saw were several hundred yards down the lake."

"I remember that old rifle of his. The action was as smooth as could be, and the trigger was perfect. Your uncle Nick was quite a gunsmith," Ron said. "By the way, what's the scoop on the body those hunters found?"

Ron Carver was the chair of our Law Enforcement Advisory Committee. He also kept his ear to the ground and was a wealth of information regarding both the community's good and bad parts.

"No determination yet. Everything points to a suicide, but there are some unanswered questions," I replied.

"I heard it was some dope dealer that did himself in. Too bad he didn't take some of his buddies with him. I've heard rumors that these clowns have moved into the area and have got a meth lab out in the national forest."

"It's not just Namekagon County. Everybody up north is seeing an increase in drug use and the crimes that come along with it.

"Well, it's a real problem for people with stores like ours. Every day, we get shady-looking characters who come in here and try to sell jewelry—the guy over at the pawnshop too. I won't buy anything unless I know the seller. Better to be safe than sorry."

"Good idea, Ron."

"Well, Sheriff, I have got to get back to it. Say hello to Julie." ❧

CHAPTER 9

I got in my squad car and took the highway north out of town. The radio traffic was light. After a few minutes, I turned off the blacktop onto one of the seemingly endless two-tracks and backroads that go across the north country. All these roads at some time were developed with a purpose. Many were used for logging operations, while some were just shortcuts between paved highways. Others were fire breaks designed to slow forest fires. Some were just trails cut into a remote lake. I decided to travel the backroads whenever practical for a couple of reasons. First, it's a more scenic drive and takes you to places you would never see. Second, it's part of my job to know the country. Len Bork and others like him had lived their whole lives traipsing around northern Wisconsin hunting and fishing. Lots of the backcountry roads and trails had unofficial names like "Skunk Lake Trail" and "Buck Saw Crossing," and local people, as well as my deputies, would use the names when describing the location. None had road signs.

Additionally, these roads were commonly used and not well maintained. In areas like this, with spotty cell service, if someone broke down, they may be there for a while. Most folks in that kind of spot just hitched up their pants and started walking. Sometimes tourists, mostly from the cities, decided to take their family van on a backroad adventure, often learning the importance of four-wheel drive and ground clearance the hard way. They might have to wait a while for someone to come by.

The road I was driving on had tire tracks on two sides with grass in the center. If two trucks met, it would take some pretty careful maneuvering to pass each other. I crested a small hill and descended into a low spot with wetlands on both sides. Someone had laid what looked like railroad ties across the wet spot in the road. I got out and looked them over. They appeared to be pretty good. On the other side of the ties were several mature trees. If I got stuck, my winch line attached to one of those trees would likely pull me out. I locked in the four-wheel drive and crept across. The timbers were solid, and I made it with no problem.

I drove for a couple of miles before I came upon an older model white four-door Ford pickup truck. It was pulled as far as possible off the road, and I could have passed easily. But I decided to stop and check it out. The back of the truck was stacked about two-thirds full with some kind of evergreen branches. A piece of plywood with a spare tire on top held them down. In the corner of the truck bed were two five-gallon plastic buckets filled with traps of different dimensions, a chain saw, and a gas can. There was a shovel, a cant hook, and a high lift jack strapped in place on the headache rack behind the cab. The cab was empty, except for what appeared to be some more outdoor gear and two pairs of snowshoes in the back seat.

It wasn't a minute or two later that I heard someone or something approaching through the woods. A man and woman stepped out onto the road. The man was hauling a black plastic sled heaped with more branches tied in place. The woman carried an axe in one hand and a lever-action rifle in the other.

They did not seem to be the least bit surprised to see me. I greeted them and couldn't help to let out a chuckle.

The man smiled, "Something funny there, Deputy?"

"No, no, I'm sorry. It just dawned on me that in the city where I used to work, if somebody was walking around carrying a rifle, we would shut down the neighborhood and call out the Emergency Response Team. Here we don't think anything of it," I replied.

"Sounds like a pretty uncivilized place, that place where you used to work."

Uncivilized is one of those things that is in the eye of the beholder. I am sure urban dwellers would find the north's bush country about as uncivilized as any place could be. It was also likely the two people in front of me would feel the same way about the land of endless pavement and traffic jams.

"It sure could be at times," I replied.

The man got out a pouch marked long cut tobacco, dumped some into cigarette paper and expertly rolled himself a smoke. He lit it, sucked the smoke in, and let go of a couple of harsh coughs.

"Gotta stop buying the cheap stuff," he said. "If we are blocking the road, Deputy, we will pack up and get out of your way so you can get going," the man offered.

"No, there's plenty of room to get by. I was just checking the backroads and wanted to make sure no one broke down out here."

"Nope, we are as good as we can be. This old truck runs like a railroad watch and hasn't let us down yet. We were just harvesting our early balsam boughs, the first ones after the second hard frost are what some of our customers want. Once we get a truckload, we take them to a buyer in Musky Falls. He ships them out, and folks somewhere turn them into Christmas wreaths and other decorations. Other people use these early boughs for traditional things. This is one of our secret spots. Balsam branches cut just right bring the best money. My wife's people call balsam Nimissé or 'elder sister.' They are an important part of tribal tradition. Half of this first load goes to the elders."

The woman spoke for the first time. "Ed, where are your manners? Introduce us to this lawman."

"Gee, sorry, she's right. I am Ed Lockridge, and this is my wife, Stella. We live out on Spider Creek a dozen or so miles from here."

"Glad to meet you, folks. My name is John Cabrelli. For better or worse, I am the new sheriff of Namekagon County, and according to what I have heard, a neighbor of yours."

"Sure, you moved into Nick and Rose's old place. They were good friends of ours. Sorry, I didn't recognize you, Sheriff, but we know all about what happened. I mean, I guess we know what happened according to the newspaper. That Jim Rawsom is a hell of a good man, I hope he heals up as good as new. Old Len Bork gave that sonofabitch just what he deserved. At least in my book. A forty-five seventy bullet was just the right medicine."

That was not an uncommon sentiment that had been shared with me frequently by citizens in our community. I had no cause to disagree with them.

Stella walked closer to me and smiled. She wore a green and black checked heavy wool shirt over an old sweatshirt and jeans tucked into winter lace-up boots with rubber bottoms. Her gray hair was in a thick braid down the middle of her back.

"By God, let me take a look at you, John Cabrelli. Do you mind turning around in a circle?"

"Stella, try to behave yourself," pleaded Ed.

Because I couldn't wait to find out what would come next, I did as she asked and turned in a circle.

"I am sorry, Sheriff, but I just had to get a good look at the guy who turned Julie Carlson's head. When I heard she had somebody, I thought two things. First, good for her. It's about time. Second, this guy must be something, like a movie star or something. I knew about you saving those kids, but I have never laid eyes on you. Not no movie star for sure, but not too bad. I mean, I am guessing you have other qualities," and she let out a loud cackle-like laugh accompanied by eyes that smiled right along with her round face.

"Oh, for crying out loud. Sheriff, just ignore my wife. She doesn't mean anything by it. Too much time in the bush. I need to take her to town for a couple of days, stay in a hotel to get her civilized again," said Ed.

Stella cackled again, louder this time.

I helped the Lockridges load the balsam boughs into the truck. They turned the sled upside down over the branches along with the plywood and spare tire to keep them from blowing out.

As they drove away, Stella rolled down her window.

"Hey, Sheriff, you bring that cute little Julie Carlson over some time for supper. You don't even need to call. We always have plenty."

I laughed as the old truck rounded the corner and was soon out of sight. I couldn't help taking a liking to the Lockridges. They were salt of the earth, as Len had said.

In urban America, a hunter-gatherer mentality entails heading to Costco to stock up or stopping by the farmer's market. The spirit may still be alive, but the opportunities to live off the land are certainly diminished. In rural America, especially the north country, hunting and gathering is still a way of life.

The fur market had suffered some financial woes as of late, primarily due to politics. But people like the Lockridges were active trappers. As soon as the ice was solid and the fur prime, they would set their traps in strategic locations and catch mostly mink, beavers, and muskrats. They would take the animals home, skin them out, and prepare the hides. Not so much with muskrats or mink, but beaver meat was very tasty, and that went into the freezer. The castor glands by the base of the tail are harvested and sold for flavoring and in the manufacture of perfume. Uncle Nick had taken me to visit a backwoods friend of his years ago. The old fellow had made beaver tail and beans for lunch. At first, I wouldn't take a bite, but with Uncle Nick's encouragement, I did, and it was delicious. We washed it down with homemade apple cider.

The upcoming deer season was as much about tradition as putting meat in the freezer. While local butchers provided expert deer processing, lots of people just processed and wrapped their own deer. The prime cuts were usually saved for the grill or special recipes. The remaining meat was trimmed and saved. And it was this meat that had become the heart of the wild game processing business. Venison summer sausage, brats, ring bologna, bacon. Each processor had their secret recipes and their following. Where you got your summer sausage made was akin to where you went to church. Each day when Uncle Nick headed off to work, he packed his lunch with two giant sausage sandwiches. I liked the garlic smoked the best.

Things seemed to be simpler up here, although not free from the ills of society from which we all suffer. Things just felt cleaner.

I drove down the road following a good distance behind the Lockridges, which was challenging because they were only doing about ten miles an hour. My phone indicated that I now had service, so I checked my messages.

That evening Julie and I sat by the fire and listened to the *Voice of the North* radio. It was one of our favorite things to do. At one time, there were small local radio stations everywhere across the landscape. Now, most of them had gone by the wayside. If they served a big enough market, they were purchased and absorbed by bigger stations. If they didn't, economic issues would lead to shutting off their airwaves, but not so with WOLF. The station manager had been in the radio business for over forty years. He took great pride in the operation of his station.

Each morning he would start with the local weather and give

updates every hour. If you live in the north country, there is likely no more important news than the weather. Three different winters, Namekagon County had gotten more than one hundred inches of snow and had temperatures as cold as fifty degrees below zero. News followed the weather, which brought in some items of national interest but mainly focused on local issues. They often featured guests with expertise spanning various topics, and they took phone calls from the public.

At noon they had the outdoor report, checking in with local hunters, anglers, and trappers as well as the proprietors of Happy Hooker Bait and Tackle and Jerry's Sporting Goods. An up-to-date weather forecast followed, along with a call-in show.

But two nights a week, it was the *Voice of the North*. It started with a mix of old-time folk and real country music, the type of music that told stories. After that, when everyone was huddled at home around the radio, a baritone voice announced the continued reading of a book. Tonight it was chapter three of Jack London's *Call of the Wild*. It was like reliving childhood memories of a bedtime story.

Morning came with a stunning sunrise. It was like the colorful leaves on the trees drank in the sunlight and were more brilliant than ever. Warmer temperatures had melted the light dusting of snow we had gotten. Although I was anxious to see the crime lab report, Julie convinced me to take a little walk down the shoreline. As we walked, I told her about meeting the Lockridges.

"They seemed like real nice folks. Amber's lucky to have them," I said.

"Yes, she is. Crystal is not the most reliable parent, so Ed and Stella fill that void. They have two rooms at their cabin that they keep made up for Amber and Crystal. If they get a call in the middle of the night, they are ready. A few months ago, when Ed and Stella filled in as school volunteers, they told me that when they get a call, they never ask any questions other than 'Where are you?' and 'Are you okay?' Then they head off in their truck and pick one or the other or both up and bring them back to their house. Most often, it's just Amber, but sometimes it's both."

———————————

I was surprised when just a few days later I received an email from the crime lab. They had tested several items.

The first was a Smith & Wesson 5906 nine millimeter semiautomatic handgun, serial number 77402. The gun contained one magazine, loaded with ten rounds of Winchester brass-cased 115 grain nine millimeter jacketed hollow point ammunition, and a single cartridge which had been removed from the chamber.

Next was a Cobray nine millimeter semiautomatic handgun, serial number 10037. The gun contained one magazine, loaded with nineteen rounds of Winchester brass-cased 115 grain nine millimeter jacketed hollow point ammunition. The weapon was in the open bolt position, ready to fire.

The Namekagon County medical examiner retrieved a single bullet from the victim.

A single brass shell casing was included.

Tests were done using both guns, firing single rounds into a water trap.

Examination of the bullet recovered from the victim and comparison to the test bullet fired from the Smith & Wesson were conclusive. The bullets in the cartridges contained in the magazine and chamber of the Smith & Wesson were a different design than the bullet recovered from the deceased. Examination of the shell casing found on the floor of the vehicle and comparison to the shell casing recovered during testing was conclusive. The shell casing found in the vehicle was not from a round fired from the Smith & Wesson 5906.

Examination of the bullet recovered from the victim and

comparison to the test bullet fired from the Cobray M11, serial number 10037, were conclusive. The bullets contained in the cartridges in the chamber and the magazine of the Cobray were a different design than the bullet removed from the deceased. Examination of the shell casing found on the floor of the vehicle and comparison to the shell casing recovered during testing was conclusive. The shell casing found in the vehicle was not fired from the Cobray M11.

The shell casing found on the floor of the vehicle was from a different manufacturer than those in the Smith & Wesson, the Cobray, and magazines. Those cartridge cases were headstamp marked WCC for Western Cartridge Company. The casing found on the floor of the vehicle was headstamp marked PMC for Precision Made Cartridge Company.

It was not a suicide; it was a homicide.

Fingerprints had been retrieved from both guns and magazines, as well as partial prints from shells that had been inserted into the magazines. Several prints were found that matched the victim. Several other prints with unidentifiable smudges were found.

I called the folks in Eau Claire County and advised them of the firearms lab's findings. They pulled the visual up while I was talking to them. They had attempted to recover latent fingerprints from the vehicle. They found several from the victim and some that appeared to be from a smaller hand from the area of the passenger's seat, likely a woman. They recovered several partials from the door handle and window glass on the passenger side. Also, there were smudges consistent with someone wearing gloves.

I called Chief Bork. "Len, any chance you could come by for a minute? I got the stuff from the lab."

"I'm on my way," he replied. ❧

CHAPTER 10

Len arrived with two steaming cups of coffee. He sat his lanky form across from me. "What did you end up with, John?"

"Do you want to hear my whole theory or just the basic lab results?" I asked.

"Your theory would be nice," he replied.

"Well, here it is. I think Devin Martin came up to the Northwoods to do business. He collected several thousand dollars from his dealers and brought fresh methamphetamines to resupply them. He ended up driving his fancy urban SUV out to the middle of nowhere on a two-track forest road. He stopped when his car was out of sight from passersby. Maybe that's where he encountered the shooter. Maybe the shooter was in the passenger seat all along and coerced Martin to drive to that location by pulling a gun. He dies there from a single bullet wound to his head. The shooter exits the passenger's door and walks away. A Smith & Wesson semi-auto and a cheap semi-auto Cobray were recovered from the vehicle. Neither gun was used to shoot Martin. The Cobray was tucked under the back seat in proximity to a duffle bag with cash and meth. So here we are. Our death investigation is now an active homicide. What do you think,

Len? Who killed him?"

In his slow, thoughtful manner, the chief took his time before replying.

"Rival drug gang, probably. We have pretty much avoided battles between drug dealers, but Lord knows drugs have been the root of a lot of violence up here. Plus, we have gotten intel from the state that dealers are moving into our area. I hate to say it, but I was reading our arrest reports that go out to the *Namekagon County News* a few days ago, and of all the arrests for the last week, more than half of them were drug related. Maybe this is what it looks like when it all gets started. I don't know. What do you think, John?"

"A rival gang makes sense. They were trying to cash in on the territory and figured it out when Martin made his delivery. They intercept him, force him to drive out into the forest, and they pop him. The shooter jumps in with someone else that followed them in, and away they go. They hid the body well enough that it wasn't found for weeks. The only thing I got here that doesn't work for me is the duffle bag. Maybe the shooter didn't open it to look inside. Maybe he or she was rattled and, for some reason, took off. I will tell you one thing for sure. No gang member or drug dealer would leave behind a pile of cash, a pile of drugs, and two guns. No way, no how."

"Unless they got disturbed. Maybe someone came along and saw them, and they spooked," Len speculated.

"That's what I was thinking. Maybe we have got a witness out there somewhere—someone who was traveling the backcountry around Ghost Lake in late August or September. There are several trout streams in that area. Maybe they were hiking in or taking their dog for a walk. You come upon something like that, and you can't blame them for turning tail," I said.

"Let's get our folks together for a joint briefing and let them know the new developments. They might be able to shake something loose," suggested Len.

"Then we'll talk to the press. This week's *Namekagon County News* is due out tomorrow. That ABC affiliate from Superior has always been good to work with, along with local radio. Should we activate the reward fund for information?" I asked.

"That's an okay idea. I am guessing the community isn't going to get too interested when they find out that a convicted felon who was likely delivering drugs to our kids was the guy who was killed. They have a real streak of frontier justice around here and a real short memory when it suits them."

"While Devin Martin is not the model citizen, a homicide is a homicide. It's not the victim we are looking for; it's the perpetrator. A killer is on the loose somewhere, maybe still in our county. We need to find him or her and put them away," I said.

"I don't disagree at all. I just know how the people of our community think. Drug dealers getting themselves killed is way down on their 'I care about that' list," Len countered.

"How much information are we going to give the press?" I asked.

"The truck, the driver, the location, and the time period. For the paper and TV, pictures of each," Len replied.

"Pictures of the truck and where we found it are no problem, but we only have a booking photo of Martin. In it, he looks like a bad guy, which I guess he is. So that's what we have. I'll give Presser a call first so he can get working on this," I said.

"I'll get the briefing together and get it out. Let's set up in the conference room at two," Len stated.

Bill Presser was the head reporter for the *Namekagon County News*. He had written a story for me about my life and how I ended up living in God's country. It made national news, and Presser won the Academy of American Journalists Award for the story. He did two follow-up pieces that also received national recognition. The job offers poured in, but they only turned his head for a moment. He was a man comfortable in his own skin. After the big story broke and the hubbub settled down, Bill Presser realized that he loved writing about the Lion's Club Fishing Contest and the Musky Queen Pageant. He wrote about the thousands of people that came each winter to ski thirty miles over wilderness terrain. He loved to tell the story of his community, his people, and he loved to fish muskies.

I called Bill and told him I needed his help. He showed up ten minutes later.

"What can I do for you, John?" Bill asked

"You remember the dead body we found out in the county a couple of weeks ago?"

"Sure, the suicide?" he asked.

"The suicide is now a homicide," I answered.

That got his attention, and his reporter antenna extended to full length.

"Homicide? Did you find out something new that changed your mind? I mean, obviously you did, or we wouldn't be sitting here. What changed?" he asked.

"Before we get rolling here, Bill, I need you to keep a lid on this until after two o'clock. That's when we are going to brief our people. You know how crabby it makes them when the press hears first."

"Got it. Tell me what you want to tell me," he replied.

"Off the record, for now, the ballistics came back. Neither one of the guns we found in the victim's truck was the murder weapon. It appears as if someone convinced him to drive to the location where we found him and shot him. We have reason to believe that there may have been a witness. No one has come forward, but we think someone else might have been there. Their presence might have scared off the perpetrators."

"Any suspects?"

"No, but it is most likely drug related. We found evidence to support that at the scene."

"The victim is Devin Martin. Is that correct?" Presser asked.

"Positive ID. It's definitely Martin."

"When you first released the name, I ran him through CCAP. He had quite a record," Presser said. "If there is a witness, do you think they might be in danger?"

I thought for a minute. Is a witness to a homicide ever not in danger? The old rule still applied: the first murder is the big one; they are just added on after that.

"I don't know, but I think it is reasonable to assume the bad guys may not want an eyewitness floating around. We have got to stress in the story that all information we get will be kept confidential."

I gave Bill all the particulars, a high-resolution photograph of the vehicle, the state corrections photograph of Martin, and several shots of where the vehicle was found. After an hour, he took off back to his office to put the story together.

"Front page tomorrow, John," Presser said as he walked out.

I had to do one more thing before the law enforcement briefing.

I called Martin's mother again. She was not happy to hear from me and was definitely under the influence of something. I told her that her son was the victim of a homicide and had not taken his own life. She was silent. I asked if she was still on the phone.

"I'm here. Drugs and gangs kill everybody sooner or later. The boy never had a chance, never had any chance at all. I raised him the best I could, but he was hard to keep track of. You might not think I am much of a mother, but I took good care of him. He was just too wild for me. Teachers used to call me and tell me he wasn't at school. I'd go out and find him and haul him back. I drop him at the front door, and he'd run out the back. So what can you do with a kid like that? Nothin'. Absolutely nothin'."

"Ms. Martin, any idea who might have done this?"

"Let me tell you something, Mr. Detective. Every one of those pieces of trash he ran with would kill each other for a dollar. They would kill their own mama. Not Devin. He loved his mother. He was always so good to me," then she hung up.

It was probably good because her speech had become so slurred that I was having trouble understanding some of what she was saying.

———————

Five different law enforcement agencies were represented at the briefing. We gave them all the information we had. Devin Martin was murdered. He was a known drug dealer with a lengthy criminal record, and based on what we found in his vehicle, he was in Namekagon County to do business. He was shot in the head and killed in August or early September. It was made to look like a suicide, but evidence recovered at the scene made a homicide more likely. I projected the image of the stolen vehicle and photo of Martin on the screen. Everyone in the room downloaded the photos.

Several people remembered Martin from his previous activities in the area. A fair number of questions were asked, and people quickly found out we were short on answers at that point.

We were looking for anyone who thought they might have seen the vehicle or Martin.

The briefing broke up at three o'clock, and people headed out of the building to find the weather had changed to windy conditions and a mix of sleet and snow. The weather report said to watch for hazardous driving conditions and bad weather.

When the weather turned bad, people hunkered down, and the further north you lived, the more hunkering you had to do. If you had to go out in inclement weather, chances were you had a four-wheel drive vehicle and had been driving in conditions like this all your life, so you could get where you needed to be.

I got home and saw that Julie had made it as well. Her suburban, paid for by my uncle Nick's life insurance, was just the vehicle for this rough weather, with positraction, four-wheel drive, and serious tires. Other than the fact that my squad was packed with equipment, they were almost the same vehicle.

Julie met me at the door. I took off my parka and hung it on one of the coat hooks. I carefully set my boots next to hers on the rubber mat designed to contain the snow as it melted and hung my equipment belt and vest on some additional hooks Bud had recently installed.

"Hi, Julie. How was your drive back?"

"Slow and careful. The plow trucks had the highway pretty clean. I just kept going."

I ate my microwaved fries and a leftover Fisherman burger. We crawled in bed, and I could hear the wind had picked up. I don't believe either of us moved the rest of the night.

On Saturday morning, we were both up at five. The sleet had turned to heavy, damp snow during the night. It was great for snowmen and snowballs but also hard to move. I wondered about accidents and called the dispatch center.

The county was quiet. Two cars were in the ditch with light damage, and the Town of School Lake Fire Department had handled a chimney fire. Chimney fires could be a dangerous thing. They usually came from not cleaning your chimney often enough. Creosote builds up, and when there is enough, it will start on fire, burning inside the length of the chimney. The fire burns hot and can cause the house to catch, especially in places where the chimney passes through the building. Flames and embers shoot out the top of the chimney and can land on the roof. Most of the roofs around here are steel so that the snow will slide off. Shingle roofs, though, are another story. In the north country, cleaning your chimney is a dirty but necessary job. Bud had showed me how to clean ours with a brush attached to a long pole. Stand on the roof and scrub the chimney, then remove the cleanout on the bottom of the stovepipe.

Julie and I had breakfast. She was dressed in sweatpants, her favorite beat-up Northern Lakes sweatshirt and fleece-lined moccasins. Her hair was tied back in a ponytail. She looked stunning.

The little woodstove had kept a few coals overnight, so it sprang to life when I added some new dry wood. I would have loved to stay home with her to enjoy the weather from inside the cabin, but it was not to be. A career in law enforcement rarely took into account the value of downtime.

I asked Julie to pull up the *Namekagon County News* on the Internet, but she could not connect. After three tries, she was frustrated and went to pour herself another cup of coffee. She looked out the window and laughed.

"Hey, John, look at the satellite dish."

The snow had stuck to the dish and covered the receiver. I slipped on my knee-high boots and walked out to clear it off. It was just the first taste of winter, which would come to the north country sooner than later. Except for a tricky February thaw almost every year, winter would pretty much stay until it decided to leave.

Before I even got back in the door Julie had the front page up on the screen. The picture of the Cadillac Escalade was on one side, and Devin Martin was on the other side. The story asked for information from anyone who may have seen this vehicle or subject. There was also a photo and a description of the location where the vehicle was found. The story ended with the fact that all information would be kept confidential. It gave the contact information for the Namekagon County Sheriff's Office and Musky Falls Police Department. I was hopeful. Police work is a strange thing. Sometimes what seems like the most insignificant bit of information turns a case. It was always a long shot, but you would never know until you asked.

I geared up, got in my squad and took off toward town. Driving conditions on the main highway were pretty good. County trucks had plowed and then spread some salt. According to the thermometer in my squad, the air temperature was twenty degrees—perfect for snow.

Traffic was light, and vehicles were traveling at a reasonable speed. I turned off on Spider Creek Road and took the back way to town.

Five miles out, I came upon a familiar white pickup truck. Ed and Stella Lockridge were standing next to it, and Stella was holding a couple of muskrats.

"Howdy, Sheriff. What brings you out on such a fine fall day?" Ed inquired.

"I could ask you the same thing," I responded.

"The law requires that we check our traps at least every four days. It doesn't say 'weather permitting.' We run a pretty long line, so we gotta be out here every day to keep up. Besides that, it's just the right way to run a trapline," Ed grinned.

I bid them a good day and walked to my squad. Then I had a thought and turned back to the couple.

"You two are out in the backcountry all the time, aren't you?"

"Every day, Sheriff."

"Here, take a look at these," I handed them copies of the photographs of the Cadillac and Devin Martin.

Ed and Stella studied them.

"Any chance you might have seen this vehicle traveling around?"

"Boy, that is a fancy-looking rig, that's for sure. Those tires look like they are almost flat, and the rims look huge. Not the kind of outfit I would think would do much good up here. Maybe it would, I guess, but I wouldn't think so," Ed responded.

"Have you seen anything like it driving around, Ed?"

"Nope, I haven't, but then the places I go tend to be a little tough going. You see anything like this, Stella? She pays a lot more attention to things like this than I do," said Ed.

"Not out here. I haven't seen anything like that. I have seen one, though," she replied.

"Where?" I pressed.

"Ed and I watched a movie the other night, and everybody was driving cars like that. Well, not exactly like that, but kind of the same," Stella explained.

"You didn't see anything around here this summer or fall?"

"Nope, sure didn't, Sheriff. Sorry we can't be of more help," Ed replied.

"That's alright, folks. You be careful. I see a little skim of ice on the lake, but I'm guessing it's awful thin. I don't want to come and have to fish you out."

"We'll be careful, don't worry, Sheriff. We've only got ten more sets to check, and they are all bank sets. Should be pretty safe. Then we're back to the shed, fire up the barrel stove, and get to skinning," Ed said.

During my drive into town, I got a call from Lois.

"Lois, what's up?"

"We got our first hit on the truck you put in the paper. A boy that works weekends at the Quick Mart over on River Street is sure he saw that truck. His name is Kenny Parson. He should be there when you get there."

At the Quick Mart, the young man working behind the counter had on a name tag that said Kenny. Being the clever, trained detective I am, I assumed that I had located the subject I needed to talk to.

"Hi, Kenny. I'm John Cabrelli. Thanks for giving us a call."

"Ah, huh? I don't think I called you."

"Kenny Parson?"

"No, I'm Kenny Bennet. We go by Kenny P. and Kenny B. around here to keep it straight. You want Kenny P."

In law enforcement, I have noticed that sometimes things are what they are until they aren't.

"Where's Kenny P.?"

"He's out back, cleaning the snow off the walk to the propane tanks."

"Thanks," I walked out the side door and almost ran right into the flying blade of a scoop shovel.

"Kenny Parson?" I asked.

"Yup, that's me."

He was a big kid with a giant gap-toothed smile. His stocking hat was emblazoned with a monster truck.

"Can we go in and talk about the truck you saw?"

"Sure, follow me."

We walked to the back of the store and took a seat in one of two fiberglass booths.

"So, you think you might have seen this truck?"

"Nope, Sheriff, I know I saw this truck, and I remember the guy driving it."

"Do you remember when you saw it?"

"It was the end of August, August 25 to be exact."

"Are you sure?"

"Yup. I even remember what time it was, around three o'clock. I usually work the shift from seven in the morning to three in the afternoon. I was counting the hours because it was the last day of full-time summer work. My dad was picking me up at a quarter after three, and we were leaving for a few days of musky fishing before school started. Anyway, the truck pulled up to the pumps. I am kind of a car guy, and a fancy tuned ride like that is hard not to notice. It had twenty-two-inch Lexani custom wheels. I could tell that the Super chrome exhaust was hooked up to something big when it pulled in. Man, that ride had the deepest black finish I have ever seen. It's called black chrome. The windows had a dark gray tint. I went out to look at the truck. The driver was just getting the pump going, and I asked if it was okay that I check out his car. He told me to look all I wanted but not to touch anything. You don't see trucks like that up here."

"What did the driver look like?"

Kenny gave me a passable description of Devin Martin. "He looked like a badass, some ugly tattoos on his arms. Talked like the gang guys you see in the movies."

"Was anyone with him?" I asked.

"Yeah, there was a girl in the passenger seat. I didn't get much of a look at her. I walked toward her door to look at the paint trim, and the driver told me to stay back and not bother her, so I didn't. He paid at the pump and took off."

"Any idea who the girl might have been?"

"Nope. With the tint and everything, I couldn't really see her."

"Did you ever see him again?"

"No, never did."

"Thanks, Kenny. I appreciate your help."

"Anytime, Sheriff," he replied and headed back out the door to finish shoveling.

I now knew that on August 25, at about three, Devin Martin was at the Quick Mart in Musky Falls, and he was still alive. He had a girl with him. The big question was, where did he go from there? I needed to find that girl and put a timeline to where he had been. ❧

CHAPTER 11

THE WATCHER

The man looked at the pictures in the newspaper. He had wondered how long it would take someone to find the car and the body. They figured out the guy didn't shoot himself pretty quick. Leaving the shell casing was just for the hell of it. Send a warning to others like Martin. He figured that's what tipped them off. He just wanted to see whether they would care enough about a dead drug dealer to follow up on things. Now that it was a murder investigation, people would be snooping around everywhere. No matter. He had covered his tracks well. In a strange way, time was on his side. ❧

CHAPTER 12

I waited until later in the morning and then called Martin's mother. She was not glad to hear from me for the third time.

"Ms. Martin, I am sorry to bother you, but I have got a couple more questions."

"You don't care about botherin' me, so don't give me that. You should be out trying to find out who killed my boy instead of talkin' on the phone!" she barked.

I proceeded anyway. "That's what I am trying to do, and if you want me to find whoever did this, we are going to need to work together. I need your help. So let me ask you something. Did Devin have a girlfriend?"

"He had lots of girls. Anybody that he wanted. He was so smart and handsome, what girl wouldn't want to be with him."

"Can you give me the name of anyone in particular?"

"No, I don't think so. He never brought them by unless they were special."

"Anyone that you remember who was special?"

"No."

"Do you have any idea why he might have been way up in northern

Wisconsin?"

"No, but I know he was up north someplace before. He came back from one trip and gave me some cash to buy myself something nice. He said he hit big at the casino."

"How much did he give you?"

"Why do you want to know? So you can turn me in? Call my caseworker and get me in trouble? It was just a present from my boy."

"No, just curious."

"I don't remember."

"That's fine, Ms. Martin. I'm sorry to bother you. I may have to call you again. Is that okay?"

"I don't care," and she hung up.

———

The newspaper photo generated another lead. This one was far more interesting.

"Sheriff, this is Joe Thomas. I'm the head of security at Flaming Torches Casino. I saw those pictures you guys posted, and I'm pretty sure I know that car and the guy who was driving it. I actually have some surveillance pictures of him."

"Any chance we could get together today?" I asked.

"I am free this morning," replied Joe.

"I will leave right now."

"Works for me, Sheriff. What's your ETA?"

"Probably forty-five minutes to an hour."

"I'll look for you. Pull around back by the offices. It dims our image when a squad car is sitting in front."

I made it in forty minutes. Joe greeted me at the door. He was a broad-shouldered giant, and at least six feet six inches tall. He had jet black hair pulled back in a ponytail and a face that looked like it was chiseled from stone. The only thing that saved him from scaring the crap out of everyone he encountered was a big smile from ear to ear.

"Come on in, Sheriff," he said as he led me to his office. "Want coffee or something else?"

"Coffee would be great."

He punched up a number on his phone, and coffee was on the way.

I handed him the picture of Devin Martin.

"Yeah, that's Devin Martin. I haven't seen him around here for a while. I was hoping that he did not appreciate his welcoming committee and moved on. Although dead is absolutely fine by me," said Joe.

"Did he hang around the casino?" I asked.

"Yes and no. He would be here for a week straight and then be gone, and we wouldn't see him for two or three weeks. One of my undercover guys made him for what he was—a drug dealer. When he'd show up here, several other people would show up too. They would book one of our better rooms for a few days, pay the bill, and be gone until the next time. As soon as we caught on, we initiated a full-fledged campaign to let them know they were not welcome here."

"When was that?"

"We don't really keep detailed track of these things. I mean, you know how it is. Sometimes you just got to do what you got to do. The details are not as important as the results. My dad was a cop in the Twin Cities in the fifties and sixties and retired in the seventies. He was never the least bit confused about who the bad guys were and how they needed to be treated."

"Your dad still alive?"

"No, he's been gone a long time."

"You didn't follow in his footsteps of conventional law enforcement?"

"Oh, I did for a while ... twelve years or so. Then the hours and the time away from home started to put a strain on my marriage. I found this job with twice the pay and regular hours."

"Must have made your wife happy."

"I don't know. She served me with papers my last day on the department. I guess she had got herself hooked up with some bolt-selling bastard at a hardware store. I haven't seen her since."

A waiter brought our coffee and set it down on the table.

"Well, Sheriff, we should get to it. I am sure you have your hands full."

"That I do, Joe. I'm just wondering if you can tell me anything else about Devin Martin."

"How about I tell you everything I can think of, and you decide what you think might be helpful. Okay with you?"

"Works for me. Anything would be a lot more than what I have right now."

"The first time we noticed Martin was in the early spring. It wasn't anything in particular, but he fit the profile of a problem child. We ran him, and he came back with a serious sheet. Still, he wasn't doing anything wrong that we could see. We identify lots of different people we want to keep track of. Usually doesn't amount to anything, but it is a big part of what we need to do to keep this place as trouble free as we can."

"It looks like a big operation. Mostly drug problems?" I asked.

"We have it all: grifters, cheats, hookers, pimps, drug users, drug dealers. You name it, and we have it. Anyway, Martin would show up every couple of weeks and book a room. Sometimes he would have a woman with him, sometimes not. He'd go down to the floor and play blackjack. If his girlfriend was with him, she played the slots," he said.

"Any idea who the girl was?" I asked.

"No, we didn't really bother with her. We were most interested in Martin. We had a couple of other things going on, and actually, as far as Martin went, we were just about to hit the ignore button.

"Then one night, Martin checks in and is down on the casino floor. Two really bad-looking joint rats show up, stop for a second to say something to Martin, and keep walking. One of my people watching Martin picks up on the meeting. Martin meets the guys in the hall, and they go to his room. Ten minutes later, they leave carrying a medium-size duffle bag. We checked the video at check-in, and it looks a lot like the duffle bag Martin had with him when he checked in."

"Sounds like a drug drop," I said.

"Yup, so we put Martin back on the top of the list. After that, he checks in with a duffle bag every two weeks, meets the same guys, gives them the bag, and they're gone. I reached out to law enforcement and let them know."

"Who do you work with in law enforcement?" I asked.

"Tribal police, your department, and a contact in DNE."

"Did anything come of that?" I asked.

"Yeah, our DNE contact showed up out of the blue one day. He walks in like he owns the place, sits down at the bar, orders a cheeseburger, onion rings, and a beer and tells them to put it on my tab. The waitress calls me to see if it's okay. I come down to see who my new dependent is, and there larger than life sits Agent Anthony Ricardo. Have you ever met the guy?"

"No, I haven't."

"It is sure to be an experience when you do."

"What did Agent Ricardo tell you about Martin?"

"Ricardo looked at our surveillance photos and got excited. He was able to ID Martin and his buddies in about a second."

Then Joe started doing something on his laptop. A minute later, the printer spits out three sheets of paper, one for each of our people of interest. He handed me the sheets with their names—Devin Martin, Jesse Gunther, and Tony Carter—and corresponding photos and rap sheets.

"They are a nice-looking bunch, aren't they," Joe commented.

"Dandy. What happened with these guys?" I asked.

"Well, Ricardo goes to work with the tribal police, and they try to put something together. He just asks us to keep an eye on things. Then a couple of days later, Martin shows up, same routine with the guys in the casino. They get the bag from Martin and head out to the parking lot. All of a sudden, a panel van, no plates, pulls into the lot, and four guys jump out wearing masks. They are all over Martin's buddies, and I mean hard. The guys jump back in the van with the duffle bag, and they take off, and they are gone. We put out an alert, but these guys are nowhere to be found. Carter and Gunther have had some serious trauma administered to them, but they don't want an EMS unit. They had nothing to say. They told us the only thing in the bag was dirty laundry. That was it. We never saw Martin or his people again," Joe paused and thought for a minute. "Sheriff, when did you say he was killed?"

"He was alive on August 25, but probably not much longer after that day."

"I think our last contact was in mid-August. Let me look here. Yup, the surveillance photo dates are August 20 and 21. The 21st would be the day the other gang, I mean, I'm guessing that's who it was, ripped him off."

"Joe, I can't thank you enough for giving me a call. Here's my card with my cell number on it. If I can help you with anything, give me a call."

"Thanks, Sheriff."

———

I drove out of the casino lot and put a call in to my old partner, Lieutenant JJ Malone, who was now the head of the Organized Crime Task Force.

His nickname was "Bear" and true to form, he answered the phone with a growl. "Malone."

"Bear, how are you doing?"

"Well, well, the sheriff of the jack pine forest. How goes it with you, Sheriff?"

"Good, Bear. I need a little help with something."

"Just like always. What do you need, John?"

I told him everything I could think of involving Devin Martin.

"Before he was killed, Martin was apparently running drugs out of a casino. The head of casino security called a DNE agent they work with. He identified Martin and two of his associates from surveillance pictures. The agent said these guys were high up in a drug gang. So far, it looks like Martin was killed sometime after August 25."

"A drug dealer that gets himself shot is not much of a big news item," said Bear.

"I know it. My problem is it happened in my county, and it looks like these guys have an operation going on up here. If that's true, I need to be on top of it. I just need you to do some checking for me."

"Alright. Send me what you got. I'll see what we can do."

"One more thing, Bear."

"Isn't there always one more thing?"

"The DNE agent that's working this area is a guy named Anthony Ricardo. Do you know him?"

"I know him. What do you want to know?"

"Just any little thing you might think of."

"Ricardo is a tough sonofabitch. He rubs almost everyone he meets the wrong way. But he is a good agent and has made some major cases, along with some major enemies. Actually, Cabrelli, he reminds me a lot of you. You guys should get along just fine. He is also one of the supervisory agent's guys who works directly with our team. Since he's in your area right now, it would be a good idea to get in touch with him. Bring him up to speed on what you got going on. My advice would be to keep him in the loop on this. I'll send you his cell number. Call him." Bear clicked off.

I received Ricardo's number and called. It went straight to

voicemail. I left him a short message with a couple of different call-back numbers.

I drove back to the office and began to go through my messages. I looked up when Chief Bork entered my office.

"Hey, Len, what's up?" I asked.

"Just wondering where you are at on the Martin homicide."

I shared what I had learned. "I am guessing this Tony Carter and Jesse Gunther are still around here. If not all the time, then now and again. It would be good to know where they stay. Let's get a BOLO and the pictures out to our people, give them a heads-up on who they might run into."

"Sounds like those guys are just what we don't need. Drug use is growing like a plague. At the chiefs' meeting this year, a guy from Health and Social Services gave a talk. Statewide, the number of ODs is out of control. Over seventy thousand people died from drug overdoses in the country last year. I guess we have been pretty lucky so far." ✦

CHAPTER 13

A week later, on Saturday night, our luck ran out. I had filled in on the three to eleven shift. At the end of my tour, I advised dispatch I was going to find my way home. A couple of minutes later, dispatch called me.

"Sheriff, we got a 911 request for an ambulance at 22 Old Lake Road about two minutes ago. Then we just now received a call back to cancel. There was a bunch of noise in the background. I am familiar with that address. My in-laws rented it for my niece's wedding last summer. It's a private lodge that someone from Chicago owns. What do you advise?"

"Keep the EMS coming. I'll swing in and see what's going on," I replied.

Deputy Delzell was also in the area and advised she would respond as well.

The massive lodge was on the edge of town, with a long driveway far enough off the road that you would have to look to see if anything was going on there. I tried to pull in, but the drive was blocked by cars, some backing up, some moving forward. It appeared as if people were trying to leave in a hurry. Delzell pulled in behind me. A girl came running up to us. She grabbed me by the arm and started to drag me toward the direction of the lodge.

"Please, my sister needs help. Hurry, please hurry," she pleaded.

At the same time, a car trying to leave lost control and crashed into the side of Delzell's squad car.

Before we could react, the reality of what we were seeing overtook us. There were kids, high school age and older, running in every direction. Delzell called for all available units as backup.

The girl tried to drag us to her sister, but we had to fight through the mob to get to the lodge. Seeing uniformed officers only exacerbated the situation as some kids started yelling, "Cops!" When we got to the lodge, we realized how bad the situation was. Kids were yelling and screaming. When we finally found the sister of the girl who had dragged us in, she was on the floor in a pile of vomit, barely conscious, while others ran over the top of her. A boy stumbled to Delzell. He had severe cuts, was bleeding profusely, and fell into her arms.

Another girl from somewhere in the crowd was screaming, "Help me. Please help me!"

Delzell wisely requested all available EMS units. We tried to do what we could, but the pandemonium was overwhelming. I picked up the girl I was trying to help and laid her on a long dining room table. I positioned her head as best I could and told her sister to hold her that way.

Our first aid gear was in the squads, but the need was so immediate that we just had to do what we could with what we had. The always resourceful Delzell came up with some linen napkins from a buffet, and I helped her use them to slow the bleeding from the injured boy.

We began a two-deputy triage protocol, trying to identify those in the greatest need, ordering the others out of the way.

Sirens screamed in the distance. EMS units from two counties and every form of law enforcement officer responded to the scene and waded into the melee. We didn't even realize that help had arrived when it did.

I found a breathing but unconscious boy of no more than thirteen or fourteen lying on the floor. I picked him up and started to carry him toward one of the long dining tables. A hand grabbed my arm, and I gratefully handed the boy to an EMT who quickly loaded him into a waiting ambulance.

I looked around the room and saw Len Bork, his arms restraining a young girl screaming at the top of her lungs, wrapped in a blanket. Len's face was bleeding where it looked like she had deeply scratched him. I only had a second to glance at him before I jumped in to help two of our local EMTs who were wrestling with a big high school-age boy who had ripped his shirt off and was fighting like he was possessed. It took all we could muster to zip tie him to a backboard.

Then I heard a call on an EMT's radio, and my heart sank. "10-33 code blue, code blue! We have a pulseless, non-breathing teenage boy. We have initiated CPR."

I don't know how long it took. It seemed forever, but eventually, everyone who needed to go by EMS to the hospital was on their way. In all my years of law enforcement, I had never seen anything like this. It was a living nightmare.

We loaded up the remaining partygoers and hauled them down to the clinic next to the emergency room, which had opened with family practice doctors and nurses coming in to help.

News travels fast in a small town, and shortly after we arrived, cars full of parents whose kids had not yet come home began to pull in.

The scene was growing chaotic as terrified parents tried to find their kids among the wailing teens. I could see the situation could get out of control any second, except for Len Bork. He directed the deputies and officers to herd all the kids who didn't need immediate medical attention into the clinic waiting room. Then he gathered the parents together in the entryway. Finally, after some cajoling,

Len had everyone's attention.

"With the sheriff's permission, here's what I would like to do, folks. We are going to match the kids we have with their parents. So if your son or daughter is here, we are going to let you take them home. If there is a child you know and would be willing to reach their parents for us, please call and ask them to come down and pick them up. Before anyone leaves, you need to fill out one of these information forms and hand it to Deputy Delzell. We will be in contact with you soon. We hope you will reach an understanding with your youngster about how important it will be for all of us if they cooperate. If you are concerned that your son or daughter may have ingested a substance they shouldn't have, go right to the clinic reception desk. They will take it from there. The kids need to understand that if they took something, they need to come forward. Do not worry about the police. Our only concern right now is to make sure everyone is safe. Do you folks have any questions?"

No one did. About half of the kids went home in the first round, and most of the rest left as a result of parents calling parents. After a while, only one remained. She sat on the floor squeezed into a corner, with her arms wrapped securely around her knees. Her face was down and covered by a hoodie, with wisps of purple hair sticking out. She would not look up or respond to the officer's questions.

I recognized the girl squatted down on the floor. "Amber, do you remember me? I am Ms. Carlson's friend. I know your grandma and grandpa. Do you remember me?"

She wouldn't look up or speak.

"Amber, will you give me your mother's cell phone number?"

No reply.

I called Julie and told her who I was with. She gave me Amber's mother's cell phone number.

"John, I am on my way to town to see what I can do," she said with resolve. I didn't argue.

I called Crystal Lockridge's number. There was no answer, so I left a message. Twenty minutes later, Julie walked in the door and right past me to where Amber was sitting. Julie plopped down on the floor beside her.

"Hi, honey," she said in a soothing tone. "Are you all right?"

Amber looked up for the first time since I arrived on the scene. Julie put her arms around her and held her tight. Amber began to sob, deep breath-robbing, painful sobs.

Julie requested a glass of water, and I responded promptly. I tried her mother again with the same result.

I took a chance and asked Amber if I could ask her a couple of questions. Amber looked up at me with red-rimmed eyes, and Julie glared at me.

"Amber, I need to know if you took anything you shouldn't have at the party. I am not asking you this for any other reason than if you did, we need to get you over to the clinic to be screened."

She whispered in Julie's ear. "John, she didn't take or drink anything. She promises."

"Amber, do you know where your mother is tonight?"

Again, a whisper. "She doesn't know," Julie relayed.

"Julie, do you have the number for her grandparents?" She did.

Stella Lockridge answered. I told her the situation, and she said that she and Ed would be there as soon as possible. Amber appeared to be glad to hear they were coming.

Meanwhile, I checked in with the hospital. Things were chaotic but getting under control. Dr. Chali's wife, Becky, had come in to help work with the families.

Ed and Stella Lockridge rushed through the door. Stella joined Amber and Julie on the floor, sweeping both up in a powerful hug.

"Oh, Amber, I am so glad you are okay. Everything is going to be just fine. Don't worry about a thing."

Ed Lockridge came over and thanked me while Julie, Stella, and

Amber huddled, talking quietly in the corner of the room.

Once the Lockridges were on their way back to Spider Creek, Julie insisted she go to the hospital to team up with her friend Becky, who was joined by Martha Bork. The three strong women were doing whatever they could, offering any comfort possible, no matter how small. Parents and some siblings were by every bed.

Those who had taken the drugs were in various treatment stages and hopefully would not have lasting health issues. The kid who smashed through the plate-glass window had numerous severe cuts that Dr. May attended to. During transport, the boy I had found on the floor had become pulseless and stopped breathing. Doctor Chali and a trauma nurse wasted no time on protocol, running right out to the loading bay when the ambulance arrived. Chali delivered what he hoped would be a lifesaving jolt of electricity to the boy's heart. At first, nothing. Chali tried the defibrillator again. No response. As he prepared for one more try, the boy coughed and coughed again. He had a pulse. He would survive.

—————

The following morning we began the process of figuring it all out. The owner of the lodge was from Chicago. It was one of a number of investment properties he owned in northern Wisconsin that he rented out via the Internet. He gave us the credit card information the person who rented the lodge had used. The name on the card was Phillip Trundle. We tracked him down easily in a suburb of Milwaukee. He lived in a senior citizen residential center. I spoke with him about his credit card. He told me that he rarely used it, and he was sure it was where it should be in the corner of his top dresser drawer. He went to look, and the card was gone. A check with the issuing company showed that several thousand dollars in charges had been put on the credit card, primarily purchases at stores that carried expensive electronics that could be bought with the stolen card and then sold for cash.

My deputies and city officers took the contact sheets and began going to each house, interviewing the kids with their parents present. The kids didn't know much. They heard through the grapevine about a big party out at the lodge. Lots of people showed up, and things started getting pretty wild. Some people there who weren't local were a little older, and many had tattoos. Several of the kids said the drugs were just in a baggie on a table. No one remembered anyone putting them there. The boy who had been cut up was the one who opened the bag and dumped the contents out on the table. He had a pipe with him and lit the meth up and smoked it, passing it around. Ten to fifteen minutes after smoking, the problems started. No one had any idea who rented the lodge with the stolen credit card. ❧

CHAPTER 14

I drove over to the sheriff's office and parked in the area behind the building. A guy was leaning against a light pole staring at me.

I got out of my truck and walked toward him. He didn't move. "Are you waiting to see me?" I asked.

"Name's Anthony Ricardo, DNE." Surliness dripped off of him. He did not look like a cop; he looked like a street thug.

"John Cabrelli. Thanks for returning my call," I said, even though he hadn't.

"Sorry, I was out detecting. Lieutenant Malone got ahold of me and figured you could use some help. So lucky you—here I am," he replied.

He immediately pissed me off. "Agent Ricardo, I have had a really long couple of days, and I really don't have any interest in smartass banter. What is it that you want?" I asked.

"Not here. I will drive east on the highway and park behind that big billboard at that auction place that's closed. You come on in about five minutes. Give me your cell phone number. If I get there and don't like something, I will call you," he said.

Five minutes later, I pulled onto a patch of gravel behind the billboard. Ricardo got out of his car and got into mine.

"It's nice to meet you, Sheriff Cabrelli. I've heard a lot about you. Some of it's even good. Sorry, no smartass banter. I forgot. It's just my nature. Anyway, I don't have a bunch of time, so here's what I think I might know.

"There is a lot of something going on in northern Wisconsin, all involving drugs and the associated crimes. Taking out Devin Martin was a big deal. We are positive he was the guy running things up here for Deacon Gunther's outfit. The only others we know he was running with are Jesse Gunther, Deacon's cousin and Tony Carter, both members of a recent graduating class of state prison. By the way, they are still around. I don't have anything for you right now on who might have taken him out. Martin was a real bad guy that ran with a bad crew."

"Any ideas about who else might be competing for the territory?" I asked.

Ricardo didn't even try to answer my question and just continued with his narrative.

"Joe Thomas told me he talked to you. He's a good man. So, about the rip at the casino. It seems that the masked guys who robbed Martin's boys at the casino would be likely suspects to look at for who whacked Devin Martin. By the way, the duffle bag that got taken from Martin's buddies was probably full of meth. Within twenty-four hours of that rip-off, a bounty of meth was hitting the street locally, so it stands to reason that the guys who grabbed it are from the immediate area. Hopefully, we'll get something from one of the local yokels and follow the breadcrumbs back to those guys. But nothing so far. The strange thing, though, is that there hasn't been any retaliation for Martin. At least no one has turned up any fresh bodies from the opposing side."

Ricardo continued, "I'm usually not interested in backwoods high school parties, but I am kind of interested in what went down here the other night. Can you help me out with that?"

"What do you want to know?"

"I want to know everything about everything, that way I can decide what's worth knowing. But in this case, though, just hit the high spots."

"Someone rented a lodge on the edge of town and threw a big party. Drugs and alcohol. Some kids OD'd."

"Geez, Sheriff, that's a lot. Tell me again more slowly so I can write it down."

"Agent Ricardo, what do you want? Quit jerking me around."

"Who rented the lodge?"

"Whoever it was used a stolen credit card issued to a Phillip Trundle in a Milwaukee suburb."

"Let me detect on this for a minute. Now just wait, Sheriff, it won't take long. I bet he's in a nursing home and didn't even know the card was gone. How am I doing so far?"

I didn't answer, not wanting to encourage him.

"Oh, oh something else. Yeah, I got something else. Is it possible that someone used that same card to buy a bunch of electronics in a one-stop shop at a local Milwaukee store? I know. Amazing, right?"

I had known Anthony Ricardo for less than an hour. In that short time, he had successfully climbed close to the top of my list of people I couldn't stand. Every word was another step up.

"Aww, come on, Sheriff. Did I get it right?"

"Ricardo, get out of my car," I said.

"Hold on, Sheriff. Just hold on."

I got out, walked over to the passenger door, opened it up, and told him to get out.

"Aww, come on, Sheriff. Give me one more chance."

"Here's your chance, Ricardo."

"Well, that gang Devin Martin was tied up with had a little side business going. The girls they ran with would get jobs in nursing homes and assisted living facilities. There is such a shortage of people who want these jobs that they could walk in the door and be working the next day. They figure out where the old folks keep their credit cards and rip them off the first chance they get. They walk out the door at the end of their shift, hand the cards off to one of the gang members, who buys expensive stuff that's easy to sell on the street. Your party may be tied to Gunther's people. I mean, there are a lot of people working credit card scams, but you gotta admit it's interesting."

"Anything else, Agent Ricardo?"

"Yeah, there is one thing. Were you able to recover the drugs that the kids OD'd on?"

"No, they were gone."

"Too bad. I would have liked to get a sample to the lab. You see, Gunther has got a lab somewhere around here. They were screwing around with some different drug concoctions. We got a sample of what they are making. It would be good to compare, but whatever. Well, Sheriff, I have taken enough of your valuable time."

Then he handed me a card. "This has my super-secret cell phone number on it. If you really have something, call me. I will either answer or get back to you as soon as I can. In the meantime, my crew and I will continue to detect. Later, Sheriff."

Ricardo got in his car and drove off.

The early dark of fall had set in as I headed back to the office to read the officers' reports from the party and interviews with partygoers. I didn't learn much that I didn't already know. No one knew who put the party together or rented the lodge. I did learn that drugs have the miraculous ability to appear from nowhere because, according to everyone we interviewed, no one knew how the drugs got to the party.

The weight of our situation sat squarely on my shoulders. I

checked for messages and felt bone-weary when I started my drive home. I parked my squad and walked up to the porch.

The night sky was clear, the stars standing out against the pitch black. Orion the Hunter dominated the southwest sky. I looked out at the impossible space. Uncle Nick and I used to stare up at the sky at night. He tried to help me understand the concept of infinity.

Johnny, someday when scientists begin to understand the true size of the universe, I think they will find that Earth is insignificant, its relative size no more than a speck of dust in comparison to the universe. But here tonight, the stars have come to greet us. Tonight, they shine for us.

The chill from the cold air was comforting, and the unfrozen lake shimmered. The door opened, and Julie came out wearing Uncle Nick's old wool sweater. She snuggled into me and put her head on my chest. I put my arm around her and pulled her close. We stood quietly, then a cold breeze coming off the lake made Julie shiver, and we went inside. The weight of our heavy wool blanket was warm and comforting as we crawled into bed. I held Julie in my arms as starlight streamed through our window, and we eventually drifted to sleep.

I slept fitfully, my hippocampus working overtime, blending recent events with events long passed. The face of young Angelina Gonzalez again came to visit me. Julie was quietly snoring when I got up at three in the morning and went downstairs. The coals in the woodstove still glowed, and I threw in a couple of pieces of split wood that soon burst into flames. I sat in the chair with my feet up, thinking about my life. It was truly better than I ever expected it would be, yet the tragedies I had been a part of were never far from my thoughts. They would always be with me. Sometimes I felt like they were waiting around the corner, hiding in the shadows, waiting to jump out. Thankfully, at some point, I fell asleep.

Julie woke me at six.

"John, wake up. You were dreaming," she said.

We showered and dressed and lingered over coffee. Julie left for school, and I drove the backroads on my way to town. I wished we could have stayed home, taken the day to walk along the lakeshore, and sit by the fire.

My cellphone brought me back to reality, and I rolled my eyes when I saw there was no caller ID.

"Hey, Sheriff, I bet you're thrilled to hear my voice so soon," Anthony Ricardo said.

I didn't say anything.

"Here is the deal. You never know when something is going to come your way. Something you might like to know came my way last night. That's if you have the time. I know you're a busy guy."

"Tell me," I said.

"I was hoping for something a little more up close and personal, and also that Chief Bork might be able to join us. What do you think? I'll make it worth your time."

"When and where do you want to meet?" I asked.

"Don't you have a cozy little cabin some place out in the woods? I could come out there. You know, sit by the fire with a nice cup of coffee. Tell you what, we could even have the chief pick up some scones from the bakery on his way out. Sounds like a nice morning, doesn't it? I hate to put you out, but we ramped things up a bit, so I got to be careful about being seen with you brave men in uniform. Your cabin seems like a safe place."

"Fine, Agent Ricardo. I'll give Len a call."

"Ah, Sheriff, could you just call me Anthony? I mean, Agent Ricardo seems so formal," he said. I hung up on him and called Len. He agreed to meet in an hour and to bring scones. I called Ricardo back to let him know the plan.

We sat around the kitchen table. It was warm in the cabin, and

Ricardo took off his leather coat. Underneath it, he was wearing twin shoulder holsters filled with two high-capacity compact Glock pistols. It looked like a custom carry double rig based on the Miami Classic.

Ricardo saw me looking and smiled, "I am a firm believer in the concept of the New York reload. So far, so good."

We drank coffee and ate the scones, but I wanted to get to the matter at hand.

"What do you have, Agent Ricardo?"

"Anthony, remember," he began. "While you have been trying to keep your heads above water busting up teenage parties—nasty scratches on your face there, Chief—I have been busy detecting, and I have detected some things of interest. It appears as though two separate drug gangs are trying to expand their networks to the state's more remote areas. One is an outlaw motorcycle gang, or OMG, based in the Twin Cities. The other is Gunther's gang, made up of our own homegrown Wisconsin ex-convicts. Both are in a class we call 'evolved street gangs.' Some have even started calling them cartels. I would not give them that much credit. However, they are spreading their wings. It started with expanding to the suburbs. They found out that middle-class kids have some money to spend and were much more reliable customers." Ricardo paused to sip his coffee. "Now they are out in the hinterland. They are finding that the wide-open spaces have a lot fewer cops per square mile, and if they keep a low profile, they can do business with less risk. Well, our bad boys from Wisconsin thought they had this sewn up.

"Then somebody makes a play and takes out Devin Martin. The bikers look like a top candidate to me. The OMG doesn't see the value in wasting time taking out street dealers. They want to make a statement, so they take out someone high up in the organization. We are going to have to pay special attention to the goings-on around here.

"I have got some people on the street. They are trying to find out what they can. We are giving this whole thing a high priority. A good portion of the state is rural, and the dopers are making a real move into those areas. There is a chance, maybe a slim one, that we may be able to get a handle on this before it really gets going. That's what we are hoping for, anyway. So, we will keep you guys in the loop, and you will keep us in the loop. My people are deep cover and real pros, but that doesn't mean they can't be found out. If you hear anything about somebody making one of my people, let me know immediately. We will do a risk assessment and probably pull him or her. For now, you go your way, and I'll go mine."

"So how sure are you it was the people from Minneapolis who killed Devin Martin?" I asked.

"Well, Sheriff, I am not sure at all. But you gotta admit, they are worth looking at, don't ya think? Stay in touch, boys." Ricardo headed out the door.

Len and I agreed for the time being to follow Ricardo's lead, mainly because it was currently the only game in town.

I spent the rest of the day in the office cleaning up the paperwork that is part and parcel of this job. My lack of sleep from the night before got to me, and I was exhausted when I loaded my gear and headed for home.

That evening, Bud joined Julie and me for dinner. Although the three of us had shared many dinners before, now that Julie and I were a couple, things were different. We were a family and vested in each other's happiness.

We dined on medium-rare venison backstrap and mushroom sauce. After dinner, we sat by the fire while Julie worked on student papers. Bud and I tried to play a game of cribbage, but I was too distracted, and Bud got tired of playing my hand for me.

"That's okay, John. I know you have a lot on your mind. I don't even know how you can think straight with all that's going on. Some kids did drugs when I was in school, but nothing like this. The most trouble we had was in the summer when the city kids would come up on vacation. Sure, some stuff happened, but this seems to be a whole bunch worse," Bud said empathetically.

"Drugs have infected our communities. There are lots of kids in our schools involved with drugs. When I get together with teachers from other districts, even the smallest ones, all are facing this problem," Julie added.

"I have no idea what to do. The only real answer is for people to stop using illicit drugs. Every cop on the street is fighting the drug epidemic as hard as they can, and every day it seems clearer we have lost the war on drugs. Bear told me that the government spent over forty billion dollars fighting the war on drugs last year. The real truth is, Julie, you are doing more than we are. Education is the key to everything. When you started at this school, you made a place where everyone was welcome, even those kids on the outside of things. I mean, where do you think Amber Lockridge would be without you and your school?" I asked.

"John, I was heartsick when you called me the other night. Amber told me that her girlfriend told her about the party. She didn't want to go, but I think she felt like she had to. She said that it was weird and wanted to go home, but her girlfriend was her ride and didn't want to. I told her if she was ever in a spot and needed a ride or anything else, no matter what time of day or night, she could call me. She has both our home number and my cell in her phone."

"Did you ever find out where her mother was?"

"'Out' is all she told Ed and Stella. They didn't say it, but I think they are concerned that Crystal might be backpedaling. I don't know."

"I saw her the other day at the store. She looked okay to me, friendly and all," Bud said.

"I shouldn't be basing this on just one thing," Julie said to Bud. "But when I went over for a parent conference, Amber said she had the flu and needed to postpone the meeting. I was no better than anyone else. I automatically assumed that she was on drugs again."

"It's hard not to go there because it's pretty much the way things work most of the time," I said.

"I know that's true, John, but maybe jumping to conclusions is part of the problem," Julie said.

"One thing you have got to remember, Julie, once someone chooses drugs, the drug begins to own them. When I first got on the street, my field training officer told me the only thing a drug addict ever thinks about is getting high. They fix up one minute, and all they think about is fixing up again. Nothing is more important to them."

The evening's conversation put us all in a somber mood. The weather settled down, and Bud headed home.

I got ready for bed, but Julie asked me to come and sit with her by the fire. She was holding a glass of red wine and handed me a glass of brandy. We sat in silence together while inside I was reveling in the fact that we were in love. I truly believed that I was the luckiest man alive.

Julie finished her wine and put her head on my shoulder. "John, I have tried all my life to never hate anyone, even when all things pointed to me being justified in feeling hatred. There is so much hate in the world, and I do not want to add to it. But, I truly hate these people who are poisoning our children—my children. I have not yet been able to rise above this hatred."

I pulled her in closer and felt her tears fall on my shoulder. Drug abuse brought pain and heartache to everyone. ◂

CHAPTER 15

THE WATCHER

The man sat in the dark on a high rise of land overlooking the trailer. There was no traffic and no one else around. He used a set of surplus binoculars to survey the area just once more, not that he could do anything in the improbable event someone other than the two guys in the trailer did show up.

Even though he had an idea where the mobile home was, it had been difficult to locate. It was hidden deep in the forest at the end of a dirt driveway connected to a forest road no one used. It was a stroke of luck that he even found it. There was a small store, more like a trading post out on the main road. He was buying fuel when a guy pulled up in a Jeep. The Jeep driver got out and walked into the store. The man had seen him before, more than once with Devin Martin. He didn't know the guy's name, but it didn't matter. The man followed him home, and for the next few days, he watched the goings-on at the trailer. He needed to be absolutely sure before he did his job. It didn't take long. People were coming and leaving with bags he assumed contained drugs made in the clandestine lab. They appeared to be doing a pretty brisk business. Two guys were there nearly all the time. They both wore pistols that he could see, and he guessed they probably had shotguns and maybe rifles stashed around the place too. They never went anywhere together, always leaving one guy to watch the place. He intended to destroy the lab and the two guys in it and send a clear message: this was an unhealthy place to do business. As it always does, his patient waiting and watching paid off. The guys in that trailer would stay up late but were asleep or passed out no later than three in the morning, and they were never up and moving before ten.

It was surprising they didn't have a dog. A barking dog could sure complicate things, but they didn't. He would have never been able to survey the place and do his work with a dog barking. He had never seen another car, truck, or person in the area between five thirty and six thirty in the morning. There would be no risk to any unintended victims, although you really could never be completely sure. In the early morning hours of the next day, he moved silently around the trailer, placing his packages in strategic places. He set the timer for six and walked back to the high hill where he would be out of danger.

He sat silently, waiting. The stars were out, but the moon was just a sliver. In the southwest sky, he could see the constellation Orion the Hunter; he was the hunter. The noise of a truck broke the silence. He looked with his binoculars and spotted an LP delivery truck as it turned onto the dirt road that went right past the trailer. The driver's timing could not have been worse. The timer he had used was dependable but could be off by as much as ten minutes. The LP truck trundled on, the man willed it to go faster, but the road was not made for speed. There was no stopping this now. The truck passed the trailer and continued on. It went another hundred yards or so when a massive fireball illuminated the woods like daylight. It went high order, as he knew it would, sending a mushroom cloud into the sky. With great relief, he saw the LP truck was still in one piece. Then the man climbed down from the hill and left the area. He had parked his vehicle a fair distance away. It was always a good idea to distance yourself from something like this. Some would say he was a fool for waiting for the explosion at all. He should have been fifty miles away. The man always needed to make sure that he had done his job. ✦

CHAPTER 16

Pagers went off across the county, and volunteer firefighters responded immediately. The Spider Lake and School Lake Fire Departments were the closest and received the first pages. A call went out for any law enforcement officers in the area. Namekagon County Sheriff's Deputy Pave and a Wisconsin state trooper were the closest and responding.

The deputy was first on the scene. What greeted him looked like some kind of large mobile home, maybe a double-wide. The basic frame could be made out, but the rest was obscured by smoke and a wildly burning fire. He noticed a vehicle in the yard just in time to witness the gas tank explode. The heat was intense, and the deputy backed off. The only thing to do was wait for the firefighters. There was almost nothing left of the structure, yet it continued to burn ferociously.

The firefighters arrived and poured water on the trailer and surrounding trees that threatened to catch. While the fire was burning stubbornly, it was almost all out and under control by the time the sun brought full light to the forest. All that remained was a burned shell of the trailer and an almost unidentifiable incinerated Jeep

Cherokee.

When it was safe, the firefighters began to look for possible victims. They found one in what appeared to be the sleeping area of the trailer and another close by. The victims were burned beyond recognition. The fire was hot enough that much of the outside aluminum siding had melted.

The two fire chiefs requested dispatch send me to the scene, and I was on my way in a few minutes. Once in my truck, the Spider Lake chief explained the situation over the radio. He further advised he had requested dispatch page out the ME and fire marshal.

I arrived on-site, and the firefighters had already run bright yellow "Fire Investigation" tape around the scene, making sure to take in as much territory as they thought was needed.

Standing off to the side, next to a big LP truck, was the driver Chad Mills. He was also the driver who delivered LP to my cabin.

"How are you holding up, Chad?"

"I am okay. Still a little shook, but I'm fine."

"What can you tell me?"

"Well, not much, Sheriff. I wanted to get an early start on my route because I had a bunch of deliveries on the other side of the county. I was kinda hoping to be done by one or one thirty and get out to my bow stand. I got some trail cam shots of a dandy ten-pointer, and there is a ton of sign. So, I took a shortcut through the forest on road 191. It is narrow but a pretty good road, and I didn't expect to run into anybody. I had just turned off the main road and maybe made it half a mile or so when all hell broke loose. There was an explosion that blew so hard it rocked my truck from side to side. I got a full load on, and it still shook the truck. Truth is, I thought I was going to blow up too. It was probably stupid, but I stopped and looked back. I could see the trailer burning like crazy. The flames had to have been burning a hundred feet in the air and roaring. I am just damn glad it didn't blow me up."

"What did you do next?" I asked.

"I drove my truck as fast as I could down the road. Then I tried to call 911 on my cell, but it wouldn't go through, and my dispatcher didn't come in until six thirty. So, I kept driving until I saw a cabin that looked like it had a phone line strung off a pole in the yard. I checked around the door frame for a key and found one. Inside, I found the phone and called the fire in."

"Chad, have you taken this shortcut before?"

"Yeah, I have every so often. Like I said, it shaves some time off."

"Did you ever notice the double-wide before today?"

"Yes, I did. As a matter of fact, I delivered hundred pounders to them every so often. They weren't on the 'keep fill plan,' but they called in whenever they needed some and I delivered it."

"Did they seem to use a lot of propane?"

"Well, now that you mention it, I have made quite a few deliveries here in the last few months. I can check with the office. They have a record of every delivery."

"Chad, do you know the names of the people who were living here?"

"Nope, Sheriff. In fact, I never saw anybody when I made my deliveries. I just stuck the slip in an envelope in the storm door. The name of the customer will be on file at the office."

"Did you notice any vehicles or anything else?"

"Not that I can recall, Sheriff. Sorry I can't be more help."

"Well, thanks, Chad. If you think of anything more, give me a call on my cell phone or through the dispatcher."

"Will do, Sheriff. Now, if it's okay, I better get back to business and get this propane delivered."

"No problem, Chad. Thanks for your help. You can go ahead and get going."

Chad jumped in the cab, released the brake, and rumbled off down the road.

The scene investigation was really moving by midmorning.

The fire marshal's office sent Jeff Wolfman, a seasoned arson investigator from the Department of Criminal Investigation. It didn't take him long to come up with a potential cause. There were bits and pieces in the mobile home, but empty cans of acetone, as well as hundreds of empty cold tablet packs and bottles, had been dumped in a hand-dug pit hidden in the woods some distance from the trailer. Remnants of glass cooking containers were strewn around the trailer's perimeter, and inside were the remains of what used to be two propane tanks. The chemicals that are used to make methamphetamines give off fumes that are very flammable and can accumulate. All it takes is a spark, and an explosion results. Meth lab explosions are not uncommon, and often the ones running the clandestine lab are the victims. Everything pointed to this being a meth lab.

"Sheriff, would you come over here a second?" the fire marshal called.

"What have you got?" I asked.

"I just happened to notice something that is likely important. Three depressions in the ground correspond with the areas where the heat was intense. The depressions are about the same size, and they are located at strategic points around the trailer. I requested the help of a crime scene unit and survey team."

"What do you think happened, Jeff?" I asked.

"I think that the explosion of the trailer was caused by some sort of destructive device planted outside. The truck driver who called in the explosion said it looked like a fireball in the sky, and that the concussion from the blast rocked his very heavy LP truck. When meth labs blow, they blow pretty hard depending on what is floating around the lab. This was a major explosion and an extremely intense fire. The explosion launched pieces of debris into the treetops and beyond. At this point, if I were to guess, I'd say that someone placed explosive charges under or almost under the trailer—maybe even used the explosives in conjunction with an accelerant. I don't know for sure, but I think there is a good chance that this was an intentional act resulting in at least two dead bodies. I think there is a strong possibility that this might be a murder," said Wolfman.

"So, how do you suggest we proceed?" I asked.

"We need to secure the scene and wait for reinforcements. They are already on their way. Once they arrive, we will first survey the area to make certain there is no unexploded ordinance. Then we'll start to sift through the debris and see what we can find. I think we will find something, though it will take a while. As soon as we do, we'll let you know. Right now, I need to get back at it."

The investigator walked back to the fire scene.

———————

I got in my truck, drove to a high spot in the road where I had cell service, and called Ricardo's secret cell number. He answered right away.

"Sheriff, how nice of you to call. I got word through the grapevine that everybody and their cousin are on the way to yet another crime scene party in your county. I don't know much else about it, but it sounds like something I would be interested in if you have the time, of course."

"That's why I called, Anthony," I replied tersely.

I told him what I knew and relayed what the fire marshal and fire chief said. I described the scene as best I could, including the trash left behind. He took some time processing the information.

"Sheriff, a meth lab blowing up is not all that newsworthy. Most of the 'chemists' working in these labs aren't on the genius list. They get all these toxic flammable fumes in their lab, and then some dummy decides to light up a smoke and *kablam!* The guys running the lab rarely survive, and if they do, they sustain some pretty severe injuries. On the other hand, if the fire marshal is right and somebody planted a bomb, that takes this to a whole new level. Without conclusion jumping too far, I think maybe we'll find out this is payback for the hit on Devin Martin."

"I'm sure it will take a while to get a positive ID on the victims. They were really burned up," I said.

"In the meantime, Sheriff, I need a little favor. Actually, it's a favor for you and me and the good citizens of Namekagon County."

"What?" I asked.

"Call your good buddy Malone and put in a mutual aid request to get some extra support for this operation. We have some new faces that have just joined us. I want to put them on the street. No contact with local law enforcement. If this heats up and your guys start rousting some likely subjects, and my people get bounced around, I don't care. It will add to their authenticity. Sheriff, I've got a feeling about this. I think we're right. This is payback for Martin. So now somebody has got to hit back. We all better be paying attention. Otherwise, this may sneak up on us."

"I'll call Malone."

"Thanks, Sheriff. Talk real nice to him. That might help."

"I doubt it," I replied.

"Me too," Ricardo said and hung up.

―――――――

The fire was out, and most firefighters returned to their respective stations and back to their regular jobs. Deputy Pave stayed at the scene with the fire marshal, the ME, and the Spider Lake fire chief, awaiting the arrival of a crime scene unit.

On my way back to Musky Falls, I talked to the people at the propane company. The person who held the account was Ervin Walder. He had a credit card on file that auto-paid for every delivery. We tracked down Mr. Walder, another victim of a credit card scam. The story was familiar. He lived in an assisted living facility two hundred miles away from Musky Falls. The attendant went down to his room, and together they checked. His credit card was long gone. He rarely used it, so he didn't even notice.

I ran the property's fire number through county records. They were able to give me the address and phone number of the owner in Minnesota, Mark Redberg. The man answered the phone as Reverend Redberg. The reverend explained that the double-wide trailer was used for years as a hunting shack by his father and family. They had stopped using it two or three years before. It seems no one was interested in going up to Namekagon County hunting anymore. The trailer had been well taken care of and was in good shape the last time he checked. They were going to sell it when they got the chance. He didn't think it would bring much, but the proceeds would be welcome. It seems he was semiretired and raising chickens on his farm in Minnesota. The money from the sale would help fund his new chicken coop. As far as he knew, no one was staying there.

He did notice recently that his electrical bill had jumped considerably. He had meant to come over and check on it but hadn't gotten to it. I was met with silence when I told him that there had been two fatalities. He spoke gently and asked the details of what had happened. I shared with him as much as I could and said that I would send him a copy of the report when our investigation was complete. He did not know if the trailer was insured. The reverend said he would pray for those who lost their lives and pray for the safety of law enforcement officers.

I had pulled over to take notes and record the contact information. When I wrapped up, I realized I was in desperate need of a cup of coffee and something to put in my stomach. When the Crossroads sign came into view, it was like an oasis in the desert. I went in and ordered a large River Blend and was thrilled to see one of their world-class cinnamon rolls left in the glass cabinet.

I walked to the back of the store and dropped down in a comfy chair. It was just what the doctor ordered. My head was buzzing, and I needed a minute to take a breath. The coffee was delightful, the cinnamon roll delicious. I had just finished and was contemplating a refill when my moment of peace was dashed on the rocks. Scott Stewart, the county board chair, stood right in front of me. I did not know him well, actually hardly at all. My interactions with him had been mostly positive, although I had a feeling that was coming to an end.

"Do you have a moment, Sheriff?" Stewart asked.

"Sure, Scott, pull up a chair."

"Can you fill me in about the fire out on the forest road?" he asked.

"Well, Scott, we don't know much yet. A double-wide trailer went up in flames. There were two occupants inside at the time, neither one survived. Once the fire was out, the fire chief started looking over the scene and found the bodies. The ME, the fire marshal, fire personnel, and one of my deputies are still processing the scene, and it's my guess they will be at it a while.

"Sheriff, does it appear that foul play was involved?" he inquired.

"I don't know yet," I replied.

"Sheriff, I have it on good authority that this trailer was probably an illicit drug lab, and that they were likely producing methamphetamines. I have also been informed that some sort of bomb may have been involved."

"Well, Scott, that's interesting. I will be anxious to see the investigator's report."

"Ah, Sheriff, I feel as though you are somewhat evasive in your answers."

"Sorry you feel that way. I am tired, and I have got a full plate right now. I am not up for a guessing game. So please just ask me what you want to know."

"Sheriff, I have heard that this explosion may have been in retaliation for the killing of that drug dealer."

"Where did you hear that?" I asked.

"Sheriff, this is a small town. Anything like this gets people talking. So, is it true? Is this retaliation?"

"Scott, honestly, I don't know. The scene belongs to the fire chief and the fire marshal right now. They are going over it with a fine-toothed comb. We will have to wait until these folks are done. I am not jumping to conclusions."

I had answered his question, but he clearly was not ready to leave.

"Is there anything else?" I asked.

"Sheriff, from now on, I want you to keep me advised and up to date on any developments in these cases. I believe it is important to the community. Maybe I can help to avoid any further missteps."

Fatigue and pressure are not a good combination.

"Missteps, Scott? What missteps would those be?" I asked.

"I am just referring to the fact that you lost valuable time regarding the Devin Martin case pursuing it as a suicide when, in fact, it was a cold-blooded killing. We need to move quickly to get things under control."

"In the Martin case, we did good police work and determined the facts of the situation. Using those facts, we have developed some theories about how this went down. We have learned a lot about the victim and a lot about the perpetrator. We are continuing to follow up on that case to the best of our ability. Are the two new bodies in some way tied to Devin Martin's death? I don't know, but we will continue to do good solid police work and try to figure that out. I will do my best to keep you advised of the status of our investigation. But unless I completely miss my guess, this thing is ramping up pretty fast. There are some parts of an ongoing investigation that can't be shared because they could compromise the case," I said.

Stewart reached into his pocket and pulled out a business card.

"Sheriff Cabrelli, that is my cell phone number on that card. I want you to understand that my request to be kept in the loop was not optional. I want to know what is going on, and I mean it. Is that clear?" said Stewart.

I didn't answer. I just said, "Nice talking to you, Scott." I got up, turned my back on him, and left.

———

On my way home, I called Malone and briefed him on what I suspected had gone down.

"Bear, I also have a request from Ricardo. He said his unit has some new faces and wanted me to request that you let him pick a couple of them to send this way."

"Ricardo must think he's got something," said Bear.

"A murder meant to look like a suicide and explosive charges used to blow a meth lab off the face of the earth are not your run-of-the-mill drug war. I think we both feel like there is something here."

"Okay, John. Ricardo's not much for wasting time or spinning his wheels. I'll get a hold of him and see he gets whatever help he needs. Just make sure you guys brief me every once in a while."

"I'll do it, Bear."

"Yeah, right," and he hung up.

A minute later, I was dispatched back to the scene to meet with the fire marshal who wanted to take me around the fire site.

The ME had just finished loading up.

"Any thoughts, Doc?' I asked.

"No, Sheriff. These bodies are burned to a crisp. At first look, it appears as if they burned to death, but you never know. I have been in contact with the ME's office in Dane County, and that's where I am taking them. Even with their help, it will probably be a while before we even know who they are. I will keep you posted on our progress."

I walked toward the former location of the double-wide. The fire chief and the fire marshal met me halfway. I could see they had been busy. Several areas were now flagged.

"What did you find?" I asked.

The fire chief spoke first. "Sheriff, there are three distinct depressions in the ground at three separate locations that would have been just under the edge of the trailer. There is a strong possibility that three explosive devices were planted at those locations. Based on what we're seeing, it appears as if the explosives may have been tied to some secondary incendiary device or substance. The fire burned with great intensity at those three locations."

Investigator Wolfman then reported. "Based on the description of the explosion by the truck driver, and the fact that we have debris from the detonation over such a large area, a bomb or bombs were likely used. If that turns out to be the case, then it certainly adds another level to this thing. The explosive device used here would not be like a firecracker where you light the fuse and run for cover. There is no way to outrun an explosion like this. So, it is likely that if it does turn out to be a bomb that the bomber used a timer or remote detonator."

"In other words, this is most likely premeditated murder," I said.

"Looks that way. I have requested some additional help from the military and other specialists in our group. When we finish the site survey, we should have some better answers," said the fire marshal.

"I won't hold you to it, but tell me what you're thinking," I asked.

Wolfman thought for a second and replied. "Here's what I think. This was a meth lab, and someone with knowledge of and experience with bomb-making planted way more explosives than they needed under this trailer, intending to blow it off the face of the earth. To that end, they did a pretty good job, including burning the occupants to a crisp. The person who did this was sending a message."

I checked in at the office on the way back. Lois filled me in on what was happening. Nothing more than the usual. We had gotten no further help from the community on Devin Martin's vehicle. I told her bits and pieces of my conversation with the county board chair, Scott Stewart. She listened attentively.

"Sheriff, Scott Stewart is a little whiney twit. I would not pay him any attention."

"I just don't want him or anyone else complicating this situation. He had a lot of information about the trailer explosion, most likely got it from one of the firefighters. If he runs his mouth around town, it could cause some complications."

"His nephew is on the fire department, so I'd bet that is probably who told him. Word travels fast around here. It can be both good and bad."

"Lois, I am headed home. I'm exhausted. I have my radio and pager on, or you can call me on my landline if you need me."

"Go get some rest, Sheriff." ✦

CHAPTER 17

The drive out to Spider Lake was, as always, an enchanted journey. A dusting of snow covered the road's shoulders. In the coming months, those same shoulders would store mountains of snow. I noticed two mailboxes that had been armored against the snowplow onslaught. One had a shipping pallet attached to one side of the box and post, while another had a piece of scrap plywood in the hope that it would prevent the plowed snow from knocking down the box. It was a miracle the plow drivers who kept the roads passable in often limited visibility situations didn't plow them all down. I felt the tension go out of me the closer I got to home. I have lived in many places, but nothing felt so wonderful as this place. It would take death or dynamite to remove me.

I walked into the cabin, took off my boots, and slipped on my new moose hide fleece-lined moccasins, the most recent gift Julie and I had given each other. Boots off by the door, mocs on. I started a fire in the woodstove and settled in. My intention was to continue reading a series of outdoor stories based on Namekagon County's history written between 1900 and 1905. Best laid plans. I fell sound asleep in the chair within minutes. I did not budge an inch until I was awakened by the front door closing. I looked up at Julie, and I was still so tired it was difficult to focus.

"John, you look exhausted."

"I probably look worse than I am, but I am tired."

"Have you had anything to eat?"

"Coffee and a cinnamon roll at Crossroads."

"That's it?"

"That's it."

"You just sit there and keep that fire going. I will be back in a minute."

I heard her in the kitchen, busy doing something. No more than ten minutes had passed, and she brought out two plates, each containing a ham and cheese sandwich, a homemade dill pickle, and Jay's brand potato chips, my favorite kind. We crunched and munched contentedly. When we finished, I took our dishes to the sink and came back to sit with Julie.

"So, how is your investigation going?" Julie asked.

"I am not sure where it's going, but it's going."

Then she listened attentively as I filled her in.

"I get the feeling that you are unsettled regarding this case. Am I reading things wrong, or is that true?" she asked.

"No, you're right. I don't have a good handle on this. The basics of these cases appear pretty straightforward. But when you look closely, they just don't make sense."

When we got up in the morning, the old adage about Wisconsin came true as it had for generations. If you don't like the weather, just wait a minute, and it will change. The day broke with sunshine and clear skies. A light wind out of the northwest suggested possible trouble later on, but right now, it was beautiful. My phone, pager, and radio remained quiet. I called into the office and found out there was nothing that needed my immediate attention. As the boss, in theory, I control my own schedule. In reality, as the boss, I work for every citizen or person who comes to roost in Namekagon County. People expect the sheriff to be there whenever they decide the sheriff is needed. This morning I was apparently not needed.

It was a day off for Julie's school but a workday for me. We were finishing our second cups of coffee, looking out the big picture window at Spider Lake. It was a crisp north country fall morning.

Julie jumped up and said, "John, I need to feel the earth beneath my feet. Let's go for a hike." I didn't object.

Boots on, we walked out the cabin's back door. After climbing a slick, rocky rise, we headed north, walking along on the southern end of the Canadian Shield—a small piece of the largest mass of exposed Precambrian rock on the face of the earth. The glacier created the landscape as it came through and scraped the surface clean. Together we hiked a land of wild, untamed beauty, too tough to be conquered by mortals. Rock hills dropped off to wetlands and lakes. Water ran off the impermeable rock and joined flowing streams and rivers. Tenacious vegetation eked out an existence with widespread roots or by growing in a crevice. We came up to a spot that overlooked a secluded wetland, a combination of shallow open water and wet meadow beauty. There we sat in silence on the top and gazed out. There is nothing like the quiet of the Northwoods. The only sounds were the whisper of the light breeze in the trees and the melodic sound of a tiny running nearby stream. As quiet as we were, our presence was too much for a dozen or so northern mallards hidden in a rice bed by the shore. They launched themselves skyward into the wind and took flight.

"You know, John, I know the lakes and rivers around here are beautiful. But it is this backcountry that I truly love. It is really like no place else. I love that we share this land with so many who came before us. People have tried to change it, to rob it of its riches, yet it remains the same."

We started back and began by holding hands, and as sweet as that was, the narrow trail would not allow us to walk side by side. Back at the cabin, I got my gear together. My pager remained silent, so I cooked up some bacon and Italian eggs for us. After breakfast, we had cleaned things up, and the last thing I wanted to do was go to work. I really wanted to kick back in an easy chair and take a little nap. Putting wood on the fire did little to change my mind. Then to top it off, Julie came back down from upstairs carrying a wool blanket and the new book she was reading. She sat in her chair, put her feet up on a footstool covered up in the blanket, opened her book, and sighed in contentment.

"Cozy?" I asked.

"Absolutely," she replied.

"Do you plan to sit there all day?" I asked.

"I don't really know. Eventually, I will probably guilt myself into doing some grading. But for now, where I am is just perfect. Any objections?"

"None whatsoever. My only issue is that I wish I could join you. Since I can't, I will proceed on my way to patrol the mean streets of Namekagon County."

Julie smiled up at me. "Be safe, honey. Bear stew for dinner."

———

Out on the road, a call came in for possible criminal damage to property in the Old Mill Trail parking lot. I advised the dispatcher I was a mile away and would take it. I pulled in at the trailhead, and there was trash strewn across the parking lot. Also, three fifty-five-gallon barrels that had been hung together in a frame and served as trash cans were now on opposite sides of the lot. One of them looked like it had been run over by a truck. I got out and looked around. There was a bunch of evidence to indicate what had gone on.

The Old Mill Trail is pretty well maintained. It is often used by mushers working their dogs out before there is enough snow to get out on the trail. Hikers and bikers use it too. There was a little-known secret about the Old Mill Trail. If you took the trail north and walked three or four hundred yards, you would come to a little footpath that breaks off the main trail. It was hardly noticeable unless you really looked for it. Len and I had taken this trail a couple of times. It led to a pretty stretch of Old Mill River that was nearly inaccessible except by this footpath. That part of the river had fast running water interspersed between deep holes. The fishing was great, with big, feisty river run smallmouth bass and, of course, the occasional musky. The river's limit was three fish per person per day, and only one fish could be over fourteen inches.

Among the trash in the lot, it was easy to identify the remains of at least half a dozen fish. It looked like a couple of anglers caught their limit, came back to the parking lot and cleaned them—probably right under the sign that read "no fish cleaning allowed." It happened fairly often. Then probably the same night, a big old black bear, with a nose better than a bloodhound, catches a whiff of the fish carcasses and, with little effort, tears the trash cans and contents apart to get at the fish remains.

I put on a pair of gloves and started picking up the trash—the glamour of law enforcement.

I was about halfway done when two joggers came off the trail into the parking area.

"Hey, Sheriff," a woman said between deep breaths. "Can we give you a hand?"

I gave the man and woman each a pair of rubber gloves to wear, and we were done in no time. The debris fit into three trash bags that I put in the back of my squad. We moved the barrels off to the side.

I thanked the joggers and started again for Musky Falls. I asked the dispatcher to send a note to the county highway crew about replacing the damaged barrels.

I parked in a diagonal stall in front of the courthouse. Chief Len Bork was standing there smiling at me.

"I heard that criminal damage call you got, Sheriff. Let me see if I can solve the case for you. Some fishermen cleaned their fish in the parking lot and threw the guts in the trash barrel. A bear cruised through and tore the trash barrels apart. And as black bears are not known for being tidy, my guess is he or she left a huge mess."

"That about sums it up, Len," I said.

"You know what I do when I catch some fool cleaning their fish in a place like that? I give them a ticket every time and for the maximum fine of two hundred fifty dollars. If they take it to court, they are usually given a choice of whether they want to pay the ticket or complete community service. The community service consists of fixing up stuff in parking areas. Hopefully, they have a new respect for how things should be when they are done.

"One time, I caught this local blowhard, who owned a car dealership north of town, and his buddy cleaning some fish on a picnic table at one of the parking areas. I wrote them both tickets and made them clean up the mess. The court date assigned to their citation came, and the car dealer's buddy showed up, but the car dealer did not. The buddy agreed to community service and no fine. The judge issued a warrant for the car dealer's arrest for failure to appear. Jim Rawsom and I went out to the dealership and arrested him. The judge let him sit for three days before he heard the case. The car dealer pleaded guilty. The judge fined him the original two hundred fifty dollars, another thousand dollars for failing to appear, and a week of community service or a week in jail."

Just then, we heard a voice from one of the courthouse windows. "Chief Bork, Sheriff Cabrelli, come on up to my chambers," Judge Kritzer yelled down to us. It was hard to tell whether it was a request or a command. We both followed the order.

Len knocked on the door that led to the judge's inner sanctum—a place better avoided.

"Come in, come in," the deep voice called.

Judge Kritzer's office walls were adorned with several mounted fish. An ashtray built into a stand that held different tobacco pipes sat on his desk. An old-fashioned coat stand stood off to the side behind the desk. Hanging from the stand was the judge's well-known and well-worn red plaid Mackinaw. Another hook held a gun belt. Crafted of fine leather, holding twenty-five or so cartridges in leather loops, the holster held a classic Colt Single Action Army revolver. A set of beautiful staghorn grips adorned the pistol.

"Len, Sheriff, what are you boys up to today? Figuring out why we have dead bodies showing up all over the county, I suspect. Well, I have a pressing issue that I need Len's help with, although, Sheriff, if you have something to offer, chime in."

"How can we help you, Judge?" asked Len.

The judge walked over to a closet and removed a long case. He unzipped it and pulled out an old but well cared for Savage Model 99 lever-action rifle. "I was at the range the other day, and this gun refused to feed the shells from the magazine on two occasions. Could you take a look at it for me and get it straightened out? Deer season is just around the corner, and I hope it's something minor."

Len knew that the judge had inherited the rifle from his father and treasured it. The judge hand-loaded his own cartridges for it. The ammunition had to be just right for it to feed from the unique rotary magazine.

"Sure, Judge, I can look at it for you. Do you have some of your ammo?"

"I have a full box right here."

"Now, Len, does Martha still have an extra place for an old bachelor at your Thanksgiving table this year?"

"Wouldn't be Thanksgiving without you, Judge. I believe dinner will be at one."

"I am looking forward to it. Martha can sure cook."

"That she can," Len agreed.

"What are you doing for Thanksgiving, Sheriff?"

"Julie, Bud, and I are having dinner together along with some of Julie's students."

"Dining at the cafeteria, I trust?"

"Yes, Your Honor, the school cafeteria it is."

"I will see you there. By the way, Sheriff, that Julie Carlson is a real sweetheart. I am happy for the both of you."

"Thanks, Judge."

=====

There was a change in fashion that spread across Namekagon County. Blaze orange was the style of the day, with some blaze pink recently authorized by the legislature thrown in. Everyone was excited for the start of the nine-day deer gun season that would begin next Saturday. Six hundred thousand hunters would take to the field, each trying to get fresh venison for the freezer. This year would be challenging again. Deer numbers were down in northern Wisconsin, and predators were most often blamed. The white-tailed deer was prime forage for cougars, black bears, bobcats (mostly on fawns), coyotes, and wolves, and those species were thriving. In some counties, it was estimated that predators took many more deer than hunters did. This set the stage for the never-ending competition between man and animals.

The annual deer hunt was not just about harvesting wild game. It was about tradition and togetherness. Families and friends across the state gathered to join in the hunt. Some folks came just to set up deer camp, play cards, drink a little, and sit by the fire. Whatever a person's reason, the white-tailed deer hunt was an integral part of the fabric of Wisconsin tradition.

The deer population in the state was much higher in the south or farmland zones than in the north, but many people flocked to the north country each year to hunt the big woods. Thousands of acres of public land gave hunters a chance to hike and hunt over the wildest of land.

The deer hunt was such an institution that the Musky Falls School District closed school for the week, primarily because only a handful of students would show up. Julie's students were no different, so she made it part of her school curriculum rather than fight it. Students who participated in the hunt were given a notebook and asked to journal the experience. Those who were out of school, but did not hunt, were asked to journal about any family tradition they experienced. Some students, because of family situations, had little to share, but they were not excluded. Julie worked hard to get those kids to join her at the community Thanksgiving feast held at the high school cafeteria. She would be aided by me, Bud, Jack Wheeler, Ron Carver, Len and Martha Bork, and many others. It was a grand time, and a ton of food would be served. ✤

CHAPTER 18

The next morning, I got a call from the fire marshal.

"Sheriff, we have finished most of our analysis, and we have determined that there were explosive charges set that led to the destruction of the trailer. The chemical residue that we uncovered indicates that the explosive was military-grade composition C-4. We have also found fragments of a couple of detonators and what appears to be pieces of a timing device. In a nutshell, someone planted three bombs and set them up with a timer. They went off at the same time. The bomber placed an accelerant, which may have included an adhesive agent, on top of or next to the explosive charges. This made certain that the trailer would burn and ignite the fumes inside. We found plenty of evidence that the trailer was a meth lab, including litter scattered around the outside of the trailer. Sheriff, you definitely have a double homicide."

"Military C-4 was used?"

"Yes, it was. There is actually quite a bit of that stuff around. When soldiers came home from overseas conflicts, you'd be surprised how many of them slipped a block of C-4 in their duffle. Some of them were farm boys who figured C-4 would come in handy for blowing up tree stumps and cattle ponds. It first saw wide usage in Vietnam, but it's still commonly used by the military today. It's out there, and you can find plenty of websites that will tell you how to set it off without killing yourself. It is very stable stuff and requires a detonator that produces a shock wave. In this case, we are guessing it was an electronic detonator triggered by a timer. Someone with a bit of knowledge could put this together. As we kind of guessed from the start, the bomber used at least twice the amount of C-4 they needed. We found pieces of the trailer a long way from the site. The Army guy who came to assist from Fort McCoy said it looked like the bomber was really pissed off."

"So far, we are thinking rival drug gangs. Maybe they wanted to send a message," I suggested.

"Probably right, Sheriff. I am just telling you what I know. I will get my report put together and ship it off to you. Any problem with me filling in Malone?"

"Nope, none at all," I said. The marshal disconnected.

I called Len and shared the report.

"We have got ourselves quite the situation here. I don't know who these most recent dead guys are, and from what I understand from Dr. Chali, we won't know for a while. Those people in the trailer were burned to a crisp. The ME is working on the ID with a forensic odontologist. Sounds like that's about all that is left to identify," I said.

"Have you heard anything from Ricardo?" Len asked.

"Not a word. But I don't think he's had time to get his people on the street yet. I hope he turns up something. Oh, I forgot to tell you, I got a call back from Douglas County. The plate on the Jeep that blew up with the trailer came back to a guy from Superior. Douglas County checked with him. He sold the Jeep on the *Northland Classifieds* a month ago to a buyer who paid cash and didn't remove the plates. They have a description of the guy that they sent over, but the seller only talked to him for a few minutes, and the description is sketchy,"

I said.

"I am headed off deer hunting this weekend. Martha would love me to bring home some fresh venison. I am hiking in off the road by Sande Landing, I'll have my pager, but if you need me, it will be a while before I extract myself, just so you know."

"Have a good time."

"Communing with nature is always a good time for me, John. Besides that, I've been keeping track of a big buck on the next valley over from the landing. I saw him there this summer when I was fishing. He's a real dandy, but I am guessing he's a wise old boy. We'll see who's the smartest."

―――――――――

I drove into the office, and there was a folder on my desk with a sticky note that read "Have a good deer season." I checked the information in the folder. The name of the person I wanted to talk to was Andy Barlow. I dialed a Superior area cell phone number. The guy who answered sounded half asleep.

"Is this Andy?" I asked.

"Yup," he responded.

"My name is John Cabrelli. I am the sheriff of Namekagon County. I was wondering if you might be available anytime today so I could ask you something about the Jeep you sold."

He hesitated before answering. "I told the other officer everything I could think of. Any chance you could come tomorrow? I work the night shift, so I don't go in until eleven. I just now went to sleep, so I am really tired."

"I'm sorry, Andy, but it's kind of important. I am actually headed your way now."

"I guess if it's important, I can stay up a while longer. Will it take long?"

"No more than a few minutes."

"How long before you're here?" Andy asked.

"Forty-five minutes tops," I replied.

"Okay, that's okay. I can finish a fish I'm working on. Do you have my address?"

"Got it, Andy, and thanks. I will be there shortly."

I pulled into Andy's driveway about five minutes early. He greeted me at the door and invited me in. The air smelled like paint fumes, and the reason why was soon evident. Andy had a small paint spray booth set up in one corner of the living room. Sitting in the middle of the booth was a taxidermy walleye that he was painting.

"Sheriff, just let me get this last coat on, and I'll be done," he said.

He flipped a switch on the wall that activated a blower fan attached to a piece of flexible duct that went to the window.

He had a small spray gun hooked to a compressor. He picked up the gun and gently turned the walleye while he applied a light coat of paint. He waited a few minutes and repeated the process. Then he examined his handiwork and applied a little more paint.

"That should do it," he said.

"That fish looks great," I commented.

"Thanks, Sheriff. I specialize in fish mounts. I hope to keep building the business so I can quit the factory and do it full-time. First, though, I have got to get myself a place to work that is not my living room. What can I do for you?"

"Andy, I need you to look at some pictures. See if one of these guys is the one who bought your Jeep."

He looked through several pictures and didn't recognize any of them until he saw the last picture.

"Sheriff, that's the guy who bought the Jeep. He got a ride over here from someone else. That could be one of those other guys. I don't know."

I was shocked for a second, and Andy caught it.

"Did I say something wrong, Sheriff?"

"No, not at all. I just need you to look at this picture again. Are you sure it's the same guy?"

"Ninety-nine percent sure. The guy had a dragon tattoo on his neck, and you can make it out a little there in your picture," Andy said with confidence as he pointed.

"Thanks, Andy. You've been a big help."

"You're welcome. Glad to help you. The guy from Douglas County told me these guys were dopers, and I've got no time for that stuff. I hope you put them in prison."

———————

As soon as I was in my squad, I called Dr. Chali, and I got his voicemail. I left him a message to call me ASAP, and then I called his pager. Ten minutes later, my phone rang.

"Doc, I think I have an ID on one of the guys in the trailer—Jesse Gunther. The other guy may be Tony Carter, a known associate of his. I don't want to put any pressure on you, but if it turns out it was Carter and Gunther in that trailer, we have got to rethink what's going on here."

"I'm headed back to the lab in Madison now. I'll call them and have them get any information they have that might help with Gunther's and Carter's IDs. How solid is the person who made the ID?"

"He says ninety-nine percent."

"Thanks, John. Good work. I'll let you know when I know something."

I needed to reach Ricardo. I called his secret cell, and he answered.

"Anthony, things are moving here, and I need some help to start sorting things out. First, I got a preliminary report from the fire marshal. It looks like three blocks of C-4 tied to some form of accelerant were detonated by a remote timer. They are going to send a report over to Malone and me. I will forward it to you. Next, it looks like the dead guys in the trailer might be Jesse Gunther and

Tony Carter. I got an ID on Gunther from the guy who sold him the Jeep that burned up at the fire. I passed the information on to the ME, and he's on it."

"Geez, Sheriff, you have been doing some detecting. I wouldn't jump to any conclusions yet, but if it turns out to be Gunther and Carter, we can safely figure that good old Namekagon County is smack dab in the middle of a drug war. The thing that gets my attention here is that someone used C-4 and a remote timer. That is not your average run-of-the-mill drive-by drug gang war. I have got to give this some serious cogitation, but at first glance, I think we better be paying attention."

"I'll send over the reports when I get them. Keep me advised on what you find, okay, Anthony?"

"Yeah, Sheriff, I will. I am actually trying to track down a possible associate of Devin Martin. I'm only getting warmed up, but I think it might be something. I'll let you know when I do."

After talking to Ricardo, I went back to the office. The preliminary report on the trailer bombing had come over. I read it and then forwarded it to Ricardo. It was not much different from what they had told me.

They had completed the survey of the scene, and they were still analyzing and examining the physical evidence. Their initial conclusion was that a party or parties unknown planted multiple explosive charges under the mobile home and detonated them at the same time. The mobile home was occupied at the time by two individuals, who likely died as a result of the explosion. However, they were waiting for the official cause of death from the ME.

I started finding what information I could regarding Devin Martin, Jesse Gunther, and Tony Carter. Their criminal lives were well documented, with notable rap sheets and overlapping time in the same joint. They were released within a few months to a year of each other. If it turned out that the bodies were Gunther and Carter, blowing up the meth lab was probably not retaliation for killing Martin. More likely, someone was trying to put Gunther's outfit out of business, and they weren't screwing around.

———————————

That night I ended up sleeping in the chair downstairs again, and once again, Julie woke me in the morning.

"John, I am beginning to think that you are avoiding sleeping with me. Do I snore too loudly or kick off the covers in the middle of the night? Does my reading light bother you?" she said with a smile.

"No, those things don't bother me."

My response caused a couch pillow to be thrown at me, which resulted in laughter from both of us.

The coffee she had made smelled wonderful. We each had a cup, and I again explained what was going on.

"I have got to get some solid information on these cases. They are clearly connected, and we should be able to get some leads from the dead guys' former associates. We just don't have anything right now. The fire marshal said C-4 plastic explosive was used in the bombing of the trailer. He told me that stuff is everywhere. I checked on other similar cases nationwide, and I found several where Molotov cocktails were used, a couple with dynamite, one even with det cord. I did find some bombings where C-4 was used. In each case, these were upper-level criminal gangs, organized crime types, fighting over big turf. Not street drug dealers. Nothing in this area of the country."

"What does Bear have to say?"

"Not much. He deals with this kind of drug gang war all the time, so it is not very high on his priority list. He is doing anything we ask, but drug dealers killing each other is the normal state of things in his world. I know this area has had drug problems on and off, just like everywhere else. This is different. Len says drug dealers come into town, but usually, they leave after the local police put a little pressure on them. Things get a little too close for them. In this case, it seems they are trying to set up shop. We have got to do whatever we can to get rid of them. If they get established, they will be here forever.

"Julie, I'm really sorry about being gone so much, sleeping in the chair. I have to say that I have had second thoughts about taking the sheriff's job. It sounded like a good idea at the time, but now I don't know. I just can't be a cop halfway."

"Well, I have always known that was going to be the case. You and I, in many ways, are cut from the same cloth. When I took over as the teacher at Northern Lakes, the school district sent every student to me who they were having trouble with. I was overwhelmed, but I welcomed them with open arms. I was their last chance. I worked night and day and still do because that is what it takes to help these kids. The reality of this is that if I don't do it, who will?

"Most people in the world seem content to talk about the idea of change to death. They express outrage on whatever issue they are outraged about at the moment in sound bites. They have meetings to discuss the issues, and in the meetings, they propose solutions and spend endless hours wordsmithing the proposals. When they have finally finished, everything is wrapped up in a neat, evenly spaced document. They walk away, patting themselves on the back for a job well done. The meeting has become the work when the real work has yet to begin. Do you think that the county board chair will step up to the task? You are faced with the same problem—if you don't do it, who will?

"As before, it will fall to you and Len and your small group willing to face the challenge. You will do whatever you need to do. The price we will pay is time together lost. The reward will be that just maybe we have saved one kid. I love you, John, and you love me, and together we are a great team. You do what you need to do, and I will keep the fire burning next to my mountain of schoolwork." ❧

CHAPTER 19

Thanksgiving morning dawned with six inches of fresh snow and sunshine. Julie had us up and at the school cafeteria early. There we met a crew of wonderful people busy preparing a dinner for everyone who walked in the door. They were also preparing to-go meals to distribute to members of the community by the local FFA chapter. Jack Wheeler and Bud had beat us there, and they were both assigned to the dinner roll making department. Jack had flour from the tips of his fingers to the top of his head. Bud was using his massive hands to knead a huge pile of dough. Next to them, Lois from the sheriff's office was placing shaped pieces of dough on a tray ready for the oven.

Julie and I were assigned to putting out tables and chairs, covering them with white tablecloths, and putting decorations made by the grade-schoolers in the center of each table. The Lockridges showed up with Amber and Crystal, who looked clear-eyed but tired. Once Amber saw Julie, she pitched right in. Ed, Stella, and Crystal began working on their own project. For as long as anyone could remember, they made a huge batch of fry bread for the Thanksgiving feast.

A happy crowd poured in and was greeted by turkey, ham, roasted

Canada goose, three different wild rice dishes, mashed potatoes, garlic reds, stuffing, fry bread, dinner rolls, vegetables, assorted pies and cakes, along with coolers filled with ice cream from the dairy.

The crowd exemplified the breadth of this Northwoods community, from an infant in her mother's arms to a man in a wheelchair wearing a cap that decreed his service in World War II. Those who needed help got it willingly, along with a liberal helping of goodness, laughter, joy, and celebration. No one was turned away. All were welcome to join in the feast. As I looked out at the crowd, I thanked heaven that there were places like this, communities like this, that still embraced togetherness and celebration.

I filled my plate with wild goose, turkey, wild rice stuffing, and two big pieces of fry bread, for starters. I was in line behind Bud, who complained in his good-natured way that the plates were too small. As people finished their second helpings, the chatter and laughter in the room began to die down—the post-Thanksgiving feast coma. Coffee was served, along with cranberry juice, apple cider, and milk. After a fifteen-minute breather, someone called out, "Who wants pie?"

The entire serving crew filled a long cafeteria table with cranberry, blueberry, apple, pumpkin, banana cream, and cherry pies. Ron Carver and Judge Kritzer were in charge of dishing up the pieces, and I was recruited to add a scoop of ice cream if requested.

When everyone was again seated, two people carrying guitars came to sit among us. The woman had shining black hair to the middle of her back with feathers woven in. The man was dressed in overalls and a beat-up old felt hat. The crowd knew who they were and quieted in anticipation.

They started to play in perfect string harmony, and then the woman broke out in a beautifully haunting voice, "On the wings of a snow-white dove, He sends His pure sweet love, a sign from above on the wings of a dove." The old song penned by Grandpappy Eli Possumtrot was made famous when recorded by Ferlin Husky. The crowd, sitting side by side, sang quietly along. When the song was over, they changed it up with "Five Little Turkeys," which set all the kids in the room and some adults to dancing. Little kids all loved Bud, the gentle giant, and they made him join hands with them as they danced in a circle.

While the music played, the kitchen crew and a few other volunteers washed up dishes, pots, and pans. Two people prepared extra meals and pie slices on heavy-duty paper plates and secured plastic wrap across the top. Then Julie came over to me.

"John, that food they just put together goes to the jail. How many guests do you currently have?"

"Two."

"How many deputies on duty?"

"Just one," I replied.

"Each year Jim Rawsom would take a plate of Thanksgiving dinner over to dispatchers, the jail deputy on duty, and the inmates. That falls to you now."

"Sounds like a good tradition. I will take it over right now."

I loaded up the box of food and drove over to the jail. The deputy was glad to see me and had clearly been anticipating the meal. I secured my weapons in the lockers in the reception area, and he buzzed me in. I set the food on a table, and the deputy took out his metal detecting wand and carefully scanned all the food and plates. He separated the servings and put a jail-approved spork with each one.

"Sheriff, do you want to do the honors?"

"Sure," I replied.

The two inmates were housed together in a six-cell block. They were minimum security, one serving time for misdemeanor theft and another for a drunk driving conviction. The deputy unlocked the door, and I put the meals on the table in the common area.

"Happy Thanksgiving, guys," I said.

"Thanks, Sheriff," they replied.

"Thanks for your help, Deputy. I am going to run down to dispatch and check in before I head back to the school and finish cleaning up. I hope you enjoy your dinner."

"I am looking forward to it," he replied.

The dispatchers were happy to get their Thanksgiving plates. They confirmed what I figured. The county was quiet. We backed up the city on a family squabble in town and escorted a rowdy patron from a local tavern to the Namekagon Express transit.

Holidays are often a mixed situation for law enforcement. In most cases, family and friends get together and enjoy good food. They may drink a little too much, but things usually stay under control. Then there are those families who haven't seen one another all year long. Not only do they not see one another, but they also avoid contact. Then they get together once or twice a year and after an hour or two remember why they didn't like each other. A few too many beers later, they are slugging it out on the front lawn or throwing dishes at each other. It usually doesn't amount to much, but there is always a distinct possibility that someone will end up cooling their heels in jail that night.

When I got back to the cafeteria, most of the crowd had gone home. The Namekagon Transit bus was loading up the WWII veteran and other diners in need of wheelchair transport. The cafeteria was spotless, with two boys I recognized from Julie's school sweeping the floor.

Once everything was put away, the custodian began locking things up. There were plenty of leftovers. Most of the food was packed up and taken over to the Birchwood Nursing Home. Each of the workers also scored a snack or two for later.

"What do you have going the rest of the weekend, Bud?" I asked.

"I thought I would get up early tomorrow and walk the ridge behind your cabin to see if there are any deer around if that's still okay with you."

"Of course. I hope you see something," I replied.

"What about you and Julie?"

"I am working the patrol shift tomorrow. One of the younger guys has got family in town and put in for the day off, so I'm taking the shift. Probably won't be much going on. I hope I'll be able to catch up on some paperwork."

"Have fun with that," Bud replied. ❦

CHAPTER 20

I slept like a rock that night. Julie had the day off from school, and even though I had the best intentions the day before, I didn't feel all that motivated to run down to the office and start finding out how behind I was on my administrative duties. Julie and I lingered over our coffee and pie leftovers we absconded with.

"John, I do think that pie may be one of the best all-around foods. It is as good for breakfast as it is for dessert."

Julie was eating a piece of blueberry pie while I was savoring banana cream, my favorite.

"Wasn't that a wonderful get-together yesterday?" Julie asked.

"It was. I loved every minute of it. I can't recall ever attending something like it. I have worked at St. Vinnie's, dishing up food to the homeless and those down on their luck before, but there was something different about this. Everyone was just together. No pretense, nothing other than goodwill."

"It is one of the treasures of living in a small town in the north country. Over the years, the fabric of the community has been woven so tightly that even if it starts to come unraveled, we can quickly stitch it back in place. This is home to most of the folks who came yesterday.

It is their family, and our family too. When Bud and I were younger and fell on hard times, it was those people who reached out to us and made us feel welcome. Sure, they came to eat good food, but mostly they came to be together. I don't think I would ever want to have Thanksgiving anywhere else. Is that okay with you?" Julie asked.

"Are you kidding me? I had a great time. It was the best Thanksgiving I can ever recall. Did my aunt and uncle participate?"

"Honey, your aunt Rose was one of the founders of the event. When you were scooping ice cream yesterday, you reminded me so much of your uncle Nick. It was sweet. What was your favorite food?"

"Tough question, but Stella's fry bread was outstanding, and by the looks of it, I wasn't the only one who thought so. People's plates were stacked high."

"Stella says it is an old family recipe. Her grandmother taught her how to make it in a *waginogan* over on Moose Lake. One of the secrets is that the oil they fry it in is rendered bear fat. Usually, Ed gets a bear every year. Sometimes though he doesn't and puts out the word that he needs the fat, and other hunters always come through."

"How are things going with Amber and her mom? They seemed to be okay at dinner."

"Amber is doing well, and she seems happy. I don't know about her mom. What did you think when you saw her, John?"

"I thought she looked tired but not high, if that's what you're asking."

Just then, a car pulled into the driveway and drove up to the front of the house. I recognized the Dodge Charger. Anthony Ricardo walked up to the door, and I met him before he could knock.

"Good morning. I'm sorry to bother you, Sheriff. I need to talk to you. Would you mind if I come in for a minute?"

"Nope, come on in. Would you like a cup of coffee?"

"Yes, Sheriff, I really would."

I introduced him to Julie.

"Anthony Ricardo, this my ah—" I never knew what to say. I hated saying "significant other," and "my girlfriend" sounded like high school. "My wife" would be the best choice, but it was one she hadn't made yet. Instead, I said, "This is Julie Carlson."

He reached out his hand, and she shook it. Julie had a firm grip, and I could see Ricardo was surprised.

"Why don't you guys sit by the fire, and I will bring you both fresh cups of coffee. I have some things to do upstairs, so I will leave you alone."

"Actually, Ms. Carlson, I would appreciate it if you'd stay."

"Call me Julie. I am glad to stay as long as it's okay with the sheriff here."

"Fine by me," I answered. "So, what's up, Agent Ricardo?"

"I have continued detecting and have a couple of operatives working the area," he replied.

"I hope they found something," I interjected, hoping he would get to the point.

"They sure did, and that something was absolutely nothing. We have not yet been able to identify another drug gang working the area. Bits and pieces are floating around, but it all goes back months ago. There is nothing current. My people have been able to score both meth and heroin, but they had to work for it, and it was pricey, meaning there is not much competition. We got IDs on a couple of local dealers, but no one who is part of a big gang trying to move in from the Twin Cities."

"Do you have any leads at all?" I asked.

"If you'll allow me to repeat some of what you already know, it will help me give you my perspective on things."

"Go ahead," I replied.

"Here goes. We have a fairly major dealer dead and probably two of his associates blown to smithereens. Other than a bit of junkie gossip, there is no real talk about it on the street, 'cuz the dopers are scared. They know that Gunther will hit back. He needs to, or he won't be in business long. They don't want to get caught in the crossfire," Ricardo stated.

"Maybe the people who took out these three guys are really bad actors. Maybe they ran the other gang out," I suggested.

"You know, Sheriff, that could be true, except that if they ran out the competition, why haven't they set up shop yet? All they want to do is sell drugs to innocent children unhindered. Looks like the coast is clear, so why are my people scratching to find anything on the street?"

"I don't know. Do you have any theories?" I asked.

"I do, but they might not hold any water. I am still working on it. It's not actually why I came by. I want to talk to you two about someone."

"Okay, let's hear it," I said.

Ricardo addressed Julie. "I am sorry to bring you in, Julie, but I need to ask you a favor." Julie didn't reply. She simply stared at Ricardo.

Finally, she said, "What is it that you need?"

"Do you know Crystal Lockridge?"

"Yes, I know her fairly well, Agent Ricardo. John and I just served Thanksgiving dinner with her and her family yesterday. Why are you asking?" Julie said, strongly defensive already.

"She was Devin Martin's up north girlfriend," Ricardo said as a matter of fact.

"Are you certain of this?" Julie demanded.

"I'm sure. We got an ID off of several pictures Joe Thomas found of her with Martin at the casino. Do you know her well enough to get her to talk to me?" Ricardo answered.

"I don't know," Julie said tersely.

"Here's the deal. Sheriff, you figured out the suicide of Devin Martin was a homicide. I read the report. Someone—probably the shooter—was at some point in the passenger side of the vehicle. The only link we might have to what went down there is Martin's girlfriend, Crystal Lockridge. We need to know what she knows. Sheriff, technically, this is your case, and I have got to say that you've done a great job with it, but Lockridge is the first solid lead we have had. We need to talk to her."

Julie looked at us and said, "She won't talk to you guys. She doesn't trust the police. She thinks that they are always trying to trick her into saying something she doesn't want to say."

"She's mostly right about that; they probably are," said Ricardo. "But we need to talk to her anyway. Any suggestions about how we get this done would be welcome. Just so we are clear, I am going to talk to her no matter what. I would like to do it in the least threatening way possible, but she will decide how that goes."

"Agent Ricardo, she is fragile, a recovering addict. She has made progress, but it's been a tough haul. She is trying to clean herself up and raise her daughter," said Julie.

"I am sorry she's had a tough life, Julie. A lot of people have. My job is to put these guys out of business before they get started. Sometimes that requires that I do unpleasant things, I don't want to, but that's the way it is. She was running around with a convicted felon and known drug dealer, who got himself killed. So now her life is my business. I know where she lives. I plan to go out there and pay her a visit. Sheriff, if you want to go along, that would be great. Julie, you can come too. Maybe it would easier for her. But I am going to drive out of your driveway and over to her house now," said Ricardo.

"Give us a minute, will you, Anthony?" I asked.

"Sure, take all the time you need. I will be outside," he replied and stepped out the front door.

"Julie, I know this stinks, but it is something that is not going to go away. Partial prints lifted from the passenger area of Devin Martin's vehicle will probably match up with Crystal. Ricardo has evidence that links the two together. Martin was a drug dealer, and he is also a murder victim, and that requires we try to reconstruct the days, weeks, months, or even years leading up to his death. Crystal's involvement cannot be ignored. If we don't talk to her, someone else will, and I guarantee they won't be as considerate as we will be. Ricardo came out here because I am the sheriff, and he needs to keep me in the loop and on his side, and because he knows about the connection between you and me and the Lockridges. He is trying to be a little thoughtful," I explained.

"He doesn't sound thoughtful to me," Julie retorted.

"He's a hard man who has gotten an up-close look at the underbelly of our world. He means it when he says that his job is to 'put these guys out of business,' and he is good at his job. That requires a certain kind of person. Tell me how you think we can best handle this, and we'll see if it's something we can work with," I offered.

"My God, John. It is the day after Thanksgiving. Can't this wait for a couple of days?"

"Unfortunately, investigations don't and can't follow the holiday calendar. Ricardo doesn't do this the day after Thanksgiving to be cruel or insensitive. He does it because it's what he has to do. Sometimes, if you wait a day, you have waited a day too long. Sometimes it can be the difference between life and death," I replied.

"Life or death, John? I think maybe you are stretching things a little far, don't you? She is just a young single mom trying to get herself straightened out. Putting her in a corner and making her talk won't save anybody. It will probably set her back months, maybe even years," Julie countered. Anger was visible behind Julie's eyes.

"Yeah, Julie, life and death. Right here in Namekagon County, life and death."

Julie stood with her arms crossed and faced me. Defiance radiated off her. "Fine, but I'm going with you, and I am going to call her to get her a little ready for what's coming," she said.

"You can go with us, but you can't call her. When we get there, you can tell her we want to talk to her, but you can't tell her why."

Julie was furious. "You want me to go with you so you can ambush her? Twist her words, try to get everything you can out of her. Destroy her and move on to your next victim?" she challenged.

It took me a moment to recover from her words, and when I did, I was Sheriff John Cabrelli. "You better stay here, Julie. I don't want to put us in a compromised situation. I am sorry, but I can't allow it. For all we know, at this point, she may have pulled the trigger on Martin. This is not like going to talk to a kid about underage drinking. This is a homicide case."

"What's stopping me from calling her the minute you two drive out?" she said with an indignant lift of her chin.

"You need to understand something. If you were to do that, you would put me in a bad position, much worse than you can imagine. You get to make up your mind about things and do what you think is right. Your statement a second ago made something clear to me. There are things that I should not share with you because it sounds like you may be willing to do something that would compromise an investigation or even my safety." Anger was rising up in me.

"How could I jeopardize your safety by calling her? That's a total overreaction," she said.

"For a smart girl, you sure are naïve. Let's just say you call her and give her a heads-up we're coming. So, she uses that time between your call and our arrival to pack her stuff and run for the hills. Or maybe she is our killer, and she uses that time to get a gun and waits for us to arrive," I responded.

"She wouldn't!" Julie shouted.

"Maybe not, but what if you're wrong?"

"I am not wrong about her. I know her!"

"Are you sure enough about her to risk Ricardo's life? My life? Because that is what you could be doing."

Her shoulders slumped; her head hung. "I am going with you, John. I'll get my coat."

"Julie, before we walk out that door, are we clear? You can't do anything to compromise the interview, no matter how it goes."

"I am very clear about that, Sheriff Cabrelli. What I am not so sure of is whether I can do this."

"Talk to Crystal?" I asked.

"No. Live with the hard side of John Cabrelli." She grabbed her coat and walked out the door.

═══════════

The three of us got into my squad and drove to Crystal Lockridge's home. The silence on the drive over was deafening.

As we approached the front door, a curtain moved aside and then fell back. Someone had looked out to see who had come calling. Ricardo palmed a gun to keep it ready, but not to advertise. I made sure mine was clear of my coat.

"Crystal, Amber, it's Julie Carlson," she said as she knocked on the door. The door opened slowly, and Amber's sweet face greeted us with tears welled up in her eyes.

"I know you've come to take her away. She's in the back bedroom. I think she's awake. Follow me," Amber said.

Crystal Lockridge was sprawled out on the bed, wearing a ratty pair of sweatpants and a t-shirt to match. She looked up at us with a glazed look, not quite putting together the pieces.

"What do you want?" she half slurred and mumbled.

Our objective had been to have a conversation with Crystal, but that would be impossible because she was so whacked out on whatever she was taking.

"How long has she been like this, Amber?" Julie asked.

"It started right after the Thanksgiving dinner," Amber replied. "I was working on my homework, and she was in her room. When she came out, well, she had the look she always gets, when ... you know. I just left her alone. She seemed like she was going to be okay.

Then she went to bed. I slept on the couch to make sure I heard her if she tried to do something stupid again, like go for a walk in the snow with no shoes or socks on. She didn't get out of bed until ten this morning and was in a horrible mood. She started screaming at me, said the place was a pigsty, and told me to get to work. Then she said all the other sweet things she usually says to me. I started cleaning, and she went back into her room. I checked on her, and she was pretty much out of it. I tried to give her some leftover turkey, but she knocked the plate on the floor. Then I left her alone."

"Amber, did you call your grandparents?" asked Julie.

"No, I don't call every time she does this. Only when I get worried about her. Like when she starts screaming or throwing things, or when I can't wake her up. Besides, Grandpa hasn't been feeling well."

At that moment, Crystal bolted out of the bedroom door and ran toward the bathroom. After ricocheting off the wall, she crashed down next to the toilet and started to retch violently. Julie ran to help her and got her head over the toilet. When she was done, she lay on the floor, her head in Julie's lap halfway curled up in a fetal position, passed out.

"She needs to be transported," Ricardo said.

I was already on the radio requesting an ambulance.

"Amber, your mom needs to go to the hospital. EMS is on the way."

"Please don't do that, Sheriff Cabrelli. Whenever that happens, she is really mad when she gets home. I almost always have to go stay with my grandma and grandpa until she settles down."

"When did she start having this problem again, Amber? I thought she was doing so well," asked Julie.

"She has been doing much, much better. I thought for sure she was cured. Then something happened just before school started in the fall. When we went to see the social worker, she even said that Mom was doing really good. But then I guess she just started slipping again. Just leave her here. She will be fine. I can take care of her."

"Amber, I am sorry, but there is no choice. You know what happened at that party. Those kids got a bad batch of drugs. No doubt some of it is still floating around. We want to make sure your mom didn't take any of that stuff," I said.

"Sheriff, please don't. Please just listen to me," Amber pleaded.

"I will be glad to listen, Amber. The ambulance is on the way."

"If she goes to detox again, they will make me move to Grandma and Grandpa's permanently or put me in a foster home. She will have no one to take care of her. The last time they said it was her last chance, and she signed on to the 'Three Strikes Program.' Please, please don't take her, Sheriff," Amber begged.

Just then, Crystal started to retch again, and her body began to convulse in some sort of seizure. Julie and Ricardo held her tightly, but she thrashed wildly. I took over for Julie for a minute.

"Julie, please call Ed and Stella and ask them to come over here. They are going to take Amber home with them. I will deal with whatever I have to deal with later. Does that work for you, Amber?"

"That would be okay, as long as my mom doesn't stop getting her check," Amber said.

"Amber, don't worry about that right now," I said.

Julie took Amber into her bedroom. Ricardo and I did our best to take care of Crystal. EMTs were fifteen minutes out; the Lockridges were ten.

When Ed and Stella arrived, they hurried up to the trailer and burst in the door. Amber ran to them. Ed was out of breath, so Stella did the talking.

"What happened, honey?" she asked Amber.

"I don't know, Grandma. She must have gotten something at Thanksgiving," Amber replied.

"Ed and Stella, I need you to take Amber home," I directed.

"Amber, pack up your stuff and let's get going," Stella said.

"Okay, Grandma," Amber said and obeyed promptly.

The ambulance pulled in, and two EMTs rushed through the door. They were fast and efficient in the evaluation of their patient, who had again lapsed into unconsciousness. Narcan was administered, and Crystal was gently lifted onto the gurney. She again began to thrash, swinging her arms and kicking with her feet. One kick landed squarely on the chest of one of the EMTs. We helped and got her restrained and strapped down. It was a scene that no one would wish to be a part of. As the EMTs wheeled her out, left in their wake were Ed, Stella, Amber, and Julie, all with tears in their eyes. A stark reminder that the addict was only one of the victims of drug addiction. Even if they were clean for years, they were just one fix away from the bottomless pit.

The ambulance left with lights flashing, taking Crystal to a place where the bottomless pit no longer existed. Six minutes out from the hospital, Crystal Lockridge, age thirty-four, had a drug-induced heart attack and subsequent respiratory arrest. All attempts by EMTs and hospital staff failed to revive her. ⤜

CHAPTER 21

Dr. Chali conducted an autopsy, and tests showed Crystal had injected a toxic drug combination of methamphetamine and fentanyl through a site on her foot, a place often used when junkies try to hide their addiction. The syringe she used was found wrapped in a paper towel in the trash basket in her room.

Crystal's funeral followed the Ojibwe tradition. She was cleansed and dressed in special traditional clothing. Food and water were laid to rest with the body to help her soul travel to the afterlife. Tribal members provided spiritual ceremony, prayed and sang for her, wishing her to a place of eternal happiness. On the fourth day, she was buried in a small cemetery underneath the branches of a balsam fir.

After the ceremony, a traditional dinner was served at the Lockridge home. I joined Ed outside, where he had gone to have a smoke.

He lit his cigarette, took a drag, and was rewarded with a rumbling cough. He pulled a kerchief out of his pocket to cover his mouth. "I gotta quit smokin' one of these days. I've heard it's not good for you," Ed said.

It was the first time we had been alone together since the incident.

"Ed, Julie and I are here to help you in any way we can. We can only imagine how you feel, but if we can do something, anything, just ask."

"Sheriff, I am sorry to say that we have been waiting years for this very day. As hard as I tried to keep her away from the bad people she traveled with, in the back of our minds, we were always waiting. Crystal just could not resist. When she was in treatment and clean, we were always so hopeful. But all it took was for her to get together with one of her so-called boyfriends, and then we were back to square one. She tried to be a good mother to Amber. She loved that girl with all her heart, but she was an addict. When I was in Vietnam, I learned a lot about addicts. They don't care about anything but getting themselves fixed up."

"I didn't know you were in Vietnam," I said.

"Yup. I was seventeen, about two months shy of my eighteenth birthday. I ended up in front of the judge for something or other. There was no doubt that I was headed in the wrong direction. That old judge was tired of seeing me and told me that he would waive me into adult court. He offered me a choice: go to jail or enlist. He gave me five minutes to decide. I told him I would enlist. The truth of it was I would have been drafted eventually. He adjourned court and walked me downstairs to the recruiter's office. I spent six years in the service, most of it in Nam. I was glad to get the hell out of there."

"Julie said that Amber is living with you now," I said.

"Yes. Technically, we already had temporary legal custody. We set that up a few years ago when Crystal went into residential treatment. You know, she was a smart girl. She could have done anything she wanted. When she would go through treatment and clean herself up, she was the sweet girl we knew, a real pleasure to be around. When she got pregnant, she stopped taking drugs cold turkey. Stella and I sat with her day and night, helping through withdrawal. She came out the other end and was determined to have that baby and raise it right. She even went back to school to get her GED. There was some concern that the baby might have some problems because of her drug use, but Amber came out just fine. She was a good mother. Then one day, the baby got sick and had a high fever. Crystal was scared to death. She begged Stella and me to take Amber to the doctor for her, said she needed some extra sleep, so we did. When we came back home, Crystal was gone. We didn't hear from her for several days. Stella sent me out looking. I found her shacked up with Travis Winslow, one of her drug dealin' friends. She wouldn't come home with me. She told me that the slimeball she was with was going to take care of her and Amber. It was another week before we saw her again. It's been the same pattern ever since. Stella and I, and Amber, for that matter, had resigned ourselves to the fact that was the way things would be."

"It must have been a tough way to live for all of you," I said.

"You know, Sheriff, sure it was tough, but there is no shortage of love in our house. We are family, and we weathered the storm. We had some rough spots, that's for sure, but we had a lot of good times too. We didn't have a big pile of money, but we were rich in other ways. The girls loved traipsing across the countryside. I guess we thought if we stuck to the homestead and kept to ourselves, we could somehow protect them. We were wrong."

"We are here if you need us," I reiterated.

"We know that. Amber is a good girl. We need to make sure she has a real chance. The other night when we came to get her from the party, Stella was just stricken with fear on the way there. She's a tough old gal but has a big heart when it comes to those girls. I hope Amber learned from her mother. Crystal dished heartache out by the bucketload, and Amber saw a lot of it firsthand."

The death of Crystal Lockridge took a toll on everyone. People in this small community had known her all their lives, and she had known them. They watched her grow up from a cute little girl in pigtails to a young teen with a pretty smile, to a mother, to a drug addict. They were all part of her successes and failures to break the iron grip of addiction. It was a story told in the past and would be told again in the future. The only thing that would change would be the name.

Len Bork and I would have had to be stone deaf not to hear the community's rumblings about the effectiveness, or lack of, on the part of local law enforcement. It was only right that it fell squarely on our shoulders.

———————

The chief and I met with Dr. Chali at the Musky Falls police station the next morning. The ME had called the night before on his way back from Madison and asked for the meeting.

"Chief Bork and Sheriff Cabrelli, we finished the autopsy report and victim identification. I have a copy here for each of you and an additional one I have been requested to give to a state investigator. I am sure you are interested in the basics more than the details at this moment so you can continue with your investigation. The victims are, in fact, Tony Carter and Jesse Gunther. Both were identified through the use of dental records retained by the Wisconsin prison system. Jesse Gunther sustained a broken jaw in prison that required significant reconstructive work that matches up with the corpse's dental work. Also, Gunther's DNA was on file, but we are waiting for the results. Tony Carter took advantage of the state prison dental program and had numerous fillings and dental work. Again, the deceased matched up with the x-rays. In our opinion, the victims did not die from the explosion; they burned to death."

"Thank you for your fast work and dedication, Doc. I am sure when you took the ME's job up here, you didn't expect to be quite so busy," I said.

"That's true, Sheriff. However, I am getting a firsthand look at how important the work of a medical examiner is. In a way, we speak for those who can no longer speak for themselves. I have learned a great deal in just a short while. When I was down in Madison, the team down there invited me to come back for a two-week training that they hold twice a year for MEs from smaller communities, so I signed up."

"Dr. Chali, we are thrilled with the work you've been doing. We're glad to have you. Are you planning on staying around Musky Falls?" Len asked.

"My wife and I love it here. We are taking cross-country ski lessons this winter and are excited to explore the backcountry trails. There is so much to do, so much fun."

Dr. Chali left, and Len and I got down to business. We were now facing four unsolved homicides, including Crystal Lockridge's death. The media would be all over us. We needed to hit this head-on and decided to call a press conference for the following morning at ten in the Sheriff Department's conference room. Len made a special effort to talk with Bill Presser at the *Namekagon County News* and the *Voice of the North* radio. I called Ron Carver.

"Sheriff, I am a popular guy today. I just got off the phone with that horse's ass county board chair, Scott Stewart. It seems that he feels you need some guidance from the county board and our committee. He wants me to put out a public notice for an emergency meeting of the LEAC," said Ron.

"Ron, the chief and I would be glad to come to your meeting, but we have called a press conference for tomorrow morning, and I am guessing that you will probably want to attend that, and you may hear all you need to hear."

"What's up, John? Fill me in," he said.

"The two guys who died in the trailer explosion burned to death. They have been positively identified as Tony Carter and Jesse Gunther, drug dealers and ex-cons, both as bad as the day is long."

"Is this tied to the other murder?"

"All the deceased are connected to the Gunther gang from the Milwaukee area."

"Even Crystal Lockridge?" he asked.

"Even her," I replied.

"Scott Stewart is spreading a rumor that the trailer was a drug lab and some kind of bomb caused the explosion. Is that true?"

"It's true, Ron. It was an active meth lab. It looks like three explosive charges were planted and set off by a timing device connected to detonators."

"Bombs, timing devices, detonators? What the hell? Do you have any suspects?"

"Some theories, but no real suspects. Gunther's gang is made up of ex-cons. They are trying to expand their drug network to the north country. An outlaw motorcycle gang from the cities is trying to do the same thing. Maybe the OMG is taking out the competition. It makes sense. If that's the case, then maybe this thing is just getting started. In the drug gang world, a rival hits, you hit back. Gunther is going to have to hit back soon, or he's going to look bad."

"Sheriff, you've got your hands full. Thanks for filling me in. I am assuming Len is in the loop."

"He is every step of the way," I replied.

"Well, good luck at the press conference. I'll be there, and I will do my best to keep that pencil neck county board chair in line," and he hung up.

Immediately after Len advised the news media of the press conference, it seemed they were all over town interviewing whoever they could, from the guys at the tavern to the minister at the Spider Lake Church.

Chairperson Stewart called me and chewed me out, accusing me of undermining the Law Enforcement Advisory Committee meeting he had requested by calling the press conference. He told me the public was very concerned about this situation and let me know that he wouldn't be held responsible for whatever happened at the press conference.

Stewart talked to any media willing to listen. He shared his dire concern for the safety of the citizens of Namekagon County and encouraged everyone who could to attend. Furthermore, even though the event was supposed to be a meeting for the press, he gave his personal guarantee that all citizens who wished to ask questions or speak would be heard.

That night, Julie and I were sitting by the fire. I was reading, and she was grading. We were both lost in our thoughts, the radio playing quietly in the background. The news came on, and the lead story was an interview with Scott Stewart. Julie reached over and turned it off. Then she held my hand.

"Julie, I don't know what tomorrow will bring. Four unsolved homicides anywhere is a big deal, much less a small county like ours. People should be concerned. Add the lodge party fiasco to that, and well, it looks like what it is—a very bad situation. I think we are going to put this thing together, but I have a nagging feeling about this case that won't go away. The bottom line is that this peaceful, wonderful community is under siege. Drug gangs are trying to move in. If they are successful, the heartaches and funerals will continue. When we get up tomorrow, I am going to go into town and take my lumps. Then I will figure out what to do next, and right now, I honestly don't have a clue what that is."

I was shocked by the number of vehicles parked in adjacent stalls next to the building when I arrived at the office the next morning. At least two TV stations had set up, and others there looked like reporters. I got out of my truck, and Bill Presser quickly came over.

"Sheriff, let me know if we can help you out when we run the story. Most of these people are here for a headline. This is my home, so let me know."

He walked off as three other reporters approached. Two stuck microphones in my face, one a recorder. Questions flew fast and furious. I didn't even hear them and kept walking into the conference room where my people were unfolding every folding chair we had. Although the press conference didn't start until ten, most of the chairs were filled by nine. The county board chair held court with some locals and a couple of reporters, clearly enjoying hearing himself talk.

At ten o'clock, Len and I stood up front and called the meeting to order. Scott Stewart came up to the front and stood next to us. It was foolish and awkward on his part, but Len stepped in and handled it well.

"For those of you who don't know me, I am Musky Falls Chief of Police Len Bork, and this is Namekagon County Sheriff John Cabrelli. Next to us is county board chair Scott Stewart. The sheriff and I have some important information to share with you, but before we get started, I am guessing Mr. Stewart has something he wants to say."

Stewart was surprised but rose to the occasion as the epitome of arrogant self-importance. He stepped up to the podium and began to give a fire and brimstone speech about the evils facing our community, and while he was a strong supporter of local law enforcement, they had shown themselves to be very ineffective in resolving the current situation. He wanted everyone in the room to know that he was ordering the sheriff to keep him informed on the status of the investigation. He intended to work tirelessly to keep our community safe.

When he came up for air, Ron Carver, who was sitting in the front row with other Law Enforcement Advisory Committee members, spoke.

"I'm Ron Carver, chair of the Law Enforcement Advisory Committee. I am so glad you are here to help us with this issue, Scott. You sure have a lot to say, criticizing our local law enforcement. I was wondering how you would solve this situation. Give us an idea of how you think we should proceed. This room is packed with people who I am sure would be happy to hear what you think."

It was too late for Scott Stewart. His big mouth had set him up for a butt whipping, and Ron Carver was just the man to give it to him.

"They need to arrest the people responsible for these crimes. Our community is facing grave danger, and we need someone to stand up to these criminals, and I am going to make certain that Sheriff Cabrelli and Chief Bork do their jobs," said Stewart.

"Let me get this straight, Mr. Stewart. I didn't hear you question the courage of Chief Bork or Sheriff Cabrelli, did I? Of course, I didn't. No one would be that foolish because no one could question the courage these men have shown. Yet I hear what you are saying, so I have a suggestion for you," Ron said mischievously.

Stewart gave Ron a suspicious look. "What would that be, Mr. Carver?"

Ron looked at me. "Sheriff Cabrelli, it is my recommendation, that is shared unanimously with my fellow board members, that in the fine tradition of Namekagon County, you immediately deputize Scott Stewart and press him into service to help in the arrest of these undeniably vicious criminals. Is that acceptable to you, Sheriff?"

I tried not to smile when I said, "Absolutely. How about right after the press conference is over?"

Scott Stewart stood there like a deer in the headlights. He didn't have anything else to say and stepped down from the podium, blending himself back into the crowd.

I continued, "Folks, thank you again for coming. We have a real situation in Namekagon County we need to discuss. If you don't mind, we would like to start by telling you what we know. After that, we would like to take questions from community members and then from the media. If that works for you, we'll get started."

Immediately a reporter I didn't recognize jumped up and fired a question at both Len and me that questioned our competence. I asked him to sit down and be patient. I again addressed the crowd that had now become standing room only.

"People jumping up like that and shouting out questions is what we would like to avoid. We'll sit here all day and night to answer your questions, however long it takes."

The reporter jumped up again, this time justifying why his question should be answered before all others.

A burly fellow dressed in Carhartts at the back of the room said it for me. "Shut up and sit down. We want to hear what the sheriff and chief have to say."

I started again, "Some of what I am going to tell you, you already know, and some you don't." Lois projected corresponding images as I shared the details of each case.

I finished up with a request. "We believe there may be other meth labs operating in the area. While we would like to be everywhere, we can't be. You need to be our extra eyes and ears. When you are out and about, keep a lookout for anything suspicious. We have a special number that will be answered twenty-four hours a day, seven days a week. You don't need to give your name, and we won't use caller ID. It is important that if you see something, you say something. Any questions?"

A local building contractor was first up. "Sheriff, Chief, my old man used to say 'good riddance to bad rubbish,' and I agree with him. Why should we even care about these bums blowing themselves up?"

Len stepped up for that one. "Bob, it's hard to disagree with you.

The only problem is that it may very well be another drug gang that's killing these people trying to move in. We want them all gone. We want to make Namekagon County an inhospitable place for them."

"Are these dead guys the ones who gave the drugs to the kids at the party?" another person asked.

"We can't prove it, but it's a strong possibility," I replied.

"I hope they suffered," shouted an angry voice from the crowd.

A grizzled seasoned citizen wearing a plaid flannel shirt, overalls, and boots with a Stormy Kromer cap on his head stood up in the front. Everybody quieted down. He was a man who had earned respect.

"Name's Durwood Sayner, Sheriff. I don't know that we have met before today, but I sure have been keeping track of you. Len and I go back a long way. How're doing, Len?"

"Got our plate full, Durwood," Len replied.

"Sheriff, I've spent over forty years as the owner of the Sayner Forestry Company. I took over from my pap when he was killed in a logging accident. We always employed local, good, hard-working folks from the community. We always paid a good wage because they earned it. I am proud to say that Sayner Forestry Company dollars raised a lot of families and put lots of our kids through school. Whenever we had a problem in town that we could help with, our people were always first to step up.

"Hell, I remember some years ago, a motorcycle gang showed up at the Musky Festival. They started raising all sorts of trouble, racing their motorcycles up and down Main Street, scaring the bejesus out of everyone. The old sheriff then and the police chief were tough characters, but they only had a few men. After the bikers took over a bar downtown and beat up the owner, the sheriff got in his car and raced as fast as he could out of town right to our yard. He told us about what was happening and asked for our help. I reckon it took us all of about ten minutes to load two stake bed trucks full of hard-working loggers. All of them had cant hooks, axe handles, and anything else they could grab, and we headed for town. Before we left, the old sheriff got on the hood of one of the trucks and swore us in as deputies. He led us right to town, the big old red light rolling around and the siren a blaring. We got there just in time. Some of our local townsfolk were going at it with the outlaws. Sheriff, I was driving one of those trucks and put my foot to the floor and crashed it into all those fancy motorcycles parked in a line on the street," the old man recalled and cackled at the memory.

He continued, "They went down like dominos, and I ran the truck right up on top of the pile. Them outlaws poured out of that bar like hornets out of a hive looking for a fight, and that was just what they got. My boys got down off those trucks, joined up with the townsfolk, and we beat the living daylights out of those motorcycle riders. Every last one of those sons a bitches got a major ass-whooping. We taught them a lesson I don't think they will ever forget. Most importantly, they haven't been back since. Sounds like maybe the best way to solve these murders is just to run this scum out of the county. We still have a couple of stake bed trucks and the men to fill them. Let 'em go someplace else and start killing each other."

The crowd gave Durwood Sayner a thundering round of applause.

"Durwood, I appreciate the offer, but I'm afraid that's not the way we handle things anymore," Len responded.

"Just so you and the sheriff know, we're behind you guys," Durwood said.

The floor was now open and the pushy reporter from earlier made sure he was first up. "Sheriff Cabrelli, isn't it true that you have no suspects?"

"No, that's not true," I replied.

"We have received reliable information that you wasted valuable time treating Devin Martin's murder as a suicide. Is that true, Sheriff? How much time did you waste? Isn't it true that it took several weeks after Martin was killed before you began to treat this investigation seriously? Come on, Sheriff, even you can't think that's reasonable. Doesn't it make sense that the same person or persons who killed Martin might be the same people who killed Jesse Gunther and Tony Carter?"

I had been there and done that before. A pushy, obnoxious reporter, looking for his byline above the fold. Throwing out rapid-fire questions, having already decided what the answer would be. What he wanted was for me to defend myself and push back in the hopes he could get the right sound bite. I didn't play.

"I expect that other reporters in the room, as well as community members, heard what I said at the beginning. But I will cover this again for those who may have missed it. Devin Martin's homicide appeared at first to be consistent with suicide. Martin was killed, and it was a while before two hunters came upon the vehicle containing the body. The body was in a state of decomposition, which made recovery of evidence and a cause of death determination more difficult. We never stopped investigating the case, not for one minute. It was this continued investigation that eventually turned evidence to support homicide. It is possible that the person or persons who killed Martin may very well be the same ones who killed Gunther and Carter," I reiterated.

"Is an arrest imminent?" another reporter asked.

"We are following every lead and continue to get new information that hopefully will lead us to a suspect and arrest," I replied.

"Do you have any suspects?"

"Many," I replied.

Then the obnoxious reporter ended the press conference for everyone by launching an attack that I was certain would be the next day's headline in the big city.

"Sheriff, why don't you just be honest with the people. There is a drug war going on in Namekagon County. Killers are running loose, and you don't have any idea who they are, do you?"

The crowd didn't like what they heard, and there was a mumbling undercurrent. I thanked everybody for coming, then Len and I walked toward the door.

The next day's headline in the big city news became the theme of the day: "Namekagon County Drug War: Four Dead, Police Baffled." ❧

CHAPTER 22

Ricardo called me first thing in the morning.

"Nice headline. The picture is definitely not your good side. Just for the record, Sheriff, did you really recommend that you load up a bunch of lumberjacks in trucks and go hunt down the drug dealers? I am not being critical. I kind of like the idea. I was actually thinking about stopping by the hardware store and picking up an axe handle or two," he said.

"What's up, Anthony?"

"I have got something for you. I need to have a sit down with you and Len and maybe bring Malone in on the computer."

"Where and when?"

"Your cabin, okay?"

"Fine. I'll call the chief."

An hour later, we were sitting around my kitchen table.

"Sorry to keep taking advantage of your humble home, but its location works perfectly for our secret meetings, not to mention the woodstove and first-class coffee," Ricardo said.

"Would you like some coffee, Anthony?" I asked.

"I never thought you'd ask."

I poured coffee and sat down.

"Let me start at the beginning with what I may or may not know. Martin and his guys are getting set up to peddle meth in the north country. They are able to keep a low profile. They like the area because there's a market for their poison, and there are plenty of out-of-the-way locations to set up a meth lab or two. Things are moving along for them, but then something changes. Martin gets whacked, and his two buddies and their meth lab are blown to bits. It is not the fact that these dopers got themselves killed; it's how they got killed. Martin's murder is set up to look like a suicide, but the sheriff figures out that it was a murder.

"The lab gets blown up along with the two clowns inside. Meth labs blow up all the time. In this case, though, the lab is blown to hell and gone. The state fire marshal and some helpers from Fort McCoy recover evidence at the scene that shows C-4 plastic explosive was used along with an accelerant and a remote detonator and timing device. What I am getting at is that kind of stuff is way too sophisticated for the average doper, at least it is in my experience. They all wish they were that clever and effective, but they're not. So, we get to the million-dollar question: Who? Who is doing this?"

"Sounds like you may have some thoughts on the matter," Len said.

"I do. I may not be right, but I have had some thoughts," Ricardo replied.

"So, what are you thinking?" I asked.

"I think there are two distinct possibilities. The first and most likely is that it is an OMG from the Twin Cities. They have been around for a long time, started in the sixties, mostly by a bunch of disenfranchised Vietnam vets. Over the last ten years, they have gone big time into the drug business and are hooked up with a Mexican cartel. Our counterparts in Minnesota and our people have got all sorts of intel that says they are already doing business around here and are looking to expand their market share. They are no strangers to violence. It's possible they decided to up their game when they ran up against Gunther and his people."

"That sounds consistent with what all of us have been thinking. A fight over territory between two gangs," said Len.

"You said two 'distinct possibilities.' What's the other one?" I asked.

"Remember that you asked because you are not going to like the answer. Here's the short story: the eastern European outfit running out of Superior Shipping and Container we busted with the feds had a bunch of people on the payroll. We took down a lot of them but not everyone. Some people fell through the cracks, mostly lower-level bosses. They are the ones who make these drug businesses work. This presented them with a golden opportunity to move up to the big leagues. They wouldn't need too many guys who know the program to put the thing back together. They know there is a ready market, and they want to move quickly before someone else takes over. They start to get things rolling and pretty quickly find that a bunch of hard cases educated in the joint have their own ideas about setting up. So, the eastern Europeans do what they have proven to be so good at—hit Gunther like a ton of bricks. Most of these guys were former military, Serbs, Ukrainians, and Czechs. They could probably put together a bomb in their sleep. They wouldn't need to send an army to get this done. One or two trained guys would be hard to spot and could handle the job."

Ricardo's news hit both Len and me like a sledgehammer blow to the chest. We sat silently. Len and I had done battle with these guys before. We had won but taken casualties.

Ricardo broke the silence.

"Remember, it's just one theory. There may be nothing to it. The next piece of information is the unfortunate reality. Some of Gunther's people are on their way here to straighten things out."

"How do you know?" I asked.

"This can't go any further. We have someone on the inside. If

Gunther finds out, he's dead. He told us people think that maybe Deacon Gunther isn't taking care of things the way he should be. That this is not a healthy place for him to be."

"Any idea who or when?" I asked.

"We don't know who, but it will be soon—very soon," Ricardo replied.

"Any thoughts on how we should handle this, Anthony?" asked Len.

"The only thing we can do is wait. If I get any more information, I will pass it on right away. In the meantime, I have mugshots and some photos of Gunther's people that have been sent to you guys. Brief your people and anyone else you think needs to know and make sure they have the pictures. Let them know who they are dealing with. If they show up, your people need to push them as much as they can. We'll know how serious they are by who Gunther sends."

———

That question was answered the next day. The newest member of the Musky Falls Police Department, Kristin Smith, made a traffic stop on the highway just inside the city limits. A dark blue late model SUV was behind a loaded hay wagon being towed by a tractor, and the young patrol officer was behind the SUV. All the vehicles were traveling in a no passing zone three miles long. The SUV driver got impatient and swung out, crossing the double yellow to pass the tractor. An oncoming car took the shoulder to avoid a collision. The officer activated her warning lights, and the tractor and hay wagon pulled over. She quickly caught up with the SUV, and the vehicle pulled over to the road shoulder.

Officer Smith parked her squad in a way that allowed her to approach the SUV safely and also offered protection from passing traffic should a rubbernecker quit paying attention to where they were driving. She called dispatch with the plate number.

Kristin walked up to the driver's side. The tinted window came down, and she was greeted by a big man with a tangle of tattoos going up his neck and onto the side of his face. Sunglasses hid his eyes. A look around the vehicle showed three others—two big men like the driver and a smaller, skinny one in the front passenger seat.

"I need to see your license, registration, and proof of insurance," she said.

"I'll need to get the registration and insurance out of the console. Okay for me to get it?"

This unnerved her, and it dawned on her who these people probably were. She realized this was potentially a dangerous situation. Nevertheless, she kept her cool.

It was common for people to keep their registration in the glove compartment or center console.

"Go ahead," she responded and put her hand on her weapon. The driver saw the move.

"Officer, there is nothing in the console but paperwork. If you want, I will get out of the car, and you can get what you need," the big man said.

"No, just hand it to me," Officer Smith directed.

The driver did as requested. Smith walked back to her squad car. She ran the driver's license and registration and advised dispatch of who she had stopped.

Dispatch responded, "Officer Smith standby. Backup is on the way."

The man driving the car was Deacon Gunther, the suspected leader of a drug gang. Gunther came back with a mile-long rap sheet, but he was not wanted nor currently on probation or parole. His driver's license was valid and registration current.

Backup came fast in the form of Sergeant Kruger and a DNR warden who had been eating lunch at a nearby café. Both were old hands and, upon arrival, positioned themselves to have the advantage if something went down.

Officer Smith issued the citation for the passing violation and started toward the violator's car when another squad car pulled up behind her with K-9 Unit emblazoned across the side. An officer from a neighboring county got out.

"Officer Smith, could you hold up for a second, please?" the officer called. She stopped and waited.

"If you have no objections, Officer, I would like to take my dog for a short walk. It won't take long," said the K-9 officer. He got the dog out of his car, which put everyone on high alert. The conservation warden had armed himself with a rifle and positioned himself behind his truck. The air was thick with tension. The K-9 officer with Officer Smith in tow approached the vehicle.

The dog handler spoke, "Sir, I am going to take my dog on a walk around your vehicle. Before I do, I would like to know if you have any controlled substances in the vehicle. If you do, and you turn them over to me, well, that might work for you down the line. If you don't tell me and the dog finds something, then we are going to take this pretty car apart piece by piece."

Gunther's hands remained locked on the steering wheel. He turned his head toward Officer Smith and the dog handler, giving them a look of pure darkness.

"You don't have probable cause to search my vehicle. A traffic ticket is not enough. You do a search and find something; it won't hold up. This is harassment," Gunther objected. He reached for the door handle to get out of the vehicle.

"Stay in your car," Officer Smith warned.

Gunther put his hands back on the steering wheel.

The K-9, a German Shepherd, began to work its way around the SUV, investigating every crack and cranny with a vacuum cleaner nose. It made one complete loop around the vehicle and then another.

"Did you find what you're looking for?" Gunther said smugly.

"Mr. Gunther, we're going to take one more walk around the car if you don't mind," the handler replied.

"Be my guest," Gunther said.

Nothing. The dog didn't alert on anything.

"If you are done, could you please give me my ticket and let me go?" Gunther said. The K-9 officer nodded to Officer Smith. She gave him the citation and instructions regarding his rights. She started to walk back to her squad when she heard a rude comment directed at her from the front passenger side of Gunther's car.

Officer Kristin Smith may have been a rookie on the force, and some people might take her for someone who could be easily pushed around. Her easygoing manner probably contributed to that. All those people who thought that thought wrong. Besides being one of Musky Fall's finest, Officer Kristin Smith was also a nationally competitive "Lumber Jill" specializing in the single bucksaw, underhand chop, and other events. All require constant training and great upper body strength. It was this Kristin Smith who approached the passenger's window, which had been lowered.

The trooper and warden moved up.

"Did you have something to say to me?" she asked.

The passenger was covered with tattoos and meth-head skinny. Her question was met with a cackle. "I just had a question, you know, just a little question to ask you."

"Weasel, shut your mouth," the driver barked.

"Oh, come on, Deac. I just want to ask her a question. It is a real honest-to-goodness question. Nothing bad."

"Weasel, I mean it. Shut up."

Weasel responded with a cackling laugh. Deacon Gunther ignored him.

"Officer, I want to apologize for that guy. He's not right. Since I have my ticket, is it okay for me to go?"

You could see the gears turning in Officer Smith's head. She wanted nothing better than to grab Weasel by the neck, drag him out of the car, and bounce his head off the pavement. But she didn't.

She did what countless law enforcement officers did every day—she let it go.

"You are free to go, Mr. Gunther," she said. This triggered another cackling laugh from Weasel.

Gunther started the SUV and slowly drove off, making sure to use his directional when he pulled off the shoulder back into traffic.

Then and only then did Officer Smith draw a full breath. She had met the enemy of her community. She hoped to see them again.

Officer Smith called Chief Bork immediately and filled him in.

In turn, Len Bork called me. "John, they have arrived, at least four of them. I'll try Ricardo and see if I can get him. We should talk things over."

We met with Ricardo outside of town on a dead-end side road.

"Well, boys, the 'A' team is here. Deacon Gunther himself, a truly bad man if there ever was one. That was a stupid move passing in a no passing zone. If Gunther had been thinking, he never would have done it," Ricardo said.

"What relation is Deacon Gunther to Jesse Gunther?" I asked.

"Cousins or something like that," Ricardo answered.

"What about the guy, Weasel?" Len asked.

"His real name is Larry Sweet, and he is as squirrely as can be. He is a real instigator and dangerous. When something bad goes down, he always seems to be part of it," Ricardo explained. "Chief, any idea where they went after Officer Smith cut them loose?"

"The trooper that backed up Smith watched them. They filled up with gas at Northern Co-op and headed north out of town. He followed them to the county line, where they pulled into that rathole tavern Outlaws."

I asked the obvious question, "So what's our plan?"

"Well, Sheriff, thanks to your call to Lt. Malone, we have additional people in the area, and they are already working this thing. Gunther and company are going to need to hook up with somebody. They didn't come for a joy ride. They are going to talk with their connections, see where things stand. They will also try to get whatever intel their people have. These guys are street smart. They are going to want to know everything they can about the opposition. So, our people are watching for them and who they connect with. I think we have this pegged right. It's a turf war. I bet Gunther and his guys won't do anything until they know everything they can know. Now we just wait."

CHAPTER 23

I drove some backroads and pulled into my cabin at the same time Julie was getting out of her car with a large Tommy's deluxe pizza and a six-pack of beer made at a small local brewery.

We sat at the kitchen table, and she filled me in on her day. Much like police work, her day-to-day activities changed constantly.

"How is Amber doing?" I asked.

"She seems better every day. I have worked with families before where the child raises the parent. The kids don't know anything better, and they just incrementally acquire more responsibility as time goes on. In Amber's case, she did almost all the household chores, besides taking care of her mother when she fell off the wagon. It seems like a lot, but in reality, kids get used to it. Then the parent gets clean or, in this case, dies, and the caretaker suddenly doesn't know who they really are. Ed and Stella are helping her through it all in the most positive way possible. Amber lost her mom, but they lost their child. They will have to work through this together. She comes to school with a lunch packed and excited and ready to be a part of our activities. Ed and Stella volunteer nearly every field day, and she seems to like that."

The next morning, Julie woke first, and I came down to the kitchen to find her cooking ham and scrambling eggs. Her hair was tousled, and she still had sleep in her eyes. She turned to me with that thousand-watt smile, and I again saw the most beautiful girl I'd ever seen.

"I had the urge to cook up a big breakfast. I've got a big day at school and will probably be late. With all that you have going on, who knows when you might get to eat."

The eggs were delicious, local smokehouse ham the best. We both lingered as long as we could. Then Julie jumped up and announced she had to shake a leg, or she would be late. While she was in the shower, I washed dishes. I was sure to treat her prized cast iron frying pan just right—no soap, no water, just a good wipe down. She taught me a properly seasoned cast iron pan cleaned up just as easily as any miracle coatings.

She came down the stairs with a bounce in her step, hair still wet but dressed for school. I helped her carry her stuff to the car. We stepped out the door and were greeted by the sharp crispness of the cold air. We loaded her car, and after a quick kiss goodbye, she drove out.

Back in the cabin, I finished wiping down the counters and set the dishes in the drying rack. I started to head upstairs for a shower when my pager went off, and a minute later the landline rang.

I answered on the second ring.

"Sheriff, it's Ricardo. I got something, and I would like to meet with you and the chief."

"Where do you want to meet?" I asked.

"I hate to impose, but how about your cabin in an hour?"

"That'll work. I'll check in with Len. If he can't make it, I'll let you know."

"Thanks, and one more thing. Could you get Lieutenant Malone to join us by phone?"

"I will take care of it. Do you want anything else?"

"Well, a cup of that good coffee you make would be great."

———————

Ricardo and Len arrived at the same time, and Malone's smiling mug showed up on the computer screen. Coffee was poured, and we all sat around the kitchen table.

Ricardo wasted no time getting started. "Locally, there has been a shortage of dope available until yesterday. Now all of a sudden, there is dope everywhere. The dealers are raking it in. They are being a little more careless than usual. We made a half dozen buys as soon as the stuff hit the street. We're putting together solid cases. So far, they're all locals. As far as we know, though, they are all hooked up with Gunther. Lieutenant, for your information, one of Musky Falls' finest made a solid traffic stop on a vehicle driven by none other than Deacon Gunther. A deputy showed up with a canine and walked the dog around, and the dog didn't indicate. We don't know who brought the drugs, but they must have come in a second vehicle. Anyway, all the junkies and dealers are happy at the moment. We won't act on our cases until we know what's going on. Maybe one of them will have some solid information they will give us in trade for a get-out-of-jail-free card. Lt. Malone, I have a question for you."

"How can I help you, Agent Ricardo," Bear growled.

"Do you have anything on the status of the eastern Europeans who were running the drug operation out of Superior Shipping and Container?"

"Well, I'll tell you what I know. The joint operation took them down hard. The big bosses have been identified, but they took off before the raid. As you are aware, they killed Mary Beth Summers, a federal agent. The Organized Crime Task Force, FBI, and DEA took them apart—every nut, every bolt. Everyone caught and charged is either in prison or on their way. Some were illegals, and they have been sent back home. The authorities in their countries were advised of what they were involved in here, and from what we know, they were not treated well upon their return. Some had outstanding warrants, and they were turned over to the proper authorities. All the property and assets of Superior Shipping and Container have been seized. The business has ceased operation. As far as I know, if they aren't dead, they are dying. Every acronym in the country is still hot after them—FBI, ICE, DEA, IRS, HS—and they are not going to let up until they run them all to ground."

"Is it possible that some of them fell through the cracks and got away?" Ricardo asked.

"Not just possible, but likely. I am sure some low-level thugs are out on the street doing what they do. I mean, crooks are crooks. That is how they make their living. Agent Ricardo, do you have anything that indicates they are back in business?" Bear said.

"No, but I think it's a strong possibility. I mean, someone is trying to shut down these guys. It makes sense that it is a rival drug gang killing off the competition. They are just a bit more sophisticated in their methods, but the result is the same."

Then the light went on for Bear. He didn't rise to the commander's position on the Organized Crime Task Force because he lacked brains or courage. One of his greatest attributes is an incredible memory. It's like he has two separate brains: one is doing the everyday work, and the other is in the background sorting through information. When the sorting through information part comes up with something, Bear puts it out.

"*Vyhazet.* It's a Czech word for get rid of everything unnecessary or unwanted. They have used this before, and I have reviewed a couple of cases. What they do is take out all the competition. They don't run them out of town; they kill them. They make it so dangerous that the ones left alive take off for greener pastures. If they come back, they're dead. It's worked well because, like it or not, we law enforcement types don't put drug gang-related homicides at the top of our priority list. Not like we would if the church lady next door gets knocked off," Bear said.

"I've heard of this before," Ricardo interjected, "never here, but I've heard of it."

"So if Deacon Gunther's there, he must be figuring on doing something," said Bear.

"That's what we think," I replied.

"Sheriff Cabrelli, Chief Bork, how do you want to play this?" asked Ricardo.

"John, what do you think?" asked Len.

"We get our people together, get them geared up, and hit the street doing what we do. Let them know that we know who they are and why they are here. If we can make a case, we'll take them down," I suggested.

Bear growled, "Everybody stand by."

It was five minutes before he came back to the phone.

"Big news, boys. La Crosse PD just made one hell of a big bust. They got three convicted felons, guns, cash, and enough fentanyl to OD everyone in northern Wisconsin. Sounds like they did a good job with the case—sharp outfit La Crosse PD is. The load was going to make a stop in La Crosse County and then was headed to the great Northwoods. My guess is Namekagon or surrounding counties. I will reach out to them and see if there is any connection between our bad guys and theirs."

The meeting broke up, and I got in my squad and followed Len into town. On the way, each contacted our respective administrative staff and asked them to have all officers and deputies, working or off shift, on vacation or not, to come in for a briefing. Most of them beat us to the office. We gathered both city officers and county deputies in the conference room, assembling our total force of sworn people. In addition, the administrative staff that is the backbone of any law enforcement agency was present. Only the dispatchers in the communications center stayed at their station. They would be briefed later.

Len started. "Folks, thanks for coming in. I know it was inconvenient for many of you, but as you know, that is the nature of law enforcement. I would like to start with Officer Smith telling us about the traffic stop she made the other day. Kristin, if you don't mind," Len directed.

"Sure, Chief," Officer Smith replied and shared the details of the stop.

"Folks, by all appearances, it seems that the drug network in the north country is wide open. The ongoing violence is a result of a turf war between drug gangs, and we have reason to believe that this will escalate. We have asked the community members to keep their eyes and ears open. Anytime you get a tip on something, follow up on it. It is critically important that we are all paying attention. You all have photos of some individuals who may be involved. These are people we know about, and there are most certainly others we don't know. Our options are somewhat limited, but I think it only makes sense that we do what we can to shut this thing down before it gets any bigger. So, let's get out there and keep our eyes and our ears open. Call in every stop, and ask for backup for anything that looks the least bit suspicious," Len concluded.

Everyone filed out of the room and resumed their normal duties. In a small town with a relatively small population and surrounded by a rural landscape, everybody knows everybody. During the height of the tourist season, thousands of people show up. Law enforcement gets pretty adept at picking out people from a crowd who may be trouble. With summer over, it would be much easier to pick out new faces.

Law enforcement officers hated the trouble that drugs had brought to the north country as much as, or more than, anyone. They would be judicious in carrying out their duties. They may push a little too hard on those suspected of bringing trouble, but that was okay. Maybe a case or two would be tossed but making sure the bad guys know they were being watched would yield great benefits. ❧

CHAPTER 24

For the next several days, things were quiet. Fall was quickly becoming winter. There were more pickup truck loads of firewood going through town than cars full of drugs. People were doing what people do in places that have cold winters and live close to the land. They were getting ready. Daylight did not break until almost seven, and darkness crept back in by five. The time available to do things had dwindled, so people hustled to get things done.

Adjacent to the north Namekagon County line was a parcel of state-owned land where, for five dollars, people could get a permit to cut and remove dead or fallen trees in a designated area. The lots were available due to a tree-killing disease and straight-line winds that had blown through the area several years before. Usually, people cut the wood to firewood lengths and stacked it close to the two-track or fire lane access. On subsequent trips to the woodlot, they would split the wood into manageable pieces, load it up, and haul it home. Although the wood was left stacked and unattended, firewood theft was rare and akin to being a horse thief in the old west. Some despicable characters tried it, but they were served a healthy dose of Northwoods justice.

A call came over the radio, sending one of my deputies to an off-road motor vehicle accident at one of the firewood cutting areas. The dispatcher said that the complainant was extremely agitated. I was a considerable distance away but started heading in that direction just in case the situation escalated. No more than five minutes from the original call, a second call came in requesting the fire department. Deputy Plums arrived at the scene shortly after and put out a 10-33 call for emergency assistance. I hit my lights and siren, arriving just as the first couple of firetrucks did. Deputy Plums waved them on to a place further down the two-track. It wasn't difficult to see where they were headed. An intense column of smoke and flames was topping the trees. In my rear view I saw more fire trucks and got out of the way to let them pass.

Deputy Plums was standing with two people. I got out of my squad and approached the group. "What's going on here?" I asked.

"Sheriff, to be honest with you, I have only gotten bits and pieces so far and was getting ready to take these guys' statements."

They provided us with ID that identified them as John and Ian Stevenson. Father and son. The father started, "Well, we heat mostly with wood, and with winter coming, we have been out here every spare minute getting everything loaded and split. We were set up here on the fire lane off to the side of the two-track road. Ian was loading, and I was running the splitter and pitching it into my truck bed. The splitter ran out of gas, and after we fueled it up, we sat down to take a little break. We were sitting here—I was having a cup of coffee and Ian his Mountain Dew—when out of nowhere comes some screwball in a hotrod pickup truck flying down the two-track, and I mean he was flying. If somebody had been coming up that road on an ATV, he would have killed them sure as I'm standing here. He swerved to miss our truck and ended up hitting our splitter hard enough that he bent the crap out of the ram. He just kept going, hit the pavement, and he was gone. He didn't miss hitting one of us by more than a couple of feet. We were cussing him out when we heard the explosion. Ian and I jumped in the truck and drove toward the boom. We got down to where the fire trucks are now, and there was single-wide mobile home burning like all get out. The flames were a good twenty or twenty-five feet high. Then Ian pointed out some hundred-pound LP cylinders and said, 'let's get out of here.' One was blowing out the top like a blow torch pointed right at the other ones. I spun the truck around and got out of there just before we heard another explosion. That one sent a big cloud into the air. We called the fire department."

"Can you give us a vehicle description?" I asked.

"Yes, sir," Ian responded. "It was a newer black Dodge extended cab. It had a loud exhaust, body lift, and big tires. There was a heavy-duty brush guard on the front—that's the part that hit our splitter. There was also a big scrape and dent about two feet long on the rear passenger side of the box."

"Could you see the driver?"

"Nope, the windows had heavy tint," Ian replied.

"Which way did he go when he got on the highway?"

"Toward town."

"South?" I asked.

"Yeah, south."

Before I finished talking to the Stevensons, the fire chief called me on the radio and asked me to come to the fire scene right away. I walked down the two-track, which eventually turned to mud from all the water, and found him.

"What have you got, Chief?" I asked.

"The fire was burning hot when we got here. But we got our equipment deployed and were hosing down the building in short order. Most of what was going to burn had burned, and we had the fire knocked out pretty quick. When it was safe to approach, one of my men and I walked up to the structure. That's when we saw a body in the yard. We checked for a pulse or respirations, but there were no signs of life. The victim was on his stomach, and we saw something in the thoracic spine area that looked a lot like an exit wound. We turned the victim over and found what appeared to be a single entrance wound. It looks like this guy was shot, not killed by the fire. We backed off and paged out the ME, and he is on the way."

"Good work, Chief. If it's okay with you, once the ME gets here, I am going to have my deputy photograph the entire scene."

"Fine with me, Sheriff."

In the meantime Deputy Plums worked with dispatch. A BOLO was issued with the vehicle description and last direction of travel. The driver was wanted as a person of interest in a death investigation. The description went out to the TV station, the radio, the newspaper, and the Internet. I wanted everyone in the county and surrounding area to be looking for that truck. Additionally, I had dispatch ask any deputies who could to come in on overtime to cover more ground. We needed to find that truck before it ended up at the bottom of a lake.

It wasn't long before Dr. Chali arrived. He went right to work and began examining the body, narrating and videoing at the same time. When he finished his initial examination, he approached the fire chief and me.

"Here's my initial finding. It looks like this guy was hit with a projectile that entered through the chest and exited through the back. Possibly a bullet, but it's hard to say right now. He was probably on the ground already when the explosion occurred. The fire must have washed over him and scorched his clothes, but he was not caught in the major conflagration. I have taken some video and will take more before we load him up. Other than that, I have nothing else at this point," Dr. Chali reported.

"Thanks. Before you move him, I want my deputy to take some pictures. He will be quick."

"Okay with me. Have him send a copy over to my office."

"We'll do it," I said.

Once Deputy Plums was taking the photos, I walked over to talk with the fire chief. "Got any ideas about this, Chief?" I asked.

"It looks like another meth lab to me. The fire marshal is on the way. My first guess would have been that it was an accidental blowup, not high order like the other one. But with the dead guy who looks like he was shot, I have second thoughts."

With our help, Dr. Chali bagged the body and loaded it for transport. They were soon on the road back to town.

The fire chief and I cordoned off the area with crime scene and fire scene tape. The fire crew was loaded and ready to get back to the station. A thousand gallons of water, boot prints, and tire tracks turned it into a mudhole. Not an uncommon situation at a fire scene. They had their job, and I had mine; we both did them to the best of our ability.

I hoped the scene would give us some idea of what happened here. I decided to wait for the fire marshal. Investigator Wolfman pulled in with two crime scene techs two hours later.

"As soon as I was requested in Namekagon County again, I advised Lieutenant Malone. He ordered me to bring extra techs," he explained.

"Thanks for bringing them," I said.

Wolfman and I walked over the scene, and he dictated his initial thoughts into a handheld recorder. The crime scene crew was ready to begin, and I left them to their work. I called Julie and, with a weary voice, told her what happened and that I would not be home until late. She said dinner would be in the fridge, and she'd leave the light on.

I called Ricardo and Len and told them what we had. Ricardo put it out to his people.

I gassed my truck and started patrolling the parking lots and backroads. I passed other law enforcement units every so often. We had to use the remaining daylight to our advantage. Five o'clock darkness would come too soon. No one had encountered the truck we were looking for.

I went back to the office. I was too keyed up to go home. Using the big whiteboard in the conference room, I wrote out my ideas about the case, erased them, and wrote them again. I went over everything I knew or thought I knew, examining each detail. Malone had to be right—some hardball players were out there and ready to take over the drug trade. The Martin killing, blowing up two meth labs, and the chemists along with them, was all about taking out the competition. These people wanted to send a message: cross them or get in the way, and you would end up dead. No talk, no negotiation, just dead. They were organized, skilled, and ruthless. Now, with the arrival of Deacon Gunther and his people, it was almost certain the body count would rise. Finding the driver of the Dodge pickup was important. Our first potential person of interest was alive. ✦

CHAPTER 25

It was long past midnight when I realized how exhausted I was. I stretched out for a minute's rest in an open seg cell in the jail. The next thing I knew, it was two in the morning, and the jailer woke me and offered a cup of coffee.

"Sheriff, dispatch needs you ASAP."

I went to the communication center.

"Sheriff, I have got Conservation Warden C160 who wants to talk with you on a secure channel. He is out of cell phone range."

I sat down at the console. "C160, this is Sheriff Cabrelli. Go ahead."

"Sheriff, this is Clark Asmundsen. I think I have your truck."

"Where are you, Clark?"

"I am on foot in an area called Big Flats, about twenty miles out of town. I am on a hill overlooking a field, working shiners. About an hour ago, I heard a truck driving down the two-track. I looked at it through my field glasses, and I could see that it was a black late model Dodge pickup. A shack and shed are at the bottom of the hill I'm on. The driver pulled the truck into the shed. I didn't see him get out, but a light came on in the shack, and I could see someone moving around behind the curtains. The lights went off in the cabin. I waited a while, and then I snuck down to look. It matches the description. On the rear passenger's side there is a scrape in the paint about two feet long. It has expired Wisconsin plates. I went back up the hill, and I have the place covered as best I can. What do you advise?"

"Have you got someone working with you?"

"I've got a new recruit on the other side of this hill," he answered.

"Does he know what's going on?"

"Not yet."

"How do you suggest we approach the cabin and shed?"

"You're going to have to walk in. There is a roughly paved town road that connects with the two-track. At that intersection, you can start climbing the hill. When you get up top, we can take up positions. This is rough country—definitely not optimum for a tactical operation."

"Clark, advise your partner to switch down to tact three. Keep an eye on the cabin. This is a person of interest in a murder and arson. When we get there, your partner can guide us to the top of the hill."

"Copy that, Sheriff. What do you want us to do if he tries to take off?"

"Stop him, Clark, but try to keep him alive."

I roused four deputies and Len Bork. They came to the office ready, and we flew out of Musky Falls, lights flashing. Deputy Holmes had hunted Big Flats with his family all of his life. He knew exactly where we were going. At the meeting point, we doused our lights. The young warden recruit was waiting for us. We hiked up the hill, and we encountered Warden Asmundsen when we reached the crest. He was sitting with his back to a tree in heavy cover with his binoculars trained on the shack.

"Hey, Sheriff. Hey, Len. You got here pretty darn quick. Must have flown low," the warden said.

"That we did," I replied with a smile.

Clark gave us the lowdown on what he had observed. The truck in question was in a shed next to the house. The shed probably had a door attached to the house. He had not seen movement since the lights went out.

Asmundsen had already scoped out positions. We agreed to get in place and wait until first light. It would be a long cold wait in rough country, but the heavy cover made visibility in the dark difficult. Daylight would work to our advantage. I would approach the shack. Two deputies with rifles would flank me using available cover. As I approached, one of our cars would pull up to the back of the truck, blocking it in and providing me with cover.

———————————

We were in position with a little more than an hour before daylight. Everybody's eyes were trained on the shack.

Suddenly, the truck in the shed fired up and backed out at high speed, taking part of the door frame with it. It spun around in the driveway, jumped onto the lane, and accelerated rapidly. The truck was flying toward the county road. He would not make it. The warden recruit blocked the road with his pickup. If he swerved off, it would be into an undrivable boulder-strewn field.

Clark had his rifle aimed at the grill of the Dodge. It didn't come to that. The deputies had deployed road spikes on the two-track in case of such a circumstance. The Dodge hit them, taking out his tires and causing the truck to swerve on the rough road into the field, where it hung up on a boulder and stopped dead. Two deputies came down the hill and approached the vehicle. The dome light came on, and the deputies could see that the individual was preparing to jump out of the truck. Then they saw a gun in his hand. He turned to face them and stopped when he saw two little red dots centered on his chest. The warden approached and took the gun. A deputy handcuffed him.

We contacted the DA. He advised us to do a thorough search of the shack and attached shed. He further instructed us to take a gunshot residue swab of both the suspect's hands before transport.

The suspect's vehicle needed to be taken to secure storage, and a deputy needed to be with it at all times until a complete search could be done.

Deputy Holmes took over the search, and the wardens volunteered to help.

I transported the suspect to the Namekagon County jail. He was identified as Tyler Winslow.

District Attorney Hablitch was waiting when we arrived. Winslow was taken into an interview room. The DA and I sat across from him. I read him his rights, and he interrupted me three times.

"You don't have to read me my rights. I haven't done anything," Winslow insisted.

I persisted and finally got it done.

"I didn't know you guys were cops. I thought you were those other guys. How was I supposed to know who you were? It was dark," Winslow said.

"What other guys?" I asked.

"The guys who killed Marcus and set the trailer on fire."

"Tyler, we've got you fleeing the scene of a homicide and arson. Then you run from law enforcement. We took a gun off you, and you're a convicted felon. Any one of these things does not look good for you. Put them all together and, well, you can see why I might be a little curious. If you've got something you need to say, the DA here and I are ready to listen. It's up to you."

"I didn't have anything to do with killing Marcus or firing his house. That is for sure," Tyler proclaimed.

"Okay, tell us your story. We're going to record it. Is that okay with you?"

"Yeah, yeah, I got nothing to hide," he said. Then he continued, "I went out to visit Marcus. I drove in on the road past a couple of guys cutting wood. Their splitter and saw were making so much noise I don't think they even noticed me. Well, I get up to the trailer and don't see anyone. Then I look closer, and I see Marcus lying face down. I started to walk up to him when this big dude steps out from behind the trailer house, and he's holding like a Molotov cocktail, and he throws it against the side of Marcus's house and runs. The place starts to burn like crazy. I had heard rumors it might be a lab, and they can explode. I took off for my truck to get the hell out of there, so I put the pedal to the metal. I am flying down the trail, and I lost control a bit and clipped a guy's wood splitter, but I kept rolling. Then I hear the explosion. I wasn't hanging around to see what happened next. I took off, and I didn't look back."

"What is Marcus's last name?" I asked.

"Johnson. Marcus Johnson," he replied.

"What happened to the guy who threw the firebomb?"

"He ran down to the other side of Marcus's trailer. I couldn't see what kind it was, but there was an SUV waiting down the hill. You see, Marcus has another driveway that takes you out the back way from his place. You know, like, in case of emergency."

"What kind of emergency would that be?" I asked.

"Like a fire or something," he replied. "It didn't take me long to figure out those guys might come looking for me, so I hid out at my buddy's shack. Then I hear you guys creeping around and, well, I thought they found me." Tyler fidgeted. "Hey, what about my truck? Those tires were pricey. Now that you know I am innocent, you should make my truck right."

There was a knock on the interview room door. One of the deputies summoned me.

"Sheriff, there is someone here to see you. He says it's important."

I walked down the hall and found Ricardo.

"John, it sounds like you snagged someone," he said.

"I don't know what is going on yet, but we grabbed a guy we can put at the scene of the latest meth lab blowup and homicide."

"Does that room have a one-way mirror?" Ricardo asked.

"Yes, you can see from the next room over," I replied.

"Let me get a look at this guy," Ricardo requested.

I went back into the room and offered Tyler a bottle of water, which he gladly took.

"Tyler, I need the best description you can provide of the guy who threw the bomb. If there is any chance you think you might know who it is, now is the time to say something. The DA is right here. We can't promise anything, but it would be in your best interest for us to work together. You are facing some serious charges," I said.

"I'm innocent. I already told you the truth. I didn't have anything to do with Marcus getting killed."

"Maybe not, but as a felon, you can't have a gun, you know, like the one we just took off you."

"Give me a break, Sheriff. I got a right to protect myself. You know the second commandment of the constitution."

"Doesn't apply to you anymore, and I think you mean amendment," I corrected.

"Honest, you guys, I don't know who they are. I can't help you. You've got to believe me. I had nothin' to do with what happened to Marcus. Nothin'," he pleaded.

"Okay, Tyler, if that's your story, fine. By the way, we are doing an inventory search of your truck. Is there anything, in particular, we might find that you want to tell us about before we do?" I pushed.

"Oh man, oh man, I am screwed," Tyler said.

Tyler Winslow was booked and put in a holding cell. Len and I sat down with Ricardo.

"Sheriff, you got yourself one. Tyler Winslow, he's a dealer alright. He just got out of the joint a few months ago. I think he did about three years on a reckless homicide rap. Sold bad drugs to a girl who OD'd and died. His brother was Travis Winslow, a doper who drowned a while ago.

"The other thing is that he's definitely not hooked up with the

Martin and Gunther crew. We are positive he is connected with the Minneapolis outfit. He connected with them about five minutes after they kicked him out of the joint. One of my people tried to score off him when all the new dope hit the street. He had nothing, or at least he said he had nothing. Maybe he didn't like the way our guy looked. My guess is that Deacon Gunther and company just hit back, more of the traditional way—firebombs, dead bodies in the yard. Are you going to let us try to flip this guy?" asked Ricardo.

"What do you think he knows that you don't?" I asked.

"He is on the other side of this thing. I bet he knows some stuff. Just think about it, Sheriff. This is a guy facing a long stretch."

Winslow's truck was taken to impound, and the search turned up five grand in cash and a significant quantity of fentanyl. Pharmaceutical grade, most certainly stolen. The quantity was enough that it could put Tyler Winslow back in prison for a long, long time, along with the other charges. ✦

CHAPTER 26

The sun was just coming up when the cabin landline came up on caller ID.

"Hi, Julie. I bet you thought I was abducted by aliens," I said.

"Not funny, John. You should have called to let me know you weren't coming home. I was worried something happened to you," she scolded.

I explained everything. She listened, but I could tell she was not happy with me. The tension came through the phone line.

I was fully expecting to get an earful when I arrived home because I certainly deserved it. That is not what happened. Instead, she sat me down at the kitchen table and fed me breakfast. After eating, I went straight to bed and slept hard. When I woke up, it took me a few moments before I realized where I was.

Julie was gone, but there was a note on the table. "There is more food in the fridge. Just nuke it for one minute. I know that you have got your hands full. Go do what you have to do. We will talk later. If you can, just let me know if you are alright. I love you, John."

I called Len and Ricardo and asked them to meet at the cabin. By the time I showered and made fresh coffee, they were there. I looked at them, and they looked at me.

"You guys look like hell," I said.

"So do you," Len replied.

We sat at the kitchen table.

"Before we get rolling here, anything new?" I asked.

Ricardo shook his head, but Len just looked down.

"Len, what's up?" I asked.

"Well, Martha has had it. She says that thirty years is enough and anything more is too much. I listened to what she had to say, and she was right on every count. As soon as we get this situation wrapped up, I will retire for good. She told me that she is going to visit her sister in Three Rivers today. That's what hurt the worst. You see, Martha has always been there for me. No matter what happened when I came home, she was there. Since the day I was first sworn in as a recruit, she has lived every day of this life right along with me, the good and the bad. Tonight when I get home, she won't be there. I cannot imagine my life without her," said Len.

We sat silently around the table, each of us lost in our thoughts.

"Anthony, do you have a wife, a family?" Len asked.

"I had a wife. I don't anymore. I got wrapped up on a case, and I was gone. When I got home, I found a note. She had been gone for over a week, and I didn't even know. This job and any kind of relationship is just not happening for me. Other guys on the unit seem to make it work, but it doesn't work for me," Ricardo replied. "How about you, Cabrelli? Have you screwed up your relationship with Julie yet?"

"I'm working on it, Anthony, and by the looks of it, I'm doing a pretty good job of it," I said. "So guys, what's our next step?"

"Our people on the street have made some cases, but I think we are close to wearing out our welcome."

"Solid cases?" asked Len.

"Each one rock-solid," assured Ricardo.

"Are you getting anything back from your people regarding the homicides?" I asked.

"Nothing other than doper gossip. Maybe it will be different with this last one, but the others, nothing. It seems to me the only potential lead we have is currently cooling his heels in the Namekagon County slammer. He's looking at some real time. My guess is that given the chance, he'll flip. He knew and was likely doing business with Marcus Johnson. I bet he can tie Johnson back to that bunch out of the cities. That makes Gunther and his boys front and center suspects, not that they aren't already. Gunther can't take the hits on his outfit lying down and stay in business. Two things happen after they get here. First, a new supply of dope appears, making the tweakers very happy. Second, Marcus Johnson gets whacked, and his trailer is torched. Shooting somebody in the front yard, throwing a gas bomb, and running away is not the same program as C-4, a timer and remote detonator. It may not be pretty, but it got the job done. By the way, one of my people says it looks like Deacon Gunther and his crew have set up housekeeping in that sleazy tavern, Outlaws," Ricardo said.

"What are you ready to pull the trigger on, Anthony?" Len asked.

"We are ready to go on three arrest warrants for people in the area who are probably tied up with Gunther. When the new drugs hit the street, the dealers must have thought it was Christmas and got sloppy. We made several buys."

"How about we sit down with the DA and draft all the charges on cases you guys have made. You are almost ready to pull your people out, anyway. Why not take the dopers down now, lock them up, and see where that takes us? Let them know that we are looking for information and ready to bargain. All of your cases are against dealers, right? All felonies?" Len asked.

"Most are. We did find a couple of our old friends that we can take for possession. But the rest are felony charges against dealers," Ricardo confirmed.

"I like this idea. Take them down as fast as we can and see what they know. They have got to know more than we do," I said.

"We used to call it a doper rodeo. Rope the dopers and haul them in. On the surface, this sounds pretty good. We do this and make plenty of noise. Len, John, your people will make the arrests. I want to limit the exposure my agents have to the media. While this is all going down, we let Tyler sit. We'll wait him out. The value of what he knows gets diminished with every arrest we make. If he knows something, and I think he does, this will go a long way to convincing him that working with us is a good idea."

"Let's run it by Bear," I said.

Malone talked the plan through with us. These were all felony arrests. Two of the suspects had histories of violence, in particular Randy Muller. He had done two stretches in state prison and had a lengthy record. Notes in his file said he should be "approached with caution" and "considered armed and dangerous." Two of the subjects met the agents at their place of residence and sold them the drugs. A third suspect met the agent at a bar, then took him back to his apartment to get heroin, which he sold to the undercover agent. The agent noted a short-barreled pump shotgun standing in a corner behind the entry door in that subject's apartment. No weapons were seen on the other two subjects. We would secure both "no-knock" search and arrest warrants against the suspects. In each case, we would treat these people as armed and dangerous and engage them as such. The takedowns were to be full tactical operations.

We met with DA Hablitch and Lt. Malone, and an assistant attorney general joined us by computer. Ricardo and his people were truly good at their job. The cases were solid. In each case, his agents had gotten into the residences, and while they couldn't provide a blueprint, they could at least provide some information on the places we would be entering.

In all three cases, they had made at least two buys. There was plenty of probable cause to indicate that they stored their illegal drugs in their place of residence. In addition, they had positively identified the dealers. The warrants were drafted, and we moved over to Judge Kritzer's office for his signature.

Hablitch called Kritzer's clerk. She checked with the judge, who said they should meet him in chambers. We knocked, and he opened the door.

The old judge gazed at us with a quizzical look.

"Mr. District Attorney, I see you have assembled quite a crew. Are you here to waste my time, or do you have something of importance for me today? Wait for a minute, though, before we get started," the judge said and turned to address the chief. "Len, thanks for working on my rifle. It works just fine, smoother than I ever remember. Unfortunately, the deer did not cooperate this year. Now, back to business. Who is going to fill me in?"

"I guess I'll start. I am Agent Anthony Ricardo of the State Department of Narcotics Enforcement. I was detailed to this area in an attempt to put a drug network out of business. We received confidential information that we have confirmed as being true. A well-established group of drug dealers from the Milwaukee area was going to set up a drug network in northern Wisconsin. While engaged in the investigation, we made contact with several individuals who sold my undercover agents illegal drugs, including methamphetamines, heroin, cocaine, and fentanyl. The specific information regarding each circumstance is detailed in the text of the criminal complaints and arrest warrant.

"There have been four recent homicides in the county. There is no question that these homicides were drug gang related. All the victims had significant criminal records, including arrests and convictions related to illegal drugs," Ricardo concluded.

"Agent Ricardo, have you and your associates developed a suspect or suspects in these killings?" the judge asked.

"No, Your Honor, we have not. We believe two other drug gangs are trying to establish themselves in the area, and the killings can be attributed to one or both of those gangs," Ricardo answered.

"Chief Bork and Sheriff Cabrelli, not a week goes by that people don't appear in my court for drug charges. It seems that illegal drug trafficking, much to my sadness and dismay, is well established here. Please help me understand why this has risen to the level of murder. I am somewhat confused by your approach here. I feel like maybe you are not as forthcoming with me as you should be. Does anyone want to help me sort this out?"

I stepped up, "Your Honor, can I be candid with you?"

"It would be a refreshing change of discourse."

"The truth is that we have some theories but no suspects in these killings. Our idea is based on several things, not the least of which is that these homicides are a step up from what usually happens. We think these killings are meant to send a serious message to the competition: if you mess with us, we will kill you. The first killing was meant to look like a suicide, and the second involved the use of plastic explosives. These homicides required planning and some sophistication. The next one that happened appears to be more of a normal retaliation. All the victims except the last one were affiliated with the gang from the Milwaukee area. They had to retaliate or pack it up. We think they shot and killed a guy named Marcus Johnson, then firebombed the trailer where he had his lab. We have a material witness locked up right now who we think is connected with Johnson and the gang out of the Twin Cities. He is being held on several charges, including felon in possession of a firearm and possession of a controlled substance with intent to deliver. He is the first real lead of any kind we have had. We believe he has information."

"So, Sheriff, and anybody else who wants to join in, you believe this rival gang out of the Twin Cities is responsible for these homicides. Is that correct?"

"Your Honor, that is where the difficulty is. We don't think they are responsible," Ricardo said.

The judge looked at us incredulously. The DA started to speak, but the judge silenced him by putting his hand up.

Judge Kritzer pulled a gold pocket watch out of his shirt pocket. He pushed a button that released the cover. He stared at the dial, then raised his head.

"You boys have five minutes to tell me what the hell is going on here. You had better be convincing because if you're not, you will leave my office immediately."

Len took the lead. "Judge, we think the people trying to take over the drug dealing in this area are most likely former members of the gang from Superior Shipping and Container. We know the feds got most of them, but they didn't get all of them. We are not the only ones who think they are trying to pick up the pieces. Lt. Malone agrees with us. They are hitting hard, moving out any competition. That is how they operate. If they are back, we need to get rid of them before they get a foothold."

The judge closed his watch. "Agent Ricardo, what do you think about this theory?"

"I believe it is highly likely. It fits the pattern that these cartels have established. They take out the competition and put their people in place. They are ruthless. The people they killed were the movers and shakers for the Milwaukee gang. They didn't waste their time taking out low-level street dealers. The Milwaukee gang doesn't get it. They are bad boys themselves. They never thought about the eastern Europeans, and they hit back at the wrong outfit. All the better for the Czechs. If they can start a war between these two gangs, it's less they have to do," Ricardo responded.

"You have three arrest warrants and three search warrants you would like me to sign. My guess is you hope to gain some information from these people. Maybe do some horse-trading. Is that the plan?"

The DA spoke up, "Yes, Judge, that's what we hope is going to happen. We also believe the person we have in custody now may be more cooperative if the value of his information has lessened because of the arrests."

"I am going to read every word of each of these complaints. Let me warn you. If you have in any way come up with trumped-up charges simply to use as leverage to get information, you will find yourselves in front of me, and I will make sure you rue the day you tried to deceive the court."

"Judge, every one of those cases is solid. We got these guys dead to rights. If we end up going to trial, they will be convicted. My people are good at what they do. No nonsense here, Judge. You have my word on it," Ricardo assured him.

"Alright, leave me alone while I do some reading. I will notify DA Hablitch when I am done. Now out."

Two hours later, the DA reported we were good to go. Ricardo immediately set up surveillance on the targets. Uniformed officers from the county, city and state patrol, and DCI agents were put into teams led by Ricardo and his people. The agents would provide positive identification of the suspects. All the places we were taking down had other residences around. We needed to make sure that these raids didn't turn into firefights.

We planned to serve the warrants beginning at seven in the morning. At six, the surveillance teams advised all persons of interest were accounted for. The go-ahead came at 7:10. The teams hit the places in full tactical gear. The apartment dweller was dressed only in boxer shorts and was tucked in his bed when the DCI agent identified him, and he was taken into custody. The next suspect attempted to run for the door. Ricardo relived his high school football glory and hit the guy with a head-on tackle, upending him and slamming him to the ground.

The warrant service on Randy Muller was a different thing. Muller lived on the edge of town in an old World War II row house. The subject had returned home at about three in the morning and had not been seen leaving again. Besides what we had found in the file, local officers had plenty of information on Muller. He was a local hard case who had done his joint time the hard way. The word was he was vying for a spot with Gunther's gang as an enforcer. The other word was something had happened to him in prison, and he had vowed never to go back inside. I guess it never dawned on him to quit breaking the law.

Chief Bork led the team with two uniformed officers and two DCI agents who covered the back door. As they approached the house, the door flew open, and Muller ran out charging officers. He dropped his shoulder and slammed hard into the chief, knocking him to the ground. He didn't, however, make it past the two-time champion Lumber Jill, Officer Kristin Smith. She grabbed the suspect around the head and neck and, in a move that she must have learned on big-time wrestling or pro rodeo, twisted his head around and dragged him to the ground. The suspect swung with his free hand and slugged Officer Smith hard in the face, but she held on. He fought viciously until a monkey pile of pissed-off cops pinned him to the ground and cuffed him.

The arrested parties were transported to the jail, booked, and put into separate cells far enough apart that they could not speak to one another.

Each residence where the arrests took place was secured. Then DCI agents, Namekagon County deputies, Musky Falls police officers, and two canine units executed search warrants on each of the houses where they recovered meth, heroin, fentanyl, a large quantity of prescription drugs, and five firearms. Everything was bagged and tagged.

After we debriefed and stored the evidence, we took our first crack at interviewing the arrested parties. An agent was teamed with a uniformed officer and assigned to each suspect. Each agent detailed the charges and the maximum sentences possible and explained to the suspect he or she was going down, but how far was dependent on cooperation. Agents explained there was a light, not very bright yet, but a light at the end of the tunnel and if the arrested parties could provide the information needed, the light might get brighter.

The first two interviewed, of course, knew about the killings. Right off the bat, both started to come up with anything they could to dig themselves out of the hole they were in. Most of what they said was street gossip, or they just made it up on the spot. They had both heard that it was people from the cities. We didn't ask, and no one volunteered any information about the Czechs, Russians, or any eastern Europeans.

Then we came to Randy Muller, a truly bad guy. Muller was a born and raised Musky Falls scumbag. Len Bork was well acquainted with him. He got around but always made his way back home. He had a long record, including being a prime suspect in a homicide, but had never been charged. His last stretch in the joint was for two counts of aggravated battery and possession with intent to deliver and delivery of heroin. He spent most of his prison time in isolation. Eventually, he was back in general population, and that's where he probably hooked up with Jesse Gunther. Maybe Gunther and his guys protected him from whatever happened to him in the joint. For whatever reason, he was now entirely loyal to Gunther. Muller was brought to the interview room wearing waist cuffs and leg shackles.

Agent Ricardo read him his rights while I watched and listened. When asked if he had anything to say, he did not reply.

After a few minutes of silence, the jailers came to take him back. Muller shuffled his feet slowly out of the interview room.

When he got to the door, he looked over at me and said, "Tell that girl who tried to strangle me I hope her face is all right. It should be a pretty shade of black and blue by tomorrow. When I get out of

236 | JEFF NANIA

here, maybe she and I can get together. You know, have a few drinks, do a little partying."

In fact, Kristin Smith's face was swollen and already turning a dark purple from where Muller had hit her. A stop at the emergency room showed no broken bones, but it would be an ugly bruise. She came back to the jail and had a surprisingly good attitude. She explained she had grown up with five brothers who, like her, competed in timber sports. This was not her first shiner.

The first round of interviews was done. I called everyone to the conference room. The agents were pros, and they each approached things a little differently. Our plan had been not to mention the eastern Europeans at all. None of the people that we had in custody said a word about people involved who had been in the drug business. Without offering anything, we let all of those people we arrested know we were interested in any information regarding the homicides. The key to success for us would be to make sure we didn't seem too anxious, too needy. The suspects we had in custody were adept at manipulating people and situations. If they thought they had something we needed, they would start playing games and be difficult to deal with.

DA Hablitch met with us and explained his intentions.

"No bail for any of these guys," he began. "The charges are solid, and we are adding felonies in at least one case. Chief Bork, please make certain that we have several photographs of Officer Smith's injury, particularly in a day or two when it looks its worst. We will charge Muller with two counts of resisting arrest and battery to a police officer, one for Officer Smith, one for Chief Bork. I would expect that Judge Kritzer will want to move forward with the prelim sooner than later. To that end, we will get all of our paperwork ready to go as soon as possible."

As Len got up from his chair to leave, he winced in pain and had to sit back down.

"Len, are you alright?" I asked.

"Fine, John, just a little bruised up from where Muller clobbered me. Nothing to it at all," he replied.

I talked to everyone else present.

"I am taking the chief over to the emergency room to get checked out."

"I'm fine, just a little bruised."

"No more talk. Get in my squad, Len. I'm driving you."

Grudgingly, he agreed.

An hour later, we returned with Len carrying his bulletproof vest with his two cracked ribs in a rib wrap. ❖

CHAPTER 27

The arrests were instant news, and the next morning our offices were besieged with media calls. DA Hablitch was prepared, and we had everything ready. He sent out a press release detailing the most recent arrests, emphasizing the attack on two law enforcement officers and that they had sustained injuries. He was very clear that this was an active situation and the ongoing homicide investigations were top priority. He detailed the arrests and identified the persons in custody. He closed the release by saying he had no further information at this time.

I spent most of the night reading the reports about the suspects. I focused mainly on Tyler Winslow. Ricardo's people were pretty sure he was connected with the people from the cities. Marcus Johnson was a known associate of his. But these were drug addicts and dealers we were working with. So, you never know what to expect. It is what it is until it's not.

My first stop was the jail. I asked the jailer to bring Tyler Winslow to an interview room. He was cuffed at the waist and was not glad to see me.

"Tyler, we need to talk," I said.

"I have nothing for you, Sheriff. I heard about all the people you arrested. Maybe they can help you out. I can't and I won't. You see, Sheriff, if I help you, I am a dead man. I don't know what you need to know, and even if I wanted to help, I couldn't," Winslow said.

"That's it, Tyler? That's your final word?" I asked.

"Yeah, Sheriff, that's it."

"I have some bad news for you, Tyler. I am asking the Department of Criminal Investigation and the DA to investigate your role in the murder of Marcus Johnson," I said.

"What? No way. That's bullshit, Cabrelli!" Winslow jumped up and toward me. I slammed him as hard as I could back in his chair.

It took him a minute before he regained his composure. I waited.

"Look, Cabrelli, you know I had nothing to do with killing Marcus. You can't put a crime on me that I didn't have anything to do with. I told you everything just like it happened. I am telling the truth. You know I am."

"I can put you at the scene when the crime was committed. You knew the victim and were in the dope business with him. You've got a sheet and had a gun. You ran from police, and on and on. Even to you, it must sound like a good case. I am getting a lot of heat from the press and have to charge someone. You could be the lucky man. Time is up, Tyler. I've gotta go," I said.

"Cabrelli, man, you can't do this! You're the police, so you got to be honest. You can't just make shit up. You can't put somebody in jail for something they didn't do. I'll be in the joint for the rest of my life," Winslow said.

"Think about it, Tyler. I'm not making anything up. It is all true, and you're right. You will be in the joint for the rest of your life."

The jailer took Winslow back to his cell.

———

My cell phone went off, and I recognized the number as Dr. Chali.

240 | JEFF NANIA

"Hey, Mike, do you have a report for me?"

"I do, Sheriff. If you are at your office, I could come over and drop it by."

"I'm here right now," I replied.

"I am on my way," he said.

Dr. Mike Chali walked into my office and handed me his report on the death investigation involving Marcus Johnson.

"Sheriff, Johnson was shot in the chest with a large caliber firearm. It could have been a rifle or a large caliber handgun. The entry wound exceeded eleven millimeters. The exit wound was significantly larger. The projectile struck the right ventricle and destroyed the heart. Other than some singeing from where it appears the fire washed over his back, there were no other injuries. He had meth and fentanyl in his system when he was killed. Did you get the report from the fire marshal and crime scene technicians yet?"

"Not yet," I replied.

"Don't expect much. Tire impressions from the scene indicated two different vehicles, but there was not much else. They sent in samples for analysis to confirm it was a meth lab."

"I appreciate you stopping by, Mike."

"How are you holding up? I saw the newspaper headline. I am sure you are under significant pressure right now."

"Doctor, this job is not for the faint of heart," I replied.

———

How long would the drug war go on? It seemed that the other side outclassed Gunther. When they hit, they not only hit hard, they did so with deadly precision. Gunther had to be rethinking bringing his drug network to the north country. I figured there would be retaliation against Gunther or his people for the hit on Marcus Johnson. When and where, who knew, but how they retaliated would tell us a lot.

We all spent the rest of the day with our sleeves rolled up, trying to put the pieces together, working with everyone involved in the investigation. Ricardo was back-checking with other agencies and people in his network to connect the dots. None of us was convinced that we had a clear picture of what was going on. We made progress in one regard with solid cases against some drug dealers. But we still had more questions than answers. Public defenders had arrived and been assigned to their various charges, and initial appearances were being set up. There was more work to do than there was time to do it.

———————

That night I tried to fall asleep, but it wasn't happening. I couldn't help but wonder if I was becoming like Ricardo. Would I find out Julie had been gone for a week before I noticed? I drifted off for at least a minute before my pager went off and the house phone rang. Julie and I bolted upright.

It was the dispatcher on the line. There had been a shooting at Outlaws Tavern. EMS was on the way, as were Deputies Pave and Plums. I had told everyone that if anything went down that was even possibly connected to our current investigation, I should be notified no matter what time of day or night. Outlaws was on that list.

I was on the road and on my way within ten minutes. I spoke with my deputies, but they knew nothing more than what dispatch had told me. EMS had been called for a gunshot victim at the bar. The caller hung up before dispatch got any more information.

The deputies arrived on the scene, and EMS followed a few minutes later. As time passed and I didn't hear anything from my deputies, I hit my lights and siren and put my foot through the floorboards. I was still a ways out when I got a call from Plums.

"Sheriff, we have a situation. Someone drove by the tavern about an hour and twenty minutes ago and fired numerous shots into the occupied building," reported Plums.

"Was anyone hit?" I asked.

"We think so, but no one is talking. The call came in as a 911 for EMS. After the ambulance was en route, someone from the bar called and tried to cancel. We had already been sent, so we continued for a check welfare, as did EMS. The patrons of this place appear to be some bad actors. The owner doesn't want to file a complaint. What do you advise?"

"Stand by in the parking lot. I am on my way," I replied.

I pulled in and noted a dozen cars, but the only people in the lot were my two deputies and three EMTs. I joined them, and Deputy Pave filled me in on the situation.

"Deacon Gunther is the new owner of the bar," Pave began. "He said around eleven someone shot up the place. He doesn't have any idea who it might have been, maybe someone jack lighting deer. A patron was hit but doesn't want or need medical attention, saying it was a minor wound. I asked to see the injured party, and a guy with a bar rag wrapped around his hand stepped up. He reiterated that he didn't want medical attention. I asked who called 911, and a woman sitting at a table nursing a drink said she did. She said she freaked out when the guy at the bar started bleeding after the shots. She said she tried to cancel the ambulance."

"Let's go in," I said.

The jukebox was playing so loudly it was shaking the windows. Nobody gave us more than a glance. I walked over and pulled the jukebox plug from the wall, and the place became quiet. At a round table in the far corner of the room sat four guys, one sitting with his back to the wall I recognized as Deacon Gunther. I walked over to the table. None of them said a word; they just glared at me.

"Are you the owner of this place?" I asked.

"Yeah, I'm the owner," Gunther replied.

"Can I see your liquor license?" I requested.

"My what? My liquor license?" he repeated.

"Yes, your liquor license," I said.

Another man wearing a leather shirt and covered with jailhouse tattoos stepped out from behind the bar.

"I am the current owner of the place. Deacon is buying me out, but for now, the license is in my name," he said, pointing to a framed official-looking document screwed to the wall. "I just renewed about nine months ago. Everything is legal."

"Any idea who might have shot up your bar?" I asked.

"I am pretty sure it was those poachers the DNR has been trying to run down. Maybe you should be out trying to arrest those guys for killing defenseless little animals and shooting holes in my bar. That's what you should be doing. Not harassing us," the owner said defiantly.

I looked straight at Gunther. "Gunther, you have any ideas about who might have done the shooting?"

"Poachers," he replied.

The old owner turned to me. "Sheriff, if you're done with us, I would appreciate it if you could leave us be. We've told you what we know. We would like to plug the music back in and get the party going again. Is that alright with you, Sheriff?"

I turned to the injured man. "Are you sure you don't want the EMTs to look at your hand?"

"It's just a nick. I don't need no EMT attention, Sheriff."

The owner plugged in the jukebox, and we left.

Pave and Plums headed back out on patrol as I went home. A drive-by shooting was typical retaliation. Deacon Gunther would now be a permanent pain in my side as the new proprietor of Outlaws Tavern. The neighborhood was going to hell. ❦

CHAPTER 28

As predicted, Judge Kritzer pushed for an early preliminary hearing. Judges always tried to clear their calendars between Thanksgiving and Christmas, then use the days before the New Year to tidy up loose ends. The first two defendants appeared represented by the same public defender. Each pleaded not guilty.

The criminal complaints put both in a perfect corner. They had audio recordings and video recordings of the transactions. The judge allowed Ricardo to testify on behalf of his undercover agents to protect their identities. Cash bail for each was set at twenty-five thousand dollars.

Randy Muller was next up and sat at the defendant's table with a different public defender. He was recorded on three occasions selling fentanyl and meth to the undercover agent. In addition, he was charged with resisting arrest and two felony counts of battery to a police officer. The DA presented his case on the drug charges. He then described the events surrounding the arrest and Muller's attempt to resist during the arrest. The next charge of battery to a police officer was described in detail. In an attempt to escape, Muller had intentionally slammed into Chief Bork, cracking his ribs.

When Officer Smith then grabbed him, he struck her in the face with a closed fist. Both Chief Bork and Officer Smith had sustained significant injuries that required medical attention. The DA then projected a photo of Officer Smith's face on the screen, and it showed a huge, ugly purple and yellow bruise. He further maintained that Muller had demonstrated by his actions that he was a flight risk. The public defender argued that he was a longtime resident and not a flight risk. The judge was not buying it. The photo of the officer's face was enough. For now, Muller would be held without bond.

Tyler Winslow, looking shaken, appeared next. He was trying as hard as he could to explain something to the public defender at the defendant's table. Soon Winslow's voice went up a couple of notches.

Then he turned to the judge and said, "Judge, can I talk to you for a minute? I mean, I need to talk to you right now. This lawyer I have got here is no good."

"Hold on, Mr. Winslow. I will get to you."

Judge Kritzer called the court to order. I looked around and noticed Attorney Jack Wheeler was sitting in the back, away from onlookers and media people, going through a folder of papers.

"First off, let's get back to Mr. Winslow's issue regarding his assigned counsel. What is the problem here, Mr. Winslow?"

"This stupid lawyer here says I might as well just plead guilty and try for a better sentence. I am not guilty, and the sheriff knows it. He has made up a bunch of charges. I need a different lawyer. This guy I got is no good."

"Mr. Winslow, do you have funds to hire your own lawyer?" the judge asked.

"No, I don't have the money to hire a lawyer. The law says that you have got to give me a lawyer if I can't afford to hire one, doesn't it?"

"Yes, it does, Mr. Winslow. I believe that is your lawyer sitting next to you at this time."

"Judge, I want a different lawyer. If this dude represents me, I will never get out."

The judge asked the public defender to approach the bench. After a brief conversation, he returned to his seat.

"Mr. Winslow, I am going to honor your request for a new lawyer," the judge informed him. The public defender was dismissed and left the courtroom with a smile on his face.

Court was adjourned temporarily. The judge requested the bailiff and I to sit on either side of Tyler Winslow until he returned. Ten minutes later, Judge Kritzer came back and called the court to order.

"Due to the recent arrests and the dismissal of counsel by the defendant, we find ourselves with an acute shortage of attorneys in the public defender's office. Mr. Winslow is charged with two felonies and is entitled to counsel. Attorney Wheeler, please approach the bench."

Jack Wheeler looked up, stunned.

"Attorney Wheeler, please approach the bench," Judge Kritzer repeated.

Jack stood up in front of the judge. "Yes, Your Honor?" he said.

"Attorney Wheeler, what brings you here today?"

"I need your signature on some papers I am filing on behalf of Northern Lakes Academy."

"Glad to hear you're helping out that school. What a fine institution it is."

"I agree, Your Honor," Jack replied.

"How is your caseload, Attorney Wheeler?"

"Your Honor, being semi-retired, I rarely have a full schedule anymore."

"That's good to hear, Attorney Wheeler, because I find myself in a difficult situation. Mr. Winslow here is without counsel. I know you to be a staunch advocate for the law, so I would like you to volunteer to represent Mr. Winslow."

"Isn't this a criminal case? I am not a criminal defense lawyer,

Your Honor. I don't really feel that I can do justice to Mr. Wheeler's defense," Jack responded.

"I can understand you being hesitant, so let me help you. You're it, Attorney Wheeler," the judge said. Then he turned to the court recorder, "Let the record reflect that Attorney Jack Wheeler is now the counsel of record for Tyler Winslow."

"I need time to look at the case file, Your Honor," Wheeler said.

"You'll have plenty of time for that. For now, it is my understanding you wish to enter a plea of not guilty to all charges. Is that correct, Mr. Winslow?" the judge asked.

"Judge, will you give me a chance to tell you something? This is all a setup. The sheriff is trying to pull one. He is trying to charge me with murder to make himself look good. I didn't kill anyone," Winslow said.

"Hold on here. What is this about? Mr. District Attorney, what are the charges?" asked the judge.

"Your Honor, charges are as follows: knowingly fleeing an officer, resisting arrest, felon in possession of a firearm, and possession with intent to deliver a controlled substance. In addition, we have an ongoing investigation regarding the killing of Marcus Johnson. We can put Mr. Winslow at the homicide scene, and he was a known associate of the deceased. However, we are not prepared to charge at this time. We are asking that Tyler Winslow be held without bail." the DA said.

"That's bull, Judge. This is a setup!" Winslow shouted.

Judge Kritzer waited until Winslow settled down.

"Are you done, Mr. Winslow? Okay, we will enter a plea of not guilty to all charges, and Tyler Winslow is to be held without bail. Any objections, Attorney Wheeler?"

Jack Wheeler just shook his head. "No, Your Honor. No objections," he responded.

The judge rapped the gavel and stated, "The court is adjourned."

Forty-eight hours later, Jack Wheeler requested to meet with me and the DA. We met at the DA's office.

Wheeler, who was my friend and neighbor, had a serious look on his face. I knew better than to think our personal relationship would have any bearing on our professional one.

Wheeler ran the show. "My client may have important information regarding the Marcus Johnson homicide. He has not shared that information with me. His offer is straightforward: he will provide you with this information if you agree to drop all the charges against him," Wheeler offered.

"Geez, Jack, a convicted felon drug addict says he may tell us something that may or may not be true, and we drop the charges. We need a little more than that," I rebuffed.

"I understand, Sheriff. I am here to float the idea of a deal, as well as one more thing. Stay away from my client unless I am present. He says you have met with him without counsel and threatened him with a murder charge. That stops now," Jack said.

"Attorney Wheeler, we are willing to consider all offers. Let us know when you have more to tell us. In the meantime, the Namekagon County Sheriff's Office, Musky Falls Police Department, and state agents shall continue to investigate the open homicide cases, including the death of Marcus Johnson," the DA countered.

Wheeler left, and the DA asked me what I thought.

"I don't think that Winslow killed Marcus Johnson or torched the trailer. I think he pulled in at the wrong time. I also think he either knows or has an idea of who did kill Johnson. If he does, then we have got something to work with," I replied.

During several visits over the next few days between Tyler Winslow and Jack Wheeler, it became clear to Jack that his client was in a bad situation. While the evidence against him for party to a homicide was largely circumstantial, it had the potential to put him away for a long time. The other charges were solid, and if we went to trial, he would be back in prison before the spring thaw.

Wheeler called another meeting.

"My client wants to make a deal. The terms of the deal will require that all current charges against Tyler Winslow are dropped. That is not open for negotiation. In addition, he wants to be put in the witness protection program," Jack said.

"What does he have?" asked Hablitch.

"Tyler Winslow saw the person who killed Marcus Johnson and threw the Molotov cocktail. He knows the perpetrator and can positively identify him. Winslow is willing to testify in court and give a sworn statement. The person he will identify is part of an organized interstate drug gang with a history of violence. It is almost certain the people who killed Marcus Johnson will try to kill him to prevent him from testifying. The information he could provide may go a long way in helping law enforcement with the ongoing homicide investigations. Due to the relationship of the person he is willing to identify with the aforementioned gang and that gang's easily proven history of violence, he is potentially eligible for the witness protection program. Before we go any further, you need to ask for a determination regarding his eligibility for the program."

We told him that we would see what we could do and get back to him. An hour later, Ricardo, Len, Hablitch, and I connected with Malone.

We went over everything again for everyone's benefit. There was little debate. We had dead bodies all over the place, and trading Tyler Winslow for a murder suspect was progress. Malone had connected with the U.S. Marshals Service.

"The marshals are on board with evaluating the threat risk for Tyler Winslow. Based on the fact that he is identifying a murder suspect and we have several unsolved murders is going to tip the scales heavily our way. If it turns out that we can connect the killer to something like the Gunther organization, Winslow's chance for a new life increases significantly," said Malone.

Jack Wheeler agreed to a meeting with the DA. They spent hours hammering out an agreement. The charges currently pending would be dropped after Tyler Winslow gave a statement that included the suspect's positive identification. Since Winslow was a career criminal, the language was very clear about what charges would be dropped and how anything else that came up would be handled.

Jack Wheeler would not allow his client to give a statement or talk to anyone until the terms of the deal were clear and the agreement signed. Jack sat in an interview room with Tyler Winslow and went over every line. At one point, we asked when they thought they might be ready. Jack answered, "When we are done." Three hours and a couple of dozen changes later, the agreement was signed by all parties. If Tyler Winslow kept up his end of the bargain, he would be a free man.

We convened with the court reporter as well as a video and sound recording device. Winslow gave us an in-depth, detailed statement. That day he picked up a load of fentanyl in the Twin Cities that he was supposed to deliver to Marcus Johnson. Tyler was then supposed to get some meth from Johnson to put out on the street. When he pulled into the driveway at Marcus's trailer, a man standing in the yard turned to face him. The guy had a gun in his hand that he put inside his coat. He and Winslow looked directly at each other. Then he reached down and picked a bottle up off the ground. He held something to it, probably a lighter, and it flamed up. He threw the bottle against the side of Marcus's trailer, and the whole side of the place burst into flames. The man ran and jumped into the passenger side of a black full-size SUV that took off. Winslow spun his truck around and took off down the road he came in on.

"Can you identify the individual you saw at Marcus Johnson's home? The individual who had a gun and threw the firebomb at Johnson's trailer?" the DA pressed.

"Yes, I can. It was Randy Muller."

"Tyler Winslow, are you prepared to testify in court that you can positively identify Randy Muller as the person that you saw at Marcus Johnson's residence?" Hablitch asked.

"Yup, it was him. I've known him for a long time. I never got out of the truck, but I could see him just fine. I am pretty sure he knew it was me," he replied.

The DA continued his line of questioning.

"At any time was Randy Muller armed at the Marcus Johnson residence?"

"Yeah, he had a big pistol in his hand when I drove in."

"Did you see Randy Muller fire the gun or hear a gunshot?"

"No, I didn't."

"What did Muller do with the gun?"

"He put it inside his coat."

"What did he do then?"

"He threw a firebomb at Marcus's place."

"More specifically, what exactly did he do?"

"Oh yeah, he picked up some kind of bottle off the ground and lit it on fire. Then he threw it at Marcus's place. It started the whole side of the trailer on fire. Then Muller took off running."

"Where did he run to?" the DA asked.

"A black SUV waiting on the other road that goes to Marcus's place. I saw him get into the passenger side of a black SUV, and the truck took off. So did I, in the opposite direction."

"Anything else, Mr. Winslow?"

"Yeah. I heard the trailer blow up."

Tyler Winslow was escorted back to his cell.

———

The next few hours were a flurry of activities. First on the agenda was to go over what had been recovered in the previous search incident to Muller's arrest. Once Muller was in custody and the residence cleared, agents and deputies followed a canine officer and his German Shepard in. According to the report, the dog alerted at two different locations. The first was a heating vent. Tied to one of the fins of the vent was a clear piece of fishing line. The vent was only held in place by one screw. With the screw removed, agents pulled up the line attached to a gallon bag of meth. The next place the dog had alerted was in a closet. A small throw rug covered several floorboards that had been neatly sawed and put back in place. The floorboards had come out easily, and this time the agents seized another plastic bag containing heroin. In addition, a large framed Taurus revolver in a nylon shoulder holster was found under the floorboards. The revolver was chambered in .44 Magnum. Two cell phones, one found in the house and the other in Muller's pocket, were also seized.

The time on our initial search warrant for Muller's residence had expired. The DA quickly drafted an amendment and took it over to the judge to be signed.

Two agents and two deputies returned to the residence. They secured the premises, which turned out to be unoccupied. They were looking for any items that might tie Muller to the events at Marcus Johnson's trailer. The search was exhaustive, and when it appeared that they would find nothing of additional value, they began to wrap things up. As an afterthought, one of Ricardo's people searched the coats hanging in a closet for a second time. But this time, he noticed a black nylon snowmobile type parka with damage to the right sleeve. It wasn't ripped; it was melted, just like what would happen if a flaming liquid was spilled on it. He turned the cuff inside out, and the fabric had melted through and would have burned the person wearing it. A disposable plastic lighter was found in the left front pocket. He seized and tagged the items.

Back at the office, we contacted the public defender representing

Muller, who said he could meet us at the jail in a couple of hours. It allowed us the time needed to prepare the criminal complaint.

I cuffed Muller at the waist. During that process, I noted a clear and recent burn scar on his right wrist. Muller and his attorney stayed stone-faced when Hablitch advised them of the new charges. We again advised Muller of his constitutional rights, and he did not respond. We advised the lawyer that we expected to have a preliminary hearing in the next couple of days. Muller remained silent. Then the DA gave Muller's lawyer a search warrant that allowed officers to examine Muller's arms. Muller was wearing a short-sleeved jail shirt over a long-sleeved sweatshirt. This was allowed during the colder months. The jailer removed the waist cuffs, and I told Muller to take off both shirts. He did not speak.

"Randy, you have to comply with their request," his lawyer said.

Muller didn't respond and did not make eye contact.

"Muller," I said. "Those shirts are coming off. Either you take them off, or we will by force."

He did not respond.

One of the jailers opened the cell door to let the DA and public defender out to the cell corridor. Muller saw an opportunity to launch an insane attack. He leaped forward, jumping on his public defender, and began viciously slugging him in the head. In a matter of seconds, the lawyer's glasses were smashed into his face, and he was bleeding profusely from several savage blows.

We tried to pull Muller off and restrain him, but his strength was animal-like, and no matter what we did, he was focused solely on trying to beat the public defender to death. The DA had the presence of mind to hit the jail alarm, and a deputy and state trooper came in from the driveway and joined the melee. It stopped as suddenly as it began, and Muller slumped to the floor like a rag doll, conscious, unresponsive, but smiling. We cuffed his hands and feet without resistance. The jailer brought up a restraint chair, and we all were relieved when he was strapped in.

Our part-time jail nurse, who was checking on another inmate, was summoned to the area. If the amount of blood pouring out of the public defender was any indication of the severity of his injuries, he was in bad shape. She started an examination and immediately told the jailer to get EMS forthwith.

The public defender was transported to the hospital.

Despite what just happened, we continued with the service of the search warrant for two reasons. First, it was during the attempted service of the warrant that the attack began, and we would have to document everything that had happened. Second, we needed to do whatever necessary to obtain the evidence we were looking for.

I took a pair of medical scissors and began to cut away Muller's shirt. I didn't have to go far. On his right wrist and forearm was a relatively recent burn. The location was consistent with what he may have gotten when the sleeve of his coat caught on fire.

I called the hospital to check on the condition of the lawyer. It was serious. The blows from Randy Muller had broken his eyeglasses, and pieces had been driven into his eye. Dr. May was at a loss when he tried to find an ophthalmologist anywhere within one hundred miles of Musky Falls, and Medflight was out on transport. Then Dr. Chali showed up and had a potential solution. An ophthalmologist close to Musky Falls had stopped by the hospital to visit and had run into Chali. She was from Houston, Texas, but had strong ties to Namekagon County and had a family lodge on Gillich's Bay. After she left, Dr. Chali did what any self-respecting person would do; he Googled her. It seems that Dr. Orengo was not just any ophthalmologist; she was a world-renowned eye surgeon. Dr. Chali had a business card with a mobile phone number, but there would be no cellular service for sure at Gillich's Bay.

Deputy Holmes knew which cabin she bought. He and his wife had looked at it but found it out of their reach. At my request, Holmes left Musky Falls at high speed. He ran as hard as he could, lights and siren. When he pulled in, Dr. Orengo opened the door a crack, the door held by a security chain. Once Holmes explained the situation, the doctor said she would be ready to go in five minutes. She came out wearing a Happy Hooker Bait and Tackle sweatshirt, jeans, and a full-length winter coat. Once in the squad car, she asked Deputy Holmes if she could talk to the hospital on the police radio. He switched to the right channel, and she was in charge, directing staff on what she would need to attempt the surgery. One of the hospital staff members she was communicating with asked her to repeat herself. Dr. Orengo did but told the person they should take notes if they had such a short memory.

They arrived at the hospital and were in the surgical suite within ten minutes. An experienced surgical nurse had been assigned to assist. When the doctor saw the victim's eye, she simply said, "Oh my God, we have a lot to do."

I had my hands full, but I knew better than to let craziness drive the situation. The public defender was being cared for, and no one else sustained injuries in the onslaught that needed attention.

Muller had been removed from the restraint chair and was locked up in a segregated cell. The cell area was equipped with two cameras, and he would be under around-the-clock surveillance. He was issued a new jail shirt and long-sleeved undershirt.

I was ready to go home, but I felt responsible for the situation with the public defender. I stopped at the hospital to check on his condition. Dr. Orengo had been at it for three hours, and there had been no communication other than the surgical nurse requested two bottles of water. It was two more hours before they were finished. The surgeon had saved the lawyer's eye. Healing would take some time, but the prognosis was good.

256 | JEFF NANIA

Ricardo called me and asked to meet back at my office.

"Things have certainly turned ugly around here. What happened with Muller's lawyer?"

I explained the situation.

"Sounds really bad. I do have some good news for you. My people and I are going to be out of your hair, at least for now. We have burned ourselves up and leaving undercover agents in place at this point would be dangerous for them. Malone has pulled the plug on our 'Up North' operation," Ricardo explained. "I wish we could have done better. Leaving a case with loose ends really pisses me off. It looks like those who are locked up are going to plead out. We got some information, but I am convinced they don't know anything about the murders."

"What about Deacon Gunther?" I asked.

"I would guess he's here for the long haul. We heard he is living in an apartment above the bar at Outlaws. He was probably driving the SUV that took Muller away after he killed Marcus Johnson. It sounds like Muller has got a real problem with going back inside. Maybe when he starts hearing the doors slamming in his sleep, he will decide to work something out," Ricardo said. "We are heading out tonight. My crew is excited to be home for Christmas. Sheriff Cabrelli, it has been a real pleasure. If you ever need me, call."

Ricardo left as he had shown up—one day a hundred percent there, the next day one hundred percent gone. ❦

CHAPTER 29

Randy Muller's preliminary hearing was set for the next Monday. The news media had run long and hard on Muller's arrest for murder and the attack on his lawyer.

Partly as a result of a shortage of available public defenders and partly because no one wanted to represent him, the clerk contacted everyone on the list and either got voicemail or no answer at all. Local lawyers avoided Judge Kritzer's courtroom like the plague. The judge ordered DA Hablitch to come to the courtroom for a status meeting.

"Mr. District Attorney, we have reached out to many lawyers who may or may not agree to represent Randy Muller. It is difficult to determine because none of them will take my calls. I suspect this has something to do with one of their own being a victim of such a severe attack. While I am somewhat sympathetic, I am not confused about the fact that the constitution provides for legal counsel. Rather than go through the trouble of bringing him into court, let's go and see him in his cell."

The judge spoke through the door of seg cell.

"Mr. Muller, I am Judge Kritzer. My staff and I have been trying diligently to find a lawyer to represent you. We have had no success.

You will have to remain in jail without any further proceedings before the court until we can secure counsel to represent you."

Muller stared cold-eyed at the judge and DA, and finally he spoke. "I'm not going back to prison. I didn't kill no one." And he retreated to the corner of his cell.

Judge Kritzer and DA Hablitch returned to the courtroom.

"I expect you will help me locate someone for this job, Mr. District Attorney."

"I'll do my best, Your Honor."

―――――――――

On my way home, I turned off the highway and came upon a truck with its flashers on at the Spider Creek bridge. I pulled up and got out to see if they needed help. I laughed when I saw that it was Ed, Stella, and Amber Lockridge. It was nice to see some friendly faces.

"Hey, you are blocking the road," I said jokingly.

"Sorry about that, Sheriff. Didn't figure anyone would be by while we checked our traps."

"How's trapping?" I asked.

"Been, real, real good. Amber, show him what you got," Ed prompted.

Amber, smiling, held up four muskrats by their tails.

"Amber set those traps herself. They're close enough to home that she's been checking them regularly. She sure got lucky today. Good fur, nice looking rats," Stella said proudly.

"But look at what Grandpa got!" said Amber.

Ed walked over to the bed of the truck and hoisted up a huge beaver. Not that I was an expert, but it was the biggest beaver I'd ever seen.

"Holy smokes, Ed! That thing is huge," I said.

"Yup, I am guessing sixty-five pounds or so. Look at the hide, almost completely black. This will make someone a nice hoop or comforter.

It will sure bring top dollar."

"With a beaver that big and old, I will have to start cooking the meat up tonight for it to be fit to eat tomorrow night," Stella added.

"She and I got different ideas what the best beaver is. For me, the bigger, the better. I like a big, beautiful hide. She likes the smaller ones. They fit in her pot just perfect."

"Say, Sheriff, I heard on the radio last night that you still got your hands full with all those troublemakers. Any idea who is behind all this?" Stella asked.

"We have one in jail for murder now, but we still have work to do."

"Yeah, the radio said it was Randy Muller you got in jail. He's a bad one, that's for sure," Ed said.

It was nice to see the Lockridges, but I had no urge to discuss the case anymore today.

"Well, I'll be on my way. It was nice to see you folks."

"Nice to see you too, Sheriff. By the way, it's going to get cold tonight and stay that way for a week. It ought to make some good ice. The fish like to school up at the point right out from your place. If you got a mind to, go down to the Happy Hooker, get yourself a couple of dozen minnows and a few chartreuse or bright pink half-ounce jigs with long gold hooks. Drill a hole about twenty or thirty feet off the point. If you did that, I think you would catch a bunch of fish. Ms. Carlson would likely be happy if you brought fish caught through what we call first ice. I know there's not much Stella likes better than first ice fish. Isn't that right, Stella?"

"I do. Maybe we should give that point a try ourselves," Stella answered.

"We might have to do just that. Maybe we'll see you out there, Sheriff," Ed replied.

I slowly drove down the road the rest of the way home.

I walked in to find Julie sitting by the fire reading. She looked up at me through her reading glasses. She hated them and said they made her look like an old schoolmarm; I thought they looked cute.

"Howdy, stranger," she said.

"Hi, honey," I said as I dropped down into my chair. I tipped my head back to the headrest and closed my eyes.

"You look exhausted," she said.

"That is because I am."

"Is there anything I can do for you?" she asked.

"The God's truth is, you're doing it. This situation has been hard on everyone. Martha Bork packed up to visit her sister after telling Len he was retiring after thirty long years. Ricardo and his crew took off to their next assignment."

"To be honest, John, I did not care for him."

"He's definitely an acquired taste."

"Does he have a family?" Julie asked.

"No, he was married once, and his wife left him while he was on a case. He didn't even notice she was gone."

"That is something we are going to get better at, John. We will figure out a way to keep each other in the loop about where we are and what we're doing. Just a short call or a text or a message, anything to keep us connected. Can we work on that?"

"We can, and we'll keep at it until we get it right."

———

Sleep would not come. My mind was going in a dozen different directions. I was missing something. There was a key out there that would open the right door when put in the lock. The other reason I couldn't sleep was that I was scared. The idea that the Czechs were behind this and starting to run their operations in the area was terrifying. They were vicious and ruthless. They would be the worst thing that ever happened to the north country. Yet, there was no other explanation. The sale of illegal drugs was big business, and this was the perfect place for them to be.

I got out of bed and went downstairs to use the landline. I called Bear's cell number, and he answered.

"Geez, Cabrelli, don't you ever sleep?" he asked.

"I need you to do something, Bear, that only you can do."

"What's that, John?" he asked.

"I need to know if it is a reincarnation of the Czech gang that is killing off people in my county. I know we think it is, and it makes all the sense in the world, but I need to know for sure."

"I can't tell you one way or the other, John, because I don't know. Nobody does. I mean, you gotta get real here. Who else could it be?"

"I need to know if it's them. I need to know where to start looking. We are nowhere. Even your investigators are spinning their wheels. I need to know," I said.

"What do you want me to do that I haven't already done?"

"Get to your contacts in the FBI. There is no way they didn't come out of that major operation at Superior Shipping and Container with a few snitches. They are masters at developing inside information networks. You need to get us to somebody that is handling somebody still on the inside."

"I don't know if I can. I don't know if I have that kind of pull," Bear said.

"Bear, just do it. Whatever it takes, just do it before things get more out of control here."

"I'll do what I can, John, but no promises."

"I need some answers, and the sooner, the better."

"Fine. I'll see what I can come up with. Now go to bed. We all know how crabby you are when you don't get your sleep."

I didn't even say goodbye. I just hung up.

I don't know what time I eventually fell asleep, but the sun was already high in the sky when I woke. Julie was long gone to school. I poured a cup of coffee and walked outside. The outdoor thermometer registered nine degrees, and there was a stiff breeze from the northwest. The lake was frozen over. I walked down to the shore. I wasn't wearing a coat, but the chilly wind felt good. The surrounding landscape was solitary. I looked in every direction and saw no one. I craved the solitude. I needed the cleansing breath of the cold winter wind. If for only a minute, I needed to escape the constant demands of the job. Soon enough, standing outside in a t-shirt and sweatpants lost its luster, and I went inside.

I got cleaned up and scrounged the refrigerator for breakfast. I put on my boots and parka and went outside again. I walked on the ice along the shore. I noticed things I hadn't seen before. With the vegetation dead and lying down, I could see the structure of the shoreline. Rocks were a common theme, some in their natural place, others carefully positioned to curtail shoreline erosion. I wondered how long people had been building things with rocks. My guess was since there were people.

After walking long enough to clear my head to some degree, I turned around and started back. I caught a glimpse of movement off the point. Soon, a line of five wolves came into focus—a pack on the hunt, leaving the land to cross the lake in search of something to eat—the magnificent predators of the north country. The predators I was chasing were likely more vicious and not so magnificent.

I made my way back to the cabin, took off my cold-weather gear, stoked the fire, got coffee and sat down with my feet up. If the world needed me right now, they were going to have to wait. I leaned my head back, closed my eyes, and drifted to sleep.

My pager and landline remained silent for over an hour before waking me up. Randy Muller had gotten a lawyer. He intended to meet with Muller that day. Due to Muller's violent and unpredictable behavior, I had left explicit instructions regarding how to handle contact with him.

The first official day of winter was upon us. Cold weather had decided to get a leg up on things. Temperatures dropped, and the landscape ruled by water was freezing in earnest, adding inches of ice each cold day. Springs and creeks fought the annual futile battle with ice. The wind picked up, which drove the temperature to a below zero windchill. The exhaust from my squad sent a cloud skyward. There were a lot of old cars and trucks still on the road in Namekagon County, and I would guess that while a fair number of them might have nonfunctioning air conditioners, none would have a heater that didn't work. In his never-ending north country education program, Doc O'Malley told me a good truck starts, drives, has functional windows, working four-wheel drive, and a good heater. Anything more was window dressing.

It was cold and snowing when I drove into town. However, the weather did not deter the hearty residents of Namekagon County. In the city park, an army of volunteers was getting ready for the winter solstice celebration. Each year the community came together to celebrate the longest night and shortest day of the year. Darkness and cold had come to the north country. It was also officially the first day of winter. After December 21, we would gain a bit of daylight each day.

I stopped to see how things were going. A huge rotisserie grill built by a local welding shop held two deer. It rotated slowly over a wood fire under the watchful eye of the chief cook. Nearby kettles were being prepared and filled with peanut oil. When the oil was hot, the plucked and cleaned wild turkeys harvested in the spring or fall would be immersed and rapidly cooked. Wild rice and cranberry dishes were prepared. Ed and Stella Lockridge were onboard with fry bread. Bud was cutting and stacking the ricks of wood for the bonfire that would be the central gathering point.

In a couple of hours, people would start finding their way to the park. Although just a few days before Christmas, winter solstice was a different type of celebration. The city maintenance crew was hauling over all the concert in the park benches and putting together a wooden stage for the annual talent show.

The official lighting of the bonfire would take place at five, and the party would begin. Locals and tourists attended the celebration. There was no charge for admission, and the food was free. There was a suggested donation of five dollars, but it was not required, and any money raised went to the Giving Tree to help provide Christmas gifts to children in the county.

I started back to my squad and saw Julie had parked behind me. Her suburban doors flew open, and kids bolted out of every seat wearing identical Northern Lakes sweatshirts. She called them together and reminded them of their responsibility to help the city crew arrange the benches and put up the bandstand.

"Looks like we are just in time. The crew is unloading the benches now. Kids, you go over and get started. I will be over in a minute. I need to talk with Sheriff Cabrelli," Julie directed.

The kids snickered and laughed.

"Boy, Sheriff, you must be in big trouble for something," one boy said, and the whole group laughed and ran off to help with the benches.

In front of God and everybody, Julie stepped over to me, wrapped her arms around me, and kissed me. She and I were careful about doing anything that might get unwanted notice, so this PDA was not expected, but it sure was welcome.

"John, I can't possibly understand all the stress you are under. I know the pressure must be incredible. I just want you to know that I will stand with you through this, and I love you."

She gave me another hug that her students did not miss, and they responded with some hoots and hollers.

"I have got to corral my students," she said. Two steps later, she was in teacher mode, heading to where the benches were being unloaded.

I drove over to the jail and checked in. My timing was perfect. Lois jumped up when I walked in.

"Sheriff, you have a visitor," she warned.

A squat man with dandruff covering the shoulders of his ill-fitting three-piece black suit charged forward to meet me.

"Sheriff John Cabrelli. Are you Sheriff John Cabrelli?"

"I am, and you are?"

"I am Sydney Cravitz, an attorney with the Public Defense Fund. I am representing Randy Muller, an inmate in your jail. Let's get right down to business, shall we? I have spoken with Mr. Muller, which is actually my first issue. I was only able to speak with him through the communication slot on a segregation cell. The deputy refused to bring him to an attorney-client conference room. He said that you had forbidden any movement without your express order. That will need to change. I demand the same access to my client as anyone else incarcerated here. If you cannot arrange that, I will be glad to go in front of the judge."

"Attorney Cravitz, do you know why I put that order in place?"

"No, and I don't care. See that the change is made. I have also noted that Randy Muller is being held in conditions inconsistent with recent court decisions regarding incarceration of more than forty-eight hours. The segregation cell where Muller is being kept appears to be a remnant of some earlier corrections era. It offers the prisoner no privacy, even when to take care of necessary bodily functions, and provides the jailers a view of the prisoner no matter where he is. It is akin to putting the prisoner in a cage, like an animal on display. This type of incarceration is being used to intimidate my client. Due to this, he is suffering from a high level of anxiety, which is preventing him from sleeping at night."

Attorney Cravitz cited several recent decisions of higher courts of which he claimed Namekagon County, the Namekagon County Jail, and I were in violation. Cravitz demanded his client be moved to more appropriate accommodations immediately or be released on bond.

He continued on. He maintained that his client was a drug user and suffering ill effects of withdrawal and had been suffering an erratic heartbeat. According to the law, Muller deserved to be evaluated by a doctor. He demanded that the situation be remedied immediately. He had already filed a copy of his affidavit with the court.

He handed me a copy, and it was at least fifty pages long.

I went to my office and called the DA to get his opinion.

"John, Kritzer just called me. He said that if this comes in front of him, he will rule against us and in favor of Cravitz's client. Do what you need to do to make this right as quickly as you can. As the sheriff and keeper of the jail, it is up to you to respond to Attorney Cravitz and advise him of your plan to rectify the situation. If you can't rectify the situation, the judge will have no choice but to consider bail."

"No way Kritzer is going to let Muller out on bond. The guy is dangerous."

"Then figure things out at the jail."

I called Cravitz's cell phone number and told him that we would remedy the situation immediately.

"Good. Let me know when it's done," he responded.

The Namekagon County jail is not a big facility, but it serves the community's needs in most cases. I had known somewhere in the back of my mind that the barred seg cell that held Muller was not going to work long term. I needed to keep Muller and Winslow far enough apart that there could be no communication. Winslow was the key to our case, and we didn't want anything to happen to him. Muller knew him and would get at him any way he could.

I called the sheriff in the next county south of Namekagon. After I explained my situation, he agreed to house Winslow in his jail. He wanted these guys gone as much as anyone. County lines don't mean much to drug dealers.

I transported Winslow, and I pushed the limits to get back to Namekagon County. On the way, I phoned in and asked for two additional personnel to meet me at the jail to assist in moving Muller. I directed the jailer on duty to do a thorough shakedown of the cell block. The last thing I wanted was for Muller to find something he could use for a weapon.

When I arrived, Deputies Pave and Delzell were ready to help with the move.

"Randy, your lawyer wants us to move you to a different cell. He feels the accommodations in this one are not as nice as they should be. We have a cell block with no other inmates in it, so that's where you are going. We are moving you now, and I hope you are not considering giving us any trouble. Are you thinking about fighting again, Randy?" I asked.

"No," he replied.

Cuffed and shackled for a move around the corner may seem like overkill to some. It's those same people who become victims of their own stupidity.

Muller was moved and locked in without incident. The cell block was outfitted with a video camera with around-the-clock monitoring at both the booking counter and dispatch center. Even so, I wanted Muller to be checked on as often as possible. I called Attorney Cravitz to let him know the move had been made and advised him the jail nurse would complete an evaluation in the morning, and if warranted, we would get a doctor to see him. Cravitz wanted to know exactly when the nurse would be there. I didn't know, but I told him I would call him when they let me know.

I needed the air and a walk and headed over to the city park. The cold felt cleansing. There was a crowd, and the mood was happy. I found Julie near the proposed location of the bonfire, watching her students. Her rule was to turn over the kids to their parents or another pre-approved responsible adult after five o'clock. All the kids had found family or were in the process of doing so. Amber was still with her.

"Hey, Amber," I said. "How are you doing? Did you get those muskrats skinned?"

"I have got them skinned and stretched, Sheriff," she responded politely.

"Good for you," I replied.

"I better go over to help Grandma and Grandpa," she said.

"One thing, Amber. Tell them to save a plate of fry bread for me," I requested.

"Okay, Sheriff, I'll tell them," and Amber skipped off to help.

"She seems like a happier girl these days," I said.

"John, the difference is remarkable. I can't imagine the stress she has been under all these years. With her mother gone and under the care of her grandparents, she is finally getting the chance to be a kid."

Our conversation was interrupted by a booming voice. Bud stood next to a neatly stacked woodpile about six feet high. The crowd quieted down. "Everyone stand back," he shouted!

Then Bud struck a single wooden stick match with his thumbnail. He held it for a second and then threw it into the center of the firepit. It was followed by a *whoosh*, and the pile burst into flames. The crowd laughed and cheered. The winter solstice party had officially begun.

Realizing I was starving, I dragged Julie over to the food line. My plate was almost overflowing before we made it halfway down the line. We grabbed lemonades and sat down at a picnic table. Bud joined us. The wild rice and venison were perfect flavor complements, and I savored every bite. Stella came over with a plate heaped with fry bread and set it on the table between us.

"Amber gave me orders to make sure you get your fill. If you need more after this, come on over," she said with a smile.

We ate and laughed, and for a few minutes at least, my troubles were swept away by the surrounding joy. Bud told us that he thought there would be plenty of ice on the lake after a few more days of the cold weather to get out and do some ice fishing.

People started to move toward the bonfire and take their places on the benches. The DJ from the *Voice of the North* was the master of ceremonies and boomed out a happy solstice greeting.

"Tonight, we are part of a tradition that has been going on for over twelve thousand years. Winter is now upon us, and so is the darkness. It is time for the earth to rest and renew, and each day from here forward, the light shines longer upon us. We have dined tonight on sustenance the land has given us, the deer that roam the woods, the Canada geese that fly past on their way south. Wild rice and cranberries that have fed generations. We are partaking in a tradition like many before us. Now we must give thanks for our bounty. It does not matter who it is you worship, your religion, color, ethnicity, or creed; all that matters is that you give thanks for what you have. If you feel that you have too little, maybe that is so, but always know there is someone with less. Now look to the sky and give thanks."

The crowd raised their faces to the celestial night, and silence reigned. The power of gratitude was overwhelming.

"Now," the DJ said, "we will begin the competition. We have ten entries for the top spot on our talent show. First up is Stan, the one-man band."

Stan took the stage wearing an old pair of coveralls and a shapeless straw broad-brimmed hat. He held an instrument that was a banjo, drum, harmonica, kazoo, and trumpet all in one. He also had a cymbal strapped on the inside of each knee. The crowd quietly chuckled in anticipation. Stan announced he would be playing a medley of north country songs, including the "Logging Song" and "Girl from the Northwoods." Then he struck up the one-man band and created a joyful musical ruckus to the pleasure of all. He ended with a harmonica and banjo number.

Stan was followed by such notables as Otto Round and the Tuba Sound, a barbershop quartet with only three members, and a folk-singing duo.

Julie slipped away for a minute, and I saw her walking with a young girl up to the bandstand. After an encouraging hug from Julie, the girl climbed on stage and took her place behind the microphone. Stan of the one-man band, who had shed all of his instruments except a guitar, joined her.

She was introduced as seventeen-year-old Eva Zachery. She smiled at the crowd, but I could see she was nervous. The audience was respectfully quiet in anticipation. Stan struck a chord and began to play the guitar, providing the cue for Eva to let it all go, and let it all go she did. She sang her song in a way that only comes from natural talent, celebrating the high notes, the low notes, and every note in between. She sang a north country ballad of hardship and happiness, rivers and forests. When the song ended, the crowd was silent. Eva stood frozen at the microphone stand. A moment later, thundering applause and cheers began. The crowd clamored for an encore, which she delivered.

The contestants came back to the stage and stood shoulder to shoulder. Audience applause would determine the winner. The DJ put his hand above each contestant's head, and the crowd cheered for their favorite.

When they got to Otto Round and the Tuba Sound, Otto took the microphone and said, "Let's not waste any more time with this."

He walked over and put his hand above Eva Zachery, and the applause and cheers made it clear who the winner was.

Bud kept the fire blazing, and people gathered around the bonfire. The party was far from over and was known to go well into the early morning hours. I, however, was done for. I sat on a bench by the fire, and Julie came to sit next to me.

"Honey, I am ready to head home," I said. "I am beat, and with any luck, I might get some sleep. The preliminary hearing for Randy Muller is tomorrow, and I have got to be at the DA's office first thing."

"Let me give you a ride over to your squad, and I'll follow you home," she said.

"Don't you have to stick around and help clean up?"

"Normally I would, but tonight they are just going to have to do without me. I am coming home with you."

The thermometer outside the house registered one degree. Inside our cozy cabin, we hung up our coats, took off our boots, and put on our slippers. I sat down at the computer to check messages.

"Are you going to work for a while?" Julie asked.

"I am going to check my messages. Then I will come to bed."

"I am going up now," she said with a twinkle in her eye. "I will be waiting for you."

Suddenly any waiting messages didn't seem so important. ❦

CHAPTER 30

I was on the road the next morning before light. Snow continued and was rapidly accumulating. I got into town, parked, grabbed a cup of coffee, and walked up to the jail.

I asked the jailer how Randy Muller was getting along.

"Sheriff, that guy is strange. He hasn't spoken one word since we moved him. I mean not one word."

I went over to the cell block where Muller was held. He was sitting on the bench at the common table.

I tried to talk to him, but the only response I got was him fixing me with his best and most intimidating stare.

"Muller, we will be here to get you for court at nine thirty. I am going to have the jailer open the shower stall for you so you can clean up. He'll put a set of clean jail fatigues through the hatch door. You decide whether to get yourself presentable for court. The shower stall will be open for ten minutes, no more," I offered.

Muller didn't respond.

The jailer and the deputy brought unkempt Muller to the courtroom. Several people from the news media were present. The judge called the court to order and began the process of a preliminary hearing.

The list of charges was lengthy: arson, battery to a police officer, resisting arrest, delivery of a controlled substance, aggravated battery, mayhem, and last but not least, first-degree intentional homicide. An impressive list, even for someone like Randy Muller.

"Mr. Muller, what is your response to these charges?" the judge began.

Again, Muller didn't reply.

"On behalf of my client, we wish to plead not guilty to all charges," Attorney Cravitz said.

"Is that correct, Mr. Muller?" the judge asked.

Again, no response.

"The court will accept a not guilty plea to all charges, Mr. Muller. Is there anything else?" Judge Kritzer asked.

"Yes, Your Honor, there is," Cravitz replied.

"Go ahead, Attorney Cravitz," the judge said.

"Due to the unusual circumstances regarding my representation of Randy Muller, DA Hablitch has furnished me with documentation regarding the charges against my client. I would ask the court to order all documentation regarding the current charges against my client to be in my possession before the end of business today, including the alleged eyewitness statement to the homicide. I believe the prosecutor has or is in the process of making a deal with the eyewitness they intend to have testify against my client. I would like to know the terms of that agreement."

"Mr. District Attorney, do you have anything to say?" the judge asked.

"Your Honor, we do have a subject currently in protective custody. He is being held as a material witness in the homicide of Marcus Johnson. He is an eyewitness to the killing of Marcus Johnson as well as the firebombing of his home. We have a sworn statement from the witness. The witness is also currently being held on criminal charges, and we have reached an agreement with him—leniency in exchange for his testimony," DA Hablitch responded.

"I would assume that the district attorney would move cautiously with any such arrangement. For now, I would like to ask the defendant a question or two. Mr. Muller, you are charged with some very serious crimes. If you are convicted of these crimes, you would be spending the rest of your life behind bars. Do you understand the gravity of this situation?"

Muller said nothing.

"Again, Mr. Muller, do you understand the seriousness of the charges against you?"

Again, no reply.

"Very well, Mr. Muller, based on the information in the criminal complaints, I find the district attorney has established probable cause. You will be held without bond. We will tentatively set the court date for January 25. Court is adjourned."

With a sweep of his robes, the judge left the bench and went to his chambers. We took Muller back to the jail and put him in the cell block.

———————

I was convinced Randy Muller killed Marcus Johnson on behalf of Deacon Gunther and believed Gunther probably drove the getaway car. I was equally sure that whoever killed Devin Martin, Jesse Gunther, and Tony Carter was still out there. As if he read my mind, I got a call from Bear.

"John, it seems as though your past adventures in law enforcement and playing well with the FBI have gotten you some additional street cred. They have some information for you regarding the involvement of the eastern Europeans in the homicides you are investigating."

He gave me the phone number. "This is a direct line to the agent in charge that is handling all this. They have sources of information and will attempt to answer any questions you might have. I suggest you call him today."

"Thanks, Bear. I'll get right on it."

"Good luck."

I called the number, and a woman answered.

"Sheriff Cabrelli?" she asked.

"Yes, this is John Cabrelli."

"I am Special Agent Cheryl Shell of the FBI. I understand that you think we may have some information for you that will assist you in the investigation of multiple homicide cases."

"That's what I am hoping for," I replied.

"Sheriff, the special agent in charge has directed my unit to provide you with any assistance you request. This is not always the way we handle things of this nature. However, we are all aware of the valuable role you played in the situation at Superior Shipping and Container. But most of all, helping to put one of our own to rest. My supervisor has briefed me regarding your situation. In addition, he furnished me with reports regarding four homicides. You may have to fill in the gaps, but let's start and see what I can do."

"Agent Shell, we have a drug turf war going on in Namekagon County. There have been five drug-related homicides, including an overdose. The most recent homicide is consistent with what I have come to expect, in my experience, from drug gangs. They shot a drug lab chemist and firebombed the mobile home used as a lab. The perp jumped into a waiting SUV and took off. We have a witness and someone in custody for that crime.

"The other killings are different. They are more thought out. I mean... I don't know. A drive-by is one thing; these are another. I know some people arrested during the Superior Shipping and Container raid were eastern Europeans running their own drug network on the side. I also know many of them had military experience. I think some of these people slipped through the cracks and set up a new operation. It is the same territory they were working before, so they know the lay of the land. I figure they are taking out the competition and making sure everyone knows that they are running the show. From what I understand, it's how they do business," I explained.

A few moments passed before she said anything.

"Sheriff Cabrelli, that is exactly how they do business. They move in, hammer the competition with extraordinary violence, and make sure those left know who is running things. A bombing using timing devices is well within their bag of tricks. Leaving one of the bosses from another outfit to rot in the sun is just standard operating procedure. So, your theory makes complete sense, except for one thing."

"What's that, Agent Shell?" I asked.

"It's not them," she stated.

"How do you know?"

"Sheriff, this is where we get into the sensitive area. The information I am about to give you is on a need-to-know basis. The SAC advised me that being anything less than completely candid with you was not acceptable. The information I am going to give you must remain confidential. The lives of several of your fellow law enforcement officers could be jeopardized," Shell warned.

"I understand."

"Sheriff Cabrelli, as you have suggested, some of them did fall through the cracks. Some did not, and they have found that working with us is a much better alternative to being deported. They feel that way because we have solid information that the first batch we deported did not fare so well on their home ground. They are either being held in a maximum-security hell hole, or they are dead. This criminal gang is somewhat unique. They are tightly knit and share information with each other, yet stab the person next to them in the back without a second thought. They are establishing a drug distribution network, but not in your county and not methamphetamines. They are in the process of developing a heroin pipeline from Mexico to the Twin Cities. They began this process within weeks of the raid on Superior Shipping and Container."

"How do you know that they aren't in Namekagon County?" I asked.

The agent chuckled, "That's the good part. They don't like you guys and are avoiding you like the virus. They have often expressed that had they not ventured into a little town and instead stayed in the city, they would not have been noticed."

"You're sure of this?"

"Sheriff, we have people on the inside, and I asked them the same question. They are positive."

"It's like good news, bad news. It is good news that they are doing business elsewhere. It is bad news that I am back to zero."

"Well, Sheriff, maybe not. My colleagues and I discussed your situation at length. We agree the murder of Devin Martin and the bombing of the first meth lab were a world apart from the killing of Marcus Johnson and bombing his trailer lab. That was just the Northwoods version of an urban drive-by—shoot somebody, start a fire, run back to the getaway vehicle, and drive away as fast as you can.

"The other two took patience, planning, and a certain level of skill. We think it is somebody sending a message, maybe payback. It's hard to know. Maybe the shell casing on the floor of the SUV was left on purpose to make it look like a suicide but left enough evidence to show otherwise. Maybe they wanted to see how smart you were. The cash, guns, and drugs they left in the car? As you stated in your case notes, 'No way a drug dealer would leave that stuff.' You covered two possibilities. Maybe the shooter was disturbed by an unexpected passerby, left the stuff, and took off. Or maybe it wasn't noticed. Then again, maybe the shooter knew it was there but didn't want it. We think there is a distinct possibility this wasn't about a drug war. Maybe this was all about the victims. Gunther and his people run with a bad, bad crowd. Devin Martin was as ruthless as

Deacon Gunther. They have no doubt made lots of enemies. Some of these guys have long memories. There might be a pattern to all this. If so, find the pattern, and you'll find your killer. Do you have any more questions for me?"

"No, Agent Shell, not right now."

"Sheriff, if you do, get in touch."

"Thanks, I will."

———

I went to the jail before I went back out on the road. Muller's change from trying to kill everyone he could put his hands on to being completely unresponsive was something we needed to pay attention to. It could be a ruse, him waiting for the next chance to get free.

"What's Muller doing?" I asked the jailer.

"Ever since you brought him back from court, he has just been laying on his bunk, back to us, and hasn't said a word."

I walked up to the cell door.

"Randy, it's me, the sheriff. Can we get you anything?"

Surprisingly, he answered. "I want to take a shower and put on clean clothes."

"I offered you that before court."

"I didn't want to then. I want to now."

"Fine. I'll have the jailer bring you back a change of clothes. Ten minutes, no more."

The jailer, backed up by another deputy, gave Muller clean clothes. Then he instructed Muller to stand in front of the shower room door. He triggered the electronic lock, allowing the door to open, and Muller stepped inside.

I left the building to clear my head. The cold air was bracing and refreshing. I was gone no more than ten minutes when both my radio and pager went off.

It was the dispatcher directing me to respond to a jail emergency. I sprinted back, knowing it had to be Randy Muller. My mind raced about how he had gotten his chance to escape and taken it. I ran up the steps to the jail as EMS screamed in.

I got to Muller's cell and immediately realized his escape had been successful.

The jailer was over the top of Muller, trying to breathe life into him. A braided long-sleeved jail shirt was wrapped around his neck. The EMTs arrived and jumped in. All attempts at resuscitation were unsuccessful. Randy Muller was dead. ✦

CHAPTER 31

It was a white Christmas. Snow began to fall on Christmas Eve day and did not stop until Christmas Day evening. Bud, Julie, and I celebrated together on Christmas Eve. I made spaghetti, meatballs, and garlic bread from a recipe I found in one of Aunt Rose's dog-eared cookbooks. The recipe was handwritten, and at the top, she noted, "Nick and Johnny's favorite." It was delicious. Bud announced it was his new second favorite just behind Julie's pan-fried walleyes.

We had a relaxed, low-key evening, talking together and listening to the radio, which played nonstop holiday oldies. Julie read while Bud and I played a game or two of cribbage. No pages, no calls. The world left us alone. We exchanged gifts that fell under the twenty-five-dollar rule. I gave Julie a pack of special tea and *Natural Connections*, a book by a local author and naturalist Emily Stone. We gave Bud a book we found in an antique store, *Common Sense Building with Timbers*. I got a set of Mepps #5, gold spinner bucktails.

The snow was piling up, and we asked Bud if he wanted to stay the night, but he declined. Once in his truck, he plowed the driveway, and we saw his taillights going down the road.

Julie was off from Christmas Eve until the day after New Year's.

We hoped to relax as much as we could and maybe even spend some time together. Perhaps we'd even get snowed in.

———

We got up Christmas morning, and Julie made coffee and started steeping her Christmas tea. I stoked the woodstove, then brought in another armload of wood from the wood bin outside. We sat quietly together, looking out the picture window. The lake was covered with snow and ice. A wind blew lightly with fits and starts, blowing the snow around. Our home weather station said the temperature was nine degrees with a windchill of five. Across the bay, I saw a half dozen colorful tents and a couple of shacks set up on the ice. Locals and tourists take advantage of the abundant snow and ice between Christmas and the new year. Skiers, snowmobilers, anglers, and snowshoers put the trails through the forest to good use.

I finished my coffee and told Julie I was going out to the shop for a minute. Hanging behind the huge woodstove in the shop were four pairs of snowshoes. Two were made of bent ash strung artfully with rawhide. The others were a long pair of "trappers" and a short round pair of "bear paws." I took them down and looked them over. They were in perfect shape, but the rawhide was drying out and needed oiling—a task to put on my list. There were also two pairs of more modern snowshoes made of tubular aluminum and flexible rubber-like material. I took both pairs down. They were ready to go. I carried them out to the porch on the front of the cabin and leaned them against the log wall.

I went inside and called to Julie.

"Hey, honey, do you want to get bundled up and snowshoe across the bay to where they're ice fishing and see what they're catching?"

"Not a chance," she said.

When I found her, I knew why. She was submerged in the upstairs whirlpool tub (installed by my uncle to help my aunt's arthritis), surrounded by bubbles, reading her new book.

"John, I have earned and fully intend to enjoy every minute of reclining in this wonderful tub. However, if it is not too much trouble, it would be perfect if I could convince you to bring me a cup of the lemon, lavender, and honey tea I have brewed in the kitchen."

"I would be delighted."

The tea delivered, I left Julie to her book and bubbles. With my cold-weather gear on, I walked outside and stepped into my snowshoes. I adjusted the binding and began my hike across the bay, cutting across the surface of the same water I swam in only a few months before. I kept a fair pace but didn't kill myself. As I walked, I realized I had become truly enamored of this landscape regardless of the season. Uncle Nick and I had ice fished one winter in this very bay. He had outfitted me with a set of junior size snowshoes. As we trekked together across the snow and ice, I remember pretending I was an arctic explorer.

Some ice anglers were in shelters, and others sat out on the ice in camp chairs or on buckets. All were dressed in standard Namekagon County winter wear: coveralls, heavy coat, gloves, and an insulated hat with earflaps. I was happy to see several adults accompanied by the next generation. School was out, and instead of sitting home glued to a screen, these kids were in training to become the next generation of conservationists.

Several northern pike lay on the ice, most of them in the twenty-four-inch range, some bigger, some smaller, and a couple of nice walleyes.

One of the fishermen sitting on a white five-gallon bucket called over to me.

"Hey, Sheriff, how's it going? You checking licenses today? I've got mine right here."

"Nope, just out for a hike, seeing what I can see."

A man wearing a blaze orange bomber hat piped up, "Well, one thing you can see is that we have caught about ten northerns to every one of any other fish. I have been fishing Spider Lake for over fifty years, best damn musky lake in Wisconsin, never even saw a northern here until just a few years ago. Now they are taking over. You want to arrest somebody? Arrest the clown who put northerns in this lake! Then we'll hang him."

I had heard of the controversy regarding northern pike establishing a healthy population in the Spider Lake Chain. As a boy, I fished quite a bit with Uncle Nick, and we never caught a northern in Spider Lake. In recent years, something changed, and northern pike were now abundant. The DNR was trying to lower the population using angler participation. The good news was that northern pike, disliked or not, were good table fare.

While I was visiting with the anglers, a youngster let out a whoop. She hooked a fish, and the battle was on.

"Grandpa, I have got a big one!" she cried excitedly. "Help me with it."

Her grandfather told her to calm down in a gentle voice and reassured her she was doing just fine. She reeled, and the fish took line. When she thought she was making progress, the fish would make a mad dash. She was using a standard size rod and reel, not a small ice fishing rig. Good thing, or that fish would have been long gone. A small crowd watched the girl's hole in the ice. They were as excited as she was. The fish finally had enough, and it came to the hole. The girl shrieked with joy as she pulled the big musky's head through the ice. The other anglers gave her a round of applause. Then people began to move quickly. The fish measured forty-four inches. Photos of the girl and her prize were taken.

The girl and her grandpa quickly carried the fish over to one of the ice shanties. The shanty's owners removed some plywood covering, revealing a large rectangular hole in the ice. Now, wearing elbow-long rubber gloves, the grandpa eased the fish into the water and held it by the tail, slowly moving it back and forth. After a few precious moments, the fish began to come around and, with a sudden, powerful thrust, it swam back into the depths of the lake. I had no doubt catching that musky through the ice was more fun than any video game.

I said goodbye and started my trek back across the ice. I decided to go the long way around, which would bring me over to Spider Creek. When I got to where the lake flows into the creek, I could see that there was ice, but even as cold as it was, there was a lead of open water. I could easily make out deer tracks that came out of the woods and down to the water but had not crossed. A set of palm-size wolf tracks followed the deer trail. Northern Wisconsin was indeed wild country.

Back at the cabin, I pulled off my snowshoes, walked over to my squad, and sat crossways on the driver's seat to limit the amount of snow I got inside. I picked up the radio and called in to dispatch to check the status of life in Namekagon County. I would have been notified if there was anything important, but it was good to check in. As I had hoped, Christmas was quiet with few calls, and it remained that way until the new year. ❧

CHAPTER 32

We kept working the case following any potential lead with little to show for it. Randy Muller's suicide complicated the situation. Jack Wheeler had crafted a solid agreement for Tyler Winslow. Winslow gave a sworn deposition as required and was prepared to testify in open court against Randy Muller. The DA and his lawyer had even gone over his testimony. There was no doubt Muller would have been convicted. Tyler Winslow had kept his end of the bargain and would become a free man. In the meantime, he was brought back to the Namekagon County jail, awaiting some action by the court or DA. We were intentionally stalling.

Deacon Gunther and the rest of the crew did not know whether Tyler Winslow or Randy Muller, for that matter, shared information with us regarding the Marcus Johnson killing. While we knew there were others in the vehicle, unfortunately, Muller had said nothing, and Tyler Winslow didn't get a good look at them. Our investigation had turned up nothing, and unless someone who knew something flipped, we would stay right where we were.

Randy Muller, operating with Gunther's gang, was responsible for killing Marcus Johnson and blowing up his meth lab, presumably in retaliation for attacks on Gunther's people and operation. But retaliation against who? Who killed Devin Martin, Tony Carter, and Jesse Gunther? Who had blown Gunther's meth lab off the face of the earth?

Several experienced law enforcement officers were convinced attacks were orchestrated by the remnants of a gang of eastern Europeans. We were wrong. The FBI had convinced me it wasn't them. Our number one suspect was a zero.

The FBI agent said to look for a pattern. Find the pattern, find the killer.

I called Len Bork. "Len, got time to sit down and talk?"

"Sure, John. Where?"

"Your office in an hour?"

"Perfect. I'll have a cup of Campfire Blend and a blueberry scone."

I showed up on time with the goods. I explained the situation to Len. I didn't betray the FBI's confidence but said I was pretty sure the info was solid.

"John, we have had everybody and their brother helping us out with this, and we still aren't anywhere. It could very well be about Martin, Carter, and Gunther. Why not? I guarantee they have done some nasty stuff in their lives, stuff that people might not be willing to forgive or forget."

"What is our next step? Where do we go from here?"

"You are going to think I'm crazy," Len began. "But I think we ought to go to the horse's mouth. Let's go to Outlaws and have a sit-down with Deacon Gunther. As bad as it makes me feel, we are all on the same side, more or less. Let's ask him face-to-face who he thinks is knocking off his people. We may learn something; we may not."

"When?" I asked

"How about now?"

"Get in my truck, Len. I'll drive."

It was still before noon when we arrived at Outlaws, and I didn't know if people who partied until dawn would be up yet. I parked in front, and we walked up to the door as boldly as we could be. The front door was locked. I knocked on it. Len didn't feel I was making enough racket, so he kicked the door several times.

A window next to the door opened. A guy covered with tattoos wearing a headscarf spoke.

"Let me see the warrant."

"We don't have one," I replied.

"Then get off the property now," he growled.

"We want to talk to Deacon Gunther," Len said.

"There ain't nobody here by that name. Now get your asses out of here," he replied.

"Is that your final word?" I asked.

He started to close the window.

"Just one more minute before you close the window," I called.

He hesitated.

"We either talk to Gunther, or I am going to call the DA to get a search warrant. We will wait right here until it shows up. When the warrant gets here, my deputies and I will disassemble this shithole board by board."

"You got nothing on us to get no warrant," he said defiantly.

"Don't worry about that. I'll make something up," I said.

"And I am going to swear to it," Len added.

"Or you can let us talk to Gunther. You've got one minute," I said.

The front door opened. It was Deacon Gunther himself, looking as evil as ever.

"So talk," he said.

"Not out here. We're coming in and are going to sit down at a table like normal people," Len said.

"But just you, me, and the chief, here. Tell your guys to go about their business," I directed.

Gunther turned his back on us, walked over to a round table, and sat down with his back to the wall. He had an open beer in front of him. Len and I sat on either side.

"What do you want?" he demanded.

Gunther was an intimidating man. He wore the scars of many battles on his face, including a Frankenstein-looking one running down the left side of his head. He lit a cigarette and sat back.

"I've got a question for you," I said.

"Ask it so you can get the hell out of here," he replied.

"Who is taking out your people? Who took out your cousin Jesse, Devin Martin, and Tony Carter? Who blew up the lab?"

Gunther smoked for a while.

"Those aren't my people. What does 'my people' even mean? If you are going to start out stupid, then this is over. Jesse was my cousin. The other two were just people I knew," he said, playing a game he knew well.

"I don't care what your relationship was. I only want to know if you have any ideas about who might have taken them out."

"You should've asked that screwball, Randy Muller. He probably did it. I'm sure he spun you a line of bullshit trying to get a deal. Good thing he hung himself. Good thing for everyone," said Gunther.

"Nope, these killings were a step above Randy Muller's talents. Whoever did those hits spent time planning. Maybe they are just getting started, or maybe they're done. I don't know. Thing is, the easiest way to get them out of your life is to help us catch them," I explained.

Gunther lit up another cigarette and smoked for a while. He rapped the tabletop, and a guy from behind the bar brought him another beer.

"You guys want something to drink?" he asked.

We both declined.

"Well, I don't know who might have done those guys. It seems to me, all their troubles started when they moved to the promised land. My cousin was all jacked up about learning to fish. They must have got crossways with somebody up here. That's all I can figure."

"You think you might be next, Deacon?" I asked.

He laughed, "I've spent my whole life thinkin' I might be next. So far, I'm still here," he said shrewdly.

"No idea who might be behind the killings?" Len asked.

"Let me be straight with you. I don't have any idea at all about who killed those guys. If I did, I would tell you. Then you do what you do. Go get 'em and put 'em away. That would be alright by me. There are too damn many criminals in the world. But I don't have any idea. If I think of something, you guys will be the first to know. How's that?" Deacon said, ending our conversation.

We left the bar, and I had an urge to take a shower.

"What do you think, Len?"

"I don't think he knows who is behind this, and I think he's a little worried we don't know. He's a drug dealer, and he has had nothing but trouble in Namekagon County. His top guy, his cousin, and his chemist all get killed. That's bad for business, maybe bad for him."

"We've got a meeting with the DA tomorrow afternoon. Any thoughts about Tyler Winslow?" I asked.

"He kept his word. We need to keep ours. He needs to go free. Truth is, we'll get him again. He won't go far. A skunk doesn't change his stripes."

Tyler Winslow had been evaluated for witness protection. Given that he was a habitual criminal, a drug user, and the person he was going to testify against had hung himself, the evaluators didn't feel that he was enough at risk. The upside for him was that he avoided going to trial and maybe doing twenty-five years.

———

I got a call from Ricardo the next day.

"Hey there, Sheriff. How goes things in Mayberry? I kinda miss the place, although my doctor put me on cholesterol medication because of my addiction to the Fisherman's deep-fried cheese curds," he said.

"I'm headed over right now for a meeting with Len and the DA about cutting Tyler Winslow loose."

"That boy dodged the bullet. The bad guy he's going to testify against does himself in. For a while, I thought Gunther might come after him just for show. I don't think that anymore. To that end, I have some great news for you. Deacon Gunther and company have fled the scenic north country. They arrived in Milwaukee yesterday evening and have reestablished residence in their old digs. The word is they just don't see Namekagon County as the place to be. I wondered if you or one of your deputies could run out to his bar and see if it's locked up. It's not important, but information is good to have," Ricardo said.

"You're kidding me. Len and I met with Gunther yesterday and asked him if he knew who was knocking off his people. He didn't have anything. Guess he didn't want to stick around to find out what happens."

"Gone is good enough," Anthony replied.

"I'll swing by there and let you know," I said.

"Thanks, Sheriff. I'll catch up with you later," and he hung up.

———

The meeting with the DA included Tyler Winslow and Jack Wheeler. When Len and I walked in, it was clear they were already in the middle of a discussion.

"Sheriff, Chief, thanks for coming," the DA said.

We settled in, and Jack began.

"You guys have not kept your end of the bargain with my client. He is still locked up," Wheeler stated.

"He is still locked up by his own choice," I clarified.

"That is because he is afraid to walk out the door. You put a bullseye on his back and no protection," Wheeler said accusingly.

"You saw the review for witness protection. They don't feel he is at risk. At your request, we appealed the decision and got the same answer," the DA said.

"I have other news that is germane to this situation," I said. "I received information this morning that Gunther and his people have returned to the southeastern part of the state. I haven't confirmed it yet, but the source is impeccable," I said.

"They are gone for good?" Jack asked.

"I don't know, but they are gone for now," I replied. "That's good news for all of us."

"My client and I have an offer we think you should consider," Wheeler said. "Tyler has seen the error of his ways and wants to turn his life around. He would like to relocate to another community and start over. He needs some money to accomplish that. We are requesting twenty-five hundred dollars from the Witness/Victim Compensation Fund to get him on his way. Let us not forget he was instrumental in clearing a homicide."

"I do not feel that paying a criminal for doing his civic duty, for once in his life, is a precedent we want to set," objected Len.

It was distasteful, but we agreed.

We had kept Judge Kritzer in the loop about the Tyler Winslow situation, and in chambers, he was advised of the current status. He had determined it was within the district attorney and law enforcement's discretionary powers to make such an agreement. He was candid about the fact that Tyler Winslow leaving Namekagon County could only be good for the community. He also agreed to Jack Wheeler's formal request to have the court proceeding closed to the public and press. The judge was a strong believer in open court, and it was a rare circumstance where he closed a proceeding. The potential threat to Winslow was enough to support that.

Our attempts at secrecy were less than successful. That evening, the local TV and radio news broadcast a story about the potential release of Tyler Winslow. The essence of their stories was pretty much the same. Winslow was an eyewitness to the homicide of Marcus Johnson. Randy Muller had been arrested and charged with the crime based on Winslow's sworn statement. Muller was found dead before he went to trial, having hung himself from the cell block shower door.

The next morning several reporters were waiting outside the courtroom for the proceedings to start. They were disappointed that when the doors opened, the room was empty. The court clerk advised them that the case was over. There was plenty of grumbling on the part of the reporters as they left the courthouse. Chief Bork and DA Hablitch went out front and addressed all questions with "no comment."

I took Winslow out the back of the courthouse and drove him to the garage to pick up his truck.

"Well, Winslow, from here on out, you're on your own. What happens from here is pretty much up to you. Good luck," I said.

"Sheriff, I am going to change my life. I'm done with getting crossways of the law. I'm done with drugs. I know I have got a second chance, and I plan to take it," Tyler promised. ❦

CHAPTER 33

THE WATCHER

The man sat in his vehicle drinking a cup of coffee, pretending to read the newspaper. He had heard on the radio that Tyler Winslow was going to be released. Just as he figured, Sheriff Cabrelli snuck him out the back of the courthouse, put him in a sheriff's car and drove him away. He followed the sheriff's car at a safe distance, watched them go to the bank and then Bill and Jack's Garage. He watched as Winslow gave the mechanic some money. They were standing next to a pickup truck. The man didn't speed up or slow as he drove past the garage but unintentionally caught the sheriff's attention, who gave him a casual wave. He waved back and continued on his way. When he got the chance, he cut through an alley and found a parking place where he could watch Winslow, who was still talking to the sheriff.

Winslow drove straight out of town on the highway, and the man followed. Tyler turned off at the first forest road and then took a series of other roads until he came to a two-track leading to the Crooked Lake dam where his brother had drowned. The man pulled off on a dead-end dirt driveway blocked from view by a hill. He shut off the engine and got out of his vehicle. He slowly, carefully followed a well-worn footpath up the hill. Soon he could see Tyler Winslow in the empty parking lot and watched as Winslow took a plastic tarp from behind the front seat and spread it on the ground. Winslow laid on his back and slid under the truck. After a few moments, he got back up with a small plastic bag in his hand. He carefully unwrapped the package, filled a small pipe, and lit it with a disposable lighter. After a minute or so, Winslow slid down the side of the truck and sat on the tarp, smiling.

From there, the man followed Tyler back to the cabin where he had been arrested. Winslow opened the door and went inside. Several minutes later he reappeared with a bottle of whiskey in his hand and headed to the woodshed. Winslow came out carrying the whiskey and a plastic bag in one hand and the large-caliber revolver he used to kill Marcus Johnson in the other. He got back into his truck, turned up the radio, and drove off. Tyler Winslow was only out for a few hours, and it looked like he was already back in business. ❖

CHAPTER 34

January started as quiet as it was cold. At the end of the first week, the temperature began to drop and stayed below zero, stubbornly refusing to move. Then arctic blasts blew through and drove the windchill to minus twenty. The coldest temperature ever recorded in Namekagon County was fifty-five below zero, and there was conjecture that the record might be broken. People who didn't need to go out hunkered down as much as possible. For others heading off to work, it was just another day in the north country. Doc O'Malley drove around with his jumper pack idling in the back of his truck. Tim the plumber had a waiting list for thawing frozen pipes and repairing broken ones. Everyone casually ignored laws regarding where and when snowmobiles and ATVs could be operated. We didn't shut our squads off.

Despite the weather, Julie's school kids still worked with the local DNR and Charlie Newlin. They were all wearing snowshoes following several different trails that led them to locations where they had placed trail cameras. Each team of kids was responsible for the cameras in their area. They recorded the camera number and location, removed the camera card, and replaced it with a new one.

Then they carefully examined the area in a hundred-foot radius of the camera, taking detailed notes and photographing anything of interest. It was exciting for all when they returned to school and got to take the first look at what the cameras had seen. Ed and Stella Lockridge helped out on almost every one of these field days. It was on one of these days that we all got some sad news.

Ed, Stella, Charlie, Julie, and the students were following the trails to the camera locations. Some snow had a crust on top, and some was powder. It was hard going. Still, youthful exuberance should never be underrated, and the kids moved quickly, making it a challenge for the adults. They all reached the point where each team would go out on their trail. Everyone took a breather, and the kids made a fire and ate some snacks. Stella noticed Ed was chilled and told him to move closer to the fire. Then Ed started to cough and couldn't stop. Everyone was concerned, but Stella said that he had spells like this before and it would pass. Soon his coughing subsided, and he began to breathe easier. Ed and Stella decided to take the rest of the day off and head back. Julie and the kids, especially Amber, wanted to go with them, but Ed insisted they would be just fine.

The one-hour walk back to where they parked took them three hours. Stella loaded him into the truck and drove straight to the hospital. He was admitted and, after a short while, moved to intensive care. They put him on oxygen and through a battery of tests.

Amber stayed with Julie and me that night. We watched *Northern Exposure* reruns, ate popcorn, and played a board game in an attempt to distract Amber, who was clearly worried about her grandfather. The next morning, Stella called and asked us to come to the hospital with Amber.

We entered through the emergency doors, and a nurse took us to the family room waiting room. A doctor came in a few minutes later with Stella, who looked as if she had aged ten years.

Stella held Amber's face with strong but gentle hands.

"Honey, we have some bad news. And just like all bad news, it is going to hurt. This time real bad. Your grandpa has lung cancer. Real bad lung cancer, the kind they cannot fix. He will still be with us for a while, maybe some months, but then we are going to have to send him on a journey."

I don't believe I had ever seen a heart shatter until that moment. Amber had lost so much in her young life. First her mother, and now she would lose the man who had loved her unconditionally, given her a home, and protected her from the evils of the world. The man who read her stories while she sat on his lap. The only man in her life. It started as a quiet sob, the kind of sob that attaches itself to those around you, the kind of sob that comes from deep inside, from that unprotected place. She cried until there were no tears left. Julie and Stella cried with her.

It was agreed that Amber could stay with us until Ed was released from the hospital, probably in three or four days. Stella asked Amber if she wanted to see Ed before she went home with us. She said no and began to cry again.

Ed improved more quickly than anyone expected and was released two days later. We met them at their cabin on Spider Creek. He looked surprisingly good, even though he was wearing a mask and carried an oxygen bottle in a shoulder pack. He got out of the old truck, and Amber ran up and threw her arms around him.

Ed had a big smile on his face, glad to be home and with his family.

"They are gonna try some treatments on me. I have to go to the hospital in Superior once a week. Stella will take me the first couple of times, and after that, I can probably take myself. We have a lot to do here in the meantime. Pulling all the traps is the first thing. I think we better get started on that right away in the morning."

"Ed, I can help you with that if you want," I offered.

"Thanks, Sheriff, but I think Stella, Amber, and I can handle it. We'll take it slow and enjoy the time in the backcountry. Who knows, we might even catch a beaver or two. Hey, I've got an idea. How about you and Julie meet us at the last trap—the one right by the Spider Creek Bridge. We should be there by noon. We'll make a fire and cook up some coffee and lunch. How's that sound?"

"That sounds great, Ed. What can we bring?" Julie said.

"Nothing," Stella said. "We always have plenty."

We worked things out so that when Stella took Ed to the cancer center in Superior, they would drop Amber off the night before. Stella and Amber picked out some of Amber's clothes and things from home. Then Julie and Amber went over to our place and had fun setting up the guest room. A few pictures, a favorite pillow, and a couple of stuffed animals helped cozy things up.

The next morning, the Lockridges pulled their traps for the last time. They had caught two beaver, a mink, and three muskrats. When they got to the location of the last trap, Julie and I already had a fire going. Stella brought out five foil-wrapped packages. She put them on the edge of the fire and banked coals over the top of them. Ed filled an old dented enamelware coffee pot from the creek and set it in the fire.

"Can't add the coffee until we get the water to a good rolling boil for a while. Gotta watch out for beaver fever," said Ed.

Each foil wrap held venison, potatoes, and onions, seasoned just right. Along with that, Stella pulled a sack out of her backpack full of homemade biscuits. Dessert was wild blueberry tarts and strong coffee with sugar and cream. It was probably the best lunch I ever had. As we were cleaning up, Ed reached in the pocket of his parka for his smoking supplies, but the pocket was empty. It was too little, too late, but now each minute of each day had more value.

I ended up helping in the skinning shed. Ed found it easier to breathe with the door open, which meant the shed was colder than either Amber or Stella liked. Even with my lack of skill, everything got skinned, stretched, and prepped for the fur buyer. Prices were good, and that made Ed happy. He was even happier when Stella came back from the mailbox with the check from Yuletide Wreath Company, payment for the balsam boughs they had harvested and delivered. He and Stella had lived a simple life and had money saved, but any extra that came their way would be much appreciated after Ed was gone.

Two days later, Ed and Stella pulled up to our cabin in the early evening and dropped Amber off. They came in for a cup of coffee, and Ed took a shot of brandy in his.

"I am kind of looking forward to seeing Gitchi-Gami again. I've known a lot of people who made their living on that lake. It's a tough way to go. But that water is really something to see," Ed said.

After a tearful goodbye, they were on their way. Julie immediately distracted Amber by suggesting she help her with some school preparation for the following day. Even though the circumstances were sad, we enjoyed having Amber with us. ❧

CHAPTER 35

THE WATCHER

The man was frustrated. He sensed the opportunity was slipping away. Tyler Winslow was keeping a low profile. The man had only seen him twice, and both times were not the right moment. He suspected that Winslow was using the remote Crooked Lake Dam road as a meeting place to make his drug connections. The man wanted that to be the place of reckoning, but he may have to change his plan.

Weeks slipped by, and just when he became most concerned that he may not be successful, he got a break. Driving down the forest road, he saw Winslow's truck turn toward Crooked Lake Dam. He waited and turned down the road after Winslow was out of sight. He pulled over to the edge of the road. A car drove down by the dam and came back and left no more than ten minutes later. The man pulled his truck into the middle of the road and lifted the hood. Winslow drove out and had to stop because of the truck in the way. He got out of his truck and came over to the man sitting behind the wheel.

Winslow was agitated and yelled as he walked up, "Hey, man, get your truck out of the way."

He looked into the cab of the truck and found a steady hand holding a worn Browning nine millimeter handgun pointed at his face.

"You! It was you," was all Winslow could say before the man shot him at point-blank range. Winslow was dead before he hit the ground. The man drove away. He had accomplished what he started. ◂

CHAPTER 36

It was a week before Tyler Winslow was found. A couple of high school kids had driven down to Crooked Lake Dam for a little privacy. They turned down the road and saw a truck in the way. The boy got out and walked up to open the driver's door. There was no one in the truck. When he looked around, he saw Winslow lying at the edge of the road on the ground. It was the dead of winter, and food was getting scarcer in the forest. The rule of nature had been applied to Tyler Winslow; creatures of all kinds saw him as a much-needed source of protein and had commenced a banquet. The boy screamed, jumped back in his car, and drove away from Tyler Winslow's body and Crooked Lake Dam as fast as he could. They were a couple of miles down the road before his girlfriend convinced him to stop and call 911.

I was at home when I got the call. It sent my heart right into my throat. Deputy Holmes was on the scene and got a tentative ID on the victim by running the truck plate. He wisely touched nothing and blocked the road.

There was no doubt in anybody's mind that our killer was back. Either out of anxiety or frustration, I flew out to the scene, lights flashing, siren wailing. On the way, I had the ME and the closest available crime lab team paged out, and I asked the dispatcher to send Deputy Delzell. I called Len Bork, and he was on the way. My final call was to Ricardo on his secret cell phone. He answered, and I told him what and who I thought I had. He would be on the way as soon as he could. I could leave nothing to chance and needed to make sure we did it by the book. If this scene had something to tell us, we needed desperately to know what it was.

I pulled in, and Holmes had his squad parked across the road, waiting patiently.

He had already photographed the scene from every possible angle. He had not touched or done anything else. The two high schoolers were parked as far down the drive to the dam as they could be waiting to be interviewed. Delzell arrived, and I asked her to interview the kids. They only knew what the boy saw. Both were pretty shaken. When Delzell had finished taking their statements, she advised both juveniles that they could call their parents, or she would. The kids showed little enthusiasm over their options. The calls were made, the able Delzell calmed the parents, and the kids were sent on their way.

I didn't know where it was, but we would wait for the crime scene team all night if necessary. Fortunately, it didn't take that long. Ricardo knew the urgency of the situation—a serial killer was out there. He used every bit of his clout and most of Malone's getting the priority one crime scene unit led by Liz Masters ordered to the scene.

I had worked with Masters and her crew before. They were the best of the best. The good news was they were in a training session just three hours south of our location—maybe two hours if they flew—which is precisely what they did.

Once they arrived, Masters and her team immediately went to

work. One of her techs assisted Dr. Chali as he examined the body. The initial and correct finding proved to be the victim was shot through his right eye. There was no exit wound. The body had sustained significant damage from being fed on. Despite that, no doubt it was Tyler Winslow.

His wallet contained a driver's license. Tucked in his waistband at the small of his back was a cheap semi-auto pistol. The frozen diluted pool of blood was now a few feet from the body. Animals, probably coyotes or maybe even wolves, had dragged the body in the process of eating it. On the ground was a single brass shell casing. It appeared similar to the one found in Devin Martin's vehicle. In Winslow's truck, we recovered a significant quantity of drugs and cash and a large caliber handgun. Len stood by me while the crime scene was processed. Delzell and Holmes assisted the tech crew.

When they were done with the scene, Winslow's truck was loaded on a flatbed and taken to secure storage. Winslow's body was loaded and transported to the morgue for an autopsy. The crime scene team had scoured the area, and nothing that had the tiniest bit of evidentiary potential was ignored.

I called the county highway department to bring barricades out to the dam and close the road. "Road Closed by Order of the Sheriff" signs were posted.

On my way back to town, I called Julie and filled her in on what was going on. She was clearly shaken by what I had told her—another murder.

She gave me some not unexpected but still sad news. Ed Lockridge had taken a turn for the worse earlier in the day and was in intensive care at the Musky Falls hospital. His breathing had become labored, and his oxygen was hovering around the critical level. Amber would be staying with us until he came home—if he came home.

Back in town, Winslow's truck was sealed up. I booked rooms for the crime scene team at the Cedar Inn, and I set up a tab for them at the Fisherman. They would process the vehicle in the morning. Once they were done, they would first take everything back to their mobile lab and see what they could determine.

Dr. Chali removed the bullet from Winslow's brain. Without comparative magnification, it was only a guess, but to him, the slug looked almost identical to the one he had taken out of Devin Martin's head a few months before. It was packaged and turned over to the crime scene team.

Len and I agreed to put pictures of Winslow and his truck out to the media in hopes of a bite. Canvasing the homes around the dam was likely to be unproductive because other than a couple of closed-up summer cabins, there weren't any.

Everything else would have to wait for the morning. I had done all I could do at that point, so I went home. Julie and Amber were in flannel pajamas, eating popcorn, and watching a goofy teenage movie. I took off my gear, poured myself a glass of brandy, sat down, and watched with them. Most of the movie was lost on me, but it had them smiling.

When the movie was over, both girls went to bed. I followed shortly after that.

In the morning, I checked in with dispatch for messages. Ricardo had come in late. He was staying at the Cedar Inn two doors down from Liz Masters. Malone wanted to be briefed at my first opportunity.

I got Julie alone for a minute while Amber was in the shower.

"What's Ed's status?" I asked.

"It is hard to say, John, but they talked to Stella about taking him home and working with hospice to make sure he is as comfortable as possible. According to her, it could be a day, or it could be a month. We'll find out more today."

"Honey, I am going to be tied up with this homicide, but if you need me, call me."

I pulled in at the motel. The crime scene team was sitting at the table with Ricardo, enjoying the free breakfast bar.

We shook hands, and I got a cup of coffee and sat down.

"Thanks for showing up so quickly. I am sorry to put this on to you, but I am at a loss. If any of you have any suggestions as to where I should go from here, I am all ears."

"Anthony here has been filling us in. It is a tough one. Protected witness gets hit, or a rival drug dealer takes him out. That's the problem with guys like Winslow. There are a thousand reasons why someone would want them dead," Masters began.

"What about doing a combined evidence review?" she continued. "It is what we have been learning about in our training workshop. We start by going over the physical evidence—everything we have—and try to tie it together. We don't consider anything but the evidence, such as blood, fibers, shell casings, and things like that. We try to develop a picture of both our victim and our perpetrator, building them out of physical evidence, so to speak.

"Then we profile the victims, identifying what they had in common that might have made them targets. In this case, they are all involved in the illegal drug trade. According to Anthony, they were working for the same outfit, except maybe for this last one. It stands to reason that his role in court testifying against another drug gang may have made him a target. Anyway, you get where I am going. You start putting everything together and start getting yeses to your questions instead of nos. Look, we're here. Why don't we all have at it? A new set of eyes never hurts."

"She has got a point," Ricardo added. "Have you ever looked at one of those hidden picture drawings where the harder you look at it, the less chance you'll see the hidden picture? You walk away and come back ten minutes later, and there it is, large as life."

I called Len to join us, and we all convened in the conference room. We downloaded complete copies of each case file. The rule was anyone could start anywhere—with the first killing or the last or someplace in between. Everybody kept their own notes.

The only thing added later was regarding the bullet removed from Winslow's head and the shell casing found at the scene. Liz set up an enlarged split screen of the bullet and shell casing and did a rough comparison to the ones recovered from the first homicide. She projected the images for all of us to see. It was not a perfect comparison, but it looked like both the bullet and the shell casing came from the same gun. It was good enough for the exercise.

Within an hour, each person had staked out space and was buried in work. I ordered in lunch, but no one stopped to eat. Midafternoon came and Liz called a break. The food brought in earlier was still edible, and Crossroads delivered a gallon of coffee. We made small talk, but people were anxious to get back at it. We worked until six o'clock. Len headed home, while Ricardo, Masters, and crew got cocktails at the hotel bar and then relaxed in the outdoor hot tub as light snow fell.

On the drive home, I realized I was getting close. Something I had seen today, or another day, triggered something somewhere inside my head. Yet, I could not for the life of me get it to come out, but I knew it would.

———————

I walked in and saw Julie had left me a note. She and Amber were with Stella and someone from hospice setting up a hospital bed and other equipment at Lockridge's. Ed was coming home tomorrow. She would check in later.

I crawled into bed, but I couldn't stay asleep. As soon as I dozed off, images of the investigation popped into my head. Julie got home just before midnight and crawled in next to me. It helped, but it didn't stop me from getting up at four in the morning. Julie, bless her sweet heart, got up with me and brewed coffee.

She shared an update. Ed, Stella, and Amber had been given end-of-life options. Ed could stay at home or go to an assisted care facility until the end. He could sign a Do Not Resuscitate order, meaning that if his heart stopped beating or he stopped breathing, he would be allowed to pass on. The family decided for home and do not resuscitate.

Amber and Stella were doing much better with the situation. Now Ed's pain was barely tolerable, even with medication. He would come home in the morning, and Stella would allow some visitors. ⤙

CHAPTER 37

I went into town and back to the conference room. I was not the first one to arrive. Anthony and Liz were already hard at it. They barely grunted hello.

I started right in. Len showed up a half hour later, and by seven, we were fully staffed.

At ten o'clock, Liz Masters called us all to attention.

"Okay, everybody. Listen up. For the next hour, make a note of your conclusions so far."

Eleven came and Liz projected what looked like a lined piece of notebook paper on a whiteboard. Each of us took our turn. Many had arrived at the same conclusions.

It was drug related and targeted at Gunther's gang except for Marcus Johnson and Tyler Winslow.

The killer was specifically after these upper-level members of the drug gang.

It wasn't competition; it was payback.

The killer had training, probably former military.

It was one or two people.

Len noted that all the murders were in places kind of off the map in the backwoods. He thought it was likely that the perpetrator did some scouting and surveillance.

Two of the senior technicians had gone through the physical evidence collected at each scene, focusing primarily on things that were somewhat unique and things that may be seemingly insignificant.

The ammunition used was unique. The two brass casings, one from the Devin Martin scene and the other from Tyler Winslow, appeared to have been extracted and ejected from the same gun. The casings were from two different manufacturers, yet they were loaded with the same type of lead bullet. Some quick research revealed that a high-power nine millimeter almost always exited. This ammunition may be of lower power. This led the techs to the idea that the killer possibly manufactured, or more likely reloaded, their own ammunition. Low-velocity stuff for a special purpose. Again, indicating the killer had some weapons skills or training.

Ricardo walked around and filled everyone's coffee cup while the technicians projected the list of hair and fiber recovered from Devin Martin's vehicle. I followed along when they were going through the list and explaining the value and location of recovered evidence. I got to the bottom of the second page, and it struck me. I jumped up like I had been poked with a sharp stick. My coffee spilled all over the table. I grabbed paper towels and tried to wipe it up. I quickly gave up and asked Len to clean up my mess. Everyone in the room looked at me like I had lost my mind. My mind had never been more focused or clearer.

"What's wrong, Sheriff?" Ricardo asked.

Len Bork, whose keen ability to read people had kept him alive over a thirty-year career, looked me in the eye. "You know who the killer is, don't you, John?"

I looked around the room, every face waiting for my answer.

"I am not sure, Len, but I have an idea and a question that needs to be answered," I replied and headed for the door.

"I'll come with you," Ricardo offered.

"No, I need to go alone. I might be wrong, but I need to follow this to its natural end."

I left the building and got in my squad.

It all fit—motive, pattern, opportunity. I drove fast but without warning lights. Tyler Winslow was not the first Winslow killed; his brother Travis was. When the body was found at the dam, evidence suggested that he was poaching walleyes and slipped while trying to make his way across the dam, hit his head on the concrete, and drowned. Each killing was tied to drugs, but there was another equally important connection.

———————

I turned off the highway onto a dead-end road I had driven many times in the past several weeks. I parked by a lean-to full of cut, dried, and split firewood. Wood from the same pile was heating the cabin, evidenced by the wisp of wood smoke coming out of the chimney. I knocked on the door, and Stella Lockridge answered.

"Hi, Stella. I just stopped on my way home to check in on you. How are you holding up?"

"Oh, Sheriff, we have our good days and bad. If you're looking for Amber and Julie, they are still at school. Amber is helping her with some work. You know, I will never be able to thank you and Julie for all your kindness. It has meant so much to us," she said.

"Stella, I was wondering if I could talk to Ed."

"Oh, he would be happy to have someone to talk to. It would be a change from me pestering him. He was looking through some old pictures. Let me see if he's awake."

Stella came back a moment later.

"He would be glad to talk to you. Says he's been expecting you. I think the pain drugs make him a little goofy."

I walked into the backroom. Ed was lying in his hospital bed, the back raised enough that he was sitting up. He had an old photo album on his lap.

"Hi, Sheriff, nice of you to stop by."

"How you doing, Ed?"

"Pretty good today. But I know I'm getting to the end. It's okay. I am ready for it. Some days I am too tired to go on."

"Ed, I've got to ask you about something. Do you mind?"

"No, go right ahead, Sheriff," he said.

"I was going over the evidence in our homicide cases with some other law enforcement officers. I noticed something that hadn't stood out for me before. A guy named Devin Martin was found dead in his SUV. It looked like a suicide but turned out to be a homicide. It was pretty likely that someone sitting in the passenger seat of Martin's car forced him to drive to a remote area and shot him in the head. When the evidence techs went over the passenger seat, they found a couple of interesting things."

"What things were those, Sheriff?"

"A piece of long gray, almost white hair and a piece of long cut tobacco, like the kind you might roll in your cigarettes."

"A lot of people got gray hair and roll their own smokes," Ed replied.

"True enough, but not everybody with gray, almost white hair who rolls their own has a daughter who was running around with the murder victim."

Ed stared at me, and then he burst out laughing. The laugh turned into a racking cough that brought Stella to the room.

"Ed, here. Take some of this cough suppressant," Stella said, handing him a medicine cup.

"No, no, I am fine, Stella. The sheriff told me a funny joke, and it got me laughing."

"Fine. I'll leave you boys alone then."

Ed handed me the photo album, open to a particular page.

I took the book and was looking at young Ed Lockridge, dressed in the uniform of Army Special Forces, with sergeant stripes on the sleeve, wearing the iconic Green Beret on his head.

"Vietnam. After three tours, I'd had enough. Came back home, married Stella, and we've been here ever since. I am guessing that's not what you want to hear, though, is it? You're damn smart, Sheriff. I knew you'd figure it out."

"The first one was Travis Winslow, wasn't it?"

"Yes, it was, but I didn't intend to kill him. It just worked out that way. Crystal was in love with him. He was a drug dealer, and Crystal did whatever he wanted her to do. She got caught dealing drugs for Travis. We hired a fancy lawyer and made a deal. If Crystal turned state's evidence against Winslow, then all the charges against her would be dropped. They would also help us get her into a residential treatment facility. We were hopeful. In some ways, Crystal was made of stern stuff. When she first found out she was pregnant, she stopped doing drugs. Stella was getting ready to be a grandma, making blankets and baby moccasins. It was a good time for all of us, and Crystal did her best to be a good mom.

"But even though Crystal's cooperation landed Travis in jail, when he was on bail, he started coming around again, and Stella said I needed to shoo that boy away. I pretty much know everything that goes on in the backcountry around here, and I knew that Travis was poaching walleyes up at the dam. He'd spear 'em on Thursday night and take them to his customers the next afternoon in time for the Friday fish fry. I parked my truck back in the bush and waited for him to show up. Eventually, there he came, drove in, and parked. He threw out a couple of coolers and started walking across the top of the dam with a spear. The fish were thick, and he had four big ones almost right away. Once he was busy, I walked down to where he was fishing. He saw me and stopped. Then he walked toward me, running his smart mouth all the way. He said bad things about my little girl.

Then he turned his back and started looking for walleyes again.

"I knew no talking to him was ever going to keep him away from Crystal. I found a stout oak branch by the edge of the road, just the right size and weight. I walked back to where Travis was fishing, got next to him, and called his name quietly. I learned to use a whisper in the war. He turned to look at me and started to open his mouth again. I swung the branch and hit him in the head as hard as I could. He fell to the ground, right at the edge of the dam. Then I just put my boot against him and pushed him into the water. That was that; no more Travis. You know what really bothered me about the whole thing, Sheriff? I had to leave the walleyes. I sure hated to see nature's bounty go to waste."

"Did Stella know what really happened with Travis?"

"No, she never did, and I never told her."

"For a while, things were good. With Travis gone, we didn't have to worry about court or him coming back. Then Crystal started running with a real bad apple. She would leave and not come home for days at a time. Amber was with us, so she was okay, but Crystal would show up at all hours. There was no doubt she was using drugs again. I tracked down her and her new boyfriend. I found out they were hanging around at the casino. I kept an eye on him as best I could.

"Pretty soon, I figured out that he was meeting one of his people every Friday in the driveway behind an old lodge by Ghost Lake. I went up there, hid in the woods, and waited. It was like clockwork. They would show up, talk for a minute, exchange duffle bags, and be on their way. The other guy always left first. Then Martin would leave a while later. The next week I was waiting when he showed up. It was no good. He had Crystal in the car with him. She got out, and they were having some sort of argument. The bastard walked up and slapped her so hard he knocked her down to the ground. I could hardly stand by and let that happen, but I had to. I just needed to wait.

"The next week, once his friend left, I snuck up on him. He was, like most criminals, cowardly. I stuck my gun in his ear and told him to drive to a spot at the end of the driveway and the beginning of the forest road. He thought I was robbing him. You should have seen the look on his face when I told him that I was Crystal's father. I told him I saw him hit her and I knew that he would never do it again. Then I shot him, and I was glad to do it. I would have liked to skin him and hang him in the woods half alive," he explained.

"Ed, where is the gun you used?"

"I was afraid you'd ask me that," Ed replied.

He reached behind his head under his pillow and pulled out a war-worn Browning high-power handgun, hammer back, and almost certainly with a round in the chamber. He pointed it at my chest and held it there, his hand steady.

I had made a foolish mistake. I was sitting a few feet from a man who had just recounted two of who knew how many murders. I let our friendship cloud my vision with his failing health making me see him as harmless. Harmless he was not; I had misjudged a killer. We looked into each other's eyes. Except for the faint hiss of oxygen, the room was deathly quiet.

"Ed, what are we going to do here?" I asked.

"Sheriff, you have got to be more careful," he replied.

In a smooth move, he flipped the gun around and gave it to me butt first. I gently took the out of his hand.

"Thanks, Ed," I said.

"Got that my first year in Nam. Holds fourteen rounds, never had a jam. I'd hate to see it sawed in half or sunk at the bottom of Lake Superior. Sheriff, I know you need to hear all this, but I am getting pretty tired."

"How about the meth lab, Ed?"

"Not willing to be done, eh Sheriff? I'll go as long as I can."

"I'd appreciate that, Ed," I said.

"They were making poison and selling it. When my sweet little

Amber showed up at that party, it damn near killed Stella and me. I made it my job to track those bastards down, and I did. I still had some blocks of C-4 brought home from the war. I used it for blowing beaver dams and the like. But I wanted everyone to know I meant business, hoping they would leave town. I took three five-gallon buckets of gas, diesel, and cheap Styrofoam cups and set them next to three blocks of C-4. I have a bunch of remote detonators and timing devices that made it home with me. Then I blew the drug lab into orbit. I want to say I am happy that LP man didn't get hurt. I never expected to see anyone else."

"How about Tyler Winslow?"

Ed's head started to droop. His eyes closed and then reopened. He didn't speak for a minute or two.

"Tyler Winslow gave Crystal the drugs that killed her. Tyler tried to talk to Amber at Thanksgiving. He told Amber he was her uncle, her dad's brother. He scared the hell out of her. She kept trying to get away from him. Then Crystal stepped in. She told Amber to go help us make fry bread. Amber did as she was told but kept watching her mother. Crystal and Tyler went to the back of the cafeteria, and Amber saw Tyler give her something. She put it in her pocket, and then Crystal came back to help us cook. She and Amber got in a real donnybrook at home that night, Amber accusing her of getting drugs from Winslow. Crystal told her that if she said anything, she'd have to go back to jail, this time for a long time. She told Stella and me the whole story after her mom died. She cried her heart out, and we tried to tell her it wasn't her fault, but she blamed herself. That poor girl through no fault of her own has been strapped with some heavy burdens."

We sat in silence for a while before Ed fell asleep again. I didn't know what to do. He wasn't going anywhere, so I got up to see Stella. When I stood, he spoke again.

"Sheriff, wait a minute. I need to tell you one more thing," he said with effort. His breathing was coming hard.

"I have one regret. I will forever be sorry that I didn't kill more of those drug dealing devils."

Ed closed his eyes and went back to sleep.

I tucked the Browning pistol in my waistband under my coat and walked out to see Stella. We talked briefly, and I left.

I took the drive along Spider Creek slowly. There didn't seem to be a need to rush. Once on the highway, I took the first turnoff I came to, taking the backroads to town. Balsam boughs were heavy with snow. Plow banks filled the road shoulder. I was back at my office, and although it felt like three days, I had been gone less than three hours.

Everybody was still busy working away when I walked in, and then the room became silent. I asked them all to sit around me so that we could talk quietly.

I told them the story of Ed Lockridge. A man whose boundless goodwill had brought so much to the community. War-hardened as a young man, Ed returned to make his home in the great Northwoods of his youth. He married Stella, the love of his life. Soon they were blessed with a daughter. They wanted nothing more than to be together and live in peace. It was not to be. Evil came to their door and threatened everything Ed cared about. He was a warrior and made a warrior's choice—eliminate the enemy. Bad men died, and it would be hard to argue that the world was not a better place for it.

No one said a word. I explained how I had arrived at Ed as a suspect. His confession and recall of the incidents sealed the case. I would talk to the DA tomorrow and ask him how to proceed. Tonight, though, I needed to go home to find my place, to find my peace.

The house phone rang at six the next morning. It was Stella. Ed had passed away in the night. He had begun his journey, and she and Amber had been by his side. ❦

CHAPTER 38

The dead-end road to Spider Creek had cars parked on both sides and all the way out to the highway. Two sheriff's deputies were on-site to direct traffic. The funeral ceremony was a mix of anglicized and Ojibwe traditions. Even though Ed was not Native American, he was known as a true friend to the Ojibwe. The minister from the Spider Lake Church offered prayers as did tribal elders. Drummers played and we sang songs of joy, songs of sorrow, and songs that told the story of our lives. Afterward, we gathered on a high hill overlooking Spider Creek, where Ed's ashes were given to the wind.

———————

Ed's deathbed confession spurred a great deal of discussion between law enforcement officers involved in the case and the DA about how to best handle the situation. Ricardo firmly believed that we should keep it our secret.

"Let the dopers think there is still somebody in Namekagon County just waiting around the corner to shoot 'em or blow 'em up. It can't help but keep some riff-raff out."

In the end, we decided to share the story with Bill Presser. For the second time since I moved to Spider Lake, the local paper was sold in bundles right off the truck. Reporters flocked to town, each looking for their own angle. Scott Stewart, the county board chair, made himself readily available to anyone who wanted to interview him.

Len, DA Hablitch, and I held a joint press conference. The room was packed. No matter how hard they tried, we would not let the reporters take us where we wouldn't go. Ed Lockridge was not a crazed backwoodsman or hermit living in a cave stalking the innocent citizens of Namekagon. He was a man who wrongly took the law into his own hands in an attempt to protect his family.

———

Amber and Stella moved in with Julie and me and stayed until the press left town. Even after they returned to their cabin, Stella and Amber sought comfort by visiting our home often. We welcomed them. Ed's death left them feeling lost. They would recover, but for now, they grieved. We were becoming an extended family of sorts— Stella, Amber, Bud, Julie, and me. We ate many dinners together, each of us taking turns at the stove. Stella loved her turn in the kitchen. She and Ed had done everything together, and she said it felt like she had lost one of her arms.

One night we had all finished dinner, and I was cleaning up while Bud, Julie, and Amber were playing Uno. Stella asked me to come outside for a minute. She walked over to her truck and removed what looked like an old military satchel, olive drab in color and well worn.

She handed it to me and said, "Sheriff, I don't think we'll need these anymore. You better take them."

Inside the bag were timers, detonators, and two blocks of C-4 plastic explosive. I looked at her, and she held a finger to her lips and said, "Shh, shh, shh. Don't ask." Then she walked back into the cabin.

———

The next morning, Julie and I snowshoed across the two-foot-thick ice of Spider Lake. There was no threat of breaking through, but in some places, the ice was windswept clean. In other places, the same wind had moved snow to depths measured in feet, making snowshoes a necessary accouterment. Today not even a breeze was blowing and there was almost no noise other than the crunching of our footgear. Spider Creek had mostly frozen over, but one area defied the cold and remained open. The hushed noise of flowing water joined us. A mature bald eagle stared down from the top of a majestic old white pine, hoping for a chance at a fresh fish dinner. The ice anglers had followed the fish to a rocky point further down the lake. At that moment, Spider Lake and all the things wild and wonderful that came with it belonged to just Julie and me.

When we reached the opposite shore, we climbed the bank and came to rest on a large flat rock gazing out at the winter panorama. The love of my life sat close to me, her beautiful blue eyes contrasting with rosy, red cheeks. Against all odds, happiness had found John Cabrelli. Life could not possibly get any better. Then it did.

She looked up at me and spoke the most wonderful words I had ever heard, "If the offer is still open, the answer is yes. Yes, I will marry you. I would love to make you Mr. Carlson." ❧

I have never arrested anyone for drugs in a duck blind.

Warden John Holmes, 1939–2017

In memory of Jerry Wakkinen—
A good man.

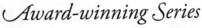

Award-winning Series

FIGURE EIGHT
BOOK ONE

After a career-ending event, John Cabrelli retreats to his late uncle's lake cabin where danger awaits—along with the truth behind his uncle's death in this award-winning first in series.

SPIDER LAKE
BOOK TWO

A missing federal agent, suitcases full of cash, a secluded cabin in the woods... Spider Lake, the award-winning second book in the Northern Lakes Mystery series, is an unputdownable crime thriller.

MUSKY RUN
BOOK FOUR

Predators stalk the Northwoods as the Great Wilderness Race gets underway. Sheriff John Cabrelli and the new Musky Falls chief of police work to keep the community calm as they try to piece together the clues before it is too late.

ABOUT THE AUTHOR

Jeff Nania is a former law enforcement officer, writer, conservationist, and biofuel creator. He is the award-winning author of four fiction books, *Figure Eight* (2019), *Spider Lake* (2020), *Bough Cutter* (2021), and *Musky Run* (2023) in his Northern Lakes Mystery series. His narrative non-fiction writing has appeared in *Wisconsin Outdoor News, Double Gun Journal, The Outlook,* and other publications.

Jeff was born and raised in Wisconsin. His family settled in Madison's storied Greenbush neighborhood. His father often loaded Jeff, his brothers, and a couple of dogs into an old jeep station wagon and set out for outdoor adventures. These experiences were foundational for developing a sense of community, a passion for outdoor traditions, and a love of our natural resources.

Jeff has been recognized locally, statewide, and nationally. *Outdoor Life Magazine* named him as one of the nation's 25 most influential conservationists, and he received the National Wetlands Award for his wetland restoration work. The Wisconsin Senate commended Jeff with a joint resolution for his work with wetlands, education, and as a non-partisan advisor on natural resource issues.

Now a full-time novelist, Jeff spends as much time as possible exploring outdoor Wisconsin with his friends and family.

Visit www.feetwetwriting.com to sign-up for email updates and read more from Jeff Nania.

 @jeffnaniaauthor   @jeffnania